They Flutter Behind You

A Novel

Brian Douglas

What Others Are Saying

"One can ask only two things of a book: is it an important story to tell and is it well told? *They Flutter Behind You* is an important story, and truly well told. It is a book of hope, but much more (if there can be more than hope) in that it resonates as real, as if drawn from fact rather than fiction, and that makes it important.

They Flutter Behind You is often dark, never dull; often poignant, never patronizing; frequently insightful, never redundant—and full of a new writer's vigour, creased with a refreshed look at situations pushed from readers' minds when they became socially uncomfortable."

-Rick Antonson, Author

"*They Flutter Behind You* is a thought provoking, powerful exposé of the human condition. Brian Douglas has woven together a story with characters who grab you the moment you meet them. As masterfully written as it is lyrical; radiating with raw emotion. It is a difficult story to pick up and perhaps more difficult to put down."

-Dr. Sharon Fischer, Stettler Alberta

"*They Flutter Behind You* is a beautifully written novel about some of the most difficult subjects of our time. Brian Douglas carries readers through powerful and painful narrative and character arcs with ease and grace, challenging us to open our minds and engage in self-examination even as we scrutinize those we may find deplorable. What is redemption? Who is redeemable? What can we forgive? These and other fundamental questions resonate throughout the book, making it a rich and deeply rewarding read."

-D. Sheldon, award winning editor

"Brian Douglas' novel, *They Flutter Behind You,* is gorgeously written, soulful and deeply existential. A *poetically* raw depiction of love and conflict, abuse and redemption. As someone who has experienced much of what the central character endures, I was profoundly moved by the horror and transcendent beauty of this story. I hope this novel is widely read. It is beautiful."

-Scott Rivers, Gabriola Island BC

"One of life's most difficult tasks is finding compassion for those who have hurt others. Brian Douglas' novel, *They Flutter Behind You,* challenges us to consider the stories of individuals whose narratives are often dismissed due to their past actions. The cast of characters brings dimension to a difficult situation with their various unique perspectives."

-E. Aisenstat, Author

"I loved each of the characters. They were well rounded and fully believable. We all need people like these in our lives."

-Fiona Tobin, Beta reader

"*They Flutter Behind You* begins powerfully and doesn't stop. It is at times so dark I wanted to stop reading but simply could not. The writing quality is very high throughout. Each character has a uniquely distinctive voice that draws the reader in and forces consideration from another's perspective. The characters are flawed yet filled with hope. I have never encountered a story such as this. It was very well put together. Read this book!"

-Jesse Savage, QuietHouse Editing

"Do you have to use the "F" word so much?"

-Brian's Mom

FriesenPress
One Printers Way
Altona, MB R0G 0B0
Canada

www.friesenpress.com

First Edition — 2024

ISBN
978-1-03-919544-8 (Hardcover)
978-1-03-919543-1 (Paperback)
978-1-03-919545-5 (eBook)

1. FICTION, LITERARY

Distributed to the trade by The Ingram Book Company

DEDICATION

This novel is dedicated to those who have suffered at the hands of another. Those whose childhoods have been shortened, impaired, or outright stolen. To face those demons, to confront the elephants in the room that are easier to skirt around, takes more courage than words could ever express. And yet, for those of us who have lost so much, hope remains. May the hope that flourishes in these pages find its way into your heart.

Dear Reader,

I have always been interested in how the novels I read came about—the story behind the story, so to speak.

The genesis of *They Flutter Behind You* lies in a particularly dark season of my life when I felt directionless, purposeless, and close to hopeless. In such times I often turn to the music of Pink Floyd. I suppose I go there not so much for relief, but rather because their music has a way of turning sadness into soul-crushing despair. Perhaps it feeds the masochist within me. When I stumbled upon the song "Your Possible Pasts," the lyrics resonated deeply. Those words! Oh my God, how they told a story—my story. As the sorrow, grief, and pain of that dark season lessened, I knew the lyrics held another story—our story—one that needed to be told. So, I began to weave this tale you now hold.

It took about six months to write that first draft, during which I often worked for twelve or more hours per day. Yet it seemed that no sooner had I begun than it was over. I remember the sense of satisfaction—jubilation even—that washed over me when I typed, "The End." (Which my editor promptly deleted.) Along with the joy, though, was a sadness. It was a bit like saying goodbye to a dear friend, something I hope you too will feel when you turn the final page. Had anyone told me the hard part had just begun, I would not have believed them, but such was the case.

What was I supposed to do with a 170,000-word upmarket psychological drama when I had traditional publishers in mind, publishers who insist on a maximum of 100,000 words? The first task was to begin cutting. In a desperate attempt to reach that acceptable word count, I slashed it down to 125,000 words, but that seemed to cut the heart right out of the story. In subsequent rewrites, I put some of the pieces back in, and the blood began flowing again—its heartbeat returned. After much painstaking reconstructive surgery, the copy you are now holding is just under 145,000 words. Because, well, because a story takes as long as a story takes to tell.

It took a couple of years before I made peace with the idea of self-publishing this novel, but right now you are holding my book in your hands, and for me, that is what matters. Within these pages I think you will find a story that intrigues you, bolsters you, and I sincerely *hope*, gives you a sense of hope and purpose. In these pages there is much darkness but also a landscape dotted with eternal blossoms of rich possibility.

Thank you so much for buying and reading Flutter. It means a great deal to this father and grandfather. I wish you much joy as you embark on this journey with Trent.

Most sincerely,

Brian Douglas
January 2024

For Sierra

CHAPTER ONE

Dear Gerald,

I should probably begin by stating that I really have no idea how, or even why, I'm writing to you. With all the years our lives have been intricately entwined, it occurs to me I have never written to you, nor you to me. To be perfectly honest—which is the sole purpose of this letter—I wouldn't be doing so now had Doctor Thackery not suggested that this practice may be somewhat cathartic.

I have been seeing Doctor Thackery once a week since arriving here in this godforsaken abyss. He has informed me that everything I say will be held in the strictest confidence unless I'm considering harming myself or others. And since I have done enough of that to last a lifetime, I am ready to begin.

Honesty is refreshing, like the spray of the ocean in your face on a sweltering August afternoon. It is also something I have rarely excelled at. I learned early, from you no less, that deceit offers instant solutions to uncomfortable situations. Although the idea of splaying my life open to someone in a profession so close to the one I no longer have fills me with trepidation. After all, the only thing that separates *therapist* from *the rapist* is a single space. Having inserted that gap and crossed that line, I am all too aware of its fragility. But I daresay I have been more honest with

Doctor Thackery in the four short months of our relationship than I have ever been with anyone. Most certainly with you.

All of that is about to change.

Doctor Thackery believes that if I am able to honestly express myself to you in this letter, I may gain some clarity and thereby discover the origin of my dysfunctions. As promising as this vulnerability may be, I am finding it a most taxing enterprise. Like tying your shoes. For the seasoned, experienced tyer, it comes naturally. For the novice, it can be a formidable challenge. However, honesty, much like deceitfulness, has an origin.

He suggests that you may be a catalyst to much of my brokenness, although you would likely never admit that. I agree with him. Not that you are responsible for my shit. What I agree with is that you would never admit to the role you played in the decrepit person I have become.

God, I hate you. There, I said it.

Of course, the only reason I'm able to tell you this is because the good doctor has told me that I will never send this letter, nor any others that may follow. Let me be perfectly clear: I am not doing this for you. It is for me alone. And there's a freedom in knowing you will never lay eyes upon it.

Doctor Thackery's hope—mine too, I suppose—is that by freeing myself to tell you all the ways I have felt dehumanized, demoralized, and less than, there may be some good added to my existence. A new freedom? Possibly. That you will never read these words matters little—not at all, in fact. Moreover, because this letter is for me and not you, I can say anything I want. You can hurt me no longer.

Oh, how bravery becomes me as I hide behind this truth, huh?

Remember the last time we were together? It was just before I came here to this place to serve my time, to pay my debt to society. We were at Claire and Robert's. I was there to visit one last time before the hammer fell, but more so to say goodbye to Mom as she clutched onto the little life that remained within her grasp. Knowing it would be the last time I ever saw Mom alive was difficult enough. The knowledge that you were coming did not make the situation easier. But you did. You left your mistress long enough to come and pay your last respects. How very thoughtful. I consider the fact that our visits overlapped nothing more than an unfortunate accident. How ill-fated for you, I know.

To be clear, by "mistress" I am not speaking of Judy, the latest notch in your bedpost. Another person could never fill the role of lover that you demand. Human beings simply do not possess the net worth for such a lofty position in your domain. I refer, rather, to that bitch you spend all your valuable time upon in these golden years. Yes, you have made it abundantly clear; nothing exists in your world that holds more value than your fucking boat. *The Endeavour* is what you christened her, right? I hear that you pronounce it "The End of Her," though, don't you? Your poor attempt at being punny was not lost upon me and was almost prophetic. Had you waited a few months longer to christen her, the name would have been more apropos.

We stood together in Claire's kitchen, you and me. After far too much awkward silence, I began dinner while Claire was visiting Mom, Robert was working, and Aaron and Stevie were at school. You suggested we make dinner together, you and I, "just like old times." But there were no "old times," Gerald. We have never made a meal together. We haven't even eaten a meal together in years. And not once have you ever invited me to dine with you.

Would it interest you to know that in ancient times the act of breaking bread—sharing a meal together—was considered among the highest of honors? It was an invitation to let your walls down and invite another person to get to know you. Ah, and there's the rub, isn't it? To get to know another person, or worse, to let another person get to know you. Why have you always been so afraid of vulnerability?

You stood at the kitchen sink and began to wash your hands. Remember? I do. I remembered then how as a child I loved to watch you come in from the fields and wash your hands before supper. We called it supper then, before we moved to the city, "got cultured," and it became dinner. I suppose that's also when dinner became lunch. I used to stand mesmerized, watching you wash.

Your toned, tired, muscular hands would turn on the rusted taps in our old, worn farmhouse. When the water reached just the right temperature, somewhere between hot and scalding, you would roll up the sleeves of your faded, grease-stained blue work shirt, the same color as your faded blue eyes. You'd wet your hands just enough, then pick up the soap from the soap dish. The hot steam rising, fogging the mirror, your face slowly disappearing, like a ship into the fog. Your big hands working together, soap rolling between them like waves rolling on the water. Lather building, back and forth, working between each finger, rising like seafoam against a rocky shore, over your strong wrists and up your forearms, the white suds turning gray, darker, almost black. Then plunged again under the faucet, the rolling, rubbing, the cleansing strokes continue, the steaming stream washing your stains, like sin, down the drain. Swirling. A dark tornado.

The water stops, the mist gives way, the ship emerges. Ninety-nine-point-nine percent pure, fresh, clean hands appear. The scent of Ivory permeates the room and my senses.

"I think I'll make a salad."

Your voice snapped me forward, back to that moment those long months ago as we stood side by side in Claire's kitchen. I so admired the way you washed your hands then, even that day, the same way you washed them when I was a child. This is the one thing, the only thing, I admire about you. That, dear Daddy, is your legacy with me—the way you wash your fucking hands.

I told you as much after you finished washing, before you made the salad, before supper—dinner, rather—before Thanksgiving, before Mom died, before prison. I say I told you as much. What I actually told you, as I recall, is how much I admire the way you wash your hands. I neglected, of course, to tell you that this is the *only* thing I admire about you. That I could never do. Cowards are rarely honest in that place where truth intersects with confrontation. Here in this make-believe letter, however, just look how brave I am.

I hate that I'm a coward.

Cowards make the greatest peacekeepers, though. We will do everything possible not to upset the proverbial apple cart. We are willing to sacrifice our values upon the altar of self-preservation. What others think of us cowards is of paramount importance. We are not among those who would ever be found uttering that all-too-common axiom: "I don't care what anyone thinks." For *all* we care about is what others think. We are driven and controlled by what others think of us. We long for the approval of others the way a drunkard longs for his next drink. It is all-consuming.

You, of course, are famous for those very words. That being said, many who commonly use that expression really mean the opposite, don't they, Gerald? Right. Honesty has never been your strong suit either.

Standing there next to you in Claire's kitchen, I try to wash my hands the way, as a child, I remember you washing yours. I have always tried to do that. After all, imitation is the finest form of flattery. I want so desperately for you to know that this act of handwashing sums up all the manly things I have ever learned from you. God, how I want you to know this. I want you to know it the way I know it. How to wash my hands like a man, this is the one thing, the *only* thing of value I have ever learned from you. I long to scream this into your reality, but I will not. I was just a boy then, but now I'm only a man; cowards both.

The very small sink in my very small cell doesn't produce water hot enough to lather. Having to use one hand to hold the button like a drinking fountain just to get the water dribbling makes working my hands together impossible. No dark tornado. The one thing of value you taught me I'm unable to accomplish here within these dark walls. In here I am unclean. Dirt, filth, and shame are my constant companions.

Claire came to visit last week. She said she hasn't heard from you since Mom's funeral. She tells me it was beautiful and that Mom was truly honored. How considerate of you not to bring Judy.

Claire tells me she's given you the prison visitor application forms but suggests I not hold my breath. I can only imagine how overcome with shame you would be, filling in those pages. Especially that one question: "Relationship to the Prisoner." Oh my, how humiliating would it be filling that box, huh?

I know something about humiliation. When you're arrested, stripped naked, forced to bend over and spread your ass for leering guards who take some perverse pleasure from your humiliation, it takes something from you. It eats away a man's character. And when there's little character to begin with, you become even less.

There's something most shameful in being caught doing that which is reviled by every part of society. Add to it the abusive treatment of powerful men, and it tears away the very fabric of one's soul. And, when a person is as concerned about what others think of them as I am, that shame is crippling. So, I share your pain, Gerald.

Shame is the most debilitating of emotions. It makes you want to crawl into the fetal position and hide from the world. The fact that you won't so much as attempt to visit your only son amplifies that shame like a soapbox preacher selling his faith. Not that I have any desire to see you. But that you have none to see me somehow aches, as unfair as that may seem. Does this make me a hypocrite? Perhaps. But I learned from the best.

And herein lies much of my anger with you: your hypocrisy. But you learned it somewhere before you passed it on to me, no doubt, and I should not be quick to throw too much raw emotion in your direction. After all, I'm a grown man, and the choices I made have brought me to this place, nothing more. But it feels good to share the pain a little.

Well, Doctor Thackery said I shouldn't just ramble on ad nauseam. This is to be as close to a "real" letter as possible. I must confess that when he first suggested the exercise, I balked, saying I wouldn't have a clue what to write, yet once I set pen to page, the words, the memories, and the pain began to flow like blood from a head wound. I'm finding it relatively easy to express myself to you. But we both know the reason—you will never read these words.

It's getting late, and my cellmate has been snoring for a while now, so I think it's safe to take a shit. I hate having to use the toilet in front of someone else, so I try to hold it until he either leaves the cell or is asleep, just one more small inconvenience in the life of a convict.

So here it is, Gerald, letter numero uno. Perhaps I'll write again.

Oh, Doctor Thackery also suggested that I should try to end on a positive note. So, thanks for teaching me how to wash my hands, Daddy.

Trent

CHAPTER TWO

Trent Reynolds was recently incarcerated for statutory rape. A thirty-seven-year-old, educated male; he was a guidance counselor at Glenwood High School until his arrest. His charges propose pedophilia, and his propensities certainly fall in this direction. Nevertheless, while Reynolds exhibits signatures of the disorder—he is an adult who has demonstrated primary sexual attraction leading to misconduct with a student under his care—other factors must be considered as well; his own childhood sexual abuse being among them.

I qualify, he is serving time for accounts of sexual misconduct with a minor. However, I have learned that in his teen years and as a young adult, he was involved with others where a significant age gap between himself and his victims existed. Modifications in the law, however, have granted him immunity against what today would be considered criminal. Therefore, I shall regard primarily the index offense as I offer guidance. However, the incidents for which he will not be charged must be considered as psychological indicators if progress is to be made. We shall explore all of these in treatment.

The patient demonstrates a normality of sexual tendencies that make him difficult to categorize. He does not fit easily into the DSM's classification. He has tested remarkably low on the volumetric and circumferential phallometry index and records moderate registration on the Abel and Becker Cognition Scale. Abel screening has revealed that Reynolds has mild predispositions but is by no means characteristically a pedophile. An early diagnosis would suggest he is an ephebophile. The question is, of course, what makes him so?

Work with criminals of this nature has revealed that cultural embracing of primarily western moral ideas should not imply that we are talking about human universals or final truths. It is my opinion that labeling an inmate based solely upon his charges seldom serves either the inmate or society well. Reynolds could be either a narcissist of the most extreme making or perhaps an empath. Time will tell.

Our sessions together are proving him to be intelligent and articulate. However, the prison culture, along with the loss of everything he once had and was, has left him broken and psychologically friable. Reynolds was a certified therapist with an exemplary record until this occurrence. I am eager to commence our work together, and there is much work to do. He offers a wealth of promise for understanding the mind of the sex offender.

I must confess that Reynolds has me somewhat confused. While I loathe his crime, I am drawn to the person I believe lives inside of him. The same cannot be said for many of those I work with in this place. I have consented to see him weekly, as I believe he may offer valuable insights into a disturbed society.

His index offense arose in a therapeutic setting where he found himself increasingly attracted to a student. He chose to continue treatment with her against his better judgment and ethical considerations. He eventually succumbed. I condemn his actions as well as the neglect for his own and the student's well-being. Nevertheless, his situation is understandable. Every therapist faces such trials numerous times throughout their practice. The difference is that Reynolds acted upon his desire and crossed that thin red line.

His victim, a sixteen-year-old female, had been a counselee of Reynolds for the better part of a high school year. As the guidance counselor in her school, he provided a listening ear, moral support, and encouragement regarding typical teenage struggles at school and at home. He had become for her, to use his own words, "a refuge in the midst of the storm that is high school." The student, Brianna Barnes, whom shall henceforth be referred to as "B," was recommended to Reynolds by her geometry teacher, Miss Thatcher, who was quite close to B. Recognizing issues that were beyond her skill set and academic training, she suggested B visit Reynolds and made the first appointment for her.

Their initial meetings were "a waste of time," according to entries from B's diary. Nevertheless, she continued to seek his guidance and after several appointments reported, "I like Mr. Reynolds. He's cute and funny, and he's helping me to see that there is more to life than high school. Why isn't there one decent guy in this entire school who's my age?"

Within two months of their initial consultation, B was initiating and scheduling up to three meetings per week with Reynolds. He did nothing to discourage or set boundaries to prevent this. Her journal suggests the cute, older guy crush had elevated into full transference. Reynolds states he recognized this yet chose to set it aside rather than address the issue as he feared it would impede the progress they were making. A seasoned therapist would have—should have—immediately recognized the faultiness of this thinking process. As Reynolds is such, his lack of response suggests he was already in denial.

Four months into treatment, Reynolds reports that her emotional attachment toward him had begun to affect progress, and he addressed the issue. This was met with repudiation, as is often the case, and her making the statement, "You wish!" then laughing it off. Reynolds admits he did indeed "wish" it was true. At that point, he began to display evidence of justification: minimizing the danger of continuing his treatment with B and magnifying the benefits of their relationship.

Countertransference—the therapist feeling inappropriate emotion toward a patient—like transference, is not uncommon in therapy, and we have many tools at our disposal to deal with this when it occurs. Reynolds did nothing. Worse, he chose the most dangerous path: denial and lying to himself. He addressed the transference but not the countertransference, a far deadlier neglect.

Within a month of the confrontation, they were secretly meeting for coffee after school and on weekends. Small gifts were exchanged, and hugs and affectionate touching became common practice.

Their first "full admission" occurred on a Friday morning before class, behind the privacy of his closed office door. From Reynolds' personal journal, I quote:

> I told her this is something I should have done long ago. I pulled her close into my arms, and we embraced. Our lips met in a slow, silent moment of deep passion. Her lips parted, and I felt the tip of her tongue against mine—electricity, a magnetic energy I had never before experienced and was completely unprepared for.
>
> The morning bell brought us back to reality. She wiped her mouth on the back of her pale hand, slowly turned on her heels, tossed her long, strawberry-blonde hair over her shoulder, and smiled seductively at me. "See you at 2:15, Mr. Reynolds," she said. With that, she disappeared through the door and down the hallway. I could hear the soft footfalls of her beautiful feet make their way to her class as my head attempted to make sense of what my heart had already confirmed. For the first time, I knew I was in deep trouble.

As I read this entry, I'm struck with the thought that Reynolds is unable to be honest with himself. His statement, "For the first time, I knew at that moment I was in deep trouble," is indicative of this. He knew well before their first kiss that he was in deep trouble. His unwillingness to admit this to himself, even in the privacy of a personal journal entry, is disturbing.

He continues:

> In the teacher's lounge later that morning, Deborah Thatcher approached me and commented upon the wonderful work I had been doing with Brianna. "She's like a different person. This morning in class she was all smiles, energetic, and full of life. I'm not sure how you do it, Trent, but whatever you're doing, don't stop.'" Those words struck like a hammer. Suddenly, I was nauseous. I went immediately to

> the vice principal and let him know I was not well. I took the rest of the day off and went home sick.
>
> At home, three times that morning I picked up the phone to call Jack Wilmott, the regional supervisor of high school guidance counselors. Three times I placed the phone back in its cradle. I rationalized that it was already too late; I had kissed her. That was enough to cost me my license and have me fired. I rationalized that no one had ever done such a terrible thing; therefore, no one could possibly understand, support, or help me. I rationalized that I had now recognized the mistake and would take preventative measures to ensure it would never happen again. I rationalized that everything would be okay.
>
> The doorbell rang at 2:30 p.m. She stood there, smiling from ear to ear. "Heard you were under the weather. Thought I would drop by to cheer you up."

A strange thing happens to a man who has never addressed severe childhood trauma. When he is at the convergence of disaster and destiny, he most often chooses the wrong path.

Reynolds invited her in.

The intake process reveals that Reynolds, regardless of his education and clinical experience, is as ignorant of the causes of his behavior as any patient I have worked with. He is self-deceived and unaware of the root issues that propel his dysfunctions, which are numerous.

Deeper exploration of his psyche has revealed significant cognitive distortions, including a buried anger and hatred toward his father at a foundational level. Therefore, we have begun clinical methodologies to explore this primary dysfunction.

The relationship between attitudes and behavior is complex. Reynolds, as he should, displays a higher-than-average understanding of these complexities. Nevertheless, his understanding as to why he entertains the attitudes that form his actions is truncated. His history with B bears witness to this.

The more we talk about Reynolds' father, Gerald, the more I am convinced that this is the proper place to begin our hard work. I have suggested that he begin by writing a letter to his father. The moment I made the suggestion, he balked. The abject horror he displayed at the very notion of communicating with his father was evidence that this was indeed the proper place to begin. I was emphatic that this would be an exercise for him only—a way to express himself, a letter that would never be sent. "Why not write a letter to your father that you will never send to him? It will be just for you. Tell your father all the things that piss you off about him. Let him know you think he has failed you miserably. Could you do that?"

He expressed doubt that he would have anything to say. I ignored this and emphasized that while he would never send the letter, he was to write it as if he would. I recommended he put it—or them, depending on whether he chooses to continue the exercise—in an envelope and even address it. This process seems to serve as a binding agent between fiction and reality. Placing the letter in an envelope and addressing it provides patients with a sense of closure and finality. I have learned that patients often feel as though this act gives them a voice and strength.

Unaddressed childhood trauma is one of the strongest predictors of offending. Every therapist who goes into practice is required to undergo personal psychotherapy as a part of their training to deal with their own internal brokenness, which we all have to a greater or lesser degree. Brennan Manning suggests that "Wholeness is brokenness owned and thereby healed." Until we can own our brokenness, it cannot be healed. Until it is healed, our ability to provide the same for others is limited.

Not surprisingly, investigation into Reynolds' personal psychotherapy reveals that he has never addressed with any sincerity some of the core dysfunctions that have led him to this place where he now finds himself.

CHAPTER THREE

Sleep in prison rarely comes easily. In fact, many nights it doesn't come at all. And on the nights it does, it comes in fits and starts. Sleep is the one thing I long for above all else. For to sleep, "perchance to dream," brings with it the opportunity to escape, ever so briefly, from the hell that holds me here. For reasons I have yet to understand, I slept better after writing that first letter to Gerald than I have in the 223 days I've been in Briar Ridge Medium Security Penitentiary.

The word "penitentiary" itself brings about a sense of juxtaposition. The idea of being "penitent" or its precursor, "repentant," simply does not coincide with the institutional model. There is nothing about the "rehabilitative process"—and I use that term loosely, for nothing like rehabilitation actually occurs within the corrections system—that would lead a man to repent. React, certainly; repent, not so much.

I'm sure the emotional exhaustion brought about by the writing of that first letter to Gerald had much to do with the decent rest I got. It takes months to get used to a prison mattress. It's about two inches thick and covered in a corrugated plastic that sticks to your skin like a leaf in the rain to your windshield—a Beautyrest it is not. Although better the plastic than whatever contagion it would have been infested with by previous inmates, I suppose. That night, even upon this god-awful prison mattress, I fell into restful slumber.

For first-time convicts, prison has a learning curve that is almost straight up. One of the more difficult adjustments to make is personal identification. We are referred to as prisoners, convicts, felons, offenders, criminals, inmates, and most often by our DOJ number. These are the official titles we bear. In essence, they are one and the same. There are many other more individuated and personal categories by which prisoners are labeled: scum, leech, skinner, banger, murderer, thug, reject, rapist, goof, cell bitch, and the list goes on. Nevertheless, one of the first difficult realities of prison life is coming to terms with these new designations. Getting used to the idea that a person's actual name is a privilege reserved for those who live on the outside of these fences takes some time. A man's identity is reduced to his crime and the label that most accurately fits that crime.

In my practice—previous practice—I made an effort to refer to students by their given names and to do so with regularity. As human beings, we have an intrinsic need for personal identity. An adjustment period is required when learning to respond to almost anything but your name.

White-collar people who commit blue-collar crimes—or worse—have a difficult time fitting in here. We are the exception, not the norm, and we have no frame of reference for what we are about to experience.

Many of my current associates are referred to as "lifers on the installment plan." They have made and are making prison a lifetime occupation, or more accurately, preoccupation. A vast majority of the men here have been in the corrections system since they were children. It's not uncommon to meet a forty-year-old man who has been incarcerated for the better part of twenty-five years, with a year or two here and there on the outside. This describes not a few of these men but the majority. They have found a way to make prison a livable situation for themselves. Or perhaps more accurately, they cannot find a way to make freedom a viable way to live.

Either way, they seem to be able to navigate the treacherous waters of prisondom in ways that the minority among us are incapable of doing. They are also able to detect the ignorance, weakness, and fear of the prison neophyte, like a shark smells blood in water. One result of these differences is that we are afraid of each other. The advantage, however, is theirs. They are keenly aware of how to deal with fear, whereas inmates like me, being on their turf, are not. We are most vulnerable.

Fear breathes fire in Briar Ridge, sucking up confidence like oxygen. Unlike me, there are many in this place who claim to be afraid of nothing. I listened in on a conversation between four inmates, all boasting about the things they weren't afraid of—cops, guards, "the man," each other, anything. The bravado was palpable. "I'd take on anyone in this fucking joint," said one brave soul. The truth of the matter, as I'm coming to learn, is that many of these "fearless" men are more afraid of *being* afraid than they are of dying. I think the proper term for this is stupid, but it would be profoundly injudicious to suggest such.

MY SISTER, CLAIRE, IS COMING to visit this afternoon! Visits are an oasis in the desert. Every word with someone from the outside is worth a thousand with a fellow inmate. Talking with another prisoner is like inhaling stale cigarette smoke. Even the best conversations are old, stiff, and fetid. There is nothing new to talk about in prison. One hears and takes part in the same conversations held hundreds of times, with subtle variations. But someone from the outside world brings a fresh newness that is life giving, like the oxygen Mom required in her final days.

Claire has been a source of inspiration and hope amidst the desperation and gloom that is prison. In our childhood, she was one of my victims. In adulthood, she is my only champion. She is grace personified. What I deserve from her is rejection, isolation, abhorrence, and disgust. What she bestows upon me instead is compassion, mercy, munificence, and love. In this regard, I am a blessed man. I only wish she wasn't so merciful with her kindness. She offers the same—freely given—to our father, something I cannot bring myself to do. I suppose that if she's willing to bequeath that honor upon me, Gerald is no less deserving of it.

I find it interesting that Doctor Thackery doesn't ask me to consider a more Claire-like compassion toward Gerald.

I stopped calling him "Dad" many years ago, for he is certainly no father to me. But "sperm donor" implies that my mother was a "cum dumpster," and I cannot go there. I call him Dad only in sarcasm. Wisely, perhaps, Doctor Thackery knows that compassion toward Gerald is a bridge too far.

But Claire Bare is coming. I haven't seen her for several weeks now. She brings with her a radiance that fills the darkest corners of my soul. It was not always this way between us. Like all siblings, we have had our share of conflict.

When she was six or seven, I was as consumed by the Pokémon craze as she was with Care Bears. My favorite was Ditto. Like all Pokémon, Ditto possessed a special power; his was the ability to transform into anything. I suppose it was this characteristic that I found so attractive. If I could transform into anything, Gerald could not get to me. More than anything as a child, I wanted to be Ditto. I would spend hours "transforming" into whatever my mind could conceive. I was the fastest horse in the world, a bird that could fly to the moon in mere seconds. Anywhere that would keep me from having to be near him.

On occasion, to piss her off, I would pretend to transform into Mr. Stevens, Claire's homeroom teacher, whom she despised. I would barge into her room as Mr. Stevens and lecture her, embarrass her, and give her more homework than all the other pretend kids in her pretend class. She hated when I turned into Ditto.

I remember the day clearly. It's hard to forget. I searched my room high and low, but Ditto had vanished. Claire was taking a bath when I barged into the bathroom; of course, she immediately screamed.

"What did you do with Ditto?" I demanded.

"Nothin'. Maybe he transformed himself into invisible 'cause he didn't like your stupid face!" she yelled.

I stormed out and headed straight to her bedroom, grabbed Funshine Bear, and ran out with it. Claire jumped out of the bathtub and, naked, chased me down the hall and downstairs. I took her favorite Care Bear outside and ran to the outhouse behind our farmhouse with Claire still in tow. It was a cold night, and she stood there dripping wet and shivering as I dangled Funshine by one leg over the outhouse hole. "Tell me what you did with Ditto!" I threatened.

"I didn't touch your stupid Pokémon!" By that point she was crying and freezing.

"Tell me!"

Nothing.

I continued to threaten, and she continued to deny. I didn't drop it in—the affection I had for her, that we had for each other—would never allow me to do that. But Claire ran screaming into the house.

When she told Gerald what I had done, he beat me mercilessly. Then he stripped me naked and threw me out the back door into a snowbank while he got dressed in his coat and boots. He dragged me by the hair into the outhouse, grabbed me by the ankles, and forced me headfirst into the hole. "How do you like it, Shithead?" he asked. He continues to call me Shithead to this day.

I found Ditto in my underwear drawer, just where I had left him. But as so often was the case in our childhood, I was pissed off at Gerald, but defenseless against him, so I took it out on Claire. For days I wouldn't talk to her. Shortly after, I began to call her Claire Bare. It began as a derogatory term because of her childish affection for Care Bears and the fact that she chased me bare naked out of the house. However, as things between us returned to normal, it became a term of endearment and something we both cherish to this day.

Claire Bare brings pure love. Just to be with her in the same room is life giving. When she comes, she will tell me all about Stevie and Aaron's soccer games, won and lost, the screenplay that Robert has nearly completed, the casserole that burned, the garbage truck that was too early, the next-door neighbor's dog that should be euthanized, and who was the latest victim of amnesia on *All My Children*. And I shall sit enraptured by every word.

In a place where every occurrence is sensational and the mundane is the exception, you long for the latter. The ordinary is extraordinary. I seek the ordinary the way a flower seeks the sun. I am coming to understand the reason so many television shows, books, and movies are set inside prisons. While tedium and monotony rule the day, even standing in a meal line is fraught with potential volatility. To escape this for even a moment is rejuvenating. For some—the regulars, the lifers—this has become their norm, their home. For inmates like me who are nothing more than unwelcome pests in other's homes, we are desperate for the peace that the primary occupants can somehow find amidst the chaos. My visits with Claire provide that. And so, I wait impatiently. She cannot visit enough.

BACK IN MY CELL, I settle—or attempt to settle—after Claire has departed. While our visits bring light and life to my existence, our farewell hugs bring a darkness that deepens with each step away from her. I watch as she walks through the doors leading her to freedom and me to this. What *this* is isn't easy to describe. It's the furthest thing from anything I could have imagined knowing anything about a few short years ago.

That dark day still hangs heavily overhead, like a cloud of mosquitoes. I was sitting at my desk in my office when the phone call from Detective Williams came, asking me to come to the station so he could "ask me a few questions."

"May I inquire what the nature of our conversation is to be about?" I asked.

"Let's leave that for our visit," he replied.

I knew full well what it was about.

The drive to the police station was filled with horror. I attempted to calm my shaking hands and racing heart with futile efforts to convince myself that he was simply looking for information about a former student I had worked with who was perhaps in trouble with the law or had committed suicide—anything but the truth that I knew I was certain to face.

The moment I entered the room, he spoke the words that I knew were coming: "Trent Reginald Reynolds, you are under arrest for statutory rape."

Blackness.

There I sat in that interrogation room for hours as events from my life, taken from the report of my lover, were revealed as pure hatred. A freefall into the deepest, darkest pit imaginable. The more he accused, the further I fell, the darker the black, the deeper the despair.

Interrogation rooms in and of themselves are a type of psychological torture. Unlike the ones in television shows, they are not large rooms with a small table in the center. This room was no more than six feet square, the door not even able to open completely before it hits the chair that Detective Williams will sit in. The cold, gray metal chair I'm placed in is intentionally uncomfortable, bolted to the floor with the back of it against a wall so that I have to sit sideways with the table between us to my left.

There are three large and ominous video cameras, each aimed in my direction. Two large speakers, which also house microphones, are mounted on either side of that large window—one-way glass—permitting who knows who to observe every word and shaking tremor that comes from my being. I'm informed of my rights, given the opportunity to contact a lawyer, and told that everything is being recorded.

The attack begins.

Hours later, as my life lies like a frog in ninth-grade biology class, dissected and flayed, held open with pins, I'm asked whether I would like a bottle of water. As Williams leaves to retrieve it, loud rap music fills the small chamber. More psychological torture.

Another detective returns in Williams' place. The music fades as she hands me a bottle of water and begins her role. I say little. With someone of my emotional chemistry, the good cop/bad cop game has little effect.

The criminal activities that brought me to this place are much like the storm that I now see building far away out my small, barred window. A dark gray line along the horizon where earth meets sky. It slowly moves toward me, building, menacing.

Escape is impossible. I'm as powerless to move out of its path as I was the path that brought me to my knees in the interrogation room that ominous day more than two years removed. Our relationship was described as acts of despicable horror, painted to show me as a horrendous fiend seeking to devour. The testimony of my closest friend and lover interpreted in the most tainted and decrepit light. I was reduced to a hideous, insolent creature of darkness.

A troll.

Memories and events once beautiful, now repugnant, storm upon me, and I'm trapped, guilty, undone. I suppose, in the recesses of my psyche, like this storm, I knew it was coming. The tempest engulfs this prison in a blanket of cold, wet misery. And somewhere in the furthest reaches of my mind, I knew that day would eventually come as well. Like this storm,

I knew it was imminent, all-consuming, and that I would experience the full fury of its wrath.

Reflecting now upon that evening after leaving the interrogation room on a bail bond posted by Claire, I recall sitting at home with Ozzy on my lap, a twelve-year-old Glenfiddich single malt in one hand, and counting my losses on the other.

In the background, behind all the clamor inside my head, Elton John softly sings:

Oh, oh, Daniel my brother you are older than me
Do you still feel the pain of the scars that won't heal
Your eyes have died, but you see more than I
Daniel you're a star in the face of the sky.

There is something mournful, sad, and yet soothing about these words. I'm well aware of the meaning behind the song: the sorrow of losing a dear friend in the Vietnam War. But for me, there is an alternate meaning, unexplainable and deeply spiritual, something in those words that connects with me and resonates within my soul in a way no other song ever has.

I can see Daniel waving goodbye.
God it looks like Daniel,
must be the clouds in my eyes.

To me, the song speaks of losses that go far beyond that of a friend.

Loss begins with regret. Counting all the "woulda, coulda, shouldas." If I would have turned away . . . I could have gone a different path. I should have resisted those strong primal urges. In those early days, right after my arrest, I had no idea how many losses were on the horizon. I was able to calculate the obvious ones, but the vast majority, the truly life-altering ones, of those I had no clue.

A loud buzzer shakes me back to the moment. Then comes an announcement: "Emergency lockdown. Emergency lockdown. All prisoners return to their cells." A scuttle in the corridors explodes as last-minute attempts are made to grind inmates for any and all types of food or anything else that might make time more bearable. I hop onto my bunk and throw the thin, threadbare blanket over my head in hopes that I will be passed by. Brakes, my cellmate, comes in with a bluster of expletives that suggest it's going to be a long few days. The last lockdown was seventeen days. During lockdown, there is no inmate movement outside of our cells aside from weekly five-minute shower privileges.

During lockdowns, we do not go to the cafeteria to eat, and meals are not served in the regular brown plastic trays. The trays won't fit through the bars. Instead, they are served on paper plates clam-shelled together and slid vertically through the bars. Whatever doesn't fall onto the floor, we get to eat. Meals also seem to get smaller the longer lockdown continues. Not surprisingly, the guards, parole officers, and program directors who make and serve the meals because the kitchen workers are locked down don't like doing what they're forced to do either.

Consequently, meals are reduced to two per day: a brunch-like thing with two slices of bread, some type of root vegetable—turnips, carrots, beets, or potatoes—a banana or apple, often rotting (culls, no doubt), and pasta or rice covered in a thick, gray, congealed goop that serves as our protein. When I was a boy, and if we had money, we would sometimes buy our dog, Charlie, Doctor Ballard's canned dog food. It was a congealment of gray and pink clumps. Haven't seen the brand in years. I think they now probably manufacture it for the prison system.

The food we are served is not easy to palate, nor should it be. We are criminals, after all. I have no misgivings about meals. I'm not suggesting we deserve better nutrition, nor am I bitching about it. As my parole officer is so fond of reminding me, "If you don't like the way things are here, Reynolds, you shouldn't have chosen to come."

The reason for lockdowns is never explained to inmates. Of course, those involved must know. It most often has to do with a death—suicide, overdose, murder—or the assault of a guard. We also have quarterly lockdowns for cell searches. They're always fun. Stripped and forced to stand naked in the corridor while your cell is turned inside out and left looking like the aftermath of a tornado. At least putting it all back together gives you something to do with your time for a short while.

A prisoner's number one enemy is time. I must find more to do with it, lest it drive me crazy.

CHAPTER FOUR

Dear Gerald,

We're now on day nine of a lockdown, and there is little to do inside my six-by-eight-foot home, so I thought I'd write. I sometimes feel that this exercise in writing is a complete waste of time, but alas, I do have time to waste. I also think that Doctor Thackery's rationale for getting me to do this may be an exercise in futility. I don't seem to get anything but angry when I write to you. But who knows? Maybe getting pissed off isn't such a bad thing.

When he first suggested it, I wasn't a fan. Yet, once he explained it, I had to agree it wasn't the worst idea. Principally, the way he recommended it: "Why not write your father and explain to him all of the heart-wrenching, fucked up, and morbid horrors that brought you to this place in life?" He was clear that I should omit nothing and include all the memories and nightmares that I'm too cowardly to tell you to your face. Would you like to know what they are? I'm sure not. But since you'll never lay eyes upon these pages, I'll proceed, with or without your permission.

Remember how Mom used to sing all around the house when Claire and I were young? Oh, how she loved to sing. She had a beautiful voice too, not that you ever noticed. She would sing to

Claire and me often, and we suggested she do something with her talent.

One winter, Claire and I must have been ten and twelve or so when we signed her up to audition for the role of Tzeitel in a local production of *Fiddler on the Roof*. She had no idea. When the script arrived, and Claire told her what we had done, she laughed and said we were silly. But we found her reading the script on more than one occasion, and the closer the audition date came, the more she considered it. She even asked us if we really thought she could do it.

Claire says she once came home from school to find Mom singing and dancing, practicing "Matchmaker, Matchmaker." But when the day of the audition came, you insisted that one, the idea was ridiculous, and two, she would not have the time because the production run was over harvest, and you would need her help. I wonder if, as she lay dying, she regretted not telling you to go fuck yourself and just went for it.

I think she stopped singing around the house by the time I was in middle school. You had given her far too many reasons not to by then.

Claire tells me you're exploring the Caribbean on *The Endeavour*. Sounds nice. You left the day after Mom's funeral? So glad you stuck around long enough to see that Claire would be alright. My parole officer told me I could apply for a "compassionate order" to attend the funeral. I would be in shackles and handcuffs with a guard on either side of me. They would take me to the funeral home, sit with me at the very back, and then return me to Briar Ridge the moment "Amen" had been declared. Ah, compassion.

Part of me desperately wanted to be there, the part that loves Mom and despises you. Mom and I talked, though, before I came here, before she died, and she asked that I not come. Interestingly, her reasons and yours for not wanting me there were similar yet so juxtaposed. She didn't want me to have to experience any more shame and degradation than I already have, and you didn't want to experience any more of the same brought upon you by me. Yeah, Claire told me.

Ever wonder how I ended up in this predicament? I do. I have been driven to the acts I'm guilty of by so many more dysfunctions than a simple lust of the flesh. Where it began and how it grew is what Doctor Thackery and I are trying to get to the root of. He tells me I'm probably not the debaucherist I think I am. I have a difficult time believing that. Society depicts those who share my guilt—my crime—as the lowest of the low. We are inhuman.

I recall with absolute clarity the judge's declaration against me that dark day now 251 days removed. His words resound today in this cell—in my mind—as loudly as they did in that chamber. "Mr. Reynolds, you are a disgrace to your profession and this court. I hereby sentence you to four years in a federal penitentiary for your horrific crimes against this young woman. Bailiff, remove this man from my courtroom." He said *man* the way a preacher might say *demon*.

My arrest happened almost a year and a half prior to that pronouncement. So, it's not like I didn't know what was coming. But with something of this nature, "knowing" holds little power to prepare you for what's ahead. While the time I will spend behind bars began a mere nine months ago, in many ways I began serving this sentence the day I was arrested. That was the day I was fired, my license stripped from me, and my crime made public. Shame, fear, and self-loathing boiled over. In this sense, I have already served almost half of my time. For there are walls that imprison, built without bricks and mortar, that are equally confining as those with. And living under your roof, I have been in a prison of sorts for most of my fucking life.

When the large, beautifully carved oak doors of the courtroom opened and the bailiffs ushered me through, the other side of the judicial system revealed its face. The polished brass, gleaming hardwood, and plush carpeting gave way to rough, unpainted cinder block and raw concrete.

Innocence begets opulence and guilt paucity.

Since you'd never ask, I thought I'd give you a glimpse of that experience. Immediately outside of the courtroom I'm turned against the concrete wall. As instructed, I place my hands on two large yellow Xs painted on the wall and my feet upon corresponding Xs on the floor. Firm, careless hands run up and down my legs, my thighs, my crotch, back, stomach, arms, chest, and through my hair. *Is this really happening*? I wonder. It doesn't seem real; it hardly seems surreal. It's like a dream, yet I'm all too aware that it is not.

Harsh words: "Turn around and place your hands on top of your head. Open your mouth. Lift your tongue." They spin me around to face the concrete once more, then yank my hands behind me. Cold, steel handcuffs are placed on my wrists and shackles on my ankles—like the judicial system—tight and unforgiving. Then they swing me around and instruct me to walk forward but to stay near the wall.

Once shackled, walking becomes a shuffle.

The long, slow trundle is utterly shameful, yet the guards talk and joke about their upcoming weekend as though I am not present. I'm not sure if it was out of curiosity or just to break the painful banter, but I ask the guard to my right (it's more of a statement than a question, I suppose): "This is just another day at the office for you, isn't it?" He doesn't look at me or even glance in my direction.

Pregnant pause—longer—nothing.

His silence says everything he wants to communicate: *You aren't worth wasting my breath on. I wouldn't give you the sweat off my balls if you were dying of thirst in the Sahara.*

I'm not sure why I'm telling you this, Gerald. It's not like you give a damn. I suppose there's a small anticipation that even though you'll never have to live this nightmare, perhaps you'll vicariously feel some of the pain if I let you in.

I can hardly fathom what it even means to let you in. I could open the door, expose my woundedness to you, but would you come in? I hardly think so. Nevertheless, I shall bear my wretchedness upon these pages, pretend that you will get them and that you might give a shit.

There, in that tunnel, as I hobble with a guard in front and one behind toward the remand center that will be my home for the next weeks as a place is prepared for me here in Briar Ridge, everything is dull. Although the overhead fluorescent lights burn brightly, it's as though they are little more than a flickering candle, a foggy yellow glow. The shackles that cut deep into my ankles are nothing more than heavy weights. I learned in those moments that there is an emotional pain—a mental anguish—so overwhelming that all physical discomfort is rendered almost non-existent. For two city blocks, I shuffle alongside my escorts, in that tunnel underneath this fair city I have grown to despise.

The short, two-block trudge seems an eternity, foreshadowing how long the days and even more so the nights of incarceration will feel. In prison, time is an obscure, shifting mechanism where clocks and calendars have no real bearing upon its movement. It has far more to do with one's mental and emotional state than with minutes and hours or even days and years, for that matter.

The more consideration I give to the elusive concept of time, the more I am aware of how artificial a construct it is. On the inside, there is always far too much, and on the outside, one can never seem to find enough.

In her last days, Mom often talked about time. She was under no illusion that she had much of it left. For her, it was as if time had become a commodity. Each person is given a limited amount, some more than others. The fairness of its distribution did not concern her in the least, but she had difficulty grasping that only a few grains of sand remained in the top of the hourglass hers was kept in. What seemed to surprise her most was how quickly an entire life could be consumed.

We enter the bowels of the remand center, itself a small city within the city, underneath the city. Police, corrections officers, general laborers, and inmates scurry like ants in a colony, back and forth, over and under and through the long, bustling corridors.

"Turn around and face the wall." My handcuffs and shackles are removed, and I'm pushed into a filthy holding tank. Graffiti covers the walls, ceiling, and door. Large Plexiglas windows on two sides give all passersby visual access to everything going on inside. A badly stained stainless-steel toilet sits in full view of everyone. Shit has been smeared on the toilet seat and the nearby wall. There is no toilet paper. Afraid to sit on anything, I stand and read the graffiti—wisdom of men gone before me.

"Death before dishonor" is scratched into the pale yellow paint. Really? The writer found nothing dishonorable about this place? It seems to me one's assimilation into this system has the specific agenda of stripping all honor from a man. Another piece of wisdom reads, "Only God can judge me." Somewhat ironic, I think, considering the fact that if you find yourself in this place, judgment by someone other than the Almighty has recently been pronounced upon you. In the ensuing months, I will see these very words tattooed upon the arms, backs, chests, necks, and faces of countless inmates—an indelible statement to the world that they are different, bound by bars but not the law that holds them.

Men who have raped, murdered, and pillaged bear the "Death before dishonor" mantra as a badge of what? Integrity? Somehow, I don't think they understand its meaning. Or perhaps I don't understand theirs, yet I am now one of them. I stand, unable to comprehend my surroundings, and attempt to contemplate the words upon these walls. Nothing makes much sense.

The door to the holding tank opens, and once again I'm instructed to follow an officer. I'm directed into a large room. This one has a full wall of floor-to-ceiling Plexiglas windows that look directly into a reception area. The reception area is teeming with police. Near the back wall, which is no wall at all but rather a sheer curtain, is a shelf with institutional clothing on it. A showerhead is mounted from the ceiling at the front edge of a large yellow square painted on the floor in the middle of the room.

Another police officer enters to join the first one. "Strip," I'm told. "Throw all of your clothes in a pile next to the wall." I follow the directions I'm given. I stand completely naked as they bark orders. I put my hands over my head, turn around, and lift my feet one at a time, to ensure no contraband is stuck to the bottom of them. I bend at the waist as far as I can, reach back, and spread my ass cheeks.

"Wider."

With latex gloves, they check to ensure I'm not harboring anything inside of me. I stand upright again, face them, and open my mouth as the gloves feel for anything I may have hidden there. Hands rub through my hair, fingers in my ears. They toss me a small plastic bottle of some semi-clear, gel-like substance and tell me to shower. The water is cold, and the shampoo/body wash has the smell of chlorinated bleach and the texture of oatmeal.

As I shower, the guards remove my clothing—every remaining earthly possession—and stuff it in a plastic bag. Everything is removed, placed into storage until my release a lifetime away.

I dry myself with a towel the size of a gunny sack and just as coarse and am instructed to dress in the clothing on the shelf near the curtained back wall. I leave that room dressed in blue overalls that are far too large in the waist and far too short in length and one-size-fits-all slippers that don't. I am taken back to the same holding cell, where I continue to ponder the wisdom on the walls around me.

Many hours later—it may have been three, it may be seven, I have no way of knowing—I'm moved to one of the units, where I'm placed into a cell. I soon learn that I will be remanded in this cell twenty-two hours per day and allowed into the center court for forty minutes, three times to grab our meal trays and watch television or use the phone before we are locked up again.

Shall I continue, Gerald?

On that first night, as I lay on the top bunk, a man—I will call him a man, with the hope of not offending him—shared with me as he undressed that he was transgender and halfway through his transition. I have come to know many in this stage of life while serving my time. This half-man, half-woman lay upon the bunk beneath me, snoring a smooth, comfortable rhythm like the slow movement of a waltz. Somehow as I lay unable to fathom slumber, he/she rested comfortably. It was there, under the dull blue light of the remand cell, that I first began to count my mounting losses.

Some things we lose are etched like names in wet cement, into permanent memories. We lose girlfriends and our mothers. And somewhere along the line, we lose hope. The loss of hope is perhaps the most painful and usually comes after so many other losses that it feels like there is little left to lose. That first night, the losses raced through my mind, and they haven't stopped to this day.

Losing my career was just the beginning. With that loss went the respect of colleagues, my reputation, my status as a professional, my sense of purpose, and with these things, any sense of dignity. One would think that the hard, concrete losses would be at the forefront—income and relationships, followed by home, then the loss of one's financial security, hope of retirement, and investment portfolio. In reality, these quantifiable losses pale in comparison to the losses not so easily measured: self-respect, emotional stability, courage, and loyalty. After all, who has ever seen a teaspoon of compassion, a linear foot of character, or a pound of faith? Yet it is these immeasurable losses, accumulating like so much snow on a rooftop, that are much more difficult to bear.

I was supposed to see Doctor Thackery this morning. However, I think that like every other activity, it too has been canceled. Time will tell. Speaking of which, it's almost time for brunch. I must get to the bars that hold me in before they slide the plates through. Otherwise I'll have to wait until supper to know what brunch tasted like.

Hope the Caribbean sun gives you heatstroke.
Trent

CHAPTER FIVE

Therapeutic interventions with Reynolds are revealing a disturbing pattern. It occurs to me that at each point of intense trauma, he arrives at the crux of the matter and there he stalls. He seems to recognize the issue he must overcome in order to break through the wall preventing him from healthier living yet is unable to summon the strength to do what he knows must be done. He is at what Carl Jung refers to as the apex of self-discovery, but he hesitates to make the leap. "A man who has not passed through the inferno of his passions has never overcome them," Jung says. I ask, more of myself than of Reynolds—for until I know what the obstruction is, it's unfair expect him to know—what's holding him back?

In the area of childhood regression therapy, Reynolds seems to be making great strides. There is evidence of vulnerability, clarity, and insight. His ability to understand and articulate his traumas is profound. But as we approach the root cause of his dysfunctions, it's as though an unidentifiable force whispers into his psyche, "This far and no further." And at this point, he seems more unable than unwilling to make further advancements. A subconscious emotional impasse inhibits vertical progress. And thus, our movement becomes lateral. I slide along with him, back and forth, looking for a tributary that might lead us forward but am met with resistance at each entry point. Again, I emphasize, it's my opinion that this blockage is beyond Reynolds' control and not something that he is even conscious of. It exists within the id but has never made it to the ego. Nevertheless, we press onward.

I have submitted a request to the deputy warden to see the patient bi-weekly, and I await the board's decision. While this is unprecedented, I am confident that my rationale is legitimate and will prevail. The prison environment has taken a toll upon Reynolds that I seldom witness in inmates. It is my belief that our progress is hindered by the duration between each session and the emotional toil he is subjugated to. If we are able to meet more often, greater progress will be made, and recidivism will become less likely.

Where definitive evidence of progress surfaces is in his honesty. When a man loses all that has ever been important to him, walls often fall. It's surprising, however, the large number of patients I work with who believe that for some inexplicable reason—whether it is a form of narcissistic moral posturing or to convince the therapist that they are not as dysfunctional as we know they are—they continue to play games in therapy, which serve them no good whatsoever. Reynolds, on the other hand, has been quick to forgo all pretense and has allowed me full access to his woundedness. His self-awareness is remarkable, as are the shame and remorse he carries. This, however, fosters a degree of self-flagellation which, in my opinion, almost exceeds the offense.

In our most recent session, I put forward the idea to Reynolds that his inner child, as wounded as it may be, longs for some intimate connection with the man he is today. His response was that if his inner child knew the man he is today, he would want nothing to do with him. The depth of his disgrace and sorrow is one barrier that seems to stall our progress. Again, I look to the wisdom of Jung: "Your vision will become clear only when you can look into your own heart. Who looks outside, dreams; who looks inside, awakes." I tell Reynolds this.

Not to be outdone, he speaks the wisdom of Roger Waters:

They flutter behind you, your possible pasts
Some bright-eyed and crazy some frightened and lost
A warning to anyone still in command
Of their possible future to take care.

On his way out after our session, he looks over his shoulder and completes the refrain:

> *Strung out behind us the banners and flags*
> *of our possible pasts lie in tatters and rags.*

Touché.

CHAPTER SIX

Three days after I last wrote to Gerald, lockdown ended. An interesting phenomenon occurs at the end of lockdown, evidence that suggests human beings, even in this place, are social creatures.

For the first day or two post lockdown, there is an almost tranquil calm throughout the prison. Even the hardest of criminals mellows somewhat. There is a longing, even amongst the most cowardly of us, for interaction with our own species. In a word, for a short while, people are decent. It's as though the human need for social interaction is greater than even some sociopaths' need for supremacy and ruin. And for a few fleeting moments, decency carries the day. But alas, that is short-lived. Once again, habitual behavior overtakes social value, and unrest is restored. Prison life returns to its proper balance.

Observations regarding the social order of prison life take me back to middle school. The ranks and antics of inmates parallel a junior high mentality, so, it's an appropriate memory.

My grade-nine Social Studies teacher taught me a lesson that now, more than twenty years later, I finally understand. Mrs. McEnroe was a rotund, stout woman, all the ammunition required for a pack of ravenous grade-nine boys. She was walking down the hall during a class break between students who were loitering against their lockers. One of my classmates uttered a quiet yet distinct "moo." Soon, a number of us joined in, and giggling from others broke out.

Mrs. McEnroe stopped and called four of us by name. She invited us to follow her to the principal's office, where she gave us an assignment to be completed by the next morning. It was a simple two-page essay. The topic: *how the conventions of civility are essential to the pacifistic functioning of society.* If we didn't understand the nature of the subject, we were to be in her classroom as soon as school got out for the day, and she would gladly explain it to us.

At 3:45, we all found ourselves in her classroom, awaiting her explanation, which conveniently took more than an hour to deliver and felt a lot like the detention she replaced with the essay.

I don't remember what I wrote in that essay, but her thorough explanation has remained like an earworm. And now, as I observe the behaviors of the inmates I encounter in this place every day, I have come to know how essential civil conventions are to peaceful living. It took this experience for me to fully realize what Mrs. McEnroe attempted to teach us.

As human beings, there are social norms we must follow to live in harmony with others. In social communities, these are most often adhered to, and when they're not, there are consequences. In the hallways of a junior high school, it is unacceptable to insinuate that your teacher is a cow.

In prison, social convention is established through violence. As a result, chaos and tyranny become the social order. The absence of civility that exists to provide structure and a level playing field creates an environment where a man's life continually hangs in the balance. Simply put, the lack of civility in prison scares the shit out of me.

CLAIRE JUST LEFT. IT WAS a surprise visit and much shorter than usual but understandably so. She wasn't planning to come until the weekend, but she rearranged a few things to be with me. Our topic of conversation was singularly focused—Gerald.

I am uncertain how to process what she told me. I see Doctor Thackery shortly and hope he will have some helpful advice. Gerald has had a massive myocardial infarction. He is currently in a coma in Lower Keys

Medical Center. Apparently, he was aboard *The Endeavour* when he keeled over. He was airlifted to Key West, Florida. They don't expect him to live.

Well, that came right out of left field. I just finished reading the letters I've written to Gerald, and I don't know what to think. I'm attempting to process this information, and I find myself at a complete loss as to where to begin.

I'm most surprised to find that somewhere in the depths of my being, I give a damn. I really thought that if this day ever came, the only emotion that would follow would be relief, peppered perhaps with a smattering of joy. Yet here I sit, and as much as I dislike it, I feel sad.

Doctor Thackery wasn't much help. He suggested I write to Gerald and tell him how I'm feeling. Of course, like the previous letters, this is to be an exercise for me alone, and I will never send this letter either, not that it would matter at this point anyway. But as he suggests, it may help to clarify some of the emotional shit that I'm wrestling with—probably not the worst idea.

CHAPTER SEVEN

Claire's recent impromptu visit didn't interrupt our routine, and she and Robert showed up to visit again today. As is each visit, it was a rich time. "Apples of gold in settings of silver," as the Psalmist says.

Sadly, even in his near-death state, Gerald stole most of the attention. Claire—as difficult as it is for me to grasp—is very upset. Apparently, Gerald's heart stopped for several minutes before he received any attention, and if he ever comes out of the coma, he will likely be unable to function with any quality of life. Judy, his latest love interest, has returned home unsure of what her role should be. So, now abandoned, he is alone in Florida, and that's eating a hole in Claire Bare. She and Robert have discussed her flying down to be with him, which I suppose is the proper thing to do. I couldn't care less, and the selfish part of me knows that since Claire can't be in two places at once, the entire time she is sitting vigil with the vegetable, she won't be here with me. I dare not tell her that, but that is the primary reason I have discouraged her from going.

I hate that I can be such an asshole.

WHEN MOM WAS ILL AND dying, Claire and I shared responsibility for her care. I suppose it only stands to reason that she feels an obligation to care for Gerald as well.

After my arrest and before my incarceration, I had a fair bit of time on my hands. For the worst part of Mom's illness, at least the worst part before coming here, I became her primary caregiver. Claire was certainly involved, but with her work schedule, the boys' hectic lives, and my unemployed and very open schedule, that responsibility fell to me, and I accepted it with gratitude.

To be honest, guilt for the pain that my shame brought upon Mom served as a catalyst for my faithful servitude. I don't know the full extent of how my offense impacted her—we rarely talked about it—but I'm certain it weighed heavily.

Mom didn't welcome truly open conversations about what I had done, so we danced around it like Swedes around the Maypole. She preferred not to know. I think she felt that was easier than knowing. On more than a few occasions, I brought the matter up, but she quickly shut it down. "We all make mistakes, Reggie." Mom often referred to me by my middle name. "What's important is that we learn from them. I love you, and no matter what anyone says or what you've done, nothing will change that fact." And that was the end of the matter. She would discuss it no further.

I think she felt like she was protecting Gerald by closing that door. When I was a kid, she was often horrified by the treatment I would receive at his hand, and I'm certain she felt it had contributed to my delinquency. If she was unaware, she could turn a deaf ear to the past. It was less painful for her than acknowledging it. I could have forced the issue, but with the physical pain she was enduring each day, I chose, rightly or wrongly, to leave well enough alone.

My days with Mom were spent listening to music she loved, helping her untangle massive balls of wool from her knitting fiascos, and planning and preparing meals. Our conversations revolved around her grandchildren, Claire Bare, and Robert's hilarious television shows, which we would often watch together.

Although Gerald was the center of attention and Robert and Claire were struggling with next steps, just having them here is like a couple of hours away from this place. I make sure I always let them know how much I value their visits. And I know that it's selfish of me to hope that

Claire chooses to not go see Gerald, primarily because then she will not be around to visit me, and I hate that narcissistic character flaw within. Just not as much as I hate being alone.

CHAPTER EIGHT

Dear Gerald,

So sorry to hear about your little mishap. Oops. Doctor Thackery told me I'm supposed to be honest in these letters. I'm not really that sorry at all. Let me start again.

I heard about your heart attack and understand you're not doing very well. Sucks to be you.

I must admit, though, that when Claire told me about what happened, something deep within me was sad. I'm still trying to put my finger on what that is. Because to be honest with you, I didn't think your demise would have brought anything but jubilation to me. It may have something to do with losing both parents in the same year. Nevertheless, a certain sense of sorrow comes with the knowledge of your condition.

I think it may be related to guilt and shame—not mine, yours. However, being a shame-bearer myself, I know something of the condition. Shame is one of those emotions I would not wish upon my worst enemy—not even you.

I hear that on the off chance you ever regain consciousness, you will be incapable of doing anything for yourself. I can't imagine how humiliating it would be for you to have someone feed and clothe you. Not to mention wipe your ass and wash your balls. No, shame isn't the right word. Shame is that emotion we feel when we've been caught in a despicable situation. Embarrassment, that's what you would feel. Sadly, being embarrassed is something you'll have to learn to live with—or not. Perhaps, if you live, you'll get used to living with a measure of guilt as well for years of brutal treatment toward those you saw as less than, as you become utterly dependent upon them.

Shame is what I live with, though, and I'm learning that guilt and shame, while closely related, are not the same thing at all. Guilt is the feeling you have when you know you've done something wrong. Shame is the feeling you get when you believe you *are* something wrong. That's the emotion that haunts my soul day in and out. I don't just think that I *have* done something bad; I think that I *am* something bad. And as I reflect upon this, I can't recall a time when I haven't felt this way. And you have much to do with it.

Long before I ever committed the crimes that brought me to this place, I felt that there was something intrinsically wrong with me. It may have come from the countless times that I could never measure up. You know, the times as a child when I would do my best to please you and was invariably chastised and punished—made to feel not as though I had made a mistake but rather that I *was* a mistake—that I am a mistake. In my previous letter, I spoke to you about what my crimes had cost me—the losses. There are some I never mentioned.

The loss of innocence, for example. You should ask your buddy Jimi about that.

Remember all those days that turned into months that carried over into years when you allowed your good buddy to spend the night because his wife had kicked him out, yet again? What would ever possess you to allow your friend, a grown man, to sleep in the same bed as your seven-year-old son? What the fuck were you thinking, Gerald?

I know times were different back then, but honest to God, people weren't. Do you have any idea what Jimi did to your son while he was lying in my bed right next to me? If you don't, ask him. Oh, that's right—you can't.

There is a greater fear lurking inside of me than what Jimi did to me. And that is that you may well have known and did nothing.

Go ahead, ask the question that begs asking: why didn't I say something? Here's the answer: What the fuck would I say? "Hey, Dad, Jimi likes to suck on your little boy's cock when he thinks I'm asleep. He also likes to shove his fingers, his cock, and other things up my ass at night." Perhaps I should have, but the reason I never mentioned it is that I was terrified. Not even as much of him as of you. Toss that around in that vegetative brain of yours for a while. Your only son was scared shitless that if he told you what your friend was doing to him, you wouldn't believe him, you'd call him a liar, or worse, choose to do nothing even if you knew what was going on. And that is what I couldn't live with.

While Jimi was doing unspeakable things to me, I would leave—not physically, that wasn't possible, but my senses would take leave of my body. I would travel to the upper corner of my bedroom, and with a bird's-eye view, I would watch as he fondled and stroked me. I could hear him grunting and moaning, as though it was not me but some horrible show I was watching on television, the sound waves reaching me at a distance. I felt his hot sperm as it splashed against my hands, my stomach, my face, my cock, my ass—whatever perversity was his pleasure that particular evening—and ran over onto the sheets. Then he would get up and wash me off with a damp rag as though it were the most natural thing in the world. But you know, Gerald, I think what was even worse than the violation is how he would wrap himself around me after he was done and hold me like I was something precious.

Ever wonder why I pissed the bed nearly every night until I was almost twelve years old? Do the math. Jimi moved out for the last time when I was eleven. Remember the morning we were all gathered for breakfast, and he laughed as he told you all about the "shower" I had given him the previous night? What a jocular moment that was, huh? You all laughed and had a grand ol' time at my expense. Ten-year-old Trent still pissing the bed. "What a pathetic sissy," you used to say to me. Wouldn't have been so funny had I said, "Hey, Jimi, was that before or after you took your fingers out of my asshole?" But I couldn't. Fear of you prevented me from seeking any kind of help.

I know exactly what you would say if this letter were to reach you: "Here goes Trent, trying to find someone to take the blame for his fuck-ups." I have never claimed that my abuse is what drove me to do the terrible things I have done to others. In fact, I have only ever told one person about it before Doctor Thackery. Claire does not even know. I don't know whether it plays a role in my own degenerate behavior or not, and somehow I doubt it does. I'm not trying to make that excuse now. What I am doing is simply telling you all the things that I should have summoned the courage to tell you as a child but could not.

Fuck, fuck, fuck, fuck! I am so mad at you.

Mom and I used to lie to you about how often I pissed the bed because telling you would result in more shaming and more abuse. As if being in grade six and still having "accidents" at night wasn't shameful enough.

My dishonesty is twofold, though. One, it was protecting what little dignity I had. And two, probably more significantly, it stemmed from rarely being believed. Why have you chosen to never believe me? Even when we both knew the truth?

Remember when I was five and told you countless times that I didn't leave the door open and let in the racoon that ripped the garbage bag to shreds and destroyed supper? You didn't believe me then, even after you beat the shit out of me, and I told you the truth. Somehow you have convinced yourself, even when you know the truth, to deny it. You are likely so self-deceived that you have forgotten the truth. You probably still don't believe me, and I'm still telling the truth. I didn't leave the fucking door open; you did! I have come to realize the hard way, that those who have difficulty trusting others usually do so because they are untrustworthy themselves. Consider the story of the boy who cried wolf in reverse. What if the first time the boy cried wolf, no one believed him? What would be the point of ever crying wolf again? Whether or not there is a wolf is irrelevant if you're never believed.

And so, the boy didn't cry wolf, and the wolf ate him.

You want to know what's even sadder than all of this other shit? My dad is dying in a hospital thousands of miles away, and even if I could somehow get there to see him on his deathbed, I have zero desire to do so. In fact, as I pen these words, Claire is doing her best to make arrangements to get down there to be with you, and I have been doing my best to dissuade her. She has a place in her heart for you that simply does not exist in mine. I wish it did; I truly do. I would have liked to have had the type of father-son relationship that certainly must exist somewhere.

It just hit me, Gerald. That's what I'm sad about. Another loss. I am mourning the fact that you and I never had the type of relationship that would stir within me a longing to be with you on your deathbed. And now the very remote possibility of any type of meaningful relationship between us is coming to a rapid end, and I could not care less.

I do not miss you. But I have, for my entire life. I have missed thirty-seven years of a relationship with the man who was supposed to be my father.

Just before I came to prison, my best friend, Bryan, came over for what I suppose was our last supper. You remember Bryan? He was the best man at my wedding and I was the best man at his, the cute kid who used to drink your beer, the one who used to tease Claire about being a lesbian, the only other person I had ever told about Jimi.

Bryan and I have always had the type of relationship that went beyond the bullshit of typical conversations about politics, philosophy, and the weather. He is one of only two people in my life with whom I have ever felt a kindred connection. Our meaningful conversations centered on our respective dysfunctions and the value of empty spaces and full hearts. I have never had deeper, more meaningful, life-changing discussions with another human being. We enriched each other's lives. Bryan changed my life for the better every time we were together.

Our conversation those few short days before my incarceration was no exception. At one point during the evening while we were out for a walk, I was leaning against a lamppost just outside of my home when he grabbed me, looked me directly in the eyes as tears streamed down his face, and told me he was going to miss me and that he loved me.

That was the first time I had ever heard those words from another man. As we were parting in the wee hours of that morning, we were standing in the foyer of my apartment, and Bryan said, "Trent, I'm going to miss our times together. I can only have these deeply meaningful conversations with one other person." I was a bit surprised since I have never held discussions as profoundly vulnerable as those I had with Bryan with another living soul.

I had to know, so I asked, "Who's the other person you can talk like this with?"

"My dad."

I was shocked. More than shocked, I was speechless. Finally, I got it out, the question begging for an answer. "You talk like this with your father?" My tone must have sounded incredulous.

He looked at me and nodded. "I know you well enough to know that you certainly don't, Trent. But that begs the question: who taught you how to be a man?"

And that, of course begs for an answer that grinds away at the very fabric of my being, day in and day out. And I have found the answer, although I don't like it. No one! That was your job, Gerald. It was your fucking responsibility to teach me how to be a man, but you left it up to Jimi.

Doctor Thackery was right again. It was a good idea to write to you once more. It helped clarify some confusion in my life. As I stated at the beginning of this letter, a part of me is sad about your imminent death. But now at least I know why. I am not sad at the prospect of losing you. I'm sad for what I lost so many years ago. For what I never had.

I sit here struggling with the best way to end this. Do I simply write, "Sincerely, Trent"? After all, I do sincerely mean what I have written. Part of me wants to write "Good riddance." And another part simply, "Go to hell." Considering the reasonable fact that you will be, and that you have made my life a living one, the latter seems most apropos.

Go to hell,
Trent

CHAPTER NINE

I head back to my cell after another session with Doctor Thackery. I find it interesting that after reading my latest letter to Gerald, his only comment was that I'm making some definite progress. On one level, I can understand this, but on so many others, it doesn't compute. When I write to Gerald, I don't feel better at all. Hatred burns deep into my soul, like molten lava burning through a mountainside. Now, I know from my own practice—previous practice—that clients usually experience greater pain prior to any sign of healing, but I'm not certain that this is what I'm experiencing. The wrath that consumes me seems to have no remedial effects.

Each time I leave his office and am escorted back—flanked on either side by men who would rather be anywhere else—the color, or lack thereof, drains me. The walls stand in stark contrast to what I have just left behind. Fifty shades of gray comprise everything along these corridors. The walls, floors, and ceilings all fall within the grayscale of the color spectrum. The cold floors are light and dark gray linoleum tiles in a checkered pattern—a large chess board upon which I am a pawn. The walls are a medium gray, high gloss—to make it easier to wash off the blood, I presume. The ceilings are a lighter gray. Even the light fixtures, cameras, and speakers are gray.

Outside, the rest of the world is gray too, perhaps paying homage to the gloom inside. The sun doesn't even attempt to pierce the grayness. I used to like the gray. It seemed to be a soothing shade that allowed more vibrant colors to stand out in rich contrast against. But when all that exists is gray upon gray upon gray, it sucks the light and life out of everything.

There is one exception to the grayness: the pea soup, green barriers that separate each unit from the main corridors and other units. These imposing floor-to-ceiling walls of steel mesh open and close only at the guards' command. Walls that separate the inmates from the guards and each other.

Once we reach my unit, the CO behind his protective glass barricade presses a button, and the loud clanking and banging starts. The large wall slides open like the entrance to the Batcave, allowing me inside. It's also an alert to every inmate on the unit that someone is coming or going. I hate that sound.

Conversely, Doctor Thackery's office is filled with color. A tapestry of rich, deep, saturated tones and textures greets you like a mother's embrace as you walk through his doorway. I like going there.

When your world is reduced to six feet by eight feet, the space inside your head grows exponentially. It seems all I do is think, process, and write—wash, rinse, and repeat. Thinking becomes a side effect of the prison experience. Not for all inmates, certainly. Some occupy their time huddled together with fellow gang members, either playing poker or around the television. Mindless activities that serve to pass the time until they are released, only to find another way back in. Or they may spend their time plotting the demise of the skinners on the unit. A skinner is what I am—anyone who has been incarcerated for a sexual offense against a minor.

Thinking consumes me. I think about Brianna often. Her smile, the way her beautiful strawberry-blonde curls would fall against her cheek, the way the sunshine caused her eyes to sparkle like raindrops on leaves after the clouds part. When she first walked into my office, I was not immediately stricken by her beauty. It was there, of course, but as a professional, I forced myself to push those recognitions to a different part of my brain. After all, high schools all across the planet are filled with beautiful young women. If that were foremost in a teacher's thinking, we would never accomplish anything.

The first thing that occurred to me the moment Brianna walked through my office door was, *Here's another student who does not want to be here.* These students are easily identifiable. They act as though there's nothing wrong, like this is going to be a complete waste of time, theirs and mine. *Let's get this over with as quickly as possible, so we can both go back to our miserable existences.* Over the years, I have learned numerous techniques to disarm such attitudes.

She came in and flopped down in the chair farthest from my desk without being invited. "The entire fucking world hates me," she began.

"Interesting you should say that," I replied. "In the staff room at lunch today, Mr. Chalmers expressed that very sentiment. He said, 'God, I hate that Brianna Barnes.' Then each of us went around the room and declared our utter hatred for you." She didn't laugh or even smile, just flipped me the bird and scowled, but the ice had been broken. "That's been bugging me all day. I'm glad you came in so I could get that off my chest. Now, what would *you* like to talk about?"

We actually made significant progress after we got to know each other. And therein lies the problem. When a person begins to feel better about themselves, their affections often turn toward their perceived saviors. I have been aware of this for years, and yet something about Brianna dislodged all inhibitors, and I fell hard for this beautiful young woman.

Ours was not a simple relationship. After we admitted our affection for each other, the counseling came to a halt. Meeting in public was always risky, so we spent much of our time driving around the city or at my home.

After my divorce, the one luxury I permitted myself was my car. It's nothing outstanding, but on a guidance counselor's salary, it was at the top end of what I could afford, a late-model Dodge Challenger. It was fairly loaded, all black, and very fast. I refused to consider it my mid-life crisis car. However, upon further consideration, it probably was.

Brianna loved to drive. Although she didn't have a driver's permit, she often reminded me that other more illegal activities had been going on inside my car, so I shouldn't be too concerned about it. She was becoming quite an expert both behind the wheel and in the backseat by the time things came crashing down around us.

The therapist in me knows full well that as an authority figure in her life, our relationship was a perilous adventure. The love we shared was not only forbidden; it was likely far more one-sided than I would care to admit. I was lonely. I had not so much as entertained the idea of getting back into the dating scene after my marriage ended two and a half years prior. I convinced myself that I preferred being alone and that time was a source of healing. Brianna's quick-witted sarcasm, her remarkable intellect, and her light, airy laugh—to say nothing of her long, slender legs—exposed my loneliness and opened a window through which I felt I could breathe again.

Brianna's love—if I can call it that—was more ideological. She fell for the man who brought a sense of order and calm to her chaotic world, a man who could identify with her struggles and show her a way through them. She was looking for a refuge in the midst of the storm that is high school, and I provided one.

I long to know how she's doing. Of course, this is impossible with the no-contact order enforced by the system. I worry about her, though, what her life is like today. Has she recovered from the fallout, the media, the exposure, and the pain I caused? Is she truly as scarred for life as the prosecuting lawyer said she is? Is she the brunt of cruelty back at Glenwood High? Do the staff and students engage her, or does she have "the plague" now? So many questions. Doctor Thackery is emphatic that this is a chapter in the book of my life that I shall never know the end of and should not attempt to read any further into. I know he's right, but in a hundred ways—no, a thousand—this is the page that has been dog-eared and which I long to keep reading.

Even with all of the time that I have had to think about this, I am unable to pinpoint the moment that I crossed the line. Oh, I'm very aware of it physically, but my heart took the leap long before my head was willing to admit it.

It's the lies that eventually catch up with you. The lies Brianna had to invent to cover where she had been, why she canceled, who she had been spending her time with, how come she no longer prioritized other friendships, what she was hiding, when would she find time to practice for her piano recital? And then there were the lies to cover the lies and those to cover those. *Oh, what tangled webs we weave . . .*

My world was infinitely simpler. I just had to deal with the lies I kept telling myself: I can handle this. I can bring this to a healthy end for both of us. I will end it tomorrow. It's not hurting her. It's not hurting me. No one will ever find out. In a couple of years, she'll be out of school, and things will be easier.

I worked hard to convince myself that our relationship was based upon far more than sex. I took a sick sense of pride in the fact that I wasn't just some pervert seeking to get my rocks off with someone less than half my age. I had pretty much convinced myself that the forbidden love we shared was genuine, pure, somehow altruistic.

One fine day as she was walking toward me in the hallway, I asked with a sarcastic sense of authority, as if I held some power over her, "Where are you headed, Miss Barnes?" As we passed, she whispered, "To the bathroom. Wanna join me for a quickie?" I didn't want to admit it, but I could not deny that I had the immediate makings of a hard-on thinking of how hot and risky that would be. I wanted to believe I was more in love with her mind and heart than her body, but an honest evaluation reveals that at that moment, I just wanted her—full stop. As I think back on all of this bullshit, I'm amazed at how I could convince myself and her that somehow, everything would be alright. I'm a sick, sick fuck. And this place is full of never-ending reminders of that.

My crime is a constant reminder of how sick and deplorable I am to the world at large. The prison community is always ready to remind me. In here, there are simple words that separate *us* from *them.* I find it interesting how words can have different associations based upon where you are.

The term "solid," for example, means something completely different on one side of these walls than it does on the other. While it is not given much value in day-to-day society, aside from its designation between a liquid and a gas, in here, it determines social status. In here it is always and only used to designate an inmate who is not a skinner. "Oh, you can trust that guy. He's solid." He may be incarcerated for swindling little old ladies out of their life savings, but at least he's not one of *them.* I think that, at one time, probably years before I got here, the word had a wider application. It likely referred to inmates who weren't rats, those you could trust to keep a confidence. It would have been an admirable character trait. But today those traits have little value, and the only thing that determines a man's character is that he is not here for sexual offenses against a minor. If you pass that test, nothing else seems to matter.

I understand the mindset. It has been shaped by the media, Hollywood, and much of society. The term "pedophile" conjures but one image in our society's collective consciousness: an overweight, jobless slob who parks his white panel van outside of an elementary school and waits for an innocent child to walk past, lures her into his van with a lollipop, drives to a secluded spot, rapes her, and tosses her body into the ditch. That's the image that culture associates with the person who is charged with a sexual offense against a minor. It's rarely accurate, and has never entered the minds of most convicted sex offenders, yet it is the brush with which we are all painted. Go ahead and tell me I'm wrong. I have been punched, kicked, spat upon, called a useless piece of shit, and am completely alienated because of my crime. I understand it. I deserve it. What I have done requires that a price be paid, and for that I am paying.

AFTER MY MEETING WITH DOCTOR Thackery ends this morning, I find myself, as I always do, at the large green barrier to my unit. The guards have as much indignation toward us skinners as anyone else, and they make no effort to cover their disgust with me. As the large, pea-soup-green gate clatters shut behind me, I make my way toward my cell.

COs rarely walk an inmate, and never a skinner, past that threshold. To do so is unsafe. I enter my cell and hear it before I feel it: a hate-filled cackle. "Die, you fucking skinner." A sharp agony burns through my lower back and drops me to my knees with pain more intense than any I have ever known. The explosion I briefly feel to the side of my head takes all the pain away.

CHAPTER TEN

Lights flicker like stars before my eyes. Once they're fully open, I realize nothing has any definition to it. Or perhaps everything has no definition. Blur, fog, and haze fill my head. Then once again, everything goes black.

When I finally come to a brief moment of consciousness, my hazy surroundings are completely foreign. Severe pain and the single handcuff and shackles that keep me tethered to the bed thwart any attempt to sit.

I have been airlifted to Bexley General Hospital, the closest trauma center to Briar Ridge with a forensics ICU. Over the following days, I piece together what happened. As I entered my cell, I was ambushed by several inmates whose assignment on our unit was to take care of skinners. And it was my turn.

A shank is any object sharpened to a point and forged into a weapon. These have several uses to an inmate: self-defense and opening letters, cans, and other paraphernalia, as well as the bodies of those who in any way antagonize the bearer. It was nothing personal; I had simply reached the top of the "fuck up the skinner" list.

My right kidney has been irreparably damaged, my jaw broken in five places—shattered, actually—by several blows to the head. Four ribs have been broken—one puncturing my left lung—my skull has been fractured, and my neck broken just above the fourth vertebra. One lower and I would be a quadriplegic. Most of the destruction occurred after I was unconscious. I was also sodomized by multiple inmates. At least one inmate also thought it would be fun to shit inside the open wounds caused by the shank. HIV tests are currently being done. Once I learned the full extent of my injuries, I questioned the need for restraint, but I'm told protocol requires it.

According to Doctor Goldstein, I was in a coma for the better part of eight days. He has reminded me frequently that I'm lucky to be alive. I don't feel particularly lucky. For the most part, aside from intense pain, I don't feel much of anything.

The first days post consciousness are filled with only two things: pain and sleep. I'm aware on some level that I have been heavily medicated. Thoughts elude me like overdue renters evade their landlord. I fight to hold on to questions, feelings, and ideas; they are as difficult to grasp as existentialism. I was booked for my third surgery, but that is being rescheduled because of an infection where my right kidney used to be. At least I think that's what I heard. I think too, but I can't be certain, that Claire may be somewhere nearby.

As the clouds lift, I begin to enter life again and can almost grasp the gravity of my situation. Apparently, Claire got back from sitting vigil in Key West with Gerald two days after she arrived there just to sit vigil with me as I was dying, or so she had been told. Before her return, she arranged for Gerald to be flown home once he is stabilized. Although his condition has not improved, life support will keep him alive, and he can at least die here, near his home.

Claire is a mess. Carl, my nurse, tells me she has been by my side day and night. She leaves only to eat, return calls, and drive the boys to their various appointments if Robert is unavailable.

Once again, Claire shines in the darkness.

I have been unable to communicate with much clarity for several weeks. My jaw has been wired shut. I have become somewhat adept at ventriloquism, though. Here's the silver lining: I can't find the words to express my gratitude to Claire anyway. The days go by, and the opiates I'm given are slowly being reduced as my awareness and my ability to tolerate pain increases.

I imagine, or try to imagine, what Claire has been living with: first Mom, then Gerald, and now me. That woman's strength never ceases to astound me.

Now that I'm conscious and no longer at risk of imminent death, they only permit Claire to visit twice per week. While this makes little sense to either of us, uncharacteristically, I'm thankful for this restriction. As much as I appreciate and value Claire's faithful loyalty, I can see the toll it is taking on her, and though she would never admit it, the truth of the matter is she needs to put some distance between herself and all that is falling apart around her. The DOJ policies do for her what she will not do for herself.

The CO whose task it is to sit outside my room and ensure I don't escape must remain hypervigilant. All I have to do is unhook myself from the multiple IVs, monitors, and devices keeping me alive, escape the traction that holds my neck stable, unlock the shackles and handcuffs, overpower him, and run like an Olympic sprinter, right out of this place.

The CO is also charged with searching every visitor. This is something I have grown to detest. I can understand that as an inmate, I am untrustworthy and every action I make deserves to be scrutinized. But why those who come to visit, who have committed no crime, are considered guilty until proven innocent makes no sense. And that pisses me right off. Each time Claire is frisked and scanned and questioned—more accurately, accused—a new sense of shame comes upon me, reminding me that my actions have harmed far more than my victim or me.

Doctor Thackery has been in a couple of times to see how I'm doing and to offer his support.

Although I was unconscious for the better part of the beating, it took an emotional and psychological toll upon me that was unexpected. A form of PTSD, I suppose. I find that whenever anyone, even Claire, enters my room, I jump, my heart begins to race, and I break out in a cold sweat if I'm not looking directly at the door and see them approaching.

Other emotional issues have begun to stir in my head as well. I wonder whether the crime I committed is truly terrible enough to warrant my assault. Perhaps it is. The shame, guilt, and remorse I was beginning to feel some relief from reappeared with a vengeance. Interestingly, I find myself not so much angry at my assailants as demoralized with myself. After all, if these men were willing to risk so much to do to me what they did, I must have deserved it.

Their aim was clear: to kill me. Their actions would have resulted in an immediate transfer to maximum security. Had they succeeded in their efforts, murder charges would certainly have followed. The fact that I survived will result in those charges being reduced to attempted murder. And each of these men on one level or another agreed that they were willing to pay the price to exact what they felt I deserved. It's difficult to get away with such an attack in prison.

Even though it occurred in my cell, where there are no cameras, once I was found, video surveillance from the multitude of cameras strategically placed through each unit would have been analyzed, and each man involved would have been observed going in and out of my cell.

Each would have been fully cognizant of this yet chose to do what they did regardless. So, with full knowledge of the impending liability, they still decided to commit the assault. My head can't escape this fact. Ergo, I must have deserved it. It has given me a new appreciation for the "Death before dishonor" tattoos borne on these men's bodies and a new understanding of the abhorrence expressed by our culture for my crime.

Here, within the prison community, my crime is worthy of the death penalty. Words that had almost disappeared from my self-flagellation resurface again, bold-faced and italicized: "I am a worthless piece of shit."

After I become semi-mobile and able to communicate more effectively, Doctor Thackery is permitted to use a private conference room to continue my therapy. He demonstrates a compassion and gentleness I have not otherwise experienced from corrections staff. He leads me in a series of meditative exercises that serve to relieve my anxiety and my pain.

Gerald has not even come up in the last three sessions, which is fine by me. I know Claire has been wrestling with whether or not to take him off life support. I have done nothing to dissuade her.

Doctor Thackery seems to feel as though I'm suffering more emotional trauma than I'm willing to admit. I don't know if I agree with him or not.

CHAPTER ELEVEN

I feel a righteous anger toward a system that can destroy a man as thoroughly and effectively as the judicial system can. What we refer to as rehabilitation is little more than lawful torture. I have given the best years of my practice to helping men recover from their own personal demons, only to stand back and watch them demonized, demoralized, and defecated upon. I had just begun to see the evidence of measurable progress in Reynolds when he was attacked.

I have now spent many hours with Reynolds in the less than favorable environment of a hospital conference room, going through remedial exercises of trauma adjustment rather than root cause analyses of his issues. Where I once reported we were engaged in the two-steps-forward-one-step-back dance, at least we were making progress. Now I find him looking around to see if he can even find a safe dance partner.

I have chosen for the time being not to discuss Reynolds' father. He does not possess the emotional framework to support this depth of work at present. Rather, our focus has been upon restoring a sense of humanity within his ego. He now demonstrates a lower sense of self than he has since our earliest sessions.

The timing for this is most troublesome. With his father's death imminent, I believe it is imperative that we reach a level of awareness of the trauma he is in denial of before Gerald dies. Otherwise, resolution, or lack thereof, becomes the ghost that will not relent. However, any attempt to force this will result in a negative outcome, creating further regression and perhaps recidivism. We now backpedal to the most basic of human requirements, the foundational level of Maslow's hierarchy of needs: Reynolds' need for safety, shelter, and stability. I patiently wait for Reynolds to embrace the true nature of his most recent ordeal and hope against all odds that some headway with his father is still within reach.

CHAPTER TWELVE

After thirteen weeks, they released me from Bexley. My temporary new home is the infirmary back at Briar Ridge. I'm here for observation and physiotherapy. I'm walking again, albeit somewhat gingerly. In all, I went through seven surgical procedures under general anesthesia and four under local. Some of the work was reconstructive, most was lifesaving.

While in the infirmary, there are no visiting privileges and no phones available. I have not seen or spoken with Claire for the better part of a month. I assume Gerald is still on this side of eternity; otherwise, Doctor Thackery or my parole officer would have informed me of his death.

My days are filled with rehabilitation therapies, sudden bouts of anxiety, dullness, and only sporadic sessions with Doctor Thackery. My nights are filled with despair and fear, as I am unable to shake these dreams that haunt me without reprieve.

Doctor Thackery and I seem to be at odds. He spends most of our time wanting to discuss the effects of my attack, of which I remember very little, rather than discussing what I believe to be more pertinent issues: those revolving around the actions that brought me to this place where my attack could happen at all.

Gerald rarely comes up. The only mention of him is when Doctor Thackery suggests I keep writing the letters that I won't ever send, if I choose to. So I may. At the very least, it will alleviate the boredom. He did tell me that he has spoken with Claire, and Gerald remains on life support. All tests suggest that his likelihood of recovery is lower than ever, and his medical team is pressuring her to allow them to remove him from all external support. She is contemplating this but has yet to make a final decision.

It seems that Doctor Thackery and I spend a great deal of our time together doing basic Psych 101. The sort of scraping the surface stuff I would do with students at Glenwood who definitely did not want to be there. I asked Doctor T about this in our last session. His response surprised me. He suggested I was more fragile than I was willing to admit. He said I've been demonstrating signs of situational depression and traumatic repression that he feels are inhibiting us from the progress we made in our earlier sessions. Well, no duh.

Then he asked something that rocked me: "Why do you think you're not angry at the men who tried to kill you?" It wasn't the direct question that caught me off guard so much as my response to it.

I cried.

It was the first time I shed tears since my incarceration. And suddenly there, amidst the bustle and busyness of the prison infirmary, a light. Clarity, like a heavy fog lifting just as you drive around a sharp curve on a dangerous road. For the first time since arriving in this hell hole, I saw something I completely missed. I feel I deserve to die. I feel like I should be dead. I deserve what I have been dealt, and worse. Not solely for what I did to Brianna but for every evil thought, every unkind word, every misguided action. I removed all responsibility from the men who did this to me, but I cannot forgive myself. In that moment, I was broken.

I have since come to realize that this moment of clarity was not so much a breakthrough into wholeness as it was a crack in the shell of my dysfunctions.

"Why do you want to die, Trent?" Doctor Thackery asked.

I responded with one of the most honest answers I have ever given: "I do not know."

I'm aware enough to know that confusion and ignorance are often the indicators of a lazy mind. They can also be the brain's way of protecting you from what is too fragile to accept. At the most basic level, I was aware of the feeling that my actions warranted my desire to be dead. But that was far too altruistic for a person of my psychological profile to be completely true. I need time to process his questions and my reactions to them, for at that moment I didn't know why I wanted to be dead, only that I did.

Doctor Thackery is helping me to recognize that what these cold-hearted bastards did to me had nothing to do with justice and everything to do with their own twisted sense of superiority. When the reality of my attempted murder sank in, I began to arrive at the truth—something not always easy to grasp and made far more difficult when lies permeate the culture. He reminded me that prison life has little to do with reality. Not that this place isn't real life; it certainly is, but virtually all who make this place a way of life are in denial. They lie to themselves, to each other, and to society as a whole. They have—we have—little ability to differentiate truth from untruth. My attackers, moreover, are men of such remedial comprehension that truth and lies are not only interchangeable, they are often reversed. In effect, when it comes to truth in prison, every day is opposite day.

My attack, he said, was more indicative of me not deserving to die than the lie that I did. Spineless men who have no fear of the judicial system, those who feel more at home in it than outside of it, are seldom afraid of it. And for these men, it has no teeth to control them.

Doctor Thackery told me something that shouldn't have shocked me, but it did: few men are not sexually attracted to teenage girls. Almost every man lusts over and desires to be sexually intimate with those far younger than himself. Most men, however, have personal standards, ethical boundaries that prevent them from doing anything more than entertaining these thoughts. Some, however, are willing to sacrifice everything to fulfill that desire. For reasons I had yet to understand, I was unable to count the cost, and I willingly endangered myself, my victims, my family, and society as a whole to engage in this taboo. There is a measure of relief that comes with knowing I'm not alone. This is tempered by the knowledge that while others may feel similar urges, I acted upon them.

Doctor Thackery suggested that the most logical explanation for my attempted murder is not that my attackers so despised my actions—such men are not often nauseated by evil—but rather that it is a reflection of something far too close to home and makes them uncomfortable. What I had done they also long to do and are perhaps even guilty of doing. This self-deception and self-denial gives them permission to feel an exaggerated sense of superiority and, based upon that, react with profound violence.

When I first arrived, I was somewhat cognizant of this. Over time, however, I forgot what I knew then: if an inmate's lips are moving, he is, in all likelihood, lying. And if he cannot tell the truth to others, it's not long before he is unwilling to be honest with himself. This has been my MO for much of my life. Why I gave a gang of savage thugs a place of superiority over me, I do not know. What I do know is that I am thinking far more clearly now than I have in months.

CHAPTER THIRTEEN

It's kinda fucked up. I'm seeing a counselor because of what a counselor did to me. When I first met Mr. Reynolds, he didn't seem like a total creep. God, was I wrong. Even after all the shit he did to me, somehow I thought it was okay. Tracy keeps telling me I was groomed—that Mr. Reynolds is what's called a predator—and from the very beginning he was out to hurt me. She says he probably began stalking me the first day he saw me, that people like him should have their balls chopped off and never get out of prison. And he should.

I'll be twenty by the time the bastard gets out. I'll be in college, and all of this will be behind me. While I'm at prom, he'll still be rotting behind bars. Good for him. Maybe he'll learn not to fuck with kids' heads and hearts. Although Tracy tells me that guys like Mr. Reynolds will never learn, that they're incurable. It's like he has a disease he can never get rid of. If you ask me, he *is* a fucking disease.

I say, "One day all of this will be behind me," but what I mean is that I *hope* one day all of this will be behind me. Sometimes it feels like he has infected me. It's not like I have a disease, but sometimes I feel like I'll never be normal again. Tracy says that's completely normal. It will take a lot of work, but one day I will wake up and not have him be the first thing I think about in the morning and the last thought that goes through my head at night.

Those thoughts aren't all completely bad, though.

The thing that hurts the most is that I really thought he liked me—even loved me. I'm so stupid. I mean, I'm not a downy or anything. I've got the right number of chromosomes and everything, but how I could believe all the bullshit and lies he dished out is beyond me. Tracy says he's like a pimp. He pretended to like me, treated me like a princess—that was his nickname for me—but was only using me. And then he shit all over me.

Tracy's smart. She's not like a genius, but she's got it together. She told me one of the things she learned when she was becoming a social worker is that guys like Trent—Mr. Reynolds, I'm not supposed to call him by his first name—are cunning. They tell you all the things they think you want to hear just to get inside your pants. She also told me that no normal man would ever want to be with a young girl. That's something that confuses me too. I didn't feel like a little kid when I was with him. Well, I haven't felt like a little kid for a few years now, but he made me feel grown up. Or maybe he allowed me to feel grown up. I don't know.

She told me that guys like Trent—him—are really, really sick. No normal person would want to be friends with a kid. And if he didn't like me, then the only explanation is that he must have just wanted me for sex. Another thing that confuses me: for a while it felt like he was actually helping me.

When my parents would fight all the time about money and stuff and I would lock myself in my room, he gave me some good advice, things I could do rather than sit there listening to their screaming. When I wrote Mom and Dad a letter, like Trent suggested, telling them how much it hurts to hear the two people I love most tearing each other apart, it really seemed to help. Even now they talk a lot more civilized to each other than they used to. At least they do when I'm around. That advice really helped, and life at home is a lot better. So, how could he be both good and bad for me?

I guess I know Tracy is right. Nothing he said can ever make up for what he did, but it's hard to believe that he didn't care for me at all.

When we first met, he was so funny. I walked into his office once, all pissed off about something, and he told me I was right, that the entire universe *should* revolve around me because I was the most wonderful person to ever grace the face of the planet. I don't even remember what I was so pissed about. I think maybe it was my turn to have the laptop for the night, and my little shithead brother convinced Mom that he needed it for homework or something. Trent always helped put things like that into perspective for me. Then he said, "Quit taking yourself so fucking seriously, Brianna. You're just not that important." I wasn't the least bit offended because he was totally right. Or he'd say things like, "Life's too short to be an asshole." That makes sense. Sometimes when I get to thinking like this, I start to miss him, then I have to give my head a shake and say, *Wake the fuck up, Bree. He never gave a damn about you!* I know that's true, but sometimes I forget. Sometimes I think I want to forget.

I'm so confused. At times I don't really want to tell Tracy all the stuff I'm feeling because I don't exactly know what I'm feeling, and it's like she gets pissed off if I ever say anything nice about him. I get that. Kinda. I mean, after everything he did to me and stuff, I should hate his guts. And I do. Except that sometimes I don't.

Sometimes I feel like I'm Dorothy from *The Wizard of Oz*. I'm caught up in this tornado, and life is spinning out of control. Like a bag caught up in a dust devil, I'm thrown this way and that, having no control at all about which direction I'm headed, where I'll land, or if I ever will. Or like a fish in the ocean just swimming aimlessly, with no sense of purpose or direction. Or maybe more like a duck with one leg in the middle of a large pond, just swimming around and around in circles, unable to get anywhere. The point is, I feel like my life has lost all sense of direction.

I used to know exactly where I was headed. After high school I was going to university to become a veterinarian. Then I'd open a small clinic just outside of the city, maybe in Wilmington, where Aunt Shirley and Uncle David live, and take care of people's pets and farm animals. My life had some sense of direction. Now I seem to have none.

Or maybe I'm more like Alice in *Through the Looking Glass*.

> *"Would you tell me, please, which way I ought to go from here?"*
>
> *"That depends a good deal on where you want to get to," the Cat said.*

"I don't much care where," said Alice.

"Then it doesn't matter which way you go," said the Cat."

And that's kinda exactly how my life feels.

I have good days and bad days. On the good days, I feel like it was just a fling. Like I had a romance with this guy who turned out to be a prick—everyone has those. For a while it's good, but then after a bit you realize he isn't the guy you think he is, and you realize that what you once thought was good really isn't, that you deserve better than this, and you can end it and find love somewhere else. I try to chalk it all up to lessons learned and move on—a good relationship that turned bad; that's all it was. Those are the good days. Or maybe they're the bad ones. I don't know.

On the really bad days, it feels like I gave myself over to a monster. He took my innocence, my virginity, and my self-esteem. I trusted him with my heart. I confided in him, told him my greatest dreams, my wildest fantasies, and my worst fears, and instead of honoring those parts of me, he ripped out my heart and trampled it underfoot. He took the most precious parts of me and dumped all over them. This is how I feel, or how I'm supposed to feel. I think. Tracy reminds me of this often. She tells me that I will carry some of the things he did to me for the rest of my life, but she will help me adjust to that as much as she can.

Tracy wants me to write a letter to him, one that I'll never give to him, but where I can vent and tell him how much I hate him and get out all the stuff that's built up inside of me because of what he did to me. He's such a fucking asshole. Maybe I will.

CHAPTER FOURTEEN

Dear Gerald,

I hear that while you and I were close to being reunited, I have progressed in one direction while you insist upon heading in the another.

I was hurt here in prison. Hurt bad. There are times when I feel that I deserve what happened to me. But this place is the full punishment I have been sentenced with, and further punishment endured at the hands of decrepit men is not part of the process. The judicial system sentenced me with what they felt was a just penalty, but others took it upon themselves to increase that sentence.

It took more time than I care to admit, but Doctor Thackery has helped me realize that my attackers were anything but vigilantic in their plan. At first I bought into a lie that hangs in the air here like pot smoke at a rock concert. By the way, you taught me early to accept lies. Lies are woven into the fabric of these walls like initials on the sleeve of a letterman jacket. Some crimes are more worthy of punishment than others. Some crimes are worn like a badge of honor while others must be hidden beneath a guise of brokenness and shame. I bought into the ideology that a murderer, an armed robber, and a pimp are better than someone who is a sex offender. In fact, everyone is better than someone like me. I have since come to the realization that superiority, flogged by inferior men, is no different than the bullying that so many of the students under my care at Glenwood have had to endure. These men are not the bearers of justice; they are simply thugs preying upon the weak. I did what I did, and I am paying the price for my actions. No one has the right to inflict any further pain and torment upon me. I am fucking furious. Oh yeah, FYI, I'm also HIV positive.

Another thing that makes me angry is how little restraint I have when it comes to thoughts of my victim. I have been making significant strides in so many areas, yet when it comes to Brianna, I stall. It's like I can't not think about her. I wonder if she hates me, if she misses me the way I do her, if she wishes for us, or wishes we had never been. I get pissed off that I can't put her—put us—behind me.

I guess I'm pissed at you as well—no surprise there. I'm mad because I can't shake the thought that if you had taught me something of what it means to be a man, something about how to flee from cowardice, I might not be in this predicament. I know this sounds like so much blame shifting, like I'm making you the scapegoat for my transgressions, but had you been involved in my life beyond the point of abuse and patronization, I may have become a different person. I may not have been a better man, but certainly I would have been a different one. And perhaps that man would have known how to deal with life after what Jimi did.

I can't help but wonder what trajectory my life would have taken if I had had the courage to tell you or Mom what was happening with Jimi. You may have done nothing, may not have believed me, but I would have told you, and that, I think, would have made a measure of difference. Hiding shit, as I'm learning, seldom gets you anywhere good. Why didn't I tell you? It was certainly more than fear or shame. I simply didn't know how to. Even now I have grown so much, learned so much of who I am and who I'd like to be, but could I confront you with this pain? Could I send these letters?

I suppose at this point it doesn't matter. You'd never be able to read them, and you'll probably be dead before they ever got to your house, which, if I understand correctly, being brain dead, you'll never return to again anyway.

So, as I mentioned, I'm HIV positive. You probably think I've become, like many in this place, "gay for the stay," as the saying goes around here. I'm not so fortunate. It happened during the beating I suffered. Nine men sodomized me, one after the other. Each one deposited his cum into my ass, tossing me back and forth like a fucking blow-up doll. Which one or two or more of them gave me the disease, I don't know, and it matters little. The point is I now have this incurable disease that can be treated and controlled to some extent, but will certainly contribute to my death eventually.

The moments immediately after learning about my newly diagnosed HIV status seemed surreal, like being in a virtual free fall and reaching for the ripcord of a parachute that isn't there. The doctor here in Briar Ridge was matter of fact. No tone of sympathy in his voice, like he was reading a newspaper, delivering facts: "Reynolds, I received the results of your HIV test. You're positive."

In a matter of seconds, I fell into a tailspin of "what if" scenarios, and my vision filled with horrific images like those from a bad movie montage. It comes so rapidly out of nowhere the moment you hear those words. Your mind races, then stalls, working in frantic fits and spurts and grasping onto the nuggets of information you try to remember about learning what it is to be HIV positive today. All the training I received as a therapist about how to talk with a student who may disclose their positive status went out the window as those words hit me.

The nurse tells me I'm going to be just fine and that HIV is a manageable disease. If I take care of myself, I can expect to live the same amount of time as I would if I were HIV negative. But still, there's an inescapable fear of the unknown. What does it mean to live with HIV? What's going to have to change in my life, and more importantly, what can I expect to remain the same? These questions and fears race through me like a tsunami. Among all the other fears and questions, the one most burning is, "Now what?"

Doctor Thackery has been most helpful regarding this new diagnosis. He tells me the first thing I must do is stop panicking. I'm the same person I was before receiving my test results. Although it may seem like everything has changed, it hasn't. He has given me some helpful things to do to ease my mind and find my way back to healthier thinking—to being okay.

The anger that arises comes with the realization that I did nothing to deserve this. I deserve a lot of things, but this is not among them. To be honest, the emotion that this condition brings even more than fear is self-pity. God, I love feeling sorry for myself. It's so easy to do, and it feels so good. I wish I could share this feeling so that others might jump aboard and join me at this party. I told Doctor Thackery about how much I despise that I love to feel sorry for myself, as if he didn't know it already. He just smiled.

The post-positive world inside my head is filled with confusion. There are times when my sense of self diminishes with each poisoned breath I take, and I want to die. But once again, as a coward, I'm unable to even take the steps necessary for this act. A part of me also longs to live and grow until I can one day look into that mirror in the morning and like the man looking back.

My life feels like a Rubik's cube—no sooner do I get one side of it in order than I turn to the next side and, in an attempt to line things up, I fuck up the first one. Confusion and sorrow mark my life in this place where I rot.

I have mentioned before that time is the enemy here. I spend far too much of it lately pondering what this disease is doing in my body. I imagine it like the cockroaches who feast upon the guano piles inside caves where bats make their homes. They eat away at all the bat shit but never make a dent in it. The guano hill grows higher and higher each day as the never-ending droppings of countless bats fill the cavern. While I know it is psychosomatic, sometimes I can feel the disease growing inside of me. Dirt and filth that can never be washed away.

In some ways, I envy you, Gerald. You lie there comatose, completely oblivious to what is happening in the rest of the world and in the lives of your children. Come to think of it, you've pretty much always been that way. I guess not much has changed.

Would you be interested to know all that Claire has gone through for you while you slumber? She has taken care of pretty much everything. While Judy abandoned you, which is no real surprise, Claire has ensured that all of your medical needs have been met, she has had the landscape company keep up on all of your gardening, she has secured your vacation homes, your boat has been dry-docked and prepared for the winter, your bills have all been forwarded to your accountant, and your mail is being collected regularly and placed in a box on your kitchen table, which is where you'd find these love letters if I had the balls to send them.

She has inquired about power of attorney in order to keep up with your affairs—pun intended—but that is out of the question since you're still alive but incapable of granting permission, so she has petitioned the courts for a guardianship, which will give her some ability to manage your life. But that process may take months. What she has given up to ensure that your life, as short as it may end up being, runs smoothly you'll never know. Suffice it to say, once again she has gone above and beyond for you. For me too.

While I may be somewhat biased, Claire is the epitome of sainthood, and you do not deserve such a daughter. I am so proud to call her my sister, although I'm certain the feelings are not completely reciprocal. I mean, how could they possibly be?

Remember how Claire and I used to fight when we were kids? She was forever getting into my stuff, reading my books, wearing my clothes. She was always such a tomboy. You probably weren't around the time she Crayola'd all the images of my grade-five science book. She said it was so boring before. "Now it's bright and fun." Mr. Wilson didn't agree, and I had to pay to replace the book with my allowance money. I think that was the time I convinced her she had Dutch Elm disease and was going to grow branches from her ears. For days she went around with cotton balls stuffed deep into her ear canals and a winter toque pulled down to her chin. I miss her so much.

In an earlier letter, I told you that Claire was one of my victims. It started and ended the year I turned fourteen, which would have made her twelve. I walked into my room one sunny morning. It must have been summer vacation because I was going inside to change into my swimsuit and spend the day in our pond with Bryan. I found her without a shirt on, going through my dresser. She smiled at me and said, "Can I wear this one?" as she held up my Green Lantern T-shirt. I just stared at her budding breasts and couldn't say anything. She tossed it over her shoulder and walked out with it dangling from one finger. As she walked past me in the doorway, her bare breasts brushed my arm, and I gasped. After that I attempted to sneak peeks of her as often as I could when I knew she would be either topless or completely naked.

We began to play this game where we would intentionally undress in places that we knew the other could see. We never spoke about it, but we both knew full well what was going on. Shortly after she turned thirteen, she came into my room one night after bedtime. She was only wearing a short nightshirt, and she sat on the edge of my bed and asked if I wanted to touch them. This became a routine. We never got more sexual than touching each other. I was most often the aggressor. This went on until she met Danny in grade eight. After that I was "gross," and it stopped. I hated Danny Malchinski.

I don't really know why I'm telling you this. I guess I thought you should know, even though you won't.

These memories are among those that fill me with shame and regret.

I love the woman that Claire has become. She is smart, confident, self-assured, and beautiful. Robert may be the luckiest man on the planet. Her children, Aaron and Stevie, are at that age where most boys find their mothers to be little more than a pain in the ass, but they still worship her.

What's it like for you these days? Do you think? Do you feel anything? Are you at all aware of what has happened to you or what's going on inside of you right now? Do you have any regrets? Do you wish that you'd done life differently—better?

A few months ago, when I was in a similar situation, I dreamed a lot. My dreams were not about a light in the distance that grew brighter as I neared death or anything of that nature. Although, interestingly, I could tell at each stage when I was getting closer to or drifting further away from life. There were horrific dreams and vibrant dreams, most involving events related to my past. I also dreamt of childhood wonders.

I was once in the ocean. The sky was cloudless, the sun high, and the water glistened like crystal. Beneath the surface were colors more vibrant than any that exist in the waking world. It didn't appear to be, nor did it feel, surreal. It seemed very, very real. Fish of all colors, shapes, and sizes swam in harmony all around me. There was no fear, only a deep desire to become one with my surroundings. I swam endlessly without tiring. I could swim as fast as the fastest of my fish companions. Dolphins and I would swim together, racing and jumping and diving to impossible depths. The joy and freedom were completely foreign. I experienced in those waters a serenity and sense of wholeness I have never known in the waking world. In such moments one realizes the limits of language, for I find I cannot put into words the ecstasy I felt. In that place, there was no shame, remorse, or regret. My life had one purpose; to experience euphoria—the freedom that knows nothing except the moment. Being in that place had only to do with now. There was no sound, no suffering, no interruptions, only pure, unadulterated bliss.

But there were others. Much more often, my dreams—elucidations—were of a different nature.

I was once tethered to a stake surrounded by men, if you can call them that. Brutal, ugly, powerful men. Men whose faces resembled those of wild beasts. Thick, coarse black hair covered their naked bodies. They taunted, poked, and prodded one another. They hit each other with blows powerful enough to knock a man flat. Blood and something else, something more vile, oozed from open wounds upon their hideous bodies. They gathered in a circle around me, communicating in a language unknown—inhuman—laughing maniacally, like crazed demons. One by one they poked me with their long talons, each one sinking deep into my flesh. The same putrid blood and bile poured forth from each wound. The stench from the toxic slime filled my nostrils. Nauseating. My demon imprisoners howled and growled as they tore flesh from my body.

I watched from a distance as the man I was on the stake became less. What remained was a corpse, eyes removed and devoured, entrails consumed by my ravenous captors. Bone, tissue, and scraps of rotting meat hung from what remained of who I had once been. The me observing the me on the stake felt no physical pain, but I felt every black emotion. My nakedness filled me with shame. My powerlessness filled me with fear. A searing, burning rage at my inability to fight back consumed me, a fury I had never known. Hatred, malice, rage, confusion, despair, and hopelessness devoured me. All that is dark and evil and twisted in humankind filled me to overflowing. I was held in a bondage that not even death could free me from.

Do you dream? If so, I hope yours resemble the latter.

Trent

CHAPTER FIFTEEN

The more I write to Gerald, the more I'm able to understand why Doctor Thackery assigned me this task. I cannot say that the process is wholly cathartic, but it is most revealing. I learn something about myself and Gerald with each stroke of the pen.

I have discovered that my attack resulted in a ten-day lockdown, during which the contents of my cell were removed, the cell disinfected, and a new inmate placed in my bunk. My cellmate, Brakes, is gone. No doubt he was one of my attackers. Marcie, my parole officer, informs me that I'm to be transferred to another institution in the next few weeks. There is only one other medium-security prison in the region, so I assume that's where I'm headed. That being said, if word of my attack—and the reason for it—has reached Dover, I may not be safe there either.

Where and when my transfer will happen, I won't be told. Prisoners are on a need-to-know-basis, and from the system's perspective, I have no need to know. So I wait.

With each passing day comes renewed strength and vitality. I look around this tiny room, my temporary cell inside Briar Ridge, and I'm still confounded. I have been in prison for a year now, and it feels as foreign as it did the day I arrived. Each morning when I open my eyes, I look at the grayish walls around me in disbelief. Since my arrival, I have been unable to grasp the reality of my situation. God, I know it's real. I live it day in and out. But with each new dawn comes the question: *Am I really here? Is this not just a dream?*

Acceptance of the fact that I'm actually here is made more difficult when I have to admit to myself why I am here. Once again, the stigma associated with my crime repulses me. I consider the pain I have brought to Brianna, Claire and her family, my profession, the shame and pain my mother took with her to the grave, and even what the staff and students at Glenwood High must bear. My selfishness often becomes too much for me to endure. Thankfully, Doctor Thackery has been more helpful than I can express in assisting me to overcome the self-flagellation I once put myself through.

I don't do that so much anymore. The honest revelation brought forward in recent meetings with Doctor Thackery has given me a measure of solace. I am not alone. All red-blooded men wrestle with similar thoughts. So, I have become a little less hard on myself. The honesty that comes in admitting that I really do not detest having these inappropriate thoughts, that I like them, otherwise I wouldn't entertain them so often, is refreshing and simultaneously disturbing. So there are times when I realize I'm growing a little after all.

The nurse startles me as she enters and hands me my medication—anti-inflammatories, antibiotics, and a plethora of different colors, shapes, and sizes of pills aimed at keeping my HIV in check. I have been off pain medication for some time now. She tells me that I will be transferred today. "To Dover?" I inquire. She shakes her head. Immediately, part of me is furious. I demand an answer. She walks out. Anger burns within me. "I may be a useless fucking skinner, but I'm still a human being. Why won't you tell me what's going on?" I pointlessly shout after her.

I have noticed that anger seems to creep in much quicker than it used to. I suppose it's one of the side-effects of the Department of Justice. That along with the loss of a man's freedom comes the loss of his humanity seems cruel, but it is the reality of prison life. I grab the book I have been reading, which sits perched upon my windowsill, Richard Dawkins' *The God Delusion*, and flip through the pages. I read but absorb nothing; the pages might as well be blank. Far too many other thoughts consume me. Days later when I finish the book, I come to the same conclusion—the pages might as well be blank. It's little more than a selfish, angry boy's tantrum, a vapid outpouring of rage upon the religious community from a man more obsessed with the destruction of a faith system that has brought hope, legitimate or otherwise, to millions over the centuries, than with promoting his own theories. Where he purports to use intellect, science, and thorough investigation to support his thesis, and states that he will not attack his adversaries based upon their faith, he does the exact opposite. When I finally set the book down, which I should have done long before the final chapter, it strikes me that Dawkins is a man even angrier than I am and with far less reason.

I find myself bouncing like the digital ball on a screensaver between anger, remorse, and self-pity. On the one hand, honest remorse for the pain I have brought into Brianna's life rises within. I took a precious child and threw her into a world she was ill prepared to handle. I knew that the moment the first inappropriate thought entered my mind. The moment she gave me a hug that lingered just a fraction of a second longer than it should have. The moment I gave myself permission to enjoy it just a fraction more than I should have.

The more Doctor Thackery and I delve into the gray matter between my ears, the more I am coming to understand the graveness of the situation. As grown up as Brianna is in some respects, she does not possess the emotional maturity to function on the level of an adult and, therefore, can only process "us" with the cerebral tools at her disposal. She must feel a certain sense of abandonment, betrayal, and exploitation. Whether these were my intentions matters little; the repercussions will be the same. And for that I am sincerely sorry. Sorrow, remorse, and anger usually surface at night, immediately after the lights in the infirmary are extinguished. I lie upon this hard, cold mattress and my mind, far from sleep, takes me to her.

I imagine her day at Glenwood High, anything but typical. She walks into class, and every eye follows her. Every student and teacher has the same thought: *There she is, Brianna Barnes, the girl who was fucking Reynolds.* This defines her. As long as she is in that school, she will forever be "the girl fucked by the guidance counselor." It's her sole identity now, and even when there are other issues at the forefront where she is concerned, that is all anyone can see. I imagine her wanting to scream, "Leave me alone! Let me just be Bree!" But she can't be. And I weep. Tears of anguish for the hurt I have brought to her sting my eyes.

I don't do well with anger. Doctor Thackery has been exploring this with me. The anger that comes upon me in fits and starts is both understandable and undeniable. In its purest form, it stems from abuses endured—from Gerald, from Jimi, from myself, and most recently my would-be murderers, which has left me with an incurable disease and paralyzing fear. In its more selfish form, I cannot deny that I feel anger toward the school board for their abandonment and utter disregard for the years of service I gave. I put them in a position of "fight or flight," and they chose the latter. It was the right choice, the only position they could adopt; nevertheless, the sting of their actions still burns. There exists as well, in the most misguided direction of my anger, some toward Brianna herself. I share with her some of the same emotions I'm certain she feels toward me, not the least of which are abandonment and betrayal.

At my trial, she was silent in my defense and vocal in my indictment. While she sat stoically on the witness stand, the prosecution painted an image of a serial rapist—the pervert in the white panel van. Brianna said nothing to repudiate these accusations. When questioned regarding her part in our relationship, she answered with a statement I must assume had been prepared by her attorney: "He told me that if I told anyone about what he was doing to me, he would hurt me and my little brother." At once, her head fell, tears welled in her eyes, and she sobbed. The prosecution allowed her sobs to echo through the chamber, like a kettledrum in a cathedral—fuel for their defense. To the average onlooker, her emotional breakdown would appear to be a natural response to the horrors she had endured. Few would have the insight to ask whether it may have had more to do with her unwillingly sacrificing me upon the altar of self-preservation than the horrors they imagined, based upon her statement.

As she was leaving the witness stand, she slowly shook her head, as if to deny the words just spoken. Our eyes met and locked, and she mouthed "I'm so sorry." At least in my eyes, this was the reality of what I witnessed, and it is this memory that stirs anger within me toward Brianna.

As a therapist, I understand full well why she did what she did. To admit that she played any role other than the helpless victim would bring opportunity for criticism, speculation, and even the justification of the accused.

It's far easier to live with the guilt of a wrongful accusation than the shame of association. My anger is subdued when I'm willing to remember this. These are the undeveloped parts of my victim. To expect any different response from her would be absurd, like expecting a dog not to chase its tail. I do wonder, though, whether there are times when that memorized, prepared statement, which sounded my death knell, haunts her, or if she feels completely vindicated. In other moments, I wonder whether my observations of her response have been fabricated in my mind as a form of self-justification.

There lingers still, in the depths of me, a penchant for self-pity. This deadly personality flaw once encompassed almost every unfair hand that I felt life had dealt me: Gerald, the poverty of my childhood, my stolen bicycle, the snowstorm on my ninth birthday, Gerald, the B+ average in grade four, being cut from the junior high volleyball team, the cancellation of *The Bugs Bunny and Road Runner Hour*, Gerald, the deaths of Rascal, Charlie, Pocket, and the cat I can't even remember the name of, Jimi, the vacation I had to postpone because of 9/11, David Roberts' recognition for the science project that *I* did all the work on, our loss to the Raiders for the little league championship, Gerald, the cast I had to wear to prom, the mortgage I was turned down for, Mom's illness, Lisa Wilson's "Dear John" letter, Gerald, my wife's affair, and the pain of my incarceration. That self-pity is now, however, reserved almost exclusively for the disease that now ravishes my body . . . and Gerald. In this respect, I have come a long way.

"Self-pity is both poisonous and highly addictive," Doctor Thackery said in our last session. "It's an exaggerated sense of your own self-worth and is far too easy to make a toxic habit out of." After a brief pause, he continued. "This is something you already know, Trent. The most destructive vice that a person can have, even more than pride, which is supposedly the number one cardinal sin, is self-pity. It destroys everything around it except itself." A long silence ensued. I can be pretty thick sometimes, but I think I'm starting to get it.

CHAPTER SIXTEEN

It has been four months since his attack, and the system has finally approved Reynolds to return to a slightly more regular schedule. We just completed our first session in my office since his attempted murder. His recovery has been remarkable. Few outward signs of physical trauma remain. The same cannot be said of his emotional well-being. Understandably, this will require a lengthier period of recovery. He has made considerable progress, but there is much work to be done before he is ready to pick up where we left off prior to his attack. His sense of humor has returned, and he displays signs of looking forward rather than inward. While there is much inner work to accomplish, the fact that he is able to look forward to anything demonstrates a level of emotional catharsis. We have advanced beyond Kübler Ross' denial stage and seem to be smack dab in the middle of anger. This is a healthy place for Reynolds to spend some time. Until now, the only demonstrations of anger have been projected toward his father. He has shown very little toward the judicial system, his previous employer, his victim, or even his attackers. I have encouraged him in this expression and have implemented numerous techniques to assist him in allowing his anger to be released in a healthier manner. To this end, he has shown substantial advancement.

I liken this progress to a musician learning scales or rudiments. They practice and practice the same movements, patterns, and strokes, repeatedly accomplishing what feels like very little. But over time, those fundamental techniques begin to develop a mind of their own, and in short order, the novice is able to play pieces that previously baffled them. It's this psychological muscle memory that I have been attempting to develop in Reynolds. And little by little, it's coming. Few things bring a greater sense of joy to a therapist than watching a patient begin to get it.

It's easy to forget how cathartic environment can be for a patient. The moment he was escorted into my office and the door shut behind him, his entire countenance changed. Tranquility. The muscles in his jaw slackened, his shoulders relaxed, and the tension fell from his handsome face. This brought a smile to both of us. He sat next to me in the chair reserved for those with whom I feel safe. Once there, a sigh of relief and a posture that said, "It's good to be home," fell over him. While I'm aware that he is far from home, his comfort suggests he is more so here than anyplace else on this taciturn campus.

Welcome back. I'm going to miss you, Trent Reynolds.

I am not permitted to tell him, but our sessions will soon come to an end. This man I have invested so much into is to be transferred to an entirely new region. This is one downfall of working for the DOJ. His parole officer has recommended he be placed in a facility on the East Coast for his personal protection. I understand this; the system has no agenda of higher importance than the physical safety of its prisoners. Lawsuits abound where this precaution is not strictly adhered to. I'm saddened at the prospect of losing Reynolds, however. We have established a rapport and mutual respect that I have found with few inmates in all my years of practice. We shall continue to meet until his departure, but this knowledge makes it difficult to pour in the required energy. I'm certain that while we may make further advancements, we will by no means achieve the healing I had hoped for.

I will forward my notes to Doctor Shamanski at Dominion with hopes that he will be able to find a place in his schedule for Reynolds, but there is little promise for much development. A connection such as that which I have established with Reynolds is rare, and the likelihood of the same being shared by another psychiatrist is remote. There is one other possibility I hold on to: that a place may be found in our protective custody unit here at Briar Ridge. I have made inquiries into this with the hope of getting him higher on the list, but I have little authority outside of the Department of Psychiatry. I hold onto this optimism lightly, however, as the wait list for PC is extremely long.

He is to be transferred from the infirmary to solitary confinement tomorrow, immediately following our session, and shall remain there until his transfer to Dominion is approved. I wish SC upon no man. There is a darkness in that place that makes being in the general population feel like a day at Disneyland. Solitary confinement is reserved primarily for inmates who are unable to function in gen pop. It serves no purpose other than to punish. Inmates are completely isolated from each other twenty-four hours a day for the duration of their stay. They are permitted to shower once every four days and do not see another inmate as they are escorted to and from the shower facilities. The only human beings they have contact with are the COs who bring their meals. In SC, inmates communicate with each other by yelling through the ventilation system and primitive forms of Morse code. No televisions, radios, or other forms of entertainment are permitted. The isolation is enough to drive prisoners mad. The only consolation a man like Reynolds has is that because he is not there for punitive reasons, he is permitted visits, sessions with me, library privileges, and weekly trips to the commissary. Solitary confinement officers do not like housing inmates who are not SC material and therefore treat them with utter contempt, especially sex offenders. I will call him for sessions as often as possible in order to give him reprieve from "the hole."

There have been no further developments in Reynolds' father's condition. Gerald Reynolds remains on life support in Glendale General Hospital. I have spoken with Claire Durst multiple times over the past few weeks. I am moved by her love and care for her brother. If more inmates had this kind of support, the recidivism rate would be far lower.

As it is, the recidivism numbers reported to the general public by the government are inaccurate. Statistics report that the recidivism rate in federal penitentiaries is approximately 48 percent. To any tax-paying citizen, this is outrageous. The truth, however, is far more frightening. Methods used to calculate this rate are suspect and difficult to understand—which is concerning in and of itself and suggests that this statistic is on the low side. The more alarming fact is that an inmate is only considered recidivist if he reoffends while on his statutory release—while he is still on parole. Once he has reached full parole, reoffending does not increase the recidivism rate; instead, it actually lowers it. An arrest the day after a man's parole is up negates recidivism. The prisoner is considered a new inmate and is processed as such. A more accurate calculation places the recidivism rate in North American federal prisons upward of 80 percent.

So, when I come across an inmate who demonstrates the potential to get out and stay out of this system, I do everything within my power to help, hence my disappointment at the imminent loss of Trent Reynolds.

Today's session suggests Reynolds is becoming much more aware of his self-sabotaging and the destructive self-talk patterns that have governed much of his adult life. We are moving ahead. I think he's willing to trust me again as his dance partner. We are edging nearer the dance floor. As he leaves, I'm sorry to see him go because I know what is in store for him.

CHAPTER SEVENTEEN

I found my safe place. It's in a small corner under the potted hydrangeas that Mom has hanging in the den. No one ever comes in this room anymore. Not since Dad moved. I dragged the big, overstuffed bean-bag chair from the rec room in here, and it fits perfectly. In the morning, the sun shines through the big French window and directly into this spot. I have a small lamp that I turn on once it gets too dark to see my reflection in the blue glass orb—a reflecting ball—that sits like a globe on a stand right next to me. It used to be in the garden out back, but I like the way it makes my face look sometimes, so I asked Mom if I could bring it in here. The glow from the lamp is soft and warm, like the Afghan I use to wrap around my body and my head when I can't stand to see the rest of the world.

Dad left about a month ago. It's not that bad, really. They've been talking about it for years, and Davy and I have been expecting it for as long as I can remember. It's interesting that they seemed to get along better once they made the decision. I even heard them doing it the night before he left—one last hurrah, I suppose. I guess it's kinda like suicide. I read somewhere that just before a person kills themselves, once they've decided to actually do it, their world becomes a better place—more peaceful. Since Trent left, sometimes I've had thoughts like these.

Mom seems so much happier now that Dad is gone. They talk a lot still, and I get to see Dad pretty much anytime I want. I've actually seen him more since he moved than I have in a long time.

We had this big, long, formal talk a couple of weeks after they decided. Davy, Mom, Dad, and I were all sitting around the dining room table—we *never* eat in the dining room—after a huge dinner from the good Chinese takeout place. We talked about pretty much everything. Davy's fortune cookie said, "Everything is hard before it becomes easy." I had to think about that for a while because when you've done something for a long time, you forget how hard it was in the beginning. Like tying your shoes, riding a bike, reading a book, or having to start living your life all over again—alone. Davy looked straight at Dad and asked, "So, living without you here is going to get easier?"

They told us it wasn't our fault, like I ever thought it was, *God.* Dad cried more than Mom. They said they had come to realize they don't love each other anymore, and rather than wait until they hate each other, they figured it was better to do it now. That makes sense. I mean, people fall in and out of love all the time, right? Look at me and Trent. I thought I loved him, but I was wrong. Everyone makes mistakes. Mom and Dad said the one thing that was certainly not a mistake was me and Davy—I guess that makes two things. Mom's fortune cookie said, "A chance meeting opens new doors to success and friendship." They told us what their relationship had been like in the beginning.

They met at a funeral, actually. It was Dad's grandmother who died. Mom was there because her mom, my grandma, had taken piano lessons from Dad's grandma, and she was always talking about what a brilliant teacher she was. When Grandma learned that her teacher had died, she wanted to go to the funeral. Mom didn't want to go, but Grandma didn't want to go alone, and Grandpa was working, so Mom went with her.

After the funeral, at the reception back at Grandpa's house—Dad's house—Dad was out back in the yard trying to sneak a beer out of the cooler on the porch when Mom came through the screen door.

"Hey! What do you think you're doing, young man?" she said.

He jumped, and said, "Holy crap! You scared the shit out of me."

Dad says he took one look at Mom and was smitten, so he offered her a beer too. They spent the rest of the afternoon hanging out, mostly in Dad's bedroom, listening to the Rolling Stones, Bob Dylan, and Janis Joplin.

Music is a great way to get to know someone. I figure that if you like a person's favorite music, you'll probably like them. That was true for Mom and Dad, and it was true for me and Trent too.

So, they were sitting there hanging out, and all of a sudden a bird flies into Dad's bedroom window. *Smack*, like a rotten pumpkin falling on the floor. Dad jumped again—he's jumpy that way. Then they went out back to check it out. It had broken a wing, so they built a little nest out of an old shoebox to keep it in while it healed. They went digging for worms and berries and took care of it.

Grandma, Mom's mom, thought that Mom must have got bored and walked home, so she left without her. After a couple of hours, Grandma called Grandpa's house because she was worried about Mom and was very relieved to find that she was still there. It wasn't that far away, so Dad walked Mom home. She went to his place every day after school until the bird died. By that time they were good friends, and their fate was sealed. "Something always grows out of death," Dad says. I suppose it does.

Because Dad practically jumped out of his skin when Mom scared him while he was trying to sneak that beer, she nicknamed him Chicken Boy—CB for short. She still calls him CB. I never asked why; I had always just assumed it was short for Christopher Barnes. It seems silly that for all these years I had no idea.

We talked around the dining room table for a long time. Pretty soon we got hungry again. Chinese food is like that. My fortune cookie said, "A good way to keep healthy is to eat more Chinese food," so we did. Dad says sometimes people confuse friendship for love, and that's probably what they did.

SO, THIS IS MY ROOM now—my safe space. Not my bedroom; I still have that. But it's my own personal getaway. The place I can come to just to escape from life, school stuff, assholes, and Davy, who's not as much of an asshole as he used to be. I think he's growing up. I come here quite a bit. It's quiet and relaxing and, well, safe.

I still think about Trent all the time. It's not like I really want to, but reminders are everywhere. When I head to study hall, I have to pass by his office—his old office. They have a new guidance counselor at Glenwood now. I don't know who she is; I've never met her, although she's left about eight notes in my box, saying she'd love to meet me. Yeah right. I'm also reminded of him whenever I see a black car. I haven't seen one like his, mind you. His was a sweet ride—black Dodge Challenger SRT with a 392 Hemi, eight-speed auto, turbo-charged, almost 600 horsepower. He used to let me drive it whenever we got outside the city. Tracy, my social worker, says I should try not to think about him or things that remind me of him. I'm supposed to use my unconditional positive self-regard to chase thoughts of him away like a bad dream. And I do most of the time. But sometimes when I'm in here all by myself, I like to remember the good times, you know?

Mom and Tracy both think I should change schools and go to St. Mary's next year, but it's my last year, and I don't want to finish high school with a bunch of strangers. Plus, why should I have to lose my school because of Trent? I've lost enough because of him. If I changed schools, it would be like admitting defeat. Then he would win. And he's taken enough from me already. Mom and Tracy don't seem to get it.

In my safe place, I have a docking station with a Bluetooth speaker for my iPhone. I listen to stuff that helps me relax. Not hip-hop and shit but other music. I love Tchaikovsky; his sixth symphony is pretty sweet. Same goes for *Swan Lake*, but *Romeo and Juliet* just makes me cry. It's like you can feel the lovers' passion in the music or something. Most of the time I listen to classical music in here. But sometimes I like to listen to old jazz, like Miles Davis and John Coltrane. When I'm really depressed, though, I listen to Pink Floyd. Trent got me into them. God, he loves Pink Floyd.

One thing that really pisses me off is when people talk about a band like it's a person. I was telling Jenny about "Black Dog" by Led Zeppelin, and she goes, "Yeah, he's great," and I'm like, WTF? Trent was way into Zep. I guess music reminds me of Trent too.

When I come into this room and listen to music and do my breathing exercises, life gets better. Davy isn't allowed to come in here or into my bedroom.

School is starting to get normal again. I took almost three weeks off after they arrested Trent. I told people it was because of the accident, but it wasn't. I wasn't really hurt at all.

When I got back to school, it was really tough at first. I was a pariah. Everyone avoided me, even Jenny and Amanda. Guys would look at me like I was nothing more than a piece of meat. I guess everyone knew that me and Trent were fucking. I got a note stuffed into my locker that said, "Hey, whore, can I get some?" and other stupid junior high bullshit stuff like that. I wrote "In your dreams" on the note, then stuck it face out on the front of my locker where everyone could read it. I saw Mr. Chalmers take it down as I was leaving school at the end of the day. But by that time, pretty much everyone in the grade eleven wing had probably read it anyway. I never got another note after that. It's those kinds of things that really piss me off though. It's hard enough dealing with all the feelings I have inside of me, and when asshats pull that kind of shit, it hurts. Before I returned, Tracy prepared me for what might happen. That was helpful. I think I'm handling it pretty well. Some guys started calling me JB, as if I didn't know it means "jailbait."

Then there's Tracy, not Tracy my social worker, Tracy Underhill. She's the school's wannabe shrink. She's a senior who is always trying to nose her way into other people's business, offering hugs and whatever she can do to try and be the one who fixes all your shit. My first day back, she came running up to me, "Oh, Bree"—nobody calls me Bree except for Dad and Davy—"are you okay? I always knew that Mr. Reynolds was a creeper. He got what he deserved. Anything at all that I can do, just let me know." She told me all this while she had me wrapped up in her arms like a wiener in a Pillsbury hot dog wrapper. Her breath smelled like eggs and coffee.

Well, you can start by getting your slimy tentacles off me, take a few steps back so I can breathe, and then introduce yourself. We've never even talked before, I hardly know your name, and you certainly don't know mine. Never fucking call me Bree again, and then you can go fuck yourself because it'll be a cold day in hell before I come running to you for sympathy, you stupid bitch.

Instead, I just pulled back a bit and said, "Uh, yeah, thanks."

In some ways this whole thing has made me more popular, although I'm not looking to win any contests. I just want my life back the way it was before all of this. But at least people know who I am now.

What I didn't expect is how uncomfortable the teachers would be around me. Even teachers like Miss Thatcher, who I used to really like, treat me like I have AIDS. They will talk to me and stuff, but when it comes to any kind of real conversation, forget it. I asked Mr. Foster for some help with math after school one day, and he almost ran away from me, like I was going to rape him. I wouldn't touch an old fart like him with a ten-foot pole anyway. Sometimes I just wanna scream, "I'm the victim here!" Maybe Mom and Tracy are right. Maybe I should change schools.

The best thing about my safe place is that it is actually safe. No one can find me here. Well, they can find me, but they don't. Mom and Davy always know when I'm in here, and they are good at giving me the space I need. I try not to milk it. I know I could. I could cry all the time and play the "poor me" card, and people would buy it. In fact, at first I did. I milked this thing and played it up for all it was worth. I think it's what everyone expected. It's what Mom and Dad and Tracy wanted me to do. So did my lawyer—especially my lawyer. But that's not who I am. It's not who I was before Trent, and it's sure as hell not going to be who I am after. I know that what he did was wrong, and in some ways fucked up. I get that.

Tracy has read me stories—case studies, she calls them—of girls who have gone through similar traumatic situations. I don't want to pretend to know what it was like for anyone else 'cause I don't, so I won't judge them. But sometimes, holy shit, these girls are messed up. And I can't help but get the sense that Tracy would like me to be more like some of them, or at least pretend to be.

When we're meeting, she spends a lot of time asking questions about the sex between Trent and me. She says the more she knows, the more she can help me. But she asks things that really make me uncomfortable, like which position he liked best and which I liked best and whether

I swallowed and stuff that I can't understand is at all important to my getting better. But I guess she's the expert. She's suggested that I'm burying my emotions because I haven't flipped out like some of the girls in her case studies, but that's just not who I am. Sorry Tracy. Actually, no. I'm not sorry at all.

CHAPTER EIGHTEEN

Hey Gerald,

Guess what? I'm in the hole. I met with Doctor Thackery this afternoon, and when the COs arrived to take me back to the infirmary, we zigged where we were supposed to zag, and I found myself here in the hole. And I thought gen pop was bad. You should see this place. I think Doctor Thackery must have known what was coming. In retrospect, he alluded to it. "Sometimes even when we're doing all the right things, life throws us curveballs," he said. Yeah, it sure does.

Solitary confinement, segregation, the hole, whatever you want to call it is nothing like being in the general population. First of all, the cells are smaller, if you can believe it. Plus, there are no lights in the cells. Well, there are, but they're so dim. Everything you look at feels like that time of night right after you turn your headlights on, thinking they should make the road easier to see, but there's enough daylight left to make your headlights useless. It's like that but worse. The only consolation is that there's nothing worth getting a good look at in this place. The cells smell like shit—literally. I think these toilets must be nearest to the septic tank, and every toilet in the prison drains in this direction. There are no windows to the outside world and no bars on the doors to let in a little more light. Instead, heavy gray metal slabs cover the entrance to each cell. A small window cut into one corner of the door allows the guards to peer in and make sure you haven't slit your wrists or strung yourself from the ceiling. No prisoners are double bunked in the hole, as if having a cellmate is a privilege. Although given enough time in a place like this, it might be.

I found a solitary confinement protocol sheet taped to one wall. We can only leave this place once every four days to shower. Otherwise, the cell doors remain locked 24/7. Meals are slid through a grate mounted at the bottom of the door. Lights out at 10:30 p.m. I just noticed there is no light switch in my room, so I'm guessing that's also controlled by the COs. And the fun just never ends. One of the COs told me to be ready at 9:00 a.m. tomorrow for an appointment. More surprises. But enough about me.

I hear that not much has changed for you, that you're still stubbornly hanging on. What are you waiting for? Walk toward the light, Gerald. Walk toward the light.

They just announced lights out in five. I guess I'll have to wrap this up in the morning.

Later,
Trent

CHAPTER NINETEEN

The sound of the heavy, rusted metal grate at the bottom of my door sliding up wakes me. It must be morning. Someone kicks a food tray through, and it stops, wedged between the toilet bowl and my bed frame. I pick it up and look into this morning's delicacies: oatmeal the texture of wallpaper paste and the color of the walls, a banana that has been squished nearly in half by the tray that was sitting on top of this one, and two slices of three or four-day-old bread, dry and crusty around the edges. I close my eyes, pretend it's toast, and choke the bread down. The rest can go back to the kitchen.

Just as I was told, at 9:00—I think it was 9:00; there's no way to tell in time here—two COs arrive at my cell and take me to my appointment.

In gen pop, most inmates refer to their cell as their house. Some even decorate them like homes. They have little carpet runners woven from stolen bed sheets, towels, and bread wrappers. Pages ripped from library books cover the large fluorescent lights, which are far too bright for the size of the cell, transforming the cold bright white into a warm glow. They make elaborate picture frames, penholders, and placemats from colorful magazines stolen from the library. Clothes bins and baskets of all shapes and sizes are molded and woven from strips of plastic ripped from mattresses. Hardcover book jackets make collages of decorative art that hang from their walls. Universal product code stickers from apples and bananas are used as tape to secure this artwork. Institutional toothpaste serves as glue when there aren't enough fruit stickers. All in all, their creative energies transform their cells quite nicely, and they do have a homey feel to them. Comfortable. I see many of these homes as I walk through the units on my way to Doctor Thackery's office.

This is exactly what I do not want. The last thing I desire is to get comfortable in this godforsaken pit of despair. I don't want this place to ever feel like home. And I suppose this is one of the things that separates us from them. Some embrace their fate, and some fight against it. The hard work they do to forge a sense of coziness within this barren landscape provides, for them, a place of refuge. I will take no refuge in this hell. Like *our* cells and *their* homes, the "us," those who refuse to become the "them," stand out in stark contrast. I think they think we think we're better than them, but that is not true. We only hope we're better than *this*. Herein lies much of the difficulty. It's a form of social prejudice, I suppose. And the "us" are the visible minority.

It has not been twenty-four hours since I last saw Doctor Thackery. His office stands in polar opposition to what I have just come from. A row of nine pearl-white framed French windows ring the feature wall adjacent to the door I'm escorted through. Louvered wooden blinds, the same color as the rich mahogany desk that sits in the center of the office, are half drawn and wrap the semicircular wall. A matching mahogany credenza with floor-to-ceiling shelves spans the entire wall behind his desk, displaying pictures of family and recent vacations, models of airplanes, and golfing paraphernalia. The outermost, glass-covered shelves are filled with books. Some are psychology texts—a few I have read—and one shelf is dedicated completely to *Psychology Today*. Many, though, are first editions of volumes from the masters: Jung, Adler, Frankl, Rogers, Freud, Erikson, Bleuler, Kübler Ross, and Maslow. The creamy-coffee walls extend to join an elaborate pearl-white chair rail and wainscoting that falls to meet tall white baseboards.

His office is clean, organized, and fresh. The smell of lemon-scented furniture polish fills the air. An elaborately embossed, dark-stained hardwood floor spans the room. Upon the floor, under his desk and the chicory brown button-tuft leather chairs that sit directly in front of it is a beautiful taupe embroidered rug, an image of olive-green tree branches woven throughout. His desk always appears neat and clean. A brass banker's lamp, leather-bound notebook, black pen, and matching letter opener are the only items ever seen upon the forest-green marble surface that gleams like a mirror in the sunlight.

"If a cluttered desk is the sign of a cluttered mind, what is an empty desk the sign of?" I asked him once. He smiled and acted as though he had never heard the question before. He is gracious that way.

I have never seen him sit in the ergonomic chair behind his desk. When I enter the room today, like most days, he stands, hands clasped behind his back, looking out a window over the wheat fields blowing in the wind below. Aside from the guard towers that loom in every corner of this campus, his office is higher than all the other wings in this huge building. We are at the heart of the prison, in a circular dome that rises above the units below.

Each time I enter, he acts as though I am a very welcome but unexpected guest. We sit together in the large button-tuft chairs that stand in front of his desk, angled so they are facing each other.

"I am so sorry, Trent." He has begun calling me by my first name since my stay in the hospital. "I knew where they were taking you after our session yesterday but was not permitted to tell you. How are you holding up?"

I relax in the big comfortable chair. "You know, it's not so bad, really."

And it isn't. I still carry a fear of every inmate I see. I imagine that the moment we pass, I will be shanked or slammed. In the hole, I don't see anyone else, so that fear is greatly relieved. I tell this to Doctor T, who nods as though he understands.

IN THE SHORT TIME THAT I've been in solitary, apart from the light, or lack thereof, the thing that takes the most getting used to is the shouting and banging through the ventilation shafts that goes on once the lights go out.

"Hey, new guy, D7. Whaddya here for?" It breaks the silence like a baseball through a picture window. In my cell, D7, immediate fear grips me. I know they can't physically reach me, but damage can still be done.

I do not respond. I don't know how to respond. I could lie, say I fucked someone over, but I have not thought through the scenario well enough not to be trapped by my own words. They know all the right questions to ask to ascertain the truth. So I remain quiet. The questions increase, their tone getting more intense, like the cymbal crash you know is coming after the crescendo of kettle drums.

Even in the protection of solitary confinement, where they can't get you, they still can. Anger rises. I remain silent. Someone shouts, "Fuckin' skinner!" and with that comes relentless banging and threats. "This ain't PC, asswipe. You're fucking dead!" The banging is unremitting, like a jackhammer pounding next to you on the street. The drone does not stop. It seeps deeper and deeper into my head, to my very bones. An hour? Maybe two—there's no way to tell time in this place—before the savages tire from their assault.

Finally, fitful sleep.

"AS WE LEFT OFF YESTERDAY, you mentioned you had been experiencing bouts of anger that left you confused. Let's explore these. When you are experiencing and expressing anger, you're not using the cortex of the brain. The limbic center is taking over. When this is taken to an extreme, we see things like road rage, assault, and manslaughter, evidence of impulse control disorder. This is not something you have dealt with much in life. In fact, you have a pattern of suppressing these tendencies. Within the limbic system is a small structure called the amygdala. It's the storehouse for your emotional memories. I'd like to spend some time in this house today."

I agree, and we begin.

My eyes are closed as Doctor Thackery leads me in a guided meditative practice. He presses a button on the arm of his chair, and quiet chamber music fills the room. He leads. I sit upright in the chair, feet planted shoulder width apart on the soft carpet beneath me; my hands resting comfortably, palms up, on my knees.

A soft bell rings. "Breathing in, I know I am breathing in." I inhale, long, slow, and deep. "Breathing out, I know I am breathing out." I exhale. We have been practicing this technique for several months now. I am to concentrate on my breathing only. Every other distraction stays behind: my disease, this prison, the losses, Jimi, the pain in my jaw, Gerald, even Brianna. As I permit myself to, all thoughts fade away, the way an anxiety dream does as the busyness of the day overshadows it.

"Breathing in, I know I am breathing in." I focus upon nothing except my breath, feeling as the air enters my nostrils, noticing that it is ever so slightly cooler than the air around me, experiencing how it causes first my diaphragm, then my chest, to rise and expand. A slight warm sensation fills the top of my lungs as they reach capacity.

"Breathing out, I know I am breathing out," I repeat after Doctor Thackery. I feel the air, soft and warm, as it slowly passes my lips. I perceive how as the air is released from my body, my shoulders relax and fall, my chest deflates, my entire body experiences relief. We remain in this mesmerizing, hypnotic cycle until Doctor T rings the bell again, a quiet tone that brings me—us—back to the moment. Our eyes open, neither of us speaking for a time, which has no bearing in this place. There is complete silence. The soft chamber music is gone.

"Anger is good for you, Trent. Stop running from it. Can we talk about a time as a child when you got truly angry? What was it like? Who were you mad at? What did you do about it?" I close my eyes again, breathe deeply, and remember . . .

I'm eight years old. Gerald has asked me to clean the garage with him. My task is to organize a large drawer that has hundreds, maybe thousands, of miscellaneous nuts and bolts, screws, nails, washers, and grommets. He has used it as a junk drawer for his odds and ends for years, probably since before I was born. I begin sorting. I put the screws in a box that has several divided compartments. I work tirelessly, separating flat head from Phillips and Robertson, placing each type in a different compartment. There are hundreds of each. Next, I go on to nuts and bolts, finding the right nut for each bolt and the right place for both. I take great pride in the work I'm doing. It feels good to be helping Dad. I'm making a difference.

As we go in for lunch, I feel like I have been accomplishing something of great value. I watch in admiration as my father washes his hands, almost like a surgeon.

After lunch we return, and I continue where I left off. I hear Dad behind the garage. He's replacing the crankshaft in an old tractor. I want to go out and be with him, but I'm not distracted; I plug away at my important work. I finish up just before Mom calls us in for supper. As we stand together near the old sink in the back, washing up for supper, I admire again how he washes his big, strong hands.

"How'd ya make out?" he asks. These are pretty much the only words he's spoken to me all day.

"Really good, Dad," I reply. "I did a great job. It'll be really easy to find anything you need now! Wanna see?"

"Nope."

And that was it. He didn't thank me or even look at me. My heart dropped. I'd given my entire day, worked my ass off to do something I thought he really wanted done, something that was important to him, and he didn't give a shit.

"And then what did you do, Trent?" Doctor Thackery asks.

"What do you mean, what did I do? Nothing. What was I supposed to do?"

"Well, then that was a cute story, and my heart goes out to the little kid whose work was neglected. But I want to hear a story about a time you got really pissed off. That's what we're here for, Trent."

"I was mad."

"Were you?"

"Yes. I worked my ass off, and Gerald didn't even have the decency to check out the work I'd done for him. Of course I was mad."

"You didn't say you were mad, and until I brought it up, it didn't even seem to be a consideration for the eight-year-old boy who'd worked so hard. In fact, I don't think you were mad. I think you were hurt. I think you felt ignored. I think you felt like your fath—Gerald—didn't give a shit about you, but I don't think you were mad. And that's one of your problems, Trent. You don't even know when it's acceptable to be angry. In fact, you're unable to differentiate anger from fear or rejection or even neglect, for that matter.

"Trent the adult, he's mad as hell. He's so pissed off at Gerald that he wishes him dead. But eight-year-old Trent, he's not allowed to get mad.

It's little Trent I would like to see get angry. Anger can be a motivating force. Let's try again."

I close my eyes again and I think. Really hard . . .

I'm five or six years old. Mom is in the kitchen making supper and calls me from the playroom to take the garbage to the shed out back. "Make sure you close the door. I don't want racoons or rats getting in." I drag the bag out to the stoop on the back porch. After closing the screen door tight, I heft the large bag over my shoulder and stagger under my load to the shed. I drop the big bag at my feet as I fiddle with the latch that keeps the shed door closed. Once it's open, I drag the bag inside, deposit it with the others, head back out, close the door, and reset the latch. Then I run back to the house, up the back steps, and inside.

"I did it, Mom," I announce as I pull my rubber boots off.

"Make sure to shut the door tight," she says again. I double check to make certain the door is secure.

I head to the playroom and continue building my fortress with my Lego set. Well, it's not Lego; it's that cheaper stuff. I don't remember what it's called. A half hour or so later, I hear Gerald yelling. "Trent, get your ass in here this goddamn minute!" I slowly walk toward his raging voice, trying to think what I could have done to piss him off this time.

My head flies forward. I feel the pain surge, and my eyes fill with tears as I'm hoisted off the ground by the scruff of my neck, his large hand squeezing tighter and tighter, pulling my hair and me higher off the floor. "You useless piece of shit. How can you be so goddamn stupid?"

He throws me into a pile of refuse. Coffee grounds, greasy paper towels, moldy lettuce leaves, last week's newspaper, apple cores, potato peelings, and assorted packages and papers. The roast beef that was to be supper lies in pieces strewn across the white and brown linoleum. Another slap, this one hard across the face. My eyes water and blood trickles from my nose. "How many times do you have to be told to shut the goddamn door when you come in?"

"I-I-I-I d-d-d-did," I try to get out as sobs choke back the words.

"And now you're going to sit there and lie to me? You little bastard." A kick that lands just where my butt meets the floor almost lifts me into the air, throwing me into the refrigerator door. "Now stop your goddamn crying and clean this mess up. I'd better be able to eat off this bloody floor by the time we get back."

I dare not lift my head to watch as I hear Claire's coat and boots being put on and Mom and Gerald getting ready to go out. The door slams, then opens again. "If this place isn't spotless and you're not in your bedroom with the door shut tight when we get back from supper, I'm going to give you something to cry about, you little bastard!" The door slams again, making the windows rattle.

There is a long silence in Doctor Thackery's office. "And then?" he asks. "Where was the anger, Trent?"

After cleaning up the mess as best as a five-year-old could, I went to my room and cried until I heard them come home. I waited, expecting my bedroom door to burst open and to be hauled back downstairs because I didn't get the kitchen as clean as he wanted. But nothing happened. I went to sleep that night without supper.

The next morning Dad was already gone by the time I got up to get ready for school. Mom had made me an extra-large breakfast. She patted me on the head and asked if I was okay as she handed me my lunch. I just nodded and headed out to wait for the school bus.

"Sorry if it pisses you off," I say, "but I wasn't really mad. Not until later that day."

When I got home from school, Dad was in the garage talking on the phone that we had in there.

"Poor little shit," he says, followed by his bellowing laugh. "I know . . . No, Jim, what had happened is, I was out on the back steps having a smoke when Louise called me in to grab some potatoes from the cellar. I took a final drag, tossed the smoke into the garden, and stepped back inside . . . That's what I'm saying. It was me who forgot to shut the door. Poor bastard."

"I can certainly understand where that would piss you off enough to scream, Trent," Doctor Thackery interjects. "What was Gerald's reaction when you told him you'd overheard him?"

I didn't tell him. I didn't say anything. I went into the house as though I hadn't heard a thing and waited. I waited all through supper, all through *All in the Family*, all through our bedtime ritual. Nothing. It was three days before I concluded that not only was he never going to admit it was his fault, he was never even going to apologize for the beating he'd given me.

That's when the rage and fury filled every part of me. That night I screamed into my pillow. God, how I hated him then. I think that's when the hatred truly began.

The next morning, I awoke absolutely certain that Gerald would never tell me the truth, and I started exacting revenge. Nothing serious, but I set about to make his life more difficult in little ways. I would steal the book of matches he needed to light his cigarettes and smile as I watched him search everywhere, getting more and more pissed off. I would do my chores half-assed, enough so that he couldn't say they weren't done but not quite to his satisfaction—not that that was possible anyway. I would pour toilet water in his coffee cup. I'd drag his favorite sweater over the spot where Charlie always slept and laugh as he spent hours picking at the little dog hairs that were matted into it.

"That's what I wanted to hear, Trent. Passive-aggressive behavior is a common expression of anger. Through intentional inefficiency, allowing problems to escalate, procrastination, and exacting hidden revenge, you used passive aggression to get Gerald to act out your hidden anger for you. Your ability to manipulate Gerald's emotions through the things you did to him gave you a sense of power that you were otherwise incapable of owning. But it can be an exhausting way to express anger, and it's the coward's way. As a child who was beaten mercilessly by your father, it was your only recourse, Trent. But as an adult, you have continued this pattern to deal with your anger, and you cannot do it forever."

I don't like hearing these words, but I have to admit they're true. Sometimes the truth hurts. We spend the remainder of our session discussing healthier coping mechanisms to deal with my anger. Doctor Thackery leads me from events in my childhood, through my teen years, and directly into the anger I have buried as a result of my recent attack and subsequent HIV infection.

I was thirteen and so was Michelle Boucher, although she didn't look it. She looked like a boy. I knew it, and so did she, but that didn't matter. Her mousy brown hair was short in a pageboy cut. She wasn't cute or even pretty, but that didn't matter either. We certainly were not boyfriend and girlfriend. We were boy and girl *friends*—buddies.

She was better than me at most things. She could pitch a baseball faster, throw a better spiral football, she was smarter and funnier, and she could skate better and faster than me. In fact, the only thing I could do better than her was piss standing up. I would get mad at her because things I had to work so hard to accomplish, she could do with seemingly little effort. She spent a lot of time at our farm the summer between seventh and eighth grade. Claire and she were fast becoming friends, and I began to think she was coming over to see Claire more than me.

One day Michelle came out of Claire's room, where they had been holed up most of the morning. Claire had given her a makeover. Her hair was done up, and she was wearing eyeshadow, blush, lipstick—everything—and she looked really good. Pretty.

"Whaddaya think, Trent?" Claire asked. Instead of saying what I thought, I laughed, I taunted, I teased. I did everything but tell her the truth. I suppose I felt as though I was losing a friend. So, rather than tell Michelle how I felt, I mocked her mercilessly. She turned around, crying, and ran back into Claire's room. After a time, she raced to the bathroom, scrubbed her face, and walked out the door without saying a word.

The moment she left, Claire tore into me. "That was a really shitty thing you did, Trent. She did all of that for you because she likes you. You're so stupid."

I didn't hear from Michelle for two weeks, and when I finally did, it was a phone call.

"Can I speak to Claire, please?" no "Hey, Trent, what's up?" no "Wanna go chuck a Frisbee?" no "Let's go frog huntin'." Nothing. Just, "Can I speak to Claire, please?" in a tone that was harsh and cold, like a blast of wind that greets you as you open the door on a frigid winter morning. We never hung out again. Just one more way I allowed my passive aggression to destroy something I valued.

Recognition of serious character flaws seldom comes without struggle. Slowly—painfully—I'm coming to understand that the tactics I use to deal with things that wound my ego are costing *me* more than anyone else.

"While I lay in the hospital recently, recovering from my attack—"

Doctor T interrupts. "Let's call it what it was, Trent. These men tried to kill you. It was more than an attack; it was attempted murder. Don't minimize this. It's part of your story now, and you must deal with it truthfully. A group of men hated you so much, they wanted you dead. Now go on."

I told him about the endless days I lay in agony so extreme I wanted to be dead. The pressure inside of my head from the built-up fluid around my brain was so intense that often I couldn't see. I could feel pieces of my jawbone moving inside my face. With every swallow, each movement brought pain so excruciating I felt nauseous. The general anesthetic used to sedate me for surgery made me so sick that I was constantly vomiting. With my jaw wired shut, the yellow bile and spit—the only contents in my stomach—forced my mouth to strain against the binds and wracked my head like a walnut in a nutcracker. Putrid bile would seep from my mouth and run down my chin. Each heave of my stomach ignited such a strong burning feeling from the shank wounds in my kidney that I felt I would spontaneously combust. I have never known such pain. The opiates added to the nausea more than they dulled the pain. Beyond anything, I longed for death. And yet some pain—a deeper pain, an emotional pain—buried inside me blocks the rage I need to feel toward those who did this.

And I'm beginning to recognize why. I have no way of expressing that anger. I only know one method for dealing with my anger, and in this situation, it's useless. Passive aggression cannot work against those I cannot reach. I'm unable to piss in their soup, to trip them as they pass, to steal anything of value, or to make them the brunt of ridicule. Nothing in my arsenal can harm them. I can't rat them out; the system has already dealt with them. No punishment they will receive can bring justice for the disease that may eventually run rampant through me. They are untouchable, and I have no recourse against them, no awareness of any outlet for anger. The anger is there, burning like a hot coal; I simply have no way to release it.

Then another pain strikes me. My victim, Brianna, is in a similar situation. All the agony and anger she must deal with cannot be expressed to me. I will never know the pain I have brought to her. I am paying for it. But the price I pay does nothing to compensate for—or lessen—the pain

I have brought upon her. I'm here, away from all she must live with, and she must walk her road to recovery alone, just as I must walk mine. The thought fills me with sorrow.

At each step along the way, we explore how I feel, what I do with those feelings, and where to go from here. The beginning of catharsis? As difficult as it is to admit, I realize I am a bitter, angry man with no means to express it. This eats away at the core of who I am. Doctor Thackery is helping me to recognize this, and with recognition comes some ability to cope. I'm learning better ways to manage this internal rage.

The coward inside of me wants to deny my anger, to exact revenge without being detected. Instead, Doctor Thackery is challenging me to do what I can to confront issues and people who anger me. "After all," he points out, "what do you have left to lose?"

He challenges me to find some correlation between my passive-aggressive lifestyle and the sexual attraction to girls that brought about the collapse of my career, my incarceration, and my disease. I'm at a loss. I can see no connection.

"Are they somehow related?" I ask.

"I'm not sure, Trent. Are they?"

I do not know.

As they usually do, our session ends the way it began. The bell rings. I settle once again. "Breathing in, I know I am breathing in. Breathing out, I know I am breathing out." A deep calm envelops me, and as much as is possible, I am at rest.

As I leave, Doctor Thackery informs me that because I'm in the hole for my own protection and not as a form of punishment, the rules of the hole do not fully apply to me. For me the hole serves as protective custody. I'm allowed to go to the visitors' lounge, the library, the gym, even the commissary. The restrictions of solitary confinement do not apply to PC inmates.

This is the thing that truly pisses off the SC guards and inmates. The inmates, with their noses pressed against the small windows cut into their cell doors, can watch as I go where they cannot. This freedom results in restlessness and agitation amongst the inmates, whose anger soars at the "injustice."

Moreover, SC guards do not like playing host to PC inmates. Not only does it make more work for them when an inmate presses the call button to renew a library book or take a shower, they have to live with the fallout that my freedom has upon the other SC inmates.

"Use this privilege wisely," the doctor forewarns.

He also tells me that I'm scheduled to be transferred to Dominion Medium Security Penitentiary, on the other side of the country. I will be given very little notice. When the transfer documentation is complete, I'll be gone, as simple as that. I'm not supposed to know this, but Doctor Thackery said it will do no harm.

Okay, now I'm really pissed. The only support I have in this fucking place is Doctor T and Claire. Now those are about to be stripped from me. I take a few more deep breaths as I wait for the COs to arrive and escort me back to hell.

In the days I have remaining here, there are some matters I must resolve. Back in my cell, I look at the letter to Gerald I began yesterday. It sits where I left it, upon the small ledge by my toilet-sink, and stares up at me like a child gazing into a candy shop window. I press the call button. My minions arrive and take me to the phones hanging just outside this dark unit. Claire will come as soon as she can. It has been far too long since I have seen my beloved sister.

On the way back, I ask the COs to take me to the commissary. They reluctantly do so. I stick my hand in the device that reads the bone structure, a safeguard against inmates stealing your money—it works well to prevent direct theft but does nothing to stop a savage from walking into your cell and taking your purchases. I enter my DOJ number into the keypad, it beeps and displays the balance of my prison account. There is enough. I purchase ten postage stamps. While it will have no impact, there is one more thing I can do as a healthy expression of my anger. With regard to Gerald, I will cower no more.

CHAPTER TWENTY

I like my coffee weak, so I rarely go to Starbucks, but it is a good place to come and think. I've been doing a lot of that lately. I order a Grande Americano from the cute blonde—strawberry blonde, I suppose—barista working the counter. "Black. And make the top two inches just hot water, please." My favorite seat, a comfortable burgundy leather armchair, is available near the fireplace in the back corner.

I have been putting off this dreaded task that looms before me, like a spider dangling in a doorway, for far too long. Robert's right, I know. But coming to the readiness to actually do it is one of the most difficult things I've ever done. In my heart, I know it's the right thing to do. The medical staff have assured me it's the right thing. Of course, Trent thinks it is. I know that pulling life support changes nothing, but doing so makes me feel like I'm the one who's killing Dad.

So this evening, Robert, the boys, and I will go back to Glendale General Hospital. I have asked Pastor Jacobs to come as well. It will almost certainly be our final visit. Dad's doctor says it probably won't happen immediately. It could take a few hours, or a day or two, perhaps as long as a week.

Yet as much as I'm consumed by Dad's situation, Trent's weighs even heavier. When we were kids, he was the most happy-go-lucky little guy in the world. Nothing seemed to bother him. Even all the stuff he had to put up with from Dad was like water off a duck's back, or at least it seemed that way.

Seeing him like this kills me. He's lost so much weight in the year he's been in prison. Every time I visit he looks a little worse. He's gaunt and pale and lethargic. The light that used to sparkle in his eyes, that once lit up the world around him, now smolders like the last flickering of a match. I worry so much about him. I feel as though I have lost my whole family this past year: first Mom, then Trent, and now Dad. Watching what this system does to Trent infuriates me. I'm exhausted with worry. I wipe away the tears, blow my nose in one of those useless little napkins with the mermaid in the middle, and go back to the cream and sugar counter for another handful. Trent has no idea what this has done to me.

It's not like I'm ashamed of him, but what he did to that poor girl fills me with shame. He thinks he's the only one suffering. I'm in prison too. Not like his, perhaps, but they share so many similarities. And I cannot escape mine any more than he can escape Briar Ridge.

The first voicemail I got from Janet threw me hard. "Hey, Claire, Janet here. I was reading the Dispatch this morning. Is that *Trent* your brother they're talking about? God, I hope not. Ring me back."

How was I supposed to respond to that call, Trent? Ever think of that? What was I supposed to do? Call her up and say, "Hey, Janet, yeah, that was my brother. No biggie, he's just a fucking perv, that's all." I haven't spoken to her since. I quit book club and volunteering at the boys' after school program. I even quit teaching Sunday school. Well, I didn't actually quit—I was asked to step down.

Graham Marshall, the Sunday school superintendent, said—how did he put it again? Oh yeah: "I think it would be in the best interest of the girls in your class." Like they were going to be vicariously molested through me. Since then we've stopped going to church altogether. Stevie and Aaron were getting bullied. Kids in their Sunday school class and mid-week Boy's Brigade program taunted and picked on them because of what they *thought* their uncle did. What did my boys do to deserve being treated this way, Trent?

The worst of it comes from teachers, though. I've been told I should probably find a different line of work by more than a few—not directly, but it has certainly been implied. Four students left my class once word got out that Trent Reynolds is my brother.

When my review was held in June, I was scrutinized more thoroughly than ever before. Questions about my personal life and sexual preferences. Questions about my relationship with my children, about the stability of my marriage, about inappropriate intimacy with any of my students. Hardly a single comment about my performance as a teacher—which has remained exemplary. With each question, I sank lower and lower in my chair. By the end of the review, I dragged myself up off the floor and slunk through the door like a student being sent to the office for cheating on a test. I sat in my car and cried for an hour.

Back here in Starbucks, I make another trip to the cream and sugar counter.

Did you consider any of this when you were providing "guidance" to little miss sunshine, Trent? You're not the only one paying for your behavior, and I have done nothing to deserve any of it!

My anger with my brother ebbs and flows like a love/hate relationship between quarreling lovers.

I was four years old when Trent became my hero, and until last year, he has remained so. Mom was in town getting her hair done, I think. Dad was supposed to be watching us—but on the farm, watching kids means staying on your property, no running to town or going to visit the neighbors. He was in the barnyard, checking the pigs or feeding the chickens or something. I decided it would be a nice gesture to make the family a cake. After all, I'd seen Mom do it countless times, so I knew exactly what needed to be done. Flour, eggs, milk, sugar, a big bowl . . . Nothing to it.

I gathered all my ingredients. The table isn't conducive to my stature, so I drag everything into the living room, where the warm rug is far more comfortable than the cold kitchen floor.

First the flour. Oops, got a bit on the rug. How much milk? About that much? Oh well, that'll soak in, and no one will know. Eggs? How many eggs go in a cake? I don't know. Five or six should suffice. Eek! Ah, that *might* soak in too. How much sugar? Perfect.

I mix all the ingredients together. Most of it stays in the bowl. Well, some of it stays in the bowl. This mixing business is hard.

Then I get a brilliant idea. I drag the bowl back into the kitchen, knocking over the bag of flour as I go, drag a kitchen chair to the counter, climb onto it, grab the electric mixer from the cupboard, climb up on the counter, and plug it in. It doesn't quite reach the bowl sitting on the floor, so I heave the heavy bowl up toward the countertop, and that's when it falls.

I am crestfallen. My cake is ruined.

The loud bang as the large glass mixing bowl splits in three or four brings Trent running into the kitchen. He simply stares. One end of the house to the other is covered in batter, flour, milk, eggs, and sugar. He finds me sitting in the midst of the mess, tears mixing with the concoction that covers my face, hands, arms, and legs.

"We gotta clean this up now!" he says. "Dad'll kill you."

We do our best—Trent does his best. I pretty much sit there and sob. He almost has the kitchen presentable but hasn't yet touched the living room where the real mess is when Dad walks in.

Trent assumed full culpability. He took the blame and the punishment: a severe beating—and I do mean severe—plus two months with no allowance to cover the cost of the wasted ingredients and the rest of the weekend alone in his room with nothing to eat. I snuck him up as much food as I dared. I think Mom did too, but it was little consolation.

This is the Trent that I want to remember. I try to push those other thoughts far away, but they keep re-emerging every time I have to deal with the fallout of his selfish choices.

Amongst all the other shit I've been forced to put up with, I've been getting anonymous emails as well. One from chopoffhisballs@hotmail.com:

> The offense your brother committed makes me want to puke. The very thought of him causes my stomach to turn. The death penalty is too good for perverts like him. He should be castrated and lobotomized. Guys like Trent Reynolds have no idea what they do to their young, innocent victims. If he ever gets out of prison, I hope I meet him on the street or in some dark alley. I'll make sure he never harms another soul. I wish death upon you and your whole family.

It was signed, "Looking out for the kids."

I got another from a member of a Parent Teacher Association somewhere in Nebraska. She felt compelled to tell me what she thinks of Trent's misconduct:

> A lotta years ago, a teacher in my son's high school villently raped a student just like ur brother did. But he came from some money and hire'd a good laywer to fight for him. Even with all of the proof against him he got off scott-free. Mosta the rest of the school took his side. He never had to ever even transfer to another school. Instead he got prompted to Vice Principle and now indangers the entire student popluation. Everyone's fraid of him. But he went around pretending that he was king shit and his don't stink and was above the law and stuff, so some men from round these parts, I won't say who, there kids went to that school and they had enough, and they brought justice on him cause the law wouldn't. You know what they did? They hobbled him. Do you know what that means? They broke both his ankles. He now has to use a walker to get around. Hahaha. Serves him right. But he then sued the school and now he has retired a millionaire. I hope your brother gets what he daserves. Not like are teacher.

It wasn't signed.

I get so angry with Trent sometimes, yet I love him dearly. He's been my best friend and biggest fan for so long. When we were kids, he was everything a little sister could ask for. He would protect me from all harm. I can't count how many times he took the blame for stuff I did so I wouldn't get punished. That bothered the hell out of me because any punishment he would get was always far more severe than anything I received. Even if we got caught doing the same thing, I might get scolded, but he'd get the shit beaten out of him. Dad was always unfair like that. I don't know why. It's like there were two sides to Dad. One side was considerate, smart, and resourceful, and the other was reserved for Trent. I've never understood it, but I can certainly understand why Trent doesn't like Dad.

I was twelve, so Trent would have been thirteen, almost fourteen, when I came into his room one night. We used to kind of fool around with each other, like a lot of siblings do. I initiated it more than Trent, I think. I slipped under his covers, and we were fooling around. We heard Dad coming up the stairs, so I ran back to my room. Dad grabbed me as I went around the corner. "What's going on?" he said. I said that I had just gone in to talk with Trent. "Get to bed!" he said, then swatted me on the backside as I whisked by.

He went into Trent's room and tore strips off him for letting me come into his room wearing nothing but a T-shirt. Then he smacked Trent around. He was always careful not to leave marks where others could see, but when I snuck back into Trent's room later, he showed me all the welts on his legs, back, and butt left by Dad's belt buckle. Somehow those things rarely seemed to bother him. But when I see Trent the way he is now, I wonder whether the way Dad treated him didn't have something to do with what he did.

I got a phone call from Allen Chalmers, the principal at Trent's old school, a couple of months back. He called under the guise of finding out how Trent was doing, but his true intentions soon surfaced. He wanted to vent, to let me know the repercussions the "incident" had had upon Chalmers and his school. Their academic rating had dropped from number three to number four in the county, several students had dropped out, and some transferred to other schools in the area. Teachers had been requesting therapy, two teachers transferred to other counties, the school's morale was on the decline, and pep rallies were anything but. He droned on and on, like a forgotten blender. He ended by asking me if I had any idea how Trent's actions affected our profession. I felt like saying: "And your scholastic rating in the county is linked to Trent exactly how? It seems to me that you're using Trent's misconduct as an excuse for every problem that has ever plagued your school. And when it comes to the impact Trent's actions have had upon others, you don't even rank in the top 100, fuckwad."

Instead, I listened politely, thanked him for his concern, then set the phone back in its cradle and sobbed like a baby.

I haven't told Trent any of this. I don't know how to. I do know Trent, though. I know him better than any other person on the planet. And I know that he is not a complete loser. He got caught up in something that was bigger than himself, he made a host of poor choices, and he didn't know how to get out of it until it was too late. But now everyone who loves him is paying for what he did.

He can't begin to fathom what it did to Mom, and I have no heart to tell him. Her heart was shattered into a million little pieces when he told her. I know she was sick and was going to die, but somehow I think that Trent's arrest brought about her death far sooner than it should have come. She died of a broken heart as much as pancreatic cancer. How do I tell him that? Do I tell him that? It won't change a thing, and every time I see him, he's so broken I don't think he could handle it.

Robert has been fantastic through this whole thing, though. He is my pillar and my strength. I don't know how I could weather this storm without him. The evening Trent came over and told us what had happened, it was Robert who provided him with more comfort than I could muster. I was in complete shock. I held Trent's hand and wept as he told us the ramifications of his offense. He had called me from the police station the previous evening. I headed straight over and paid his bail. He hardly looked at me. "Please give me a day," is all he said. "I'll come over tomorrow and tell you everything." As his story unfolded, I had no ability to comprehend that it was even Trent speaking. The story he told could not be his. Things kept coming at me and fleeing from me in rapid succession. I would reach out for comprehension, and it was gone again. By the end of the night, I understood as much as my mind could hold: Trent had been fired from Glenwood, arrested for statutory rape, and was going to prison. Nothing else really mattered. I had no clue that he would not be sentenced for more than a year and a half, that his life would crumble out from under him, or that the impact of his actions would be so widespread.

When a person is arrested, in many ways their sentence begins at that moment, even if their actual incarceration is months away. At that moment they lose everything but their freedom. When they are then forced to wait years to get to trial, they have been paying dearly for their crime long before they are ever behind bars. I watched this thing begin to destroy Trent from the day he confessed everything to Robert and me, five hundred days before he ever saw the inside of a prison cell. This is an injustice of justice.

I must focus on this evening, though. The boys haven't really ever been around death. While they watched Mom die along with us, she put such a brave face on whenever they were around, I don't think they had any idea how sick she was. For them it was like Grandma was here one day, and the next she wasn't.

Even though there is only a slim chance that Dad will die tonight while we're there, they are going to be very aware of its possibility. And I worry. Not so much about Aaron but about Stevie. He's such a mama's boy.

CHAPTER TWENTY-ONE

Hey Gerald,

It's been a few days since I've written. As I'm sure you can imagine, I'm as busy as a vampire at a blood donor clinic in this place. So much to do and so little time.

They're shipping me out of here. Apparently, since my attempted murder, word is out. The powers that be are afraid there are inmates who want to finish the job, and I've got a target on my back. So they're sending me pretty much as far away as they can. I'm not sure when that will happen, but it could be any day now. I'm going to miss Claire so much. She'll do her best to see me a couple of times before I'm transferred.

Here in the hole, time seems to almost come to a standstill. Days drag on like weeks. As much as I'm not looking forward to leaving Claire behind, it will be good to get out of the hole. I'm going to miss Doctor T as well. Not you, though. I'll miss you like a hangover. It's rather unfortunate; it feels like so much of the personal inner work I have neglected to do my entire life I was actually beginning to accomplish with Doctor Thackery's help. He says there's a good shrink in Dominion, but the chances are slim they will place me on his caseload any time soon.

Doctor Thackery and I have been doing some helpful work in the area of anger. Turns out, "I'm mad as hell, and I'm not gonna take it anymore." We've been looking at expressions of my passive-aggressive tendencies and how unproductive they can be. When I think of all the energy I have spent to exact my anger upon you, it makes me, I don't know, angry? A man would have confronted you to your face. A coward would not.

Remember the summer I got my driver's license? For weeks I had been working up the miniscule amount of courage I possessed to ask Lynette Peters go with me to Rockfest on the Beach at Lake Delaware. It was to be the event of the summer, thirty thousand people gathering for a full day of our favorite music. The tickets alone cost a fortune. I used almost an entire paycheck from my job at Chevron to pay for them. Mr. Lemming reluctantly gave me the day off, and you promised that I could take the Lexus. I should have known that your promises were empty, but for some foolish reason I took you at your word. Is any of this ringing a bell, Gerald?

I spent the better part of Friday afternoon and evening getting ready. I washed the car inside and out, even waxed it and polished the rims. It hadn't looked better since the day you drove it off the lot.

Before she left for the weekend, Claire helped me pick out the right clothes: Ocean Pacific beachwear for the day, Calvin Kleins, a Gekko T-shirt, and an OP hoodie for after the sun went down. She made me try it all on and model it for her. Then on Saturday morning, she did my hair, kissed me on the cheek, and told me I looked hot. All ready to go, I went to ask you for the keys.

I remember it like yesterday. The sun was already warm; it was going to be the perfect day. You were sitting at the round glass table on the balcony, the one supported by three green marble dolphins. You were reading the paper.

"Hey Dad, can I get the keys for the car?" I asked. You never looked up from the paper, never even glanced in my direction. You pretended to be deeply engrossed in an article about how to breathe new life into old furniture.

I stood waiting.

I knew what was about to come. The long silence was for effect. You'd then dangle the keys in front of me, as if taunting a dog with a steak. And then the lecture would begin about the responsibility that comes with being behind the wheel. "Four thousand pounds of metal moving at sixty miles per hour is a weapon," you'd say. "Do you have any idea how hard I've worked to earn the money for this car?" you'd say. "Bloody kids these days think the world owes them a living," you'd say. "There better not be so much as a crumb on the floor when you get back." you'd say. And then, just as you were about to let the keys fall into my hand, you'd pull them back, like the steak from the dog, and you'd drone on for another five minutes or so. That was the way getting anything out of you was. You're so predictable.

But not that morning. No, that morning you diverted from the usual. "Yeah, no, Trent, that's not gonna work." You never so much as lifted your eyes from the newspaper. You offered no explanation, no rationale, nothing. You just sat there with your stupid glasses perched on the end of your nose like some university prof studying a dissertation and allowed the pain of your words to sink deep into me. It dawned on me as I stood there in disbelief that you had planned this all along. You had watched me working my ass off spit-polishing your fucking car the day before and decided at that point to exert your authority and change your mind at the eleventh hour. You knew what this meant to me. You knew, and you chose to hurt me . . . yet again.

"What're ya standin' there for? Grab the truck keys and get your skinny ass out the door." The truck was a piece of shit left over from the farm days. I was so pissed. "Well, what're ya lookin' at? Move yer ass. Your sweetie's a-waitin'."

"Shoulda known," I mumbled as I walked away.

You can move fast when you want to, and you were up in a nanosecond. "What did you just say to me?" Then you cuffed me across the side of the head. "Well, now you can't have the truck either. Looks like you're shit outta luck." I think it was the first time I ever told you to "fuck off" to your face. The beating was worth it. Lynette never spoke to me again, and little things began going wrong with your precious LS 400 shortly after.

"Some son of a bitch smacked the corner of my car in the parking lot this afternoon, Louise."

I just smiled. But this has been the pattern of my life for as long as I can remember. Rather than expressing my anger at the object of its intent, I hide it and bring it out when no one is looking. It's the coward's way. I've mentioned my cowardice many times. And I have come to a decision. I'm going to mail these letters I've been writing. I know you've been *dying* to read them. Did you catch the pun?

Again, my cowardice pushes through though. There's probably not a chance in hell that I'd dare send them if there was a snowball's chance of you ever getting them. I spoke with Claire yesterday, and apparently she's doing the deed tonight. Pastor Jacobs, your old buddy, is coming to town so Robert, Claire, Aaron, and Stevie can have a little ceremony for you before your doctor flips the switch. A farewell party, so to speak. My contribution will be the letters I send.

So, it looks like this is the end. I'll probably write again after you're six feet under, but for now I just wanted you to know that as little as it will matter, I at least summoned the courage to send you all my heartfelt thoughts while yours is still beating. I know it's not much; it's most certainly no demonstration of true bravery, but it's a little less cowardly. I won't hold my breath waiting for a purple heart, but it's better than nothing.

Bon voyage,
Trent

CHAPTER TWENTY-TWO

The judicial system never ceases to amaze me. I have recently learned that Trent Reynolds is not being transferred to Dominion after all. Like so many of the events that unfold in this place, it's a mystery. Perhaps another inmate's paperwork was misplaced, Reynolds' DOJ number was entered on the wrong line in the database, or a spreadsheet was misread. Whatever the reason, I shall likely never know, but suddenly he is at the top of the list for transfer to the protective custody unit here at Briar Ridge. Two inmates from PC are to be released on parole at the end of the week, and he will be placed there by the weekend.

When I first learned I was losing him as a patient, my discontent was significant, bordering upon depression. He had been making such great strides. The idea that it was all for naught was extremely discouraging. I eagerly look forward to resuming the deeper work of therapy. He is displaying signs that lead me to believe we can begin tapping into the woundedness of his inner child once again. With his father still alive, I hold out hope for significant growth.

I must confess that when I received the news that he is not being transferred, I was surprised at my internal response. A sense of joy, almost jubilation, overtook me. I found myself wanting to run to the hole and tell Trent the good news. However, the more rational, logical man I am knows that as easily as he was placed at the top of the PC list, he could just as quickly return to the bottom. Until he physically arrives in PC, there are no guarantees. I'm intrigued, however, at my own emotional reaction and must explore it.

Just as therapists in private practice gravitate toward some patients more than others, the same holds true in this setting—perhaps even more so in this setting. I feel a fondness for Reynolds that I have felt for few other patients. When I look inside myself to determine the power of this attraction, I recognize a commonality: Reynolds and I share an affinity for peace and order. Like him, I enjoy quiet and solitude over noise and distraction. He is thoughtful, a deep thinker. We also share a love for similar writers and composers. And perhaps above all, I sense within this wounded, broken man an inscrutable longing for wholeness. For a therapist in this dry and dusty land, he is an oasis.

However, if this growth is to occur, I must rely upon wiser men than I to pave the way for the work Reynolds and I must forge together. "Between stimulus and response there is a space. In that space is our power to choose our response. In our response lies our growth and our freedom," says Viktor Frankl. My next challenge is to help Reynolds spend some time in that space between stimulus and response—a sort of no-man's land, if you will, a place no one likes to spend much time. I shall incorporate a seldom-used therapeutic strategy in this effort. Logotherapy is a school of psychological practice given merit by very few practitioners in a culture that emphasizes the quick fix.

Since their inception, the schools of psychoanalysis and psychotherapy have ruled the North American psychiatric practice. Adding to our arsenal everything from lithium and electroshock treatment in the 1950s and 1960s to more recent breakthroughs of selective serotonin reuptake inhibitors such as sertraline, fluoxetine, and citalopram, we attempt to alter mood, and thereby improve the quality of life. Artificial intelligence and virtual reality are now being researched as potential additional sources of therapy in our attempt to conquer mental and emotional disorders. My practice has been built upon these methodologies. Sadly, I must confess that for many patients, even our best efforts provide only temporary improvements and at worst can destroy the lives of the very people we have set out to help.

This science, the study of the brain, is the most recent branch of medicine. We are merely in its infancy. We have only been using our brains to examine our brains for a few short decades. The brain is the most complex and difficult mechanism humankind has ever attempted to understand. Imagine a device so potent and intricate it has the power to create. This machine has imagined, designed, and constructed virtually everything around us. Yet this small organ weighs less than two pounds and can fit in the palm of your hand. The problem is, it contains more nerve cells than there are people on the planet, and we're just beginning to scratch the surface in our understanding of it. It is most difficult to fix that which we do not understand. While we have come a long way, I still concur with Carl Jung's proposition that "modern psychiatry is little more than a chaos of arbitrary thought."

In my work with Reynolds, I have chosen to abandon traditional methods in an attempt to bring about healing. I will seek guidance from the past rather than the present or even the future. Logotherapy works from the assumption that every human life has meaning. If a man can grab his sense of purpose—the reason he was placed on this planet in the first place—he can soar. As Nietzsche posited, "He who has a why to live for, can bear almost any how." William McCartney put it more poetically: "The two most important days in your life are the day you're born and the day you find out why."

Before Reynolds can discover any sense of purpose, however, we must conquer what has created his profound sense of purposelessness. Neuropsychological profiling has verified the pattern I have witnessed. Repression of a disturbing nature has become rote practice. A man who tells himself over and over again that what is actually occurring in his life cannot be, begins to believe it. When a child does this, it can define his life path.

When it comes to the development of personality, early childhood is old age. By five years of age, the personality is almost fully developed. From this point forward, a person can adjust, but without significant effort and intentional determination they have little power to dramatically change. For proof of this, one need look no further than the men I am surrounded by. Traumatic events that span years in a child's life create lifelong personality traits that cannot be changed. Armed with this knowledge and faith in the power of logotherapy, in this man I shall attempt the improbable: to change Reynolds' personality.

The search for purpose can be long and difficult, and the process can damage a man's sense of worth. Yet search for it we must, for until the pearl of great price is found, it has no value.

Much like growth, linear regression is hierarchical. By examining the effects of parental trust and alienation, purpose can become a predictor of self-esteem. Parental alienation significantly reduces the opportunity to establish and develop purpose and self-worth. Conversely, parental trust moderates the association and fosters both. Results suggest that parent-child relationships characterized by high levels of parental alienation may exacerbate the malevolent effects in one's search for purpose. Few things have impacted Reynolds' formative years more than parental alienation. Getting him to recognize and admit the origin of his self-sabotaging is key. The next step is to move beyond recognition to the implementation of change.

I have been criticized by my peers for the depth and thoroughness of my reports. They suggest that it pulls valuable time away from other patients. But I have always found these recordings to be the progenitors of paths toward solutions. When written immediately post session, they provide a lens through which I am able to process the effects of the counsel I provide. But more than this, they bring clarity and direction that would otherwise remain uncharted.

I know where I must begin. Reynolds permitting, we shall at once begin excavating the mine of his psyche, burrow through the muck and mire of pain submerged deep in his unconscious mind, and arrive at truth that shall open the door to self-examination—the portal to new beginnings.

I hold out much hope for rediscovery. There is, after all, much to be hopeful for. Hope is a powerful motivator. Not so long ago, with his transfer looming, I held little hope for Reynolds. This had less to do with any sense of messiah complex—I gave up on that years ago—and more to do with a thorough understanding of the judicial system. My hope rests in the goodness that I know exists inside him. In a place such as this, goodness is a rare quality. When one finds it, he holds onto it like a precious gem.

Upon news of Reynolds' transfer, I experienced a sense of loss for any further progress with him. That sense brought with it a desire to give up the fight, so to speak. Knowing he will remain with us breathes new life into that hope, and I can say along with Tolkien, "There's some good in this world, Mr. Frodo, and it's worth fighting for."

CHAPTER TWENTY-THREE

When the car finally came to a stop, I felt the blood trickling from my nose. Although I didn't even know I had hit my head on anything. With all the spinning, I didn't feel a thing.

It was the weekend before final exams, and Trent and I wanted to go to the beach together. We could never go to Alum Creek Lake—that was way too close and way too risky—so we drove for two hours to Pelican Point on Lake Delaware. It's just as nice, much safer, and there are a lot fewer people. I told Mom that I was spending the night at Jenny's—that was my go-to story whenever I slept over at Trent's—and that Jenny, Amanda, and I were going to the beach. We got up at about nine, which was an hour later than we planned to leave, but we were up way late the night before, which isn't a shocker, so we were in a bit of a hurry. We showered—we could have gotten away earlier, but whenever we showered together, one thing always leads to another and, well . . . you know. Then we hopped in the car and took off.

I have Trent well trained. At the Starbucks just before the highway, he pulls in, and we order coffee and then switch places. He still doesn't want me driving in the city, which makes sense since I still don't have my driver's license. I fishtail out of the parking lot and we're on our way.

We have the tunes cranked and the windows down. Life doesn't get much better than this. I'm with my boyfriend, driving a hot car, and it's a gorgeous day.

We were best friends. When I first went to see Trent a lifetime ago, I wasn't really attracted to him. I mean, what fifteen-year-old goes looking for love in someone twenty years older? But we just sorta clicked. He was so helpful and smart and funny, and he really is hot. Not Jack Dylan Grazer hot, but Trent's really cute, and he's got a pretty rockin' body for thirty-seven. The first time I saw his body, I was surprised. When you're hanging with your girlfriends and talking about older guys, you're always like, "OMG, can you imagine seeing *that* naked?" And then you all laugh. But I was really, I don't know, pretty amazed by his body.

All that stuff aside, he really is—was—my best friend. I could tell him anything. I suppose it helps when your relationship begins by telling him your most intimate stuff. That's probably what attracted me to him in the first place.

When he was still my guidance counselor, I was telling him about this guy, Rusty, that I had it hard for. He was in my math and bio classes and was always kinda flirting with me. The more he did it, the more I wanted to get to know him, but I didn't know where to begin. It's not like I hadn't had a boyfriend before, I'd had plenty—well two, two before Trent—but that was enough, and I knew what to do. But Rusty seemed somehow completely out of my league.

He was popular, had his own car, he was really cute, *and* he sang and played guitar. I mean, anyone would have died to go out with him. So I was in Trent's office, spilling my guts about how much I liked him, when Trent just cuts in and says, "What are you waiting for, Brianna? Ask him out."

I was like, "Whaaaat? I could never do that."

"You know, Brianna," he began. He used my name a lot when he talked. I asked him why once, and he said it gives a person a sense of value when they hear their own name. I think he's right. "You only live once. And if you really feel that strongly about Rusty, go for it. Think about it like this: if he says no, you'll be in the exact position you're in right now. It changes nothing. But if he says yes . . ." And so I did. And Rusty told me he was flattered, but I was the wrong gender. God, was my face red. Anyway, shortly after that I started to like Trent, and he started to like me. And, well, that's what got us to this place.

On the final approach to the entrance into Pelican Point, as we were rounding the corner, I was going pretty fast, too fast, I know, but the day was so perfect. I just wanted to grab my bikini and hit the sand. Trent had just said, "Slow down. Where's the fire?" when the front tires lost traction on some sand in our lane and we slid across the yellow line. It happened really fast. The front of Trent's car hit the back of an oncoming car, and we both went spinning like coins you flick with your finger on the table when you're bored. I have no idea how many 360s we did, probably eight or so. When we finally stopped, Trent was already leaning over, asking if I was okay. He said we should probably switch places, but by the time I figured out what he was talking about, two witnesses and the driver from the car I hit were standing next to us.

Trent did everything he could to defuse the situation. He was taking phone numbers and exchanging insurance information as though we could just drive away and take care of things later. That was going to be a bit tough with our front fender and right wheel floating in the lake. I guess he was in shock too. By the time the police arrived, I could see the resignation on his face. It was like he had aged ten years in that hour. I didn't have a clue, but he knew this was it. The jig was up.

It took a long time to sort everything out. Paramedics showed up. They checked me out in the back of an ambulance, and because I said I was a bit dizzy, they decided to take me in for a "once-over," just to be sure. Trent rode in the ambulance with me. He didn't say more than a handful of words the entire ride back, which was unusual for him. I must have apologized a dozen times for wrecking his car. He said it didn't matter. I know how much he loved that car, so I couldn't wrap my head around his careless attitude. I had no clue what the ramifications of our little fender bender were going to be, but he knew all too well. The police had contacted my parents and told them to meet us at St. Joseph's.

Mom and Dad ran into the examination room, as pale as sheets. After being convinced that I was okay, they wanted to know how Jenny and Amanda were . . . and then where Jenny and Amanda were. And that's when the walls came crumbling, tumbling down.

Even though Dad had made eye contact with Trent when they arrived, the connection had not yet fused. Trent was standing next to me at the head of my bed. Mom and Dad had met him a few times because of all the counseling and stuff. Dad stared at Trent for about ten seconds with this quizzical expression on his face, and only then did the light go on.

As Trent lowered his head, my dad walked up and stood nose to nose with him. "How could you do this to my little girl?" he asked. Mom had no idea what Dad was talking about, and I had just clued in. "Get the fuck out of here," he growled through gritted teeth. I had never heard him drop an F-bomb before.

That was the beginning of the end. I totaled my boyfriend's $75,000 car, his career, and his life in one fell swoop. There are days when I hate myself for it. I know it's not really my fault, but when I consider how quickly his entire world collapsed around him, I can't help feeling somewhat responsible.

Sometimes I cry myself to sleep at night, thinking, *Oh my God, what have I done?* It's not just his car, his money, and his job. He's in goddamn prison! The place where guys get fucked up the ass when they drop their soap in the shower. Every day, I wake up and my life is pretty much just like it was before Trent. Every day, he wakes up, eats pig slop, and has to wonder if today will be the day he's going to die. He's not meant for that kind of life, and I put him there. Tracy keeps telling me that I *didn't* put him anywhere; he put himself there, and I know she's right, but it *feels* like I put him there.

The whole court shitshow really messed with my head too. I had this lawyer. I guess she was really good. She was really tough; that's for sure. When she first told me what she expected me to say in court, I was like, "No fucking way. I'm not doing that to Trent." Then she said if I didn't say it just like she wrote, Trent's lawyer would tear me apart. He was going to insinuate that I was a slut and that I was the one at fault. She said he would paint a picture of me that would ruin my reputation. And then, because the media had full access to court reports, it would be in the newspaper, probably on the news, and spread through Glenwood. And my life would pretty much be over.

At first, I still refused to say it, then my lawyer told me the same thing that Tracy had been telling me, that Trent was sick and needed help. If I said anything that made it sound like I was okay with what happened, he would never get the help he needed, and because Trent had a serious illness, the next person he harmed—and there would be others—may not be so lucky. He might really hurt—or worse, even kill—the next girl to get sex because he couldn't control that urge in himself. "If you care about Trent and want to help him, this is the only way you can do it," she said. And so I did. As soon as those words came out of my mouth in court, I felt like I was going to puke. I hate myself so much some days.

The judge sentenced Trent to four years. When the bailiffs, or whatever they're called, took him through the back door of the courtroom, I prayed so hard that he would look at me, and just before he went through, he did. He looked absolutely finished. Our eyes met and locked. I know it was only for a moment, but it felt like an eternity. At that moment, we communicated something to each other. I think a part of him had died. I wished he could feel my sorrow. I wished he could know that I hated saying the things I said. I won't say that anyone made me say those words—one of the first things I learned from Trent is that no one can *make* you do anything, that we always have a choice—but I felt trapped into saying them. And most of the time, I'm sorry I did. I know that it made little or no difference as far as Trent going to prison is concerned. What we did was against the law, and he was going to prison no matter what I said. I think that's one of the things that really hurts. I chose to protect myself and throw Trent to the wolves to save my own reputation. I try to comfort myself by saying it made no difference to Trent's sentence, but it matters to me. I have to live with the knowledge that I lied to save my own ass.

Everyone tells me it's not my fault and that it's stupid to think about him and the tough time he's probably having. And they're right. But try to stop yourself when thoughts of someone have consumed you day in and day out for so long. I suppose it's like Davy's fortune cookie: "Everything is hard before it gets easy."

This is hard. Life is hard. And I don't feel like there's anywhere I can go or anyone I can talk to who will understand.

When I try to talk to Mom about it, she just gets pissed at me for not being pissed at Trent. Tracy is even worse. She either wants to know only about the sex we had or how much I hate Trent. When I try to tell her how difficult it is getting over him or how sorry I am for what happened, she won't listen. "Do your self-talk, Brianna. The longer you focus on that piece of shit, the longer it's going to take for you to get better. Do your self-talk."

My life is divided into two eras: BT and AT. Before Trent, I was lonely and insecure, awkward, unsure of myself, and miserable. After Trent, I'm *confused*, lonely, insecure, awkward, unsure of myself, and miserable. The only time I felt anything at all was that very short DT period in my life. During Trent, I was confident, beautiful, self-assured, and hopeful.

Now I'm just lost.

I live in a fantasy world of "what ifs." What if I hadn't been driving so fast? What if Ms. Thatcher had never told me to go see Trent in the first place? What if I took care of my issues on my own and didn't go to see a counselor? What if Rusty wasn't gay? What if Trent didn't start to like me and treated me like any other student he counseled? What if I didn't start to like him and treated him like every other teacher? What if I wake up tomorrow and this is all just one long bad dream? What if I didn't ever let him kiss me? What if I slit my wrists? What if he gets out of prison and sweeps me off my feet and takes me away and we *do* live happily ever after?

I hear Tracy's voice: "Do your self-talk, Brianna."

I'm perfectly fine the way I am. I'm strong. I'm intelligent. I'm full of promise. I'm perfectly fine the way I am. I'm strong. I'm intelligent. I'm full of promise. I'm perfectly fine the way I am. I'm strong. I'm intelligent. I'm full of promise.

Here in my safe place, I repeat this mantra ten times, fifty times, a hundred times. Mr. Reynolds cannot hurt me anymore. Mr. Reynolds cannot hurt me anymore. Mr. Reynolds cannot hurt me anymore. I do my breathing exercises and hold onto these words. They become one with me. They become me, and I become them. I try to believe these things I'm told I need to believe. These are the things that will help me recover from the damage inflicted upon me by a sick, selfish human being. I do believe this. I do believe this. I do believe this. I want to believe this. I want to believe this. I want to believe this. I'm trying to believe this. I'm trying to believe this. I'm trying to believe this. I doubt I can believe this.

This is the cycle that I have spent far too much time in as of late. But wait until tomorrow. Tomorrow, I may be as filled with hate for him as today I am with hope.

CHAPTER TWENTY-FOUR

Glendale General is about twenty minutes away. Stevie wants me to sit in the backseat with him while Aaron sits in the front so he can comfort me. He won't say these words; he doesn't express himself that way. He just says, "Hey, Mom, wanna ride back here with me for a change?" Of the two, Stevie is the sensitive one. Aaron is all boy. He is courageous, independent, and assertive. He knows what he wants, and he goes for it. They are the same traits that attracted me to his father when we met, the same things that I find so attractive in him today, eleven years later. Aaron is like Robert in so many ways. They are "no bullshit" men. Aaron sees what he wants and goes after it. He can be a bit like a bull in a china shop at times.

Stevie is kind, compassionate, vulnerable, and sensitive. Of course, this can be a source of major conflict in our home. It shows up in the words they use. "Aaron, please just leave me alone" versus "Stevie, get your stinkin' butt outta my face or I'll kick your head in." They mean the same thing; they just express themselves differently. One is no "righter" than the other. It's just who they are. Once I figured this out and stopped interfering so much, our home life became a lot simpler. Some battles are not worth the effort.

Stevie is the first person to notice when something is bothering me and the first to try to comfort me. He doesn't handle conflict well and would rather hide and hope that the problem simply goes away than face it head on and deal with it. He's definitely the comedian of the household, though. His smile alone can make you laugh. And so I sit in the back with Stevie resting his head against my breast. He strokes my hand and whispers, "It'll be okay, Mom. It'll be okay." Stevie is so much like my big "bother" that sometimes I accidentally call him Trent. He doesn't mind, though; he adores his uncle.

The boys don't fully know why Trent is in prison, only that he did something bad. We're going to have to tell them soon. At nine and ten years old, they don't ask a lot of questions, but they will almost be teenagers by the time he gets out in two more years, and they're damn sure not going to accept "Uncle Trent just made a boo boo" for an answer.

"It'll be okay, Mom." I hope it will be.

When we gather around Dad's bed, he looks at peace. That makes it easier. I meet with Doctor Morrow in his office. He has all the paperwork laid out on his desk when I arrive. He has been so gracious and supportive throughout this ordeal. I don't even read through the waivers and documents. There's no need. I'm the type of person who needs to know everything well in advance so I can process it. I recognize them from the samples I've studied online. I'm self-aware enough to know that my comprehension level will not be at the top of its game come showtime, so I've prepared well ahead.

Back in Dad's room, Doctor Morrow stands at the head of his bed and explains what he's going to do and what will likely happen—which is nothing. He suggests that we may want to step out of the room while they extract the ventilation tube inserted through Dad's mouth into his lungs. He warns us that Dad will choke and gag just like any living person would as they pull the tube. We stay. They do. He does. And then nothing happens. It's sort of funny. I could tell that Aaron was almost disappointed, but Stevie was relieved. I love my children exactly as they are. They complete our family perfectly.

Doctor Morrow turns off the ventilator, which was the only machine still connected to Dad. An IV remains, providing fluids and nutrition, and the finger-grip heart monitor so they can tell when he dies, but otherwise the many other devices have already been removed. It's almost anticlimactic. The only change is that the room gets very quiet. The heavy, swooshy, gurgling sound of air being forced into and out of Dad's lungs stops, and the room goes silent except for the soft beeping of the heart monitor. In all the months I've been coming to see Dad, I've never heard the room so quiet. We stand around, breathing the silence, anticipating, waiting. Finally, Aaron breaks it. "Is something supposed to happen?" he asks.

"No one knows," Pastor Jacobs replies. "He's in God's hands now."

WHEN TRENT AND I WERE kids, somewhere around the age Aaron and Stevie are now, Charlie got a snout full of porcupine quills, again. It was the third or maybe fourth time since I had been alive that it had happened to him. Dogs are a lot like people; some just never learn. Charlie was older than me by a couple of years. We got him as a pup just before Trent was born. I think Trent always felt as though Dad was fonder of Charlie than of him, which I suppose is why, as sensitive as Trent is, he wasn't as upset as me when Dad put Charlie down. Or at least he didn't show it. Dad sometimes referred to Charlie as their firstborn, although Mom never liked the implication of that comment.

So, Charlie came home one day with his nose full of porcupine quills—twenty-seven, if memory serves correctly—*and* reeking of skunk. He must not have known what hit him. When he came whimpering up the back steps, Mom shooed him away from the porch. His pain bothered her, no doubt, but not as much as the thought of trying to get the smell of skunk out of everything he came near. When Dad got home, it would be his problem to deal with.

The natural thing to do would have been to take Charlie to the vet and have him sedated and remove the quills. But these were the days before Reynolds' Baling Systems, and there was no money for such extravagances. That first evening, Dad tried to pull a few quills out with pliers, but the skunk smell was so overpowering that he couldn't do it. Two days and a tomato juice bath later, Dad was back at it. By then the smell had diminished enough that Dad could stomach it. But Charlie's nose was getting infected. Dad spent most of the day with Charlie. He would pull one out, Charlie would howl in pain, growl, and try to bite him, then

Dad would hold and pet him until Charlie calmed. Then he would start the process all over again. I think Charlie knew Dad was trying to help, but when pain meets the instinct to survive, instinct reigns supreme. I know this is true in dogs. For Trent's sake, I hope it's true of humans too.

Trent and I watched through the back window on and off throughout the day. I would watch until I couldn't bear to look anymore, then run away crying. Trent didn't. He just stayed. When the last of the quills had been extracted, Dad came into the house to wash up. The toll it had taken upon him was apparent. He was more emotionally exhausted than he was physically, even after wrestling with Charlie all day. That night, I heard Trent crying as Charlie lay whimpering next to him in his bed. I went to Trent's room and peered in through the crack in his door. He was stroking Charlie's head and whispering, "It'll be okay, Charlie. It'll be okay."

About two weeks later, Charlie was still unable to eat. The infection just kept getting worse. He was in agony all the time. Dad picked up some medication from the vet that was supposed to help, but I think it was too late.

We were startled awake early one Saturday morning. The loud crack of the gun ripped through the air and my dreams like a thunderclap. It woke Trent as well, and he came into my room. "What was that?" I asked.

He looked at me, fighting back tears. "I think Charlie's gone."

We had a funeral for Charlie the next day. Dad put him in a potato sack, put that potato sack in another one, and then put both sacks into a hole he had dug the day before. It wasn't like *Old Yeller*. Charlie was nobody's best friend; he was just a scruffy farm dog that everybody liked to have around. He brought a little comfort to our family.

At the funeral, Dad said what a good dog he was and that we were all going to miss him. It wasn't much. Then he shoveled dirt on him. Trent asked if he could shovel some, but Dad shook his head and kept shoveling. Trent and I trudged back to the house.

Dad said less at Mom's funeral than he did at Charlie's. When Mom first got sick, they diagnosed her as having a gastric ulcer. By the time they discovered the cancer, it had spread throughout her esophagus, stomach, liver, and lower intestines. There was nothing they could do. I've been told that even if they had caught it early on, the chances of doing much about it were minimal. It didn't make me less angry, though, watching the life being sucked out of her like the air from a bouncy castle. Her decline was perceptible each day. Every time I visited, she looked worse.

Cancer is a horrible thing to watch and even worse to endure, or so I imagine. It destroys everything it touches. It can eat away at the very heart of a person and their entire family. It stripped almost everything from Mom, but it could not take her dignity. Right until the last few days, she would wake up in the morning and get dressed in her nicest clothes, as difficult as it was. She would put her makeup on—in the last days, I did much of that. She would fix her hair, which had almost completely grown back, the best she could and make herself presentable.

It didn't matter whether she was going to have a house full of visitors or if the only people she saw were the respite workers taking care of her, she wanted to look her best. She was doing it for herself and no one else. I think it gave her a sense of dignity that the cancer had done its best to strip from her. When I would encourage her to just stay in her housecoat and slippers, she would get mad at me. "What's wrong with you, girl?" she'd say. "It's nine o'clock in the morning. What? I should sleep the day away?"

I doubt I'll ever know the toll it took on Trent. When he was still out after his arrest, when he had so much time after losing his job, he spent long days and evenings with her. I wasn't there the day she asked him why he wasn't at work, and I can't begin to fathom how difficult that conversation must have been for Trent to tell or for Mom to hear. Once he got to Briar Ridge and his prisoner phone card was activated, he would call her every day—until he couldn't.

Each of our visits were filled with questions about Mom and little things that I should know. "Even though she hates it, make sure to puree her food so she can sip it easily through a straw. When you leave, if the sun is shining, close the shades. The bright light hurts her eyes and gives her headaches. And make sure she has her First Alert bracelet with her at all times."

"I know, Trent. I've taken care of her more than you."

"And please tell her I love her and that I am so sorry." The walls that keep him inside and prevented him from seeing Mom added much to his misery. And that misery consumed him the way cancer did her. When Dad left, Trent was Mom's strength. When Trent left, she crumbled.

On her last morning, we sat together, Mom in her finest dress. I think she knew. I asked her to sing Trent's favorite song.

"You are my sunshine, my only sunshine . . ." She could only get out portions of the verse before she needed to rest.

"Please don't take my sunshine away," I sang, finishing for her.

When Trent was young, she used to hold him and sing this song over and over whenever he was upset. And with Dad's unexplainable wrath toward Trent, that was a lot of the time. In the same way that I'm Dad's favorite, Trent was Mom's. But now she's gone, and in a few short hours, Dad will be as well. I'm about to be an orphan.

Somewhere in the middle of that thought, I'm interrupted by Pastor Jacobs asking me if I would like him to pray. Pastor Jacobs has been a long-time friend of Dad's. They golfed together, drank beer together, and worshiped together. I think the priority has always been pretty much in that order. He leads us in a prayer, reads from the Bible, and provides the right amount of support. Not overly preachy, not too sentimental. He departs with Doctor Morrow, leaving us to wonder, now what? As a family, we stand together, huddled at the foot of Dad's bed, unsure of what to do next. We watch, we wait, we listen.

Maybe we'll hear him stop breathing. We don't know. After far too long, Aaron says he's hungry. Robert agrees, and we decide to stop at the Pizza Palace near the edge of town.

In the back seat of the SUV with Stevie nestled close again, I hear his soft voice once more. "It'll be okay, Mom. It'll be okay." But it isn't always. It wasn't for Charlie. It wasn't for Mom. It's not going to be for Dad, and I can only pray it will be for Trent.

CHAPTER TWENTY-FIVE

Before we moved to the city, after Gerald shot Charlie, between grades four and five, Claire Bare and I searched beneath the canopy of the hayloft, looking for newborn kittens. We were sure they would be up there since it was the place all the barn cats came to have their litters. It was the safest place away from predators.

This is what I've been branded: "predator: one that preys, destroys, or devours."

It's so easy to define a man by a single action. All that Brianna and I shared has been reduced to the instincts of a wild animal—theirs for survival, mine for conquest.

We found them nestled below the hoist, behind the hay rack, between two bales, beneath the loft, their eyes just beginning to open. Few things bring a bigger smile to Claire's face than holding a kitten. She wraps the tiny, helpless creature beneath her sweater, next to her bare skin, and purrs into its ear. I'm to believe that Brianna was just like that, a helpless creature that I wrapped in my clutches, next to my bare skin, but with very different intentions.

Watching Claire with a kitten is like watching snow fall ever so gently, building a protective layer to insulate the tulips before they bloom in the spring. She knows how to shawl them so they believe nothing in the world can harm them.

She named this kitten Pocket, as she often carried him like a joey in its mother's pouch, inside the kangaroo pocket Mom had sewn into her large, comfortable sweater for just that purpose. As she lays in the hayloft, Pocket nuzzles closer to her. He climbs, slowly making his way to her earlobe, where he latches on. He closes his little eyes and nurses upon her. They purr together.

I suppose there is a correlation. Brianna latched onto me, looking for protection, comfort, and nurture. The kitten sucking on Claire's earlobe finds comfort and warmth, but Claire was as unable to provide the nutrition required for his survival as I was to give Brianna what she needed to thrive.

Instinctively, I know this. I'm well aware of the damage that is inevitable in inappropriate relationships between a student and a person in a position of authority. I have breached a sacred trust and with that broken the law, my own ethical, moral boundaries, and Brianna's heart. As aware as I am of this, I find it incomprehensible that Brianna is as helpless as the system wants me to believe and works so hard to convince themselves that she is. Moreover, I know her well enough to understand that reducing her to "helpless, demolished victim" will piss her off and thwart her healing more than it will assist her in it.

The kitten's mother, Rascal, has no mistrust or fear of Claire's intentions. She instinctively knows that her kittens are not at risk. Rascal is a good mother. This is not her first litter, far from it. She bathes and feeds her little ones with love and tenderness. When she hears the approach of Remington, in all likelihood the kitten's father, she rises in defense of them. No one, nothing will bring harm upon them. She will fight to the death to save them.

Claire melts under the charms of the kittens' affections. She falls back into the soft hay and invites all seven into her tenderness. They crawl over her and each other, each striving to be the center of her love. I sit upon a bale above them and watch this magic unfold. Claire Bare, omnipotent in her strength and her love for each one, giggles with joy. They are completely unaware that her sheer size and strength is something that, wielded in anger, could be their demise. They only know that her love is so all-encompassing, she poses no threat whatsoever.

Rascal picks up the kittens by the scruff of their necks and helps Claire to keep them upon her. There is no mistrust of Claire; Rascal is self-actualized in her confidence. She observes without concern. Knowing that her babies are in good hands, she can go mousing without apprehension or thought that anything bad will befall her children.

Rascal, now both predator and mother, leaves. She is on the prowl. She seeks out the prey that will sustain her, providing nutrition to care for her family. I follow Rascal, who is in full predator mode. She slinks low to the ground, listening, smelling, sensing; she knows that what she seeks is close. Perched on a hay bale behind, I cannot see what she can, but I know she is within striking distance. She squats into the pounce position. Still. Not a whisker seems to move. She goes in for the kill. The mouse runs as if its life depends upon it. The chase is on. I follow. Around the bales, toward the big door leading to freedom. It suddenly stops and darts between two old tractor tires and into a corner behind the big barn door. A fatal mistake. The mouse is trapped. Terrified. Paralyzed. It has literally had the shit scared out of it. Rascal hovers over it. There is no escape. It is helpless, knows its fate, and is powerless to do anything about it.

It dawns upon me in that moment, before Rascal's lethal pounce, between grades four and five, beneath the hayloft, behind the barn door, between the tires, that I have this same feeling each time I hear Jimi climbing the stairs late at night, making his way to my bed. And I cannot imagine that Brianna has ever felt the same when I have approached her. Can she have?

MY CELL DOOR OPENS, AND the bright corridor light seeps in like smoke up a chimney. "Reynolds, pack your bedroll. You're moving out." I know what's coming. In conversations with other inmates before the hole, before the hospital, I learned something of the transfer process. I will be taken to a holding cell, stripped, and searched; every potential hiding spot thoroughly examined. While all sense of dignity and modesty took flight long ago, one never becomes remotely comfortable with that form of intrusion. The very thought of a cavity inspection throws me back to nights long ago.

I feel Jimi's warm skin next to mine. It always begins the same. I roll onto my stomach and feign sleep. If I lie on my back, he begins at my front. His hands rub my back. "Trent," he whispers. If I acknowledge him, he will simply wait. The inevitable is coming; it always does. I have learned it is best to get it over with. Big hands. Hands rough like the stucco on the side of our farmhouse. Their caress feels like the stroke of a cheese grater. Moving lower. Fingers, almost imperceptibly slow, lift the back of my underwear. I feel a finger slide from the top of my bum where my cheeks meet and travel downward. He is at the entrance of that forbidden place he knows so well. I can hear his breath deepen, feel his heart speed up. His hand pulls upward toward the blanket that covers us, pulling my underwear away from my body and then downward. They rest just above my knees. When his finger returns it is warm and wet. It enters slowly like the head of a turtle emerging from its shell, twisting, turning, stretching, burning. I press my head hard into my pillow, willing myself not to cry. It's hard breathing like this, and I wish I wasn't. A second finger enters and begins to stretch, as if trying to make a peace sign. But there is no peace. If it's a bad night, a third will enter, and I know what is to surely follow.

I relive this horror each time I'm forced to endure the inspections of the corrections staff. I try to block these thoughts from consuming me, but it's no easy task. Even so many years later, the moment my mind begins to think of the "Jimi days," fear grips me as the images force their way into my mind like a fetus through the birth canal. I am as powerless against those memories as I was against the evil that invaded my bed.

I'm told that after the strip search, I will be dressed in a blue jumpsuit, handcuffed, shackled, and placed in a cell no larger than a phone booth. Then, after any amount of time—maybe one hour, maybe six—I will be chain-ganged with the other prisoners who are also being transferred. We are no longer inmates, for we have no prison to be "in," so I suppose we are only mates. We will be escorted by a platoon of guards flanking us on all sides, armed with batons, tasers, and pepper spray, to a bus similar to a Greyhound, but that is where the similarities end. Inside the bus are stainless-steel compartments, one for each prisoner. Throughout the milk-run to every federal penitentiary across the country, we will be locked away until our arrival at whichever prison will serve as our home for the remainder of our stay. I have been forewarned to stop drinking well in advance of the journey. Piss breaks are frowned upon and rare.

None of this occurs.

Instead, I'm taken to another unit as far from the hole as you can possibly go in Briar Ridge. I stand before the "bubble"—that sacred, round, bulletproof glass room where the guards spend the majority of their days—and there I am processed.

As I walk with the two guards through the corridors of Briar Ridge to this unit, holding my bedroll in one hand and the rest of my earthly belongings in the other, I'm overwhelmed with the thought that this is everything I have remaining in life, and I'm okay with that. I have life. Not so long ago, even that was questionable.

I am approaching year two of my sentence and may only have to serve two thirds of it behind bars. If all goes well, I will spend my final year outside on parole. Therefore, I am well past the halfway mark, and with that comes a certain incentive, a hope. Hope is something I've had little of in this place. Now there's a hint of it. A glimmer of hope, like a weak ray of sun that breaks through the clouds on a socked-in day. I have found something I haven't known since long before my arrival here. It feels good. It brings something close to the beginning of a smile upon my face.

Just before I walk through the large gate separating the guards from the inmates, I notice the mailbox mounted to the wall. I drop in Gerald's letters, all six, and that smile begins to spread. As I walk through the large gate, I realize that I will see Doctor Thackery again and soon shall see Claire Bare once more. I have much to smile about.

This is protective custody, the place where people like me, "skinners," are safe from what others do, and have done, to people like me. I will spend the rest of my sentence in this unit. It looks like every other unit. The guards are the same as every other unit, and so are the inmates. The only difference is that here, in this wing, we are all being protected. Not from each other, of course, but from those in gen pop who are out to get us. Because we aren't protected from each other, it can still be a very dangerous place.

CHAPTER TWENTY-SIX

Hey Gerald,

I'm no longer in the hole. Funny story. Long before I ever went to solitary confinement, I was talking with an inmate who had just been transferred to Briar Ridge. He told me all about the transfer process, so when the guards came into my cell last week and told me I was being shipped out, all the images from my conversation with this inmate came flooding back. In my head, I see the entire thing unfolding, and it is not a pretty sight. Then suddenly, I find myself here, in the protective custody unit. The idea of being transferred was probably worse than the transfer itself would have been, but since my attempted murder, I find myself often thinking to extremes.

It's surprising how the uncertainty of every move I'm forced to make in this place affects me. With each change of location comes a new fear and a new hope. The fear is that somehow things will be worse, more difficult, more dangerous than they were previously. The hope, which is something recently renewed within me, is that this place will be a little better than the last, that my cell might have a window, that my cellmate doesn't snore, fart continuously, talk incessantly, or rape me. Since my return from the hospital almost five months ago now, this is the first time I have been in a regular cell. I was pleasantly surprised to see that there's only one bunk in my cell. I won't have a loud, stinky, obnoxious cellmate. Can life get any better?

I have another hope, something I've been learning about myself in the work I've been doing with Doctor Thackery: I hope that I can begin to express my anger in better, more acceptable, braver ways as I grow. We've been talking a lot about anger recently. He tells me that anger is a healthy emotion. In the back of my head, I know this. I've been trained to know this stuff. I help—helped—others work through anger issues many times, both as a guidance counselor and in private practice before then. But you know how mechanics usually drive cars on the verge of breaking down? I guess it's a little like that. They spend so much of their time fixing other people's vehicles, they neglect their own. My psychic car has been misfiring for some time now—well, for the better part of my life. The engine light has been on for years, but I ignored it. Somehow, I have managed to navigate the emotional highways of life without a major incident until now. But just as the mechanic's car will eventually break down, mine has. So, Doctor T and I are looking under the hood, so to speak, and trying to get me running again.

The point is, I have used only one technique to deal with anger much of my life, and it has not been a good method. You have been the recipient of it much of the time and have been the cause of it far more often. It's the coward's way—no surprise there. The only way I know how to express anger is passive aggressively. I get hurt, I get mad, and I react. My reactions are somewhat retarded, though. Not in a developmentally delayed sort of way—well, perhaps in a developmentally delayed way, but I'm slow to respond. Things that would piss others off in a nanosecond, I bury and allow them to fester and consume me. Then I plan covert ways to exact my anger, and not always upon the recipient of my wrath.

Case in point: I was eleven years old, and Jimi had finally moved out. I wish I had known it was the last time; it would have made life much easier. You had just begun designing the first prototype of the Reynolds Wet-Dri baler. I came into your makeshift office, that corner of the garage where you piled up boxes to keep me out, and told you that Mom wanted you to burn the garbage in the burn barrel behind the house because it was attracting coyotes, and she was afraid for Charlie and the cats.

Remember what you told me? "You do it." I told you I was afraid that with the strong wind, I would catch something on fire. And all you said was, "Just make sure you don't." Then you tossed me a book of matches and said, "Get out of my hair. I'm busy." Well, you know what happened next, or at least you know part of what happened.

I went to the burn barrel and assessed the situation. There was so much garbage in it that I was pretty sure the fire wouldn't stay contained, so before lighting it, I began pulling out some of the stuff. I was up on a small box so I could reach down and grab a couple of things that were wedged deeper in the barrel: a broken table lamp and a stack of old newspapers. That's where I found him.

Why the hell would you destroy the one thing from my childhood that was sacred to me? I reached in almost as far as I could and grabbed Mr. Snuffles by the ear. True, I hadn't played with Mr. Snuffles in a while, maybe a year, but so what? He was *my* rabbit. *My* toy. *My* security. I had him sitting on my dresser for a reason, Gerald. He was there to protect me. I used to hold him and squeeze him as tight as I could when Jimi was doing what he did to me. He allowed me to feel as though I wasn't enduring the torture alone. Mr. Snuffles kept me sane. And you stole him.

To be fair, you would have had no way of knowing that. But you also had no right to take him. You're the one who was always bitching, "If it's not yours, don't touch it." Mr. Snuffles wasn't yours. Actually, I'm pretty sure you knew how much he meant to me. Otherwise why would you do it? As far back as I can remember, you only did things to me that you knew would hurt. I think it was an act of spite.

Why do you hate me, Gerald?

About two weeks before that, you came barging into my room to give me shit for who knows what, and on your way out, you grabbed Mr. Snuffles off my dresser and threw him at me. "And get rid of this goddamn doll. You're not a girl, and you're not six years old anymore either."

I can only assume that because I didn't, you did.

After loading all the garbage back in the burn barrel, or as much as I felt was safe to begin with, I started the fire. I watched it carefully to ensure that no embers or pieces of garbage flew out and into the trees or buildings nearby. I had loaded the last of it in the barrel when you came to make sure I wasn't burning the farm down, one of the few fatherly things you'd ever done. When you saw me standing there holding Mr. Snuffles, you flew into a rage. Seconds later Mr. Snuffles was reduced to a pile of singed hair and ashes, and I was reduced to tears. I stood back watching my protector go up in flames. The saddest part was—the reality was—Mr. Snuffles never had the ability to protect me, and the person who did was standing next to me, smiling as Mr. Snuffles, my illusory protector, turned to ash.

Sometimes I think you would do those things to provoke me into battle. Realizing I could never win in that arena, I took the fight to my turf. Your first set of hand-drawn blueprints for the baler, would you like to know where they mysteriously disappeared to? You'll find them among the ashes in the burn barrel, alongside Mr. Snuffles.

I wish you could read this. God, that would infuriate you. If you knew this, I'm sure you would argue that the two acts were on a completely different scale. My action cost you a couple months of hard work. Yours cost me nothing. After all, it was just a stupid stuffed rabbit, right? But from my childhood perspective, you stole the only hope I had of security. In my mind, the two were—still are—unbalanced in your favor.

In case you haven't figured it out by now, passive aggression is my default. It's the way I level the playing field. I'm learning that this action—well, reaction—isn't the best way to handle life's disappointments. It's exhausting, cowardly, and unfair to both parties. Every morning when I take that handful of pills to keep the HIV at bay, I get angry. But more and more, I'm channeling that anger in healthier directions. This is difficult when those I'm most pissed off at are unreachable, so I do the only concrete thing at my disposal. I rage at the nurse who gives me my pills, I vent to Claire and Robert when they come, I express my anger to Doctor Thackery, and I write about what I'm feeling deep inside. No one deserves to be the target of my wrath aside from the assholes who did this, but at least I'm not keeping it buried deep inside, where it grows and festers, ravaging and eating away at my soul until I respond in ways that are destructive to me and those around me.

I'm beginning to get visibly pissed off. It may appear to be a bad thing—it certainly feels that way sometimes—but it's good. Allowing this anger has another benefit. When I'm able to express my wrath, it reduces the self-pity that consumes me as powerfully—perhaps more so—than the anger.

Anger has no conscience and no compass. Direction comes from the knowledge of where a person wants or needs to go. Anger is directionless; it follows the path of least resistance. It just needs to get out. If it's kept under the pressure that someone who is passive aggressive keeps it under, it's not reduced over time, like the fizz in a beer that is dropped and then drunk last. The pressure continues to increase and accelerate. And because anger can't navigate itself, when it blows, the fallout is directionless. Everyone in its path is destroyed. Hence the term "blind rage," I suppose.

Unlike me, you never kept yours in, so it always had a target, usually me. In this respect, as much as I hate to admit it, you're probably healthier than I am. Sadly, you weren't always the recipient of my wrath, which you deserved.

I found Claire's friend Sam going through my jacket pockets when I was fifteen. She was a couple of years younger than Claire, maybe eleven or twelve. She was a cute, feisty kid who would flirt with me whenever she was over playing with Claire. Sam no longer went to school with Claire. They had been in the same school the previous year, but since Claire had moved to middle school, the only time they saw each other was at soccer games and when Sam came over. I snuck up behind her and grabbed her around the waist. "What are you looking for?"

"Um, I was just checking to see if you had any matches or a lighter."

"For what?"

She held up a pack of cigarettes.

"You're a bad little girl, aren't you?" I said.

She laughed. "You have no idea. Wanna smoke?"

We headed out back together and lit up. I asked her where Claire was, and she said that Claire hated the smell of smoke, so she stayed up in her room.

I mentioned that Sam was cute, and she was. But she was only a child. Puberty was something she was looking forward to but possessed little physical evidence of. There were no real external indications of anger or self-pity in what I did next. And for it to be interpreted as anything but the perverse actions of a horny fifteen-year-old boy would take a psychological understanding of the human condition that I had no ability to grasp at the time.

She handed the cigarette we were sharing to me. I took it with my right hand and then slid my left hand under her T-shirt and began to caress her chest. You could not call them breasts, for they were little more than puffy nipples, just beginning to stick out from her shirt. I asked her to show them to me, and she lifted her shirt right over her head. I bent forward and sucked on each one. Her response was far more confused curiosity than sexual excitement. I took her hand and put it down the front of my jeans. She wrapped her hand around me but had no clue what to do and likely no desire to do anything more. That did not matter to me. I simply wanted to hurt her.

Claire came around the side of the house and looked at us in disgust, then turned around and went back into the house. Sam attempted to take her hand away and put her shirt back on to follow Claire, but I forced her to continue. I pulled my pants down and made her stroke me until I was finished. She took her sticky hand away and held it up to examine this stuff she had never seen before. I picked her T-shirt up off the ground, used it to clean myself, then tossed it back to her. "Thanks," I said. Then I turned and walked away.

Inside, I went to Claire and said, "Your friend's a little skank."

She looked at me like I was a piece of shit and said, "You're gross."

Sam continued to come over on weekends after soccer games and occasionally throughout the summer. Every opportunity I had, I used her. It has taken me years to process why I did what I did to her, because it was hardly sexual. I mean, without question, it was a form of sexuality. And for years I thought I was nothing more than a disgusting pervert for doing the things I did to her. It has taken me a lifetime to recognize that while it was a sexually abusive act, it was far more than that.

Sexuality, like anger, builds, and over time it requires release. For me, with each release of sexual tension also came a release of anger. I found myself a little less angry at you, at Jimi, at the world. I found that the pain and anger that raged inside of me, burning like red-hot lava, somehow subsided when I degraded and demoralized others. It was nothing more than a misdirected passive-aggressive attack. I couldn't hurt you, so I hurt Sam.

Making atonement for this feels impossible.

In the twelve-step recovery program of Alcoholics Anonymous, they speak of the critical importance of completing steps eight and nine if there is to be any long-term recovery. The alcoholic is to make a list of all persons harmed and become willing to make amends to them. Then they are to make direct amends to such people, unless to do so would injure them. How do I make amends to Samantha? Where would I even begin? How is it remotely possible to undo something as damaging as what I did to her? Sam was little more than the conduit through which my brokenness was played out. And I consider whether I must place Brianna in this same category.

Sam, I'm so sorry. Gerald, I'm so fucking pissed.

Ever so slowly, I approach a new recognition: the power and destruction that passive aggression wields. It's a two-headed beast that devours itself and its prey. Passive-aggressive people are often so removed from their own emotions they don't even recognize anger when they feel it, even when their bodies send a signal that they are upset. In fact, inside my head, it's as if the lines between anger and sexuality get crossed, like when you're fishing with a friend and he moves to the other side of the boat to reel in his line. Suddenly, he's pulling on your line. You both cross back and forth to untangle the mess, but in the process you make matters far worse, and in short order, it's almost impossible to untangle. As a confused and angry man, I ask myself—and must inquire with Doctor Thackery—have I crossed the lines so often that, emotionally, I'm unable to differentiate anger from sexuality? I feel as if I have created a complete mess of my emotions, and as I'm powerless to discern which line is which, the person most deserving of my anger, you, goes unscathed while I leave a trail of undeserving victims in my wake, the least of whom is certainly not Brianna.

With Brianna, however, I made matters worse by falling in love with her. Or at least the closest thing I have ever known to love. You think my emotional life was a confusing mess before? You should have seen how fucked up things became after. I created such a web of self-deceit and manipulative bullshit that I think I probably convinced her as much as myself that what we had was real. I wanted what we shared to be real. I still do. It's when I begin thinking this way that I suspect the lines are crossed. In the end, though, I'm learning some things about truth. And lies.

So, here I lie on my new bunk, in my new cell, in a new unit, wondering what this new adventure will bring.

I think Claire Bare is coming in the next couple of days. Nothing brings life to this place more than her visits. I miss the boys, though. Years ago, when they were five and six, I promised Aaron and Stevie that when Aaron turned ten, I would take them camping for a week to the ocean, so we could snorkel and swim with the dolphins. That's next week. Another promise turned into a lie.

Claire says the boys don't know why I'm in prison. That brings a certain sense of relief, yet along with the relief comes the realization that at their age they might have checked me out online or heard from others at school. I want to be a man they can look up to and respect, yet am all too aware that respect is easily destroyed in children—adults too. My fear is that with their active imaginations, they will fantasize about what could have brought me here. Of course, as kids, their minds will gravitate toward the most obvious: *Uncle Trent killed someone*. What a terrible thought. But what's worse is that, culturally, that idea is far more palatable, and acceptable, than the reason I am here—and the reason, I'm guessing, most of the men in this unit are here.

Doctor Thackery has the fishing lines of my life in his hands. He does not untangle them for me. That's not his job. He has no more ability to do that than he does to take a piss for me. But he is showing me the knots, and I'm examining them to see which line goes over, in, through, under, or around. It's difficult, and if I pull the wrong line, I could make the knot even worse. So I'm taking my time. I think I've got a handle on the direction I need to pull next, although I'm not looking forward to it, and I fear the knot will rise up to choke me.

Oh yeah, I mailed your letters this morning. I'm aware it changes nothing. Your heart will have beaten its last long before they arrive. Nevertheless, I receive a certain satisfaction knowing that I have had the heart and strength required to do this insignificant act while yours still beats. I hope you die better than you lived.

Die well,
Trent

CHAPTER TWENTY-SEVEN

I went to visit Trent this morning. Claire was planning to come as well, but she's been under so much stress lately that I suggested—or rather, insisted—she take a spa day and allow me to go myself. There have been many things that I've needed to talk with Trent about that Claire has been resistant to, and to be honest I'm hesitant to do it with her present. So I'm glad I forced her hand.

There is a hardness in Trent that didn't exist in him two years ago before all of this started. It's not bad; in fact, it's actually good to see. He is developing, for lack of a better word, a backbone. I can only imagine prison will do that to any man. In the time Claire and I have been coming on these visits, I've watched Trent decline and shut down rapidly. His deterioration has impacted her profoundly. She has spent far too many trips home after a visit inconsolable. I share her concern, without question. Watching as Trent withdraws from life is an unpleasant thing. I do have a perspective, however, that she cannot understand. I love Trent deeply, but I have also been exposed to the effects that childhood sexual abuse can have on its victims. This is something I have needed to share with Trent for a long time.

My mother, Aaron and Steven's grandmother, was the victim of horrific abuse at the hands of her uncles. The toll it took upon her was immeasurable and impacted her for life. But it didn't impact her alone. Everyone within her reach was impacted. Years of depression, followed by substance abuse, destroyed her and our family. My father took the brunt of her anger, which sent him to an early grave. My brothers and I were never trusted. What I wanted Trent to know is how far-reaching his actions are, that they affect so many more people than just him and his victim. While I know he must certainly be aware of this on some level, I felt he needed to hear firsthand what his selfishness has done to his sister.

As I told Trent these things, he became agitated at first. But little by little, he calmed and listened. "Trent, Claire is coming unglued," I said. "It's not completely your fault. With your mom's death, your dad's condition, and the pressure she's under from school, she's more fragile than I have ever known her to be. But you have brought more pain into her life than you will ever know. You need to consider how widespread the impact of your actions has been.

"That girl, your victim, carries a burden that you and you alone are responsible for. You forced her to make choices way beyond her ability, and she must live with the consequences of the choices.

"Please know that I don't for a moment believe that I'm in any way above you. I have been guilty of terrible things, and if at some point you wish to address those, I will try to be as gracious with you as you're being with me at this moment. But right now, there are some things that I need to say and you need to hear.

"I understand that you're paying, have paid, and will continue to pay a heavy price for what you did. I love and care for you, Trent, but you and that girl are the least of my concerns. My sole concern at this moment is Claire, Aaron, and Steven. And I need you to know that.

"When I consider the harm your selfishness has had on Claire, I shudder, and I get angry. Claire's pain cascades down to the boys, who feel its effect and take it out on each other. There's a ripple effect to what you did that impacts everyone who knows you, but most significantly, it touches those of us who love and care for you.

"Claire has not been sleeping. She picks at the food on her plate, pushes it around, and eats only enough to survive. The laughter and joy that once radiated from her is pretty much nonexistent. Our sex life has dwindled to almost nothing. She has stopped attending her book club, yoga, and Pilates; she simply has no energy for them. Her attention span has become as short as her fuse. You remember how much of the boys' antics she could once put up with? Not anymore.

"When she comes to see you, she puts on a brave face and makes it seem as if everything is just grand, but it isn't, Trent; it's far from it. She comes home from school with horror stories about what it's like being the pariah, the ostracized one, the one whose brother is a sex offender. That's the label she now wears like a tattoo across her forehead. It's sucking the life out of her, and it's all because of you."

I paused as I told these things to Trent to allow the weight of my words to sink in. As I spoke, he became very quiet, very gracious, and very broken. The truth often hurts, but it will also set a man free. It has no power to do so, however, unless he knows the truth. The hardness I had seen in Trent melted away as the weight of my words sank deep into his heart.

There are few things in the world, perhaps none, that hold a higher value to Trent than Claire. As the recognition of the depth of sorrow and grief his actions have brought upon her were revealed to him, it broke his heart once again. While I know little about the prison system, I know enough. Signs of weakness in this place are not tolerated.

I chose a table in the visitors' lounge as far away from other inmates and their guests as I could, but as the morning progressed, the lounge filled. We were surrounded by others on all sides, so I was somewhat reluctant to unleash this upon Trent the way I had, but once I began there was no stopping. For Claire's sake and for Trent's, what needed to be said outweighed his need for privacy and protection. His eyes filled and then overflowed, his shoulders heaved, and his breath came in gasps. When he was able to pull himself together, he looked deep into my eyes. "Thank you," he whispered. And I knew that he had heard.

"These things I have told you today, Trent, have been more difficult to speak than I can express. This has been one of the most unpleasant tasks I have had to do in a very long time. But please know that I *had to* do it, for Claire's sake and mine, but mostly for you. I take zero pleasure in having to tell you these things. But I believe with all my heart that you need to hear them."

I'm not an emotional man for the most part, but tears streamed down my face too as I spoke these hurtful truths to him. But as I told Trent, they needed to be said.

I had been thinking about what I was going to tell him for months. In fact, I wrote it all down and read those words often. I hope it didn't come across like a rehearsed speech. I don't think it did. It was certainly heartfelt.

When I arrived back home, Claire was already there. She said that as much as she had wanted to see Trent, she was glad I insisted she take the day for herself. She was in a better space than I had seen her in a while. Of course, she wanted to know how our visit went. I said it was fine. I haven't yet told her the nature of our conversation. I will, but I know it will bring her more pain, and she was in such a great place that I didn't want to dampen her spirit.

IT WAS TRENT WHO INTRODUCED me to the love of my life. Trent and I have been friends for a long time. I've known him since his first year of university. We met at a production of *David Copperfield* that I directed. I invited a few of the cast for beer one night after rehearsal, and Trent and I clicked. We began to hang out a fair bit. As a freshman, he was just getting a feel for the campus, and I took him under my wing. It was in his third year that he introduced me to Claire. He said it took him that long because he knew that Claire and I would get along well, and he suspected that we would end up together permanently. He wanted to make sure I had the depth of character required to date his precious sister.

Trent and Claire are as close as any siblings I have ever known. This is one of the things that make it so difficult for her. The summer he graduated with his master's, Trent, Michelle—Trent's wife, or ex-wife, rather; they were only dating at the time—Claire, and I went to Europe for a month. It remains among the fondest memories of my life.

We spent a week in Venice, without question one of the most romantic spots on the planet. One evening began at Za Lucca's. We started with antipasto and a pumpkin flan that was out of this world. Claire had spaghetti and mussels. She was raving about how amazing it was, so Trent stuck his fork in to try it. Claire took a forkful at the same time. As they began to eat, they realized they had each picked up the opposite end of the same strand of spaghetti and proceeded to act out the scene from *Lady and the Tramp* to perfection, complete with fluttering eyelids and all. It ended with their noses touching and Trent giving Claire a big kiss. It may have been the second carafe of red wine, but I started giggling like a schoolgirl, and soon we were all in hysterics. We laughed so much that entire month.

As a sitcom writer, I'm surrounded by teams of funny people, and I take a certain sense of pride in my ability to make people laugh, but Claire is one of the funniest people I know. Together, Trent and Claire are piss-your-pants funny.

Later that evening, we were walking through San Marco. During the day, it can be crowded and touristy, but at night the square clears out, and the quartets in front of the restaurants begin to play. The flickering lights of the piazza, the sunset, and the beautiful music all work together to create an irresistible atmosphere of romance. We had walked to the tower of San Giorgio. It offers a breathtaking panoramic view of the city and its surroundings. The island itself is isolated from the rest of the city and gets much less foot traffic than the tower in St. Mark's Square. It's the perfect place to be alone with your partner or two or three of your closest friends.

We were passing one of the few small groups of tourists on the street when, out of the blue, Trent crossed from our side of the piazza to theirs. He got down on all fours a short distance in front of them and muttered under his breath. As they approached, one gentleman from their entourage asked Trent what he was doing.

"Sorry I'm in your way," Trent replied without missing a beat, "but I dropped a contact lens, and I have to find it."

As any kind-hearted souls would do, they offered to help. Pretty soon, all five of them were down on their hands and knees, looking for Trent's non-existent contact. Trent slowly backed out of the group, got up, and crossed back to our side, and we carried on our merry way. For all I know, they may still be there, searching.

The moment we rounded the corner, Michelle slapped Trent. "You're an ass," she said, but we all laughed hard and very long.

Claire and Trent have many gifts and skills. Music, however, is not one of them. In London, we were touring among the vendors and buskers in Piccadilly Square. Suddenly, Claire removed the cute beret she was wearing, placed it upside down near a lamppost, and broke into the Beatles' "Yellow Submarine." Trent immediately joined in. They were terrible and completely butchered the song. The moment they finished, they began "Eleanor Rigby." A small crowd began to gather around, certainly not because of the talent but because of the bravery and audacity the two displayed. Trent didn't know many of the words, so he sang "blah, blah, blah, blah" even louder at the parts he didn't know. As soon as they finished a song, Claire would bow and shout, "Thank you, thank you very much." They ended their less-than-thrilling set by completely destroying "Hey Jude." It was hilarious. Some of the growing crowd joined in on the chorus. The best part was that by the time we left, Claire had six pounds twenty in her beret. "Easiest money I've ever made," she declared, then started humming "Money for Nothin'" by Dire Straits as she pocketed her earnings.

Fond memories like these make it difficult to be as hard on Trent as I was today, yet it is our closeness that gives me permission to do so. And it's only because I love him like a brother that I did it. He was the best man at our wedding. I think had I not asked him first, Claire would have asked him to be her maid of honor and that would have been awkward. I believe our relationship is strong enough to handle such brutal honesty, or at least I hope it is. Time will tell.

Claire and I made love tonight. What a wonderful experience that was. I will go back to see Trent again soon, this time with Claire. She misses him so much.

For some bizarre reason, I forgot to tell him that his father is still alive. Not much has changed, but no one expected him to last this long after removing him from life support. I suppose it's only a matter of time, but I probably should have told Trent. I should also have told him that the hostility between him and Gerald takes a huge toll on Claire as well. But that can wait for another occasion. In a few days, once Gerald dies, it won't be an issue anyway. But the way Trent and Gerald have treated each other for as long as I've known them was completely unfair to her.

But alas, life is unfair.

CHAPTER TWENTY-EIGHT

I have been in phone conversations with Tracy Mathis from Child and Family Services. She has under her care Brianna Barnes, Reynolds' victim. While I don't make a practice of discussing my patients with other therapists—much less social workers—I consented to lend her an ear, which, as I listened, seemed to be all she wanted. In the midst of her rant, I identified an interesting hypothesis that had not previously occurred to me but may lead toward redemption for both the victim and the offender.

It is an unfortunate cultural bias, held by much of society, that maintains we must seek redemption at all costs for the victim but not at all for the offender. A shift in this mindset must take place if society is to become a safer place.

She inquired at length about the sentence Reynolds is serving and voiced her displeasure at its brevity. I refused to provide her with details vis-à-vis his therapy, his attempted murder, or his progress, which angered Ms. Mathis further. Conversely, she felt compelled to inform me in graphic detail all the damage my patient has caused in Ms. Barnes' life. While she stopped short of accusing Reynolds of being a serial rapist, she made it clear that her patient was severely damaged and might require institutionalization. This disturbed me, as it seems to contradict reports I have read from the police, her intake therapist, and several teachers at her high school. I listened openly, however, as traumatic regression has been known to occur in victims of childhood sexual abuse. However, it's rare with a child of sixteen and is virtually unheard of where the victim has no further ability to encounter the offender. And never have I come upon regression to the point of institutionalization among someone who wasn't previously mentally ill or violently attacked in multiple succession. Therefore, I inquired as to the nature of her treatment and challenged the accuracy of her statement, whereupon she became accusatory, offended, and verbally abusive.

It's a regrettable problem within the mental health community, but some counselors, thankfully very few, do more harm than good. If Brianna Barnes is suffering needlessly at the hands of an incompetent social worker, this must be addressed. I'm thinking about asking Leland Philips, the chief medical investigator, to look into this matter.

Ms. Mathis further reports that her patient is displaying evidence of complete denial regarding the trauma she has suffered as a result of the damage *my* patient has inflicted. I informed her that this is common. Victims typically respond to abuse in one of two ways. The first is with complete brokenness of spirit, denial of any personal gain from the association, and rage for the injustice brought upon them. The second is with sympathy for the offender and justification for his behavior. Neither is healthy, neither is restorative, and neither is accurate, but both are common.

One of the more difficult hurdles for any victim of sexual abuse to overcome is biological response. Humans are sexual beings. A culture that propagates the "If it feels so good, it cannot possibly be bad" mantra further serves to complicate the scenario. The victim certainly experienced intense pleasure from the intimacy shared with the offender. Both her conscious and unconscious mind reinforced this actualization and sent the message that, therefore, *this must be good*; *this must be love*. All association with any negative reckoning is promptly dismissed, and confusion ensues.

However, unless we have no choice, we do not stay involved in relationships that offer us nothing. If there is no personal gain from an interaction that we are free to leave, we leave. My understanding from Reynolds and B is that she felt nothing in her association with Reynolds that compelled her to stay. Her journal entries, and her own admission, indicate that she was free to leave if she chose, regardless of the prepared statement she read in court. What kept B in her relationship with Reynolds was the basic human need for love, security, and stability. It's similar to the reason gang members stay with gangs. She felt these needs were being met. Again, this is nothing out of the ordinary. To confuse pleasure with love is as common among humans as eating when we're no longer hungry. What differs for the victim in this case—in fact, what renders her the status of victim at all—is that her confusion was introduced by a person in a position of authority. Therefore, their sexual relationship was illegal.

It is not common for me to offer unsolicited advice to professionals I don't know personally in regards to their therapeutic approach, but I felt that in this case it might prove helpful. I suggested that if the counseling techniques Ms. Mathis was implementing were not working, perhaps she could give B permission to feel what for her is authentic rather than attempting to convince her it is not. Discrediting a person's experience devalues them and erodes the foundation of trust required for therapeutic progress.

This guidance was not received well. Apparently, I have "no right to tell her how to treat her patient" and am stuck in an antiquated approach to therapy "that went out with the dinosaurs."

Hmm . . .

My focus, however, must remain on Reynolds. I hesitate to involve myself with the treatment of his victim, and it may be perceived as a conflict of interest to do so. Nevertheless, I hold on to an "antiquated" philosophy that I have experienced some success with. It's a rare event, but there have been occurrences where a powerful psychic union has been established between people who have been intimately involved. The religious call this a "soul tie" and attempt to remedy it with exorcism.

It's similar to the phenomenon reported by identical twins who share thoughts, emotions, and, at times, physiological sensations—twin telepathy. This theory suggests that acts of extreme intimacy can create a bond between the participants. This connection remains long after the acts themselves are over.

Some studies suggest it may establish a lifelong link, joining the participants emotionally. For evidence of this, one needs to look no further than to those who have experienced dozens or even hundreds of sexual partners. Statistics reveal that such promiscuous individuals often report much lower levels of emotional intimacy. Their ability to be emotionally invested in their partners, past or present, has been "watered down." If this can transpire, as the evidence purports it does, logic suggests the opposite may be true as well. For many who have had only one or very few sexual partners, they are on an equal emotional wavelength, so to speak, and a psychic union can occur.

If my hypothesis is correct, it explains the difficulty I have been experiencing in helping Reynolds enter the deeper levels of emotional work required to obtain healing within his inner child. It would further explain the unconscious blockages I referred to earlier, and perhaps also the problem Ms. Mathis is having with her patient. She certainly does not possess the wherewithal to make such a diagnosis. There are techniques I will implement to test this theory, and if correct, I will take the necessary measures to help Reynolds and his victim break free. However, as with so many psychological efforts, the patients must be willing, or headway remains unattainable and regression probable.

My conversation with Ms. Mathis, combined with my therapeutic knowledge of Reynolds, leads me to consider that B and Reynolds may be connected in this way.

To clarify this supposition, both B and Reynolds are experiencing tremendous difficulty in separating truth from reality. They share an emotional attachment that is preventing them from seeing the true nature of their association. This is not unusual for a young victim like B. However, Reynolds, himself being a therapist, has the cognitive ability to understand the reality of the situation. Nevertheless, he seems unable to make the leap between his cognitive awareness and his emotional attachment.

For all the progress I have seen in him, Reynolds still romanticizes his association with his victim. This is not uncommon. The offender feels a certain justification for his actions if he is able to convince himself that his intentions were more altruistic than they actually were and divorce himself from the truth that harm is being, or has been, done. "Able," however, is the operative word. If he were simply unwilling, that would be another matter altogether. There is a gargantuan difference between the two.

Since my conversation with Ms. Mathis, I'm less confident that proceeding in the direction of my current focus will provide Reynolds with insight into the reasons for this minimization and, therefore, the healing that he so desperately longs for. He may be unable to make the connection. It may require a more radical approach involving both victim and offender. It further may explain why Reynolds has been so resistant to accept criticism of his minimizing.

Occasionally, ignorance is beneficial. Ms. Mathis has unwittingly opened the door to previously unavailable knowledge. In light of this, I am beginning to suspect that psychic union disorder may be preventing both the victim and the offender from the necessary breakthroughs they require. However, I may have to visit the victim to know for certain.

CHAPTER TWENTY-NINE

When I was in grade seven, Mr. Desmond, my homeroom teacher, used to embarrass me every chance he could. It wasn't just me; he did it to almost everyone in class. I did an assignment once on what I wanted to be when I grew up. I said that I was going to be a "vetrinarian." In front of the entire class, he ridiculed me. "You know, Brianne"—he never called me Brianna, he always shortened it to Brianne, probably didn't even know my real name—"it takes a lot of brains to be a vet, and if you can't even spell the word *veterinarian* properly, you probably should consider doing something else. Maybe you should be a receptionist or a janitor. Something that's a better fit for you."

That pissed me off because Mom is a receptionist. It was like he was saying not only am I stupid, so is my mom. I felt like saying, "I can see why you became a teacher. It's the perfect job for you 'cause it doesn't take a lot of brains to humiliate a little kid, you stupid asshole." But, of course, I didn't. I just sat there feeling like a puppy that missed the training pad and pissed on the carpet and had her nose rubbed in it. She doesn't have a clue why her owner is doing this to her. She just figures, *Even after I do what I'm supposed to, I get punished.*

Almost every time I come home from a meeting with Tracy, my social worker, I feel like I did in class that day, like I'm having my nose rubbed in it. Maybe I just don't get it. But it's like she expects me to be, I don't know, different somehow. Like I should pretend to be completely fucked up instead of just sad and lonely. Don't get me wrong; she is helping me. She has given me some great books to read about improving my self-image and things like that. *What Color is Your Parachute?* is awesome. It's about job hunting and career planning and stuff like that, but it's more about figuring out who you are as a person and what you want out of life . . . I still want to be a "vetrinarian."

Tracy also offers good advice when it comes to handling some of the fallout from my affair with Mr. Reynolds that I still get from time to time in school. But she also feels compelled to tell me all the things that she thinks I'm doing wrong: I'm not being truthful about my feelings, I'm not as angry as I should be, I'm not as broken as I should be, I'm not as open as I should be, I'm not as anxious as I should be, I'm not as emotional as I should be, I'm not as depressed as I should be, I'm not as introspective as I should be, I'm more optimistic than I should be, I'm more forgiving than I should be, and I'm more content than I should be.

Maybe I'm wrong, but isn't the whole purpose of therapy to move me from a negative, self-defeating direction into a more positive frame of mind? And how does she know how I should feel, anyway?

So, here I sit, way past midnight in my beanbag chair, with my small lamp illuminating the blue orb next to me, looking at my face in it, wishing that my nose didn't look so wide in the thing, and wondering what the fuck is wrong with me. I hate that I have to see a therapist because of what Mr. Reynolds did. I hate that I'm not as angry as I should be or as empty or as broken. I think of all the things I want out of life and wonder how the hell I'm ever going to get there. And I wonder about what things would have been like had I not smashed up Trent's car.

I would get shivers up and down my spine anticipating his arrival when he picked me up after school in our secret meeting place. I would see the front of his car pull around the corner, behind the Seven-Eleven, next to the big blue garbage bin—I hated that spot, but it was safe. I'd wait behind the bin. If no kids from school were in sight, he would pull up, open the door, and I would hop in. Once I was inside, we were pretty safe because even the front windows of his car are—were—tinted black, and unless someone came right up to them, they couldn't see in. He would lean over to me and give me a soft, gentle kiss. The scent of his cologne would stir things inside of me. "Hello, princess," he would say. He loved the taste of my lip gloss. It's not cotton candy or bubble gum, like I used to wear, it's Burt's Bees Mango Butter.

If it was nice out, we'd often go for a drive; we both loved to drive. As soon as we got to the ring road, it was my turn. We would usually spend our drives talking about life and dreams and hopes and our future together.

He wants—wanted—to take me to Italy after high school, where we can—could—be open about our relationship. He went there after he finished his schooling. He said I would love it because I'm a romantic at heart, which I suppose I am. He also said that when the sun sets in Florence along the Arno, there's nothing like it. It's like the entire world stops and wraps itself around you in a blanket of breathtaking magic. In that instant, nothing else matters, all cares fall away, and for a fleeting moment everything is perfect. I wish I was there now . . . with him.

Our drives gave us the opportunity to talk about the day. I would tell him all about mine, and he would do his best not to wear his guidance counselor hat and just listen. He was a great listener. I'm sure there were times that he wanted to counsel me and make suggestions about the choices I was making and stuff, but we talked about it just before we started going out, and he said that one of the choices I needed to make, without his input, was whether I wanted him as my guidance counselor or as my boyfriend because he couldn't be both. I respect that and understand why he made me choose. It would be like if your gynecologist was your dad.

He would tell me all about his day too, although he never talked about who he was counseling, which I was okay with because then I knew he would never tell other people about all the things I'd confided in him.

If my parents were both working or at one of Davy's games, we would either go out for dinner—Trent introduced me to sushi, proof that there is a God—or back to his place. He was a great cook and taught me a lot of helpful cooking tips, like how toasting herbs and spices before you use them brings out their full flavor and aroma and to be patient and stop moving and poking your steak because it won't speed up the process, and each time you move it, it prevents the caramelization that adds to the flavor, or how saving a little of the pasta water and adding it to the sauce makes for a richer, tastier sauce. Cooking together was so much fun. We had our share of food fights, "I dare you to eat this," and "Try saying the alphabet with a mouthful of apple cobbler" moments. There were times when we laughed so much we cried. I said he was my best friend, and he really was. But dwelling upon the past will not help me get to the place I need to be, as Tracy is quick to remind me. My thoughts when I come to my safe place are to be focused on getting better, not reminiscing about the Trent days. But when I come in here, it's the perfect place to remember.

At lunch one day, I dropped by his office. I wasn't feeling well. Some beefy, brainless asshat in my phys. ed. class had thrown a dodgeball at my head that hit me so hard it knocked me off my feet. My head started pounding a few minutes later, so I went to tell Trent that I wasn't going to come over after school. I was gonna go home, take some Tylenol, and try to sleep it off. Instead, he offered to take me to his place, where I crashed, and he went back to school.

When I woke up, school was over and he was home. He took me by the hand and led me into the bathroom, where he had candles lit, Loreena McKennitt playing softly in the background, and the most luxurious bubble bath drawn. A bath bomb from Lush filled the room with the scent of the rainforest just after a tropical storm. I had undressed in Trent's room and was just wearing one of his T-shirts. He lifted it over my head and helped me into the tub, then turned around and left to make us scallop and cavatelli pasta with white truffle sauce.

Trent was a bit of a wine sommelier. He said it's a little-known fact, but the Aussies make some of the best red wines. Wolf Blass Blue Label is heaven. He often had a glass while we were cooking and one with dinner, never more. Sometimes he would allow me to have a glass either before or during dinner with him, but never both. At first that pissed me off 'cause in so many other respects he would treat me like we were equals, yet when it came to drinking, he was always cautious. I figured it out, though, and it makes me respect him more. It was like he was saying, "There's no way I'm going to get you drunk so I can take advantage of you." As fucked up as it sounds, he was always careful to make sure that he never pressured me into doing anything I wasn't perfectly comfortable with.

In fact, we didn't have sex until I was sixteen. We both wanted to, *desperately*, but that was a line he would not cross. We made out a lot, and I even slept over naked with him a few times, but until I was older, he insisted we wait before going all the way. I knew it was killing him.

When we finally did it, four days after my sixteenth, it was the most incredible thing I have ever experienced, pure magic. Trent asked me probably a dozen times if I was sure. I finally told him to just shut up and fuck me.

He was gentler and more passionate and careful than I could have possibly asked for. It didn't hurt at all; it was absolute bliss from start to finish. Sex is one of those things that words are pretty useless for trying to describe. It has a power and a mystery that defies description. Nothing is more indescribable than the feeling that overtook me when we stared into each other's eyes and came together. It wasn't so much about the orgasm as it was about the connection that we made in the moment. Over the five months that we were sexually intimate, it was always amazing. I wanted it more than Trent did, and I think I often wore him out. I guess I was a bit like a kid with a new toy. It was so wonderful and new and fresh and exciting that I couldn't get enough. Even so, as mind-blowing as the sex was, it was only a small part of what we shared.

I was trying to tell Jenny about it, but I don't think I did a good job because she didn't seem to understand where I was coming from or where I was going. Like I said, it's hard to describe. I've been trying to tell her how bogus it feels when all people think about when the topic of Trent comes up is what he did to me, and I know they're referring to the sex. Yes, he fucked me, okay? God, I get it. We had so much more than that, but people can't seem to get past the fucking. I'm aware that it's the defining point of our relationship and what made it so wrong, but it was not our entire relationship, and I need someone to understand that. Jenny says she does, but I don't know if I believe her. Any time we're talking about Trent and I say things about the music we loved or the places we shared or the books we read together, her eyes kinda glaze over. I know where her mind is going, and when she can't hold it in any longer, she blurts out, "But he fucked you, Brianna," and I kinda give up again.

Tracy asks a lot about the sex, and I do mean *a lot.* I've tried telling her it wasn't just sex. Sex was just a small part of what we shared. But she doesn't get it either. I know it was the sex that was illegal and stuff, but my God, give it a rest, lady. I hate having to share details about my orgasms and favorite positions and acts that I performed. I want to say that it's none of her damn business, but I guess until she knows everything, she can't help me fix everything, or at least that's what she tells me.

I'm perfectly fine the way I am. I'm strong. I'm intelligent. I'm full of promise. If I *am* perfectly fine the way I am, why does Tracy try so hard to change me? And what is she trying to change me into? When you change a tire on a car, the new tire does the same thing as the old tire, right? I mean, it's not like a caterpillar. When it wraps itself in a cocoon, it becomes something completely different from what it was. Is Tracy trying to change me into a butterfly or just another tire? I feel like she wants me to go back to being this boring, shy, hollow entity. But something has come alive in me, and I want to know more about it. I'm self-aware enough to know that Trent woke me up sexually, but there's more to it than that. He brought another part of me to life as well, and I kinda like it. I've become more of a risk taker, more adventurous, and I like that part of me. Trent woke that in me too, but I don't know how to be that way without him.

When I first learned to ride my bike after Dad took the training wheels off, I noticed something interesting happening. As long as he was running alongside me, I could ride like a pro. He wouldn't be holding onto my seat or touching my bike at all, just running alongside, and I would be fine. But as soon as he fell back and let me go on my own, I'd wipe out. Or if he held onto the seat too long, I would try to break away and fall. This kinda feels like that. I need someone to run alongside me so I don't fall. I don't need them to hold me, just be there. I think that's what Tracy is supposed to be doing, but she's holding on, and as I try to break away and go on my own, she grabs the back of my bike and I fall. And sometimes it feels like she does it on purpose.

It seems like no one understands this mess I'm in or knows how to help me figure this shit out, and that's when it gets really lonely. And when it gets really lonely, that's when I miss Trent the most, and when I miss

Trent the most, I start feeling depressed and sad. And when I start feeling depressed and sad, I start feeling angry. And when I start feeling angry, I want to talk with someone about it who will understand, and when I look for someone to talk with about it, the only person I want is in jail. And when I find no one to talk with about it who will understand, I get lonely, and the cycle never seems to end. Am I fine just the way I am? Am I strong? Am I intelligent? Am I full of promise? The only thing I know I am at the moment is empty and afraid.

I watch tears roll down my face in the blue glass orb. They look like snakes creeping toward my neck, like worms working their way into the core of an apple, then devouring it from the inside. On the surface, the apple still looks pretty good, but inside it's being eaten away; all that is good is being devoured. The person I used to be is being consumed by this thing that has worked its way inside of me, that I have no control over. When it gets fully inside, I can almost forget that it's there, but then I feel it emerge, and with it comes the recognition that I'm being eaten alive. It burrows back into me, and I feel it grow and move and consume.

CHAPTER THIRTY

Claire was standing at the top of the spiral staircase in our massive new house with Greg, her prom date, by her side, looking down upon us like a goddess from the heavens. Mom wanted a few pictures before they left. She looked stunning. She had just returned home from a complete makeover; her makeup, her hair, her Coco Chanel dress—she was going to be the "belle of the ball," no question. As I stood at the foot of the stairs, watching this unfold, I couldn't remember a time that I had been more in awe of or prouder of my sister, and it was not because of how she looked.

A couple of months earlier, she had broken up with Arnie, a rich, pompous punk who was looking for nothing more than arm candy and a good lay. It took Claire about three dates—two longer than it should have, in my estimation—to figure him out, but once she did, she dropped him like a microphone at the end of an award-winning performance. The only reason she had expressed any interest in him in the first place was because of the sudden windfall our family was privy to after Gerald sold Reynolds' Baling Systems. It affected us all differently. I think Claire was overwhelmed by the abrupt disparity. But now she was with Greg, and she was thrilled. He was grinning from ear to ear at his precious treasure. When we looked at the pictures later, we all agreed that we had never seen Greg more overjoyed, more confident, more dignified.

In her senior year, she volunteered as a special needs assistant in a grade eleven class and was assigned to Greg. Greg is mildly autistic and socially awkward, to put it respectfully. He has difficulty making friends, paying attention, and maintaining conversations. When excited, he expresses himself with wild hand gestures, and his inside voice remains outside. Claire invited him over a few times after school, before prom. It was easy to see why she liked him. He was kind and compassionate and possessed a gentleness of spirit that was magnetic. While he displayed signs of semi-erratic behavior around others, Claire's mere presence settled him in a way no one else could. Around her, he was the perfect gentleman. He wouldn't forget himself and pick his nose or yell for no reason. She brought out the best in him, and Greg made her glow. They didn't date, and they were not boyfriend and girlfriend. In many ways, they shared something more.

Claire invited him to prom because she truly wanted to spend that special evening with him. She said she thought of asking me, but that would be awkward. She made it clear to Greg that they were not going to be a couple and that this was not an act of sympathy toward him. She cared for him and could think of no one she would rather spend prom with.

A host of guys had asked Claire to go with them, but she turned each one down, saying she already had a date. One week before prom, she asked Greg.

It was the last class on Friday afternoon, and she was going to her regular volunteer shift in Greg's class. She walked in with a single white rose. Greg, as he always did, approached the front of the class to meet her. Then in front of everyone, she said, "Gregory David Williams, would you please do me the honor of being my escort at the Westmount High School prom?"

Claire tells the story much better than I do, but apparently, he stood before her, his eyes filling with tears, speechless. The classroom fell pin-drop quiet as they stood face to face, just looking at each other.

"You're not joking?" he asked. "Just making fun of me?"

"Oh my God, no! Never," she said. Then she handed him the rose, gave him a long hug, and kissed him on the cheek. The entire classroom broke out in applause. Mrs. Roth, Greg's teacher, excused herself from the classroom for a few moments while she composed herself. Later, she told Claire that that had been the most special moment of her teaching career.

Claire had called Greg's mother the day before to make sure she was okay with it and that she felt confident it would not negatively affect him afterwards. Greg was the only grade eleven boy who was an escort at the prom, and he was on top of the world.

It didn't end in the romantic way that fairy tales often do. They weren't voted prom king and queen or any such thing, and a few assholes did their best to try to ruin things for Greg and Claire, but she put a quick end to their attempts.

Arnie, her ex, approached her. "What's the scoop, Reynolds? Couldn't find a man to go with, so you found a retard?"

She stopped in the middle of her dance with Greg while he hung his head in embarrassment and grabbed Arnie's tie. "Now, you listen to me, you pathetic, arrogant, slimy fuck. Greg has more class in his little finger than you have in your entire body. Greg is everything any decent girl would want in a date. I've seen everything you have to offer." She gestured to his crotch. "And Greg is more man than you'll ever be." Greg beamed as she threw her arms around him and gave him a long, slow, passionate kiss. By the time they finished kissing, Arnie was nowhere to be found. It was her finest hour.

They had no further hassles all night long. They danced almost every dance together. She even slid Greg's hand down over her ass as they slow-danced in front of Arnie.

She didn't arrive home until very late that night. Well, early the following morning. I don't know whether or not they had sex; I've never asked her. It would never have been expected by anyone, certainly not Greg. But I suspect that Claire may have made it the best night of Greg's life. Like I said, I've never asked, and she would never tell. If they did, it will remain a special and private part of their memories.

Even now, years later, Claire remembers the evening with great fondness. Every time we mention it to Greg, he is radiant. They still stay in touch. Greg was an usher at her and Robert's wedding.

That's who my sister is, an amazing woman who always puts others first. She is still defensive of the marginalized and less fortunate and usually fonder of them as well.

But something has changed. Robert came to see me a few days ago. All is not well in their world, and I'm directly responsible.

When you throw a stone into a still, quiet lake, it makes ripples. At first there's a large disruption near the point of entry, but little else. As time passes, the initial splash subsides, but the trajectory of the impact spreads rapidly in all directions, and on a still day, you can see the effects from shore to shore. Claire is one of the many who is feeling the ripple effects of my stone. However, to call what she is living a "ripple effect" is the furthest thing from the truth. She is living with the full, blunt-force trauma of my affair. The damage and disruption from my selfishness is destroying her in ways I never imagined. Her life is unraveling like a cheap sweater, and I'm pulling the yarn.

If I'm honest with myself, I have to admit that I must have known about at least some of the pain I had brought upon her, but I have been unwilling to admit it. To do so would mean taking an even deeper look into myself, being willing to concede that I was prepared to jeopardize much more than my own career and security, or even Brianna's well-being, that I was willing to disgrace and destroy the one person I love more than any other for my own selfish fulfillment. That is a thought I did not relish living with. So an equally selfish part of me has buried it, hoping I never have to look at it.

Robert forced me to look.

I cannot say I'm filled with gratitude for his holding my hand to the flame, but I recognize his need to do so. Hearing the devastation that I created was like hearing I'm solely responsible for the plague. I hate the way it sounds. I hate the light it puts me in and the implications of it. But what I hate even more is myself.

When I first began having feelings for Brianna—*admitting* my feelings for Brianna—there was a popular song on the radio at the time. I hadn't yet made the decision that I would shortly make, to abandon everything for this one thing, but I was seriously considering it.

Like anything that will bring about large-scale change in a person's life, you count the cost, you weigh the consequences, and you measure its impact. Whether it's a new job, a move, or even a vacation, you consider what the ramifications of taking that step will be. Just days before that life-altering morning when I first kissed her in my office, I was sitting at home one evening doing just that, considering the potential aftermath. This song came over the airwaves and struck me like a sledgehammer. I wondered how the songwriters could have known what sat on the horizon of my life.

If I traded it all
If I gave it all away for one thing
Just for one thing
If I sorted it out
If I knew all about this one thing
Wouldn't that be something . . .

I swayed there, on the cusp of trading it all for this one thing. It was nothing I had planned. I didn't know that first day when Brianna walked into my office where fate—our passions, my lust—would take us. But the closer I came to that thin red line, the less willing I was to look at the possible fallout.

Even though I knew, I didn't want to know. In the recesses of my mind, the costs I could calculate at that time were clear, and I willingly took that step across the thin line between decency and decay. My mind had been made up. I knew what I was going to do. I didn't want to know, but I knew, and I hated the sound of it.

I can color it, shape it, disguise it any way I choose, but it still sounds the same. A cacophony of ugliness. I hate how it sounds, but I did it anyway.

The problem, however, is that I only *thought* I knew the full-scale potential impact of my decision. In reality, I had little clue. I knew that I could—and was willing to—jeopardize my career, my security, my reputation. I even thought of the damage I could inflict upon Brianna. But I didn't consider everything else. I gave no consideration whatsoever to how it might impact Claire. As I sat listening to Robert reveal the devastation my selfishness was bringing upon his family, I couldn't escape the final refrain of that song. I heard the words he spoke loud and clear, yet that mournful refrain was just as prominent:

Even though I know
I don't want to know
Yeah, I guess I know
I just hate how it sounds . . .

It ran through my head like a freight train speeding toward a chasm in the mountains where the track has washed out. The ripple effect of my actions is far vaster than I ever imagined possible.

I want to believe that if I *truly* had known the full impact of my actions, if I had been able to calculate the mass destruction, I would have chosen a different path. Logic says anyone would. Yet even now, if I'm fully honest with myself, I cannot say that I know the answer would be *absolutely not.* Isn't that something? I admit here and now that I am in desperate need of help.

I CAN SEE CLAIRE STANDING at the top of the spiral staircase in our big new home. Looking down at me but not looking down *on* me, and I wonder, does she look down *on* me now? She should. I have given her every reason in the world to do so, but she probably doesn't; that's not her nature. She is grace personified. I consider the wreckage that remains in the path of the tornado that is my life and hope to God that I can begin to dig through the mire of disintegration and find one or two building blocks upon which to rebuild the foundation of trust and love that the storm of my choices has swept away.

CHAPTER THIRTY-ONE

Doctor Thackery often talks about being able to separate truth from feelings. As far back as I can remember, this has been a battle for me. As a child, my feelings would get hurt, and it felt like the entire world was out to get me.

In grade three, I dressed up as the Green Lantern for Halloween. In retrospect, it's easy to see why he was my favorite superhero. The power of his ring made my make-believe world a safer place. If I could harness a person's willpower, like the Green Lantern could, I could be happy. I could make Mr. Brown, my teacher, stop making fun of me, I could make Gerald like me, and I could make Jimi stop touching me. I could point my ring in their direction and my world would be a better place—a safer place.

Prescott Elementary School placed a great deal of emphasis on Halloween. Everyone was encouraged to dress up, even the teachers. All regular school activities were postponed for the day. In the morning, we would sit at our desks, watching as each class came through, showing off their costumes. When our class was called, we would line up in single file to be paraded through every classroom in the school. It was our turn to show all the other students our "cool" costumes. In the afternoon, we would have a school party in the gym.

It always started great. As I walked through the younger grades' classrooms, I felt like I had the perfect costume, but the nearer we got to my own grade level, the less sure I became, and by the time we got to the grade five and six classrooms, I felt ridiculous. It was like that every year. But the year Mom made my Green Lantern costume would be different. Somehow I knew, when I slept with the power ring under my pillow the night before, I would wake to find it actually possessed power to control people's minds. Everyone, even the grade six kids, were going to be in awe of me and my costume. It was perfect. At least, in my mind.

I knew the previous Halloween, when I was in grade two—the year Mom dressed me up as a kitten—that this year, I was going to be the Green Lantern. I had saved my allowance for two months and ordered an "authentic" Green Lantern power ring from the back of a comic book. When it arrived, I was ecstatic. We couldn't afford to buy the "authentic" lantern, but Mom promised she would help make me one that was every bit as good.

Spandex was unheard of in our home, so Mom gave me a pair of her black nylons to wear. They were a little big and looked silly with just my underwear underneath, so I wore a green—well almost green, more like bright yellow—swimsuit over top. It was a bit tight, but it looked pretty cool anyway. I had a green shower cap on my head. Mom had bought it just for me. I also wore a green bodysuit of Claire's that was part of her ballet costume, the kind that snaps together at the crotch. It was far too small and a little uncomfortable when it was done up, but it was tight, and it worked perfectly. Instead of the Green Lantern mask, Mom used makeup to cover my eyes and nose. It wasn't the perfect color, but it was close. It was witch's make-up, but who cared? It was green, and you could hardly even notice that the eyeshadow Mom put on me was more blue than green. I got to wear the only green towel we owned as a cape. It was forest green and frayed along the edges. Mom used a diaper pin with a bright blue clasp to fasten it. My white gloves were borrowed from Mrs. Hall, a neighbor. They were satin and had pink daisies embroidered around the cuffs. The final touch, the lantern, we made from a milk carton covered in mostly green Christmas wrapping paper. I used my aquamarine crayon to cover the white snowmen.

Just before the school bus arrived, I stood in front of the bathroom mirror to examine the end result. The shower cap was a little big, and folds that looked like a fat lady's ankles ran along one side. The makeup on my face was slightly too dark and a bit streaky. Claire's bodysuit hurt my armpits, and my balls were already beginning to ache, but it was the right color. The gloves looked a bit like the fat lady's ankles on my head, but it didn't matter, and no one would notice the pink daisies. My skin-tight swimsuit was great because I could stuff all the excess of Mom's black nylons inside so they looked like they fit. They were a tiny bit too see-through, but no one would be able to detect that. My lantern looked more like a Christmas present than a lantern, but people would get the idea. Ah, but my ring! It was perfect. And after all, with the power I could wield with that ring, nothing else mattered. I gave Mom a huge hug, took one last look at the superhero in the mirror, gave my reflection a confident nod, and was out the door.

Like every year, our class sat impatiently, chomping at the bit, waiting for our turn. "Mr. Brown's grade three class," was finally announced over the intercom, and off we went. This year was going to be different. I walked with my head high through each classroom. I tried my ring out on a couple of my classmates as we walked to the grade one class, and it worked! They were joking about my gloves, but when I pointed my ring at them, they stopped.

When we arrived at the other grade three classroom, I began to suspect that I'd used too much power on my own classmates. One girl asked me why I was wearing pantyhose. I was tempted to take control of her mind so she would see the truth, but chose to save the power for the kids who mattered, the grade five and six kids.

Grade four was going to be the test, though. I walked in, and a whole row of them began to snicker. I held my ring discreetly, so they wouldn't know I was controlling them, and shot my mind-controlling power in their direction. It was a waste, though, because I soon realized they weren't laughing at me; they were laughing at Taylor Reid, the kid in line right behind me, who was wearing a store-bought Superman costume—dumb.

In the grade five class, a big stupid kid grabbed my cape and ripped it off as I was walking past. When I bent over to pick it up, Mom's nylons pulled out of my swimsuit and flopped around my ankles like skin on an elephant's legs. I felt the power from my ring draining fast.

When we were leaving the first grade five class, their teacher asked me what I was dressed up as. Idiot. As I entered the next classroom, I noticed that my power ring was missing. I must have dropped it when I was trying to put my cape back on, which I was now carrying over my arm like a limp dishrag. I knew before I had gotten past the first row that without my ring, I was in big trouble. I was powerless.

Jeremy Schmaltzy started it. "Hey, kid, what's that green stuff on your face? Is it snot? Are you Snotman?" I felt the tears begin to well as the entire class broke out in laughter. My head sank low, and I fought hard to keep from crying. My eyes stung. I used my towel—it certainly was no longer a cape—to wipe my eyes. Blue eyeshadow mixed with puke-green makeup smeared across my face. I looked at Mrs. Hall's beautiful white satin *lady's* gloves. They were covered in green makeup and the actual snot that was running down my face. By the time we arrived back at our classroom, Green Lantern had been reduced to Snothead, Snotman, Snotboy, and the Great Green Vomit. Once again, I was demoralized.

"Maybe you should go to the bathroom and clean all the snot from your face, Snotboy," Mr. Brown said to me as I was leaving for lunch.

I sat in the corner of the gym with my head down for most of the afternoon while the Halloween party was going on all around me, pretending to read a book but really crying and wanting to disappear. Claire sat with me for much of the time. She said she didn't think I looked like Snotman; she thought I looked like Rowdy Gaines, the Olympic gold medal swimmer.

As I was waiting for the bus after school, Mrs. Richmond, the school receptionist, came up to me. "I think these belong to you, sweetheart." She handed me the blue diaper pin and my Green Lantern ring and gave me a sympathetic pat on the head. When the bus dropped us off at the entrance to the driveway of our farm, I threw that useless ring into the ditch as far as I could.

Like Doctor Thackery has so often told me, the truth is simple, but we tend to complicate it. I was not Snothead, nor was I the Green Lantern, but I believed I was as much the former by the end of that day as I believed I was the latter at the beginning of it. In fact, neither was true.

Yet somehow, even today, I have a difficult time separating truth from fiction. I convinced myself that I could get away with my relationship with Brianna without getting caught. In the same way, I convinced myself a fake plastic ring could overpower someone else's thoughts. Somehow I believed that I could ruin my own life without affecting Claire's in the same way as I thought that a little girl's green dance costume and Mom's nylons made me look like the superhero on the cover of the comic book. I know this truth, even though I don't want to know it, and I hate that I don't want to know it. But truth is truth, and deception always seems to lurk just behind the door.

CHAPTER THIRTY-TWO

The autumn I entered grade seven was wet and miserable. Each day, Dad would come in from doing chores and checking the fields looking the same: wet and miserable. Each day was exactly like the day before and the one that followed.

Our livelihood lay soaked and rotting on the ground. There would be no salvageable crop this year, which was like pouring salt on a wound because it was a bumper crop that lay drowning in the pasture that had become a swamp. Even the straw and hay were spoiled. So there would be no bedding or food for the cattle.

Dad had been negotiating the sale of the cows because we could not afford to buy the feed they would require over the long, cold winter ahead. He had no bank balance to speak of, no credit, and no leverage to purchase anything. The only option now was to sell off the livestock. It was the worst time of the year to do so, as the cows were mostly pregnant. A pregnant cow in the fall had nowhere near the value of a cow and calf in the spring. Without the feed to keep them alive over the winter, however, his hands were tied.

We watched as day after day, Dad sold a few cows or pigs and dropped a little bit lower, admitting defeat and becoming a little less of a man with each wave of his hand to the neighbor who happily drove off with our livelihood.

Mom and I did our best to assure Dad that things would work out. He would smile and try to reassure *me* that I didn't have to worry; he wasn't about to let us starve.

My big "bother," a nickname I'd given Trent the previous year, made himself scarce during that time. With Dad in the headspace he was in, Trent knew the ice under him was thin. After doing what little he could each day, Dad would take off in our old pickup to the bar in town and return late in the evening in even greater despair. When there were precious few cattle left to sell and still no hope of recovering the crop, he would bury himself in the garage behind a bunch of boxes he'd stacked up to form a makeshift office. That is where the Reynolds Wet-Dri Baler was invented. "The only reason we are in the position we're in, Louise," I heard him say to Mom one night, "is because you can't bale a crop that's soaking wet. What if you could dry it and then bale it?"

I don't pretend to understand the work involved or possess the technical knowhow required to design and build such a device, but Dad did, and that's all that mattered. He worked all that autumn, through winter, and well into spring, and the end result was the formation of Reynolds' Baling Systems Inc. Dad had invented and designed an implement that would pick up soaking wet straw, hay, or alfalfa, feed it through a system of tumblers and driers and then into the baling mechanism, and what came out the back end, delivered directly upon a pull-behind bale wagon, was a perfectly uniform dry bale. It had never been done before.

Dad patented the concept and approached investors, who ran with the idea. They hired engineers to create blueprints from Dad's drawings, and the following autumn, the first prototype of the Reynolds Wet-Dri Baler was turning saturated crops into edible delicacies for hungry bovine. A manufacturing plant came next, and soon balers were rolling out the doors as quickly as they could be built.

The biggest problem was keeping up with demand, and before I was in grade nine, we had more money than any of us had dreamed possible. We moved to the city when I began high school, and the following spring, a huge implement manufacturer made Dad an offer he could not refuse. They bought RBS for an obscene amount of money, plus stock options. And the rest, as they say, is history. Of course, it radically altered our lives.

Mom and Dad began to drift apart at about the same time as the money was drifting in. Mom says that Dad simply couldn't cope with the boundless influx and it changed him. Dad colloquialized that you could take the girl out of the farm, but you couldn't take the farm out of the girl. According to him, Mom just couldn't handle their new jet-set lifestyle. They were probably both right. Call it a midlife crisis, call it the opportunity of the affluent, call it whatever you want, but Dad began to care less and soon became careless. He traveled a lot and took vacations without Mom, but certainly not alone.

When you come from a life of abject poverty, and suddenly riches abound, it does something to you. It certainly had an impact upon me, and not always a good one. I made some ridiculous choices, a few of which I regret to this day. I hesitate to say that money can't buy happiness; that is such an old, overused cliché. And while everyone knows it's true, many who have money are too quick to forget how miserable they were before. I'm not foolish enough to believe that money made Dad happy, but the lack of stress that poverty had brought upon him was clearly evident.

He began to thoroughly enjoy life. The sad part is, he did it at the expense of his family. I suppose at the end of the day, he was so sick of how the lack of money had controlled every decision he made that he allowed the limitless surplus to control and consume him in much the same way as our poverty had.

When he returned from one of his getaways, he would lavish gifts upon me. At first I received them with gratitude, but soon I realized they were little more than an attempt to buy my allegiance and appease his guilt. The luster quickly faded. It's one of the things I wish I had talked with Dad about before his heart attack. I wish I could have said it was unfair for him to attempt to purchase my love.

That wasn't the only reason he went overboard in his affection toward me. There was a darker side to his grandiose generosity. He rarely gave Trent a penny. He would revel at Trent's lack and our affluence. Trent got a job at a service station to earn a fraction of the money that Dad would toss at me. I would try to give Trent money and things to even the score, but Trent wanted no part of that. It was an affront for him to accept even the crumbs that fell from the rich man's table.

When he was a senior in high school, a group of Trent's friends were planning a ski trip to Jackson Hole over spring break. It was to be their "last hurrah" before they all graduated and parted ways to different universities scattered across the country. Trent worked every weekend and as many evenings as he could to save for the trip.

Dad had bought me a brand-new Mazda MX 5 convertible for my sixteenth. After much pressure from Mom, he bought Trent an old, beat-up Honda Civic, which Trent reluctantly accepted.

A couple of weeks before Trent's ski trip, they booked a suite at Snow King Mountain Resort and made travel arrangements. After dinner one evening, Dad took Trent outside and demanded that he pay him back for the car *loan*. Trent was shocked. He didn't say a thing, though. He just canceled his trip with his friends, got as much of his deposit money back as he could, and left an envelope with $1,500 on the counter. After that he disappeared, and we didn't see him at home for three days. I saw him every day at school, but he wouldn't come home until Dad left on another one of his excursions. What really pissed me off is that Dad always carried at least that much cash with him at any given time anyway. It was nothing more than pocket change for Dad and just another way he trampled upon Trent.

That, I suppose, is the other thing I would like to have been able to tell Dad: how hard it was to play Dudley Dursley to Trent's Harry Potter. Not that Trent ever thought that my receiving from Dad was unfair. He was thankful that I could wear nice clothes, have nice things, and fit in after all the years of being a reject. But it made me feel like the ugly stepsister in *Cinderella*, getting everything while Trent got shit upon. It was unfair for Dad to put me in that position, and it placed an enormous strain on Trent and me, a strain similar to what we are experiencing right now.

Robert and I are going to visit Trent in Briar Ridge tomorrow. It has been a couple of weeks since I've seen him, although Robert went last week. I know Robert as well as I know Trent. He wanted to visit Trent by himself—that is, he needed to visit Trent by himself. They are very close, probably best friends. So it didn't strike me as unusual when Robert suggested I take a day for myself while he went alone. But when he got home, I knew immediately that their conversation had been more than sunshine and roses. It took a few days before Robert filled me in.

I love Robert dearly, and I know that he only has my best interest at heart. Trent's too. He showed me a printout with a detailed outline of the things he had said to Trent. And if it were possible, I might love him even more for doing it. Trent and I are sometimes too close. Some might even say we're enmeshed, although I doubt that—which, of course, anyone who is in a codependent relationship would say. The one thing I do know is that being aware of the pain Trent is currently experiencing and had lived through at the hands of Dad for most of his life creates within me a desire to ensure he doesn't suffer more. Few things in life are more important to me than Trent's well-being. When he suffers, I suffer, which is exactly what's been happening. The difference now is that he brought his suffering upon himself, and I'm simply feeling the repercussions of his actions.

I do get angry at Trent, though. It surfaces most often when I see how the boys are affected by his actions. Aaron has the utmost respect for his uncle but is unsure how he's supposed to feel about him—how he's *allowed* to feel about him. Last night, we told the boys exactly why Trent is in prison. It was no big revelation to them; they both know how Google works, and they had heard stories from kids at school. But it seemed to give them permission to ask questions and speak openly about it. Robert and I agree that we should have told them much sooner. As parents, though, you always hope and usually assume that your kids are far more innocent and unaware of human malevolence than they are.

Aaron wanted to know what the difference between statutory rape and rape was. My immediate thought was that for months he'd been holding the image of his favorite uncle ripping the clothes off kids as they came into his office, throwing them to the floor, and fucking their brains out, then giving them a pat on the head and sending them off to their next class. I regret not telling them sooner, and I get furious with Trent for putting me in a position where I had to tell them at all.

Stevie wants to know "why Uncle Trent did that." That question demands an answer, but the only one that I can give him is "I have no bloody idea." So I try to explain it in a way that an almost nine-year-old will understand.

"Uncle Trent made some really poor choices," I say, sounding like a digital personal assistant. "You know how Dad and I talk with you both about the importance of choosing well?" Now I sound like an advice columnist. "Uncle Trent is a bit sick."

"I read this thing on Facebook that said Uncle Trent is really sick in his head and that when he gets out, he's going to keep doing this, and he might even kill people," Stevie says.

I try to explain the politics of cultural persuasion, but all I get in response is a blank stare. "Uncle Trent isn't going to kill anyone, Stevie," I say, although I'm seriously considering killing Trent for putting me in this position.

"He's no different than he ever was. He did something really stupid, and while it's all his fault, he never meant to hurt anyone. When he was a little boy, life was really hard for him."

"Why?"

"Grandpa and Trent didn't have a very good relationship."

"Why?"

"Because Grandpa didn't really like Trent."

"Why?"

"I think because Grandpa and Trent were so alike."

"Why?"

"Uhm. Well, because they both worked very hard and didn't feel like people appreciated their hard work."

"Why?"

And about that point, I realize I'm just blowing smoke, and I don't have a clue why Dad always treated Trent like shit, and it makes me really mad at him too—one more thing I wish I'd been able to ask Dad about.

Finally, I give up. "Stevie, I don't have the remotest idea what your uncle was thinking when he began having sex with one of the students at his school. I wish I did, I truly do, but I do not know and can't figure it out. I know that Uncle Trent is wondering the same thing, and I don't think he knows either. He's seeing a man who has been helping him figure out what's broken inside of him that would make him even consider hurting that girl the way he did, hurting himself the way he did, and hurting us the way he did. It hurts inside when you think about what Uncle Trent did, doesn't it?" Stevie and Aaron both nod. "It hurts me too," I say as tears begin to flow down my face.

"Maybe when Uncle Trent gets out, we can all help him get better," Stevie says. He reaches over and strokes my arm. "It'll be alright, Mom. It'll be alright. We'll all help Uncle Trent."

Tonight, as we put the kids to bed and say their prayers with them, Aaron wants to say a special prayer for Trent. He seldom prays and *never* out loud.

"God, help Uncle Trent get better, and fix his head so he won't wanna have sex with girls anymore. And help us help him. Although I don't know what I can do. The end." Aaron could never understand why we say an entire prayer in English and conclude it in Hebrew, so he just says, "the end." I get that.

I FLOP DOWN ON THE sofa that sits across from the fireplace in our family room and lay my head in Robert's lap. There is something comfortably mesmerizing about watching fire. The flames flirt and flit and dance like sugar plum fairies. I suppose it's the randomness of it all. There's something relaxing and inviting as the flames jump and stretch, a form of controlled chaos. I guess that's what I long for in all of this but seem to be unable to find. Amidst the chaos of life—Mom's death, Dad's imminent death, Trent's incarceration—I long for a bit of control within the chaos. And that is the one thing I cannot find.

I force myself to break free of the fire's hypnotic pull, and my eyes rise to the pictures above the mantle. One photo of Trent, Aaron, and Stevie completely covered in mud, soaking wet, and grinning from ear to ear makes me smile. The boys had just turned six and seven. Every summer during the second week in August, Trent would take the boys for the week. He had been doing it since they were out of diapers. He called it "giving Robert and I a break," but the reality was far less altruistic. He adores Aaron and Stevie and loves to spend as much time as possible with them.

That summer, they spent the better part of the week going to ball games and making day trips to the zoo, the beach, and the old farmyard. The boys love to run through our old, abandoned farmhouse and the barn, the outbuildings, and the fields. They can't believe that people could "actually live in a place like that."

Trent would play hide-and-seek with them there, which was completely unfair because he had hundreds of hiding places he discovered as a child—mostly to keep away from Dad—and their chances of finding him were slim.

The weekend before Trent brought the boys back home was always reserved for their camping trip. That August, they were going to the coast. Trent found a great campground, complete with a swimming pool, water slides, a go-kart track, and horseback riding. The plan was to get as much of those things in as possible.

It poured rain from the moment they pulled onto the expressway and kept raining until the moment they pulled back into the driveway. They all agreed it was the best weekend of the summer.

As they were driving to the campsite, however, Aaron began to complain. "Ahh, Uncle Trent? It's gonna suck. It's supposed to rain all weekend."

"I heard that too," Trent replies. "So why don't we try to see if we can get as wet as possible all weekend? We can't change the weather, but we can change the way we feel about it. What if it's better to be wet than dry? This weekend is going to be 'Wet Weekend'!" Then Trent dumped his water bottle over Aaron's head. That was where the fun began, and it didn't stop 'til they got home. Trent has lost much of that optimism over these last couple of years, and no wonder. I hope he can find it again.

At some point, as I was immersed deep in thought, Robert slipped away and went to bed. I sit here weeping. I weep for my children, for my big bother, for my dad, for Robert, and for myself. Maybe I need a change of perspective, a "wet weekend," so to speak. This is a hard season of life, the hardest I've ever gone through. I'm powerless to change much of what I'm facing today, but I can change the way I face today. I don't have to enjoy it, but I can endure it better than I have been. Telling the boys the truth about their beloved uncle was a good start.

I need to tell Trent some truths as well.

CHAPTER THIRTY-THREE

This blackness is darker than anything I have known, although it is not so much the dark that carries the ice-cold fear as it is the emptiness—the loneliness. I have lived within this cavern of misery for untold days. In this place somewhere between life and death, I'm aware. I wish I wasn't, but I am.

I wasn't, but I am again.

I lived once, somewhere, at some time. I lived poorly. Now I live in death. In this place, emptiness echoes like a gunshot. It's not physical; it's so much worse, like the inside of a bubble filled with unimaginable horrors. Decay, decline, and despair are all that exist. Deep inside I think I know that I wasn't always alone. I wasn't always dead. I wasn't always in torment.

I lived once, not well. I loved once, not well.

My son sought to love me, but I rejected him. My son wanted my love, but I withheld. I'm aware that a presence much greater than me is holding me hostage for the misery I brought upon my child. He was a treasure that I threw away like so much trash.

TRENT IS YOUNG AND HAPPY and hopeful. The sun burns high and long in the midsummer sky. Clouds, like wisps of clean vapor, steal across the vast blue expanse above. Beautiful fields of golden wheat bow and bend like a chorus line at curtain call. Flax strong, blue, and bountiful stands straight and proud, like my son next to me. We gaze together upon these fields, our lifeblood. My son is strong and courageous. At age three, he proudly carries loads that are much too heavy in order to please his father. At age four, he is able to tell whether a crop is ready for harvest. At age five, he knows. At age six, he stands away, apart, wary of his father, his faith is shaken, his trust hesitant, his hope faltering.

On that beautiful summer day, we walk together in the pasture, among the cows. A young heifer is not well. She is listing to the right and limping. I come alongside to check what's the matter. She has a large thorn in her foot. The tissue is inflamed and warm. I stroke her, trying to settle her, but she resists. I attempt to lift her leg. She fights, and anger stirs in me. Trent stands close, wanting to help. I tell him to back away. I pull hard at the leg, planted firmly on the earth. The heifer snorts and kicks. The blow hits me hard in the leg. I'm furious. I strike out but not at her, at my son. I strike with the back of my hand, sending him into the barbed wire fence. "I told you to stay back, you stupid little shit!" I hit him again, then one more time. He cries. I tell him to shut his goddamn mouth or I'll give him something to cry about. He stifles his tears. I go back to the cow. I am not sorry.

WE STAND, I AT THE bottom of the cellar, he on the landing above. I want to rebuild the trust I know has eroded—I know I have eroded. There are no stairs in our cellar; a ladder is the only way down. The lights, all three, are on. One is at the far end, one near the center, one directly above me. "Jump," I say. He does. I catch him. He laughs. We do this again and again.

I place him back at the top, walk to the far side of the cellar, and pull the string. The light goes out. The cellar dims. I return to the space below my son. "Jump."

"It's dark, Daddy."

"I'll catch you." He does. I do. He laughs. I pull the string just above my head. Now I'm only a silhouette.

"Jump."

"Daddy, I'm not sure where you are." I hear the fear in his voice.

"Jump." I can see him clearly. He hesitates. "Jump." He does. I catch him. There is no laughter. I place him back at the top. I pull the final string. Blackness.

"Jump."

"Daddy, I can't see you."

"I'm right here. Jump." I can barely see him. He cannot see me. "Jump." Nothing. "Damn it, Trent, jump," I command. He whimpers. "Jump!" He jumps. I miss. No, *he* misses. I hear the thud. He screams. I flail for the string above my head. Light. A tooth is missing, and blood streams from his mouth and nose.

His mother races to the threshold above. "What happened?" she asks. I squeeze his arm. The message is received.

"He fell. He's fine." I do not like this boy, this child of mine, and I do not know why.

I LIE UPON A LARGE, circular golden bed, wrapped in magnificent Egyptian linen. Two stunningly gorgeous young women half my age lie naked beside me. Heaven. We are resting now. Not long ago, they performed upon me and each other sensual acts of pleasure unknown to me short days ago. I try to bask in the glory of these delights, but their splendor vanishes like vapor rising on a hot road. I cannot hold on. Too many reminders of betrayal, infidelity, and adultery fill me with guilt. I inhale another line from the buttocks of the vixen next to me and am able to forget momentarily. But his face comes to me as I try to remember to forget. "Adulterer, monster, infidel, quitter, betrayer, coward!" he shouts. I cannot escape the accusations, his or my own. Hell.

HE MUST HAVE BEEN TWELVE years old. I despised everything about him. The light-colored curls that graced his forehead where mine had receded far beyond a widow's peak. His bright, crystal-blue eyes, mine narrow and pale in comparison. His thin but developing torso beginning to show signs of the muscular chest sure to follow, mine beginning to sag and bulge in all the wrong places. His strong, tanned, handsome face already turning girls' heads, mine never receiving a second glance. I should have been proud of him. I should have rejoiced in his maturity. Instead, I ridiculed him, mocked his masculinity, shamed his manhood.

In this dark place, my arrogance and jealousy have become my shame and sorrow.

He ran to me once. He now runs away.

I long to exist again, only better. I long to live again, only better. I long to love.

I feel ruined, but I do feel. This thing I feel is wet and crawls down my face like the slow melting of icicles on a warm spring morning. To feel anything more than deep despair is good.

CHAPTER THIRTY-FOUR

Self-discovery is one of the beautiful side-effects of personal introspection. Our most recent session has just concluded. It occurs to me that after all we have been through together and the hard work Reynolds has done, he is beginning, finally, to get it.

It's unfortunate that much of a therapist's energy is expended upon helping patients unlearn. Society sends messages, subliminal and intentional, that shape the perceptions of culture. Truth, as simple as it is, often gets buried within the snare of the lies we are sold and sell to ourselves. Some of these are as simple as "You deserve a break today." Others are more complex, like the lies Reynolds has spent much of his life believing. Lies we tell ourselves often enough, over a long enough period of time, in situations traumatic enough, weave their way into the material of our unconscious mind, reshape themselves, and return to our consciousness as fact.

Lies are the nemesis of the psychiatrist. They too will fall away, but seldom before they have wrought irreparable damage in a person's life. Reynolds is beginning to come to terms with the irrefutable evidence of the destruction brought upon him and others by the fabrications he has accepted as truths. Some of these surface in our renewed efforts to explore his relationship with his father.

He tells of events in his formative years that have shaped some of his sexual aberrations. He was six years old and had just wet the bed again.

Enuresis is not uncommon among children, although there are psychological factors that may contribute to it, and in Reynolds' case, I'm certain they did.

Wearing only his underwear, he went looking for his mother to ask her to help him change his bedding. She wasn't in. His father asked what the problem was. Reynolds was reluctant to tell him. With the history between the two, this is not surprising. Reynolds said his father was sitting at the kitchen table, smoking a cigarette, and called him over. His underwear was drenched, and he smelled of urine. Gerald grabbed Reynolds by the hair, pulled his underwear off, and shoved them in his face. He then proceeded to "teach him a lesson he would never forget." He forced his son onto his back on the floor, spread-eagled, sat upon him with his knees upon Trent's spread legs, and held both of Trent's arms over his head with his left hand while he burned the tip of his penis with the cigarette he held in his right. He didn't simply touch the glans with the tip of the cigarette; Reynolds' father extinguished his cigarette on the head of his son's penis. As Reynolds is circumcised, it resulted in a scar that remains, albeit ever so faintly, to this day. Then he told his son that if he ever pissed the bed again, he would "chop his prick off and force him to eat it." Freudians would have a field day with this trauma. Suffice it to say, far more than Reynolds' penis was scarred that day.

For a six-year-old boy, the notion of life without a penis is horrifying. The images circulating in his mind range from turning into a girl to bleeding to death and everything in between. The psychological damage this stirs within a child can be lifelong. For Reynolds, this propagated an entire childhood of lies and concealment. He could never again allow his father to learn that he had ever wet the bed. From that moment forward, bedtime elicited deep-seated fear at the possibility of wetting the bed, being found out, and losing his manhood. It had no power to prevent enuresis, though. In fact, the terror that consumed him proliferated the act. Bed-wetting became almost a nightly occurrence from that day until age twelve.

Reynolds endured severe balanitis as a result of the cigarette burn. The inflammation and subsequent pain were excruciating. As healing from the torture progressed, he began to touch himself to see how much it still hurt. It was this action that introduced him to the act of masturbation. The pleasure he received from the sensation of touching his healing penis had a threefold effect. First, it felt good. It also brought about significant confusion. Then a tertiary psychological effect occurred: Reynolds began to associate sexual stimulation with fear, pain, and disgust.

The idea that his penis was the cause of so much pain in his life—the bed wetting, which resulted in the torture, which resulted in fear and shame—created in him a detestation for all things related to his penis, both pleasurable and painful. Anything having to do with his penis was interpreted with utter confusion. It felt good, but it was bad. It brought pain, fear, and shame, and yet it *still* felt good. Therefore, *he* was bad, scared, and ashamed. Lies come to us in many forms. The most difficult to navigate are those embedded in our existential pain.

His sexual abuse contributes to this in no small way. At seven years of age, Reynolds became the victim of severe sexual molestation at the hands of his father's best friend. The abuse occurred almost nightly, on and off, over the course of four years. This, in concert with his negative predisposition toward the nature of all things sexual, manifested itself in a form of sexual stasis—the inability to receive sexual pleasure from anyone who could pose a threat. Many whose sexual development is halted at an early age find they have difficulty with normal sexual progression and therefore find themselves sexually attracted primarily to those who pose little or no threat to them. It's not that they are unable to have sexual thoughts or feelings toward someone of similar age, gender, or stature, but they prefer being with those whom they can control—those who pose no threat. Clearly, this is where Reynolds is halted.

The silver lining to Reynolds' situation, if there is one, is that with diligent effort, he may be able to overcome this paralysis. During our times together, we have explored at length, with his inner child, the effects of his abuse. Trent has made a rapid union with the boy who has suffered so much, and I observe a wonderful bond developing between them.

One of the more difficult steps is helping the boy trust the man who allowed the suffering: himself. Reynolds shows great promise for rapid recovery. I'm grateful for this, as it allows us to move forward with haste.

The next hurdle we must overcome to expedite healing for Reynolds and his victim is to address the psychic union disorder that I am now convinced exists between them. Having conducted further research into the matter, as well as holding lengthy discussions with trusted colleagues, we are ready to move forward.

I have also been in dialogue with Leland Philips, the chief medical investigator, who has examined the disturbing issues arising from my discoveries regarding Brianna Barnes' therapy. He has held consultations with the victim's therapist, Ms. Tracy Mathis. Leland agrees with my assessment that her management of the victim's abuse and her qualifications for treatment are insufficient, and he has terminated her involvement.

The victim is now under the care of Doctor Linda Knox, a well-respected psychologist for whom I have the utmost regard. Doctor Knox and I have collaborated on numerous occasions, and I'm confident that she will make great headway with the victim.

Linda has proposed a joint therapeutic session involving her, the victim, and me. I'm considering the matter. However, two concerns come to mind. The first is the affection I have developed for Reynolds. In fact, I find I'm having to repeatedly remind myself that he is the offender. I realize he has done considerable harm to his victim; however, he has also endured unspeakable horrors and is, in that respect, very much a victim as well. The second consideration is the awareness that knowing as much about Reynolds as I do, I may approach the victim with biases that impede the desired outcome.

CHAPTER THIRTY-FIVE

I've been in PC for almost two months now, and it's really just more of the same. I actually thought—I suppose hoped—that because all of us are here to be protected from something or someone, it would be different from gen pop. Somehow better. It isn't. In some ways, it's more difficult. The difference is that I'm on the opposite end of it now. I'm becoming more like *them* and less like *us*.

There is a chain of command on this unit that is more brazen and defiant than on others—"one ruler to rule them all." I thought, or perhaps I had convinced myself, that a man's response when placed into a protective environment would parallel something close to gratitude. It does not. I thought that knowing the system found one valuable enough to take him out of harm's ways would instill a sense of appreciation. Such, I am learning, is not the case. Rather than being grateful for this shield of protection, the men who surround me now are even more bitter, if that's possible. It's as though our presence in this place has made a statement to the rest of the prison that we aren't strong enough to make it in gen pop, so we have to prove otherwise.

Picasso is one such inmate. I don't know the man's given name; everyone calls him Ramone, although I don't believe that's it either. In his previous life, Picasso was a drug lord. He doesn't know how many men he has killed or has had killed, nor does he care. He stands six feet eight inches tall. He's a large man who spends as much time as he is able in the gym, getting even bigger. He is the supplier of steroids to much of the prison population and has a booming business.

I call him Picasso because his face looks as if the famous artist created it. In the drug bust that brought him to our little family, he was shot multiple times, including once in the face at close range with a shotgun. While not quite killing him, the blast did a masterful job of rearranging four of his five senses. His eyes aren't where they once were. Well, one is. The other rests a bit more to the left than it previously did. His nose—what remains of it—now resides an inch or so lower than it once did. His mouth rests to the right of his chin, and the flap of skin that was once his left ear flops around like a panting dog's tongue. All in all, he is a work of art not suited for the faint of heart.

On day three of my new adventure in the world of protective custody, Picasso entered my cell without invitation. Well, he didn't quite enter my cell; he stood in the doorway. And he didn't quite stand in the doorway so much as he consumed it, two of his minions standing just behind him.

"Whaddaya hea fo?" he demanded. Having learned from previous mistakes, I concocted an elaborate tale about an Internet scam that allowed the victim to believe they were looking at their bank balance when in reality it was sitting in an offshore account with my name on it. My best friend, Bryan, helped with this fabrication. With him being overseas, our communications have been primarily via letters and the odd phone call. While I was still in the infirmary, though, I'd sought his computer expertise. Using pictures and info from my actual charges, he created several fake news articles and Internet posts about the scam, and since they were posted after my actual conviction, they would appear before any of the posts on Google searches which were there prior. Namely, those related to my statutory rape charges. Because they can't do it themselves—the Internet isn't available to prisoners—they get outsiders, usually ex-cons, to search for a fellow inmate. They seldom search for long. It wasn't bulletproof, but considering the attention span of most convicts, I hoped it would suffice.

After I spun my tale, Picasso stared at me for a long time, working out in what little brain remained whether my story was plausible. He would have already checked, of course. No one ever takes a convict at his word. He continued to stare at me. Finally, he stuck his gargantuan fist out front, the invitation for a fist bump. "Righteous," he said, though it came across as "recluse." Apparently it's acceptable to swindle little old ladies out of their life savings. It took me a bit to figure it out, but I was in. I will be okay in here.

In the hierarchy of protective custody, no one ranks higher than Picasso, and he rules the unit with an iron fist. It's not uncommon to watch him approach a skinner carrying his meal tray and slap it out of his hands or to use a skinner as a punching bag. Sure glad I'm not one of *them*.

Picasso's word is like that of an English monarch, so what he says becomes law and is above contestation. I'm a welcome member of Picasso's posse. I don't do anything with that power, but I'm privy to all the rights and privileges that come with membership. The only difference between the person I was then and the person I am now is that I can walk the hall of the unit with less fear of attack. And that I receive as a gift. I have had few encounters with Picasso after that first one, but word has gotten out that I am "solid," and that's all that matters.

Doctor Thackery is pleased with the progress I'm making—that we're making together. I would be stumbling around in the dark without him. My visit with Robert was a wake-up call. I take all the things that I'm realizing—or, in Robert's case, have been pointed out to me—and those I recognize in myself to Doctor T. He almost always has some valuable advice or profound insight that I have somehow missed.

Turns out I have become a victim of the lies I have believed and, every bit as much, those that I tell myself. Gerald used to lie to me all the time. I must have been fifteen or so before I realized that. Claire was working on an assignment for her English Lit class. She was writing a story about the only family vacation we ever took while we still lived on the farm.

I would have been eight the summer of that vacation to the Poconos. About an hour from the Pennsylvania border, we stopped for fuel and a bathroom break. Gerald was under the hood, checking the oil, and I was standing beside him. He looked down at me. "Go ask the man in the service station if he has any fan belt fluid. But it has to be twelve-volt fluid. The twenty-four-volt is only used in tractors."

I dutifully headed off on my quest, then returned more embarrassed than humored. But Gerald got a kick out of it, and that was all that mattered to him. He used that to illustrate my stupidity many times over the years.

When we arrived at the campground, we began setting up our site. Mom and Claire were gathering firewood. I was helping—or thought I was helping—Gerald set up the tent.

"I don't need your fucking help," he said. "Take the bucket down to the creek and get some water." He paused. "And get as many red-spotted tree frogs as you can find. They're delicious roasted over a fire. There should be hundreds of them." He threw a bag at me. "Here. If there are too many, you can carry them in this. Get at least a dozen. If you can't find them at first, don't give up like you always do. Keep looking. You may have to walk a ways to find them. The important thing is not to make a lot of noise, or you'll scare them."

I had no idea where the creek was, so Gerald pointed me in the right direction and I headed off. As I walked along the path, I began to suspect that the elusive red-spotted tree frog was about as real as twelve-volt fan belt fluid, but I kept an eye out just in case. I continued walking down the path Gerald had placed me on, listening for the sound of the creek, but I heard nothing. After a good twenty minutes, I figured I must have missed it, so I headed down an offshoot and then another. It didn't take long before I was utterly lost. I kept looking for the creek or my way back. I knew that if I found the creek, my family would eventually find me because that was where they would search first. What I didn't know was that there was no creek. The camping guests got their water from a well just behind our campsite. But I didn't learn that until I was helping Claire with her English Lit assignment seven years later. She had known and so had Mom. Gerald told them both shortly after we arrived when Claire had asked him if we could go swimming.

It was a park ranger who found me about six hours later, close to midnight. I was covered with mosquito bites, shivering, starving, and had pissed my pants. When he returned me to my parents, I was so relieved to be safe and reunited with my family that I forgot it was Gerald who had placed me in jeopardy in the first place. It was seven long years before

I put the pieces together. Gerald had intentionally sent me off in pursuit of that which I would never find because it didn't exist. He did it for one reason: so I would get lost. No, he did it for two reasons, the other being because he hates me.

Doctor Thackery has suggested I have been lied to and misdirected so often in life that even when the truth presents itself in plain view, I'm both unable and unwilling to believe it, just like I couldn't see the reality of my Green Lantern costume. This is not a debilitating problem in and of itself, but it becomes so when I do the same thing to myself, Brianna being the textbook example. The truth about the inevitable outcome of our relationship was plainly visible, yet to me it was as unrecognizable as Gerald's lies. The lies surrounding Brianna had been affecting my life and perspective in ways I was unwilling and unable to admit.

Fridays had always been pizza night at my place with Claire's family. They would arrive at about 7:00. I would have all our favorite ingredients: hot capicola, Genoa salami, spicy Italian sausage, shrimp, portabella mushrooms, anchovies, fresh mozzarella, vine-ripened tomatoes, arugula, sun-dried tomatoes, sweet white onion, avocado, and fresh herbs. I love to cook, and we have such a great time doing it together. The sauce was a secret recipe made from scratch. Aside from the usual ingredients, it included puréed Kalamata olives, minced garlic, and mizithra cheese.

Stevie and Aaron had their own table with their own special ingredients, things the rest of us wouldn't dream of putting on a pizza—pineapple, pepperoni, and cheddar cheese. Our weekly pizza nights were a special bonding time for all of us and included games we could all enjoy and often a movie.

Once Brianna came into the picture, however, those nights became a rare event. I convinced myself that the lies I told to get out of pizza night didn't affect anyone except me. But Robert reminded me what a treasured time those evenings had been and how upset it would make not only the boys but also him and Claire when I would call late Friday afternoon to cancel. It wasn't just the lies I told to get out of pizza night; it was the lies I told myself so that it wouldn't bother me so much. I willingly traded a valued tradition to feed my own selfish, carnal pleasure.

I'm gaining a new understanding of the devastation my lies have wrought. They say that admitting you have a problem is half the battle. That's a lie. It's merely the tip of the proverbial iceberg, but it is essential to the development of new and healthier life choices.

I'm having the most difficult time getting my head around one particular lie. This lie centers on my feelings for Brianna, which I'm still wrestling with. I understand the futility of my feelings, but that does nothing to diminish their effect on me. To the best of my knowledge, I have been in love only one other time, and unfortunately—sadly—it was not with Michelle, the woman I married.

Her name was Megan. I was in my sophomore year at Ohio State, where we attended evening psych classes together. Our first significant encounter was when we were working together on an early childhood development project. We never dated, and as much as I pressured her to, we had never even kissed. She had made a personal vow not to get romantically involved at all during her academic career, and she stuck to it. When love strikes, however, we know it. Many emotions can be mistaken for love, but the authentic thing is unparalleled, or so I thought—think. It is this unequaled experience that Brianna and I shared.

In every capacity, Brianna seemed to be my equal. On so many levels, we had a natural affinity. We shared intimacy, compatibility, romance, and trust. I remember many occasions where we agreed that we felt more relaxed and closer to each other than we had ever been with another human being. To be fair, she had little to compare that to, but I had much.

In the summer between grade ten and eleven for Brianna, we visited a veterinary clinic. I suggested she check it out with the hopes of perhaps doing some volunteer work in their animal shelter. It was the clinic where I had often taken my cat, Ozzy, over the years, and I knew the vet quite well as a result. He welcomed Brianna and gave her a complete tour, even allowing her to observe a surgical procedure that he performed on a golden retriever. Before we left, he offered her the opportunity to apprentice under him when she reached that point in her program. She was completely enraptured the entire day, and it solidified her decision to pursue this as a career path.

Shortly before we left that afternoon, I stood in conversation with Doctor Cho, watching as Brianna sat on the floor of the shelter surrounded by puppies. Her love for them and the affection she displayed reminded me so much of Claire. That was the moment I knew for certain that I was in love with her.

Back at my place as we ate dinner—baked eggplant parmesan with a spinach and gruyere soufflé—I listened as she shared her dreams with me. She foretold our future in great detail: her schooling, her apprenticeship with Doctor Cho, our home just outside of the city, not so far that it would be too much of a commute for me to get to Glenwood but far enough that she could have a private practice that would serve both city and country veterinary concerns.

We laid together that evening, sharing the sofa as we watched an episode of *Blue Planet*. As we watched, I thought to myself, *This is her, the woman I want to spend the rest of my days with.*

When we retreated to the bedroom, our lovemaking was slow and gentle. There was no urgency, no hesitation, no boundaries, only utter and complete surrender. Even our shared orgasm was a moment of unhurried, unfathomable ecstasy and wonder. As she lay sleeping naked next to me, the rise and fall of her breath was an invitation to join her on this rare, limitless adventure that few will ever know: true love.

True lies?

I try to deny this feeling—these passions—I have for her. But to do so feels like one of the lies I'm attempting to eliminate from my life. And this makes things far more confusing than I can explain. Doctor Thackery says he has a hypothesis as to why this is and wants to explore it with me but is unwilling to speak further about it until he gathers more information.

Physically, I haven't been feeling well. I haven't been able to eat much or to keep it down, not that there is much worth wanting to eat or keep down in this place. But I'm rapidly losing weight, and I can't afford to lose much more. During pill parade, I mentioned this to the nurse who gives me my daily meds. She says an upset stomach is common with some of the medication they are feeding me, so they have adjusted my HIV meds—a cocktail, they call it, although it's certainly nothing like a Black Russian.

I do wonder whether Brianna ever thinks of the good parts, of the love and passion that I think we shared.

CHAPTER THIRTY-SIX

Aaron and Stevie were in a heated battle over World of Warcraft when the call came in. I recognized from the call display that it was Glendale General. Robert and I had just been to see Dad the previous evening, so I was certain there was only one reason for such a call—Dad had passed. I tried to settle the boys, calm myself, and answer the phone without completely losing composure. I watched as if in slow motion as my shaking hand picked up the receiver.

DAD HAD ALWAYS BEEN BIG on life lessons, tools to place in our—my—spiritual toolbox so they would be there to take out and use whenever we—I—needed them. These helpful offerings were foundational in the development of emotional balance, which has served me well in life. Had Trent been included in these "teachable moments," I think it may have saved him from much of the pain that has marked his life.

On a beautiful Sunday afternoon when I was nine years old, I went to the barn to check whether the new litter of kittens we had been expecting had been born yet. The car had hardly stopped when I bolted toward the barn. "Margaret Claire Reynolds! Don't you dare think of going into the barn in your Sunday dress." Mom said. I reluctantly turned around, ran to my bedroom, changed, and then headed back to the barn.

You know how there are times when you're really looking forward to something, and then something else grabs you and you forget the thing you were so excited about in the first place? That was one of those days.

I scrambled up the ladder to the hayloft, pushed aside a bale of hay that mother cats often had their litters behind, and saw Remington. Dead. Remington was Rascal's kitten from her first litter and was also likely the father of most of Rascal's future litters. He was a big old tomcat. He was kind and gentle and perfect to have on your lap when it was cold out because he was so big he could warm you from the waist up. And there he was, dead. And cold. I sat down beside him, stroked his head, and cried. At that moment, I couldn't remember ever feeling sadder. The sadness was like a heavy weight sitting in the pit of my soul, preventing me from moving.

Dad often came and helped me find the kittens, as long as Trent wasn't around. He found me in the loft behind the bale just as I'd been since finding Remington. He sat with me for a long while and said nothing as I wept. He stroked my head as I did Remington's. A long time passed before I spoke. "It hurts so bad, Daddy."

"I know it does, Claire, I know it does. But this too shall pass." I had no idea what he meant, so he explained it in a way a child could understand. He took me by the hand and led me down from the hayloft, out of the barn, and over to the small flower bed that Mom had running along the length of our old farmhouse. He squatted next to it and set me on his knee. Then he told me about the life cycle of a Morning Glory. The flower was in full bloom. It was beautiful. We smelled it and touched its velvet-like petals.

"A while ago this was nothing more than a seed, Claire, and in a few days it will wither and die. Everything in life is like that. We're born, we grow, and we die. Remember that Lion King song, 'The Circle of Life'?" I nodded. "It's important that we cherish what we have when we have it because it won't always be here."

"Just like Remington?" I asked.

"Just like Remington. The more we love things, or cats, or people, the more it hurts when we no longer have them. But there's something else that is going to pass, too: the pain you feel right now. It hurts because you just lost someone—something—you love. It will take time, but the sadness in your heart will fade, just like everything else in life."

It's a lesson I have tried to instill in Stevie and Aaron as well. This is the side of Dad that Trent never saw. Everything passes. Even the pain of losing your mom, your brother, or your dad.

"HELLO . . . YES, THIS IS CLAIRE Durst."

Another Remington moment. The same as the day I went to the hayloft as a nine-year-old, expecting to find life but instead found death, and in the shock of the new discovery I forgot what I went expecting to find.

I was fully expecting to hear that Dad was dead. Instead, I was told the opposite. Doctor Morrow said that for some inexplicable reason, he seems to be waking. There is strong evidence of brain activity. His eyes are moving beneath his eyelids just as they do in REM sleep. And he's been crying. Tears are rolling down his face, and small sob-like cries are escaping his dry lips. Doctor Morrow wouldn't call it a miracle, but he did use the phrase "medical mystery." Robert and I will head back to the hospital shortly.

I haven't told the boys. I don't want to get their hopes up, like mine are. A new hope is being birthed inside, though. I want to tell Trent when we visit on the weekend, even though I'm all too aware that this news will certainly not stir in him the same emotions it has in me.

ROBERT AND I WERE MARRIED in the summer. It was a fairytale wedding that had the potential to become a nightmare. Dad spared no expense. I have never seen the tally of all the costs, and I don't want to. Robert did some calculations, as things were, in his estimation, getting way out of hand. He figures the total cost would have been in excess of $250,000. All of us—Robert, Mom, and I—tried to dissuade Dad on multiple occasions before we finally gave up.

My favorite flower is the bird of paradise. It's certainly not the most fragrant of flowers; in fact, as they get old they begin to smell rancid. But in my estimation, they are the most beautiful expression of God's creative hand. I wanted one in my bouquet, with white roses, and a couple on the head table as a centerpiece. Dad only heard, "Claire likes birds of paradise." He relayed it to the wedding planner, who passed it on to the florist, and come wedding day, several hundred birds of paradise plants were beautifully arranged amidst perhaps thousands of white roses in almost every nook and cranny of our backyard.

Ever since I first heard the song "Butterfly Kisses," by Bob Carlisle, when it came out in the late 1990s, I knew it would be a part of my wedding one day. So what did Dad do? He contacted Mr. Carlisle's agent and flew him in to sing the song live at our wedding. Don't get me wrong; I loved it and very much appreciated the idea, but it felt excessive. Like Mom, I'm just a simple farm girl at heart, and I was overwhelmed by Dad's enthusiasm.

Mom and I planned the reception dinner. I say "planned," but we certainly didn't execute it. Once again, as a farm girl, I wanted a basic meat-and-potatoes dinner, beef of course. Dad said he'd take care of it. The next thing we knew, he had hired Chef Ling Ngan and his team from LA to cater the affair. Kobe beef was flown in directly from Japan at Chef Ngan's request. There was also Maine lobster, Chinook salmon, black Ayam Cemani chicken, foie gras, Almas Iranian beluga caviar, and so many other delicacies it was difficult to keep track of them all. He even had Robert's and my name embossed on the dance floor.

Trent was very quiet on the evening of the event, which was nothing unusual when he and Dad were together in the same space. He did the toast to the bride, and a more eloquent recitation I have never heard. He spoke of the honor and gift it was to have me for a sister. He didn't repeat the typical idioms of how beautiful I looked in my stunning Gucci gown or reminisce about the funny things we had shared and done as children. He spoke of character and substance and purity of heart. When he finished, I thought, *This is my finest hour.*

After the first dance—the bride and groom dance—Bob Carlisle stepped onto the stage for our father-daughter dance. It was a moment I will never forget, though not for the reasons one might expect. First, because so much attention was drawn away from Dad and me because of the star on the stage, but more so because of what Dad whispered in my ear during the dance. He had been drinking a fair bit, so I took that into consideration, but as the great bard once said—or maybe it was someone else, but it sounds Shakespearean—"the second glass of wine brandishes truth from thy lips."

As Bob sang the words, "I must have done something right, to deserve a hug every morning, and butterfly kisses at night," Dad said, "I hope you are enjoying your special day, sweetheart. I did this for you because my love for you knows no bounds. I want you to know how much you mean to me . . . and I want Trent to know how much more important you are than he could ever be."

At that moment, the music stopped. Bob Carlisle's voice faded in the distance, the beautiful lights went dim, the mirror ball shattered, the flowers withered and died, the perfect, warm summer evening became as cold and dark as the barren arctic in midwinter, and the caviar became rancid bile. For me, the dance was over. I continued to hang onto Dad, but only out of fear I would fall without his support.

When the song ended, I turned away. I didn't look at Dad, and I couldn't even look at Mr. Carlisle to express my thanks. I went back to Robert, held him close, and told him how much I loved him.

It was during the fourth dance, a slow waltz, when Trent approached us. He bowed and said in an amateurish English accent, "Excuse me, fair matron, may I perchance have this dance?" I clung to him like a lost child who had just been reunited with her mother, placed my head on his shoulder, and wept. To this day I'm certain that Trent believes they were tears of joy.

When Robert and I go to see Dad this evening, I will push the darkness of that memory, the darkness of that part of his character, into the furthest recesses of my mind and remember only the good in him. He is, after all, my dad. And to me he has been, for the most part, a good role model and a good father.

I wonder, though, how one person can be both benevolent and malevolent simultaneously. How the same man can be so filled with wisdom and compassion one moment and so shallow and cold the next, so generous and yet so self-serving. As I consider what Trent has done to that girl and his family, I have to ask the same question. Dad and Trent are not so different after all. Perhaps that's something I need to address with them both. Maybe now I'll get the chance. What did Dad do to deserve butterfly kisses? What did I do to deserve Dad's love? What did Trent do to deserve his hate?

CHAPTER THIRTY-SEVEN

This may well have been the worst Starbucks shift I have ever worked, one shithead after another. I'll be so glad when it's over. To be fair, it's not completely the customers' fault. I botched quite a few orders today. I don't know where my head is at.

Linda says the energy required for me to do the hard work—and it will be hard work—that I need to do can lead me to be distracted and lose focus. She says I shouldn't be too hard on myself about it. I like the way she puts it. She says I have to "learn to be kind to my woundedness." Linda's my new therapist, Doctor Linda Knox.

I got a call from Tracy, my old therapist, a little while ago, saying because she has way too many cases, she has to prioritize, so she will no longer be working with me. That was it. Short, direct, and to the point. She was never like that in our sessions. You have to be pretty fucked up to be dumped by your therapist. I got a call the same day from Doctor Leland someone-or-other. Mom talked to him, mostly. I guess he's the head honcho of all the shrinks in the city or something like that. He recommended I see Linda instead. She specializes in victims of child sexual abuse. He made all the arrangements, and now I have an actual shrink.

Linda is the real deal. She only has three rules, which she told me when we first met. The first is that I have to be completely honest with her. The second is that I'm not allowed to call her Doctor Knox; she says that would be the equivalent of her calling me Student Barnes, and we should be identified as the person we are, not by the things we do. Cool. Oh yeah, the third rule: I'm to be completely honest with myself. I think that rule might turn out to be the hardest.

From the moment we met, it felt so different than with Tracy. Not that Tracy was bad; it's just that Linda isn't at all concerned with things like what I think of her. She seems to want to get to the issues rather than impress me with all her education or how busy and important she is, or how many other patients she's working with. She won't even talk about another patient with me, kinda like Trent wouldn't. In some ways, they're a lot alike. They both make me feel relaxed and welcome. She never seems like she's in a hurry. Even when I'm quiet and have nothing to say or am struggling to find the words to express myself, she doesn't rush me, and that helps me be more open with her. Talking with her just feels, I don't know, right. Like talking with Trent did. She's so chill. So much different than Tracy. She doesn't talk much unless she has something she feels is important for me to hear. Instead, she listens.

I asked her why she says so little. She said that if she's talking, she's not learning, and the only way for her to help me is to learn about me, and the only way to learn about me is to listen to me. That's why it's important for me to be honest too. She says that listening is twice as important as talking, which is why God gave us two ears but only one mouth.

I watch her sometimes when she's listening to me. It seems like she's working so hard, working things out. She calls it active listening. She looks right into my eyes when I'm talking. I'm not used to that. Most of the time, people look at your mouth, your nose, or all around the room, but when Linda is listening, she looks directly into my eyes, and I can feel that she's really listening. If I say something that doesn't make sense or is confusing—which I probably do a lot—she waits until I complete my thought and then asks me to explain again, differently, what I mean.

Sometimes, though, I think she asks me to say it again because I'm the one who's missing the point, and when I say it differently, I'm the one who understands things better. Most people only listen to you in order to know what they can say to make themselves feel better or smarter or whatever. Or they're just waiting for you to take a breath so they can talk. Linda listens because she really wants to know. Sometimes she just nods, not like one of those bobble-head dogs that people put on the dash of their cars, but like she really understands what I'm trying to communicate. And that helps me to know that she's getting it too. When I finish a thought or a story, she summarizes it, usually in a sentence or two, to let me know she heard me.

In our first meeting, I told her how hard it was not to be able to talk with anyone about how I really feel because every time I do, I get shut down, even with Tracy.

"Well, for what it's worth, it would help me to know exactly how you *really* feel about Trent," she said. She doesn't make me call him Mr. Reynolds. I really like that.

So I told her.

Just before I began, she asked me to remind her of the three rules.

"'Cause you forget?" I asked.

She smiled. "Humor me."

"Rule number one: I have to be completely honest with you. Rule number two: your name is Linda, not Doctor Knox. Rule number three: I have to be completely honest with myself."

WE HAD BEEN DATING FOR about six months, I guess, which means Trent hadn't been counseling me for almost a year. I started seeing him as my counselor when I was a freshman, and we started dating that spring. The following autumn, a couple of weeks into grade eleven, was the junior retreat. Every year the grade eleven students go on a weekend retreat to Corkscrew Falls in Hocking Hills State Park. Trent was one of the chaperones. For some stupid reason, he chose to ride on the other bus rather than the one I was on.

"Was it really 'for some stupid reason' that he chose not to ride on the same bus as you?" Linda asked.

I frowned in confusion. "Why?"

"Well, it occurs to me that you probably know exactly why Trent rode on the other bus, and if you're *honest* with yourself, you would have to agree that not only was it not a 'stupid reason,' it was a very good reason. And since you agreed to be completely honest with yourself, this might be a good place to start."

Wow! She was *really* listening to every word I said. It took me a while to get used to that. And I became much more aware of how I said what I said after that. Not in a way that made me scared to be open with her, more like the opposite. I knew she really wanted to help me, so it was important for me to share my story as honestly as possible.

When we got to Corkscrew Falls, they divided us into groups and we took our stuff to our various cabins. My cabin was at the end of a long stretch of pine trees. Only two other girls, Donna and Tammy, were in my cabin. As we were getting ready for bed that first night, Tammy said, "Hope you have a great night," as they packed up their stuff. I asked where they were going, and they said they were going to a party in cabin four with a bunch of their friends and wouldn't be back until the sun came up. Then they picked up their stuff and walked out. They didn't ask what I planned to do; they certainly didn't invite me along. They just giggled as they walked out. I guess even then I was a pariah.

Sitting there all by myself, I texted Trent. He texted back immediately: "I miss you!"

"Can you drop by my cabin?" I replied. "There's no one here, and there's something I really need to show you."

"Is it important?"

"Yes. Very!!!"

"Give me ten."

When he knocked on the door, I was lying on my bunk, naked, so I called for him to come in. When he did, his mouth dropped open. He scanned the room to make sure we were alone, then stood in the doorway just staring at me, saying nothing. It wasn't the first time he'd seen me naked or anything, far from it, but every time he saw me without clothes, it was like the first time. I loved that I could do that to him. Then he turned around, walked out, and slammed the door behind him. About five minutes later, I got a text from him saying that our relationship was complicated enough and there was no way that, as much as he wanted to, he would have sex with me while we were at an event he was chaperoning.

I was so pissed at him that I avoided him for the rest of the weekend. Every time I saw him coming in my direction, I would walk the other way. If we were at one of the group activities, I would sit as far away from him as possible and not even look in his direction. I could tell it was hurting him, but I wanted to hurt him for what he had done to me.

On the bus ride back to the city, he texted to say he would really like it if I came over that night so we could discuss this *issue*. I didn't respond. When we got back to school, Mom picked me up, and as we were leaving the parking lot, Trent was pulling out too. Our eyes met, and I sent him a text saying I'd be over at 8:00.

When I got to Trent's place and he opened the door, I threw my arms around his neck and gave him a long kiss. Then we had our first fight, sort of. We talked about everything that had happened over the weekend. He told me how he felt I had put him in a very difficult position, and I told him that his walking out of my cabin made me feel rejected. We didn't yell at each other or anything, but I could certainly feel the tension. I wasn't scared we were going to break up; I knew this was something that happened to couples, and we could work it out. Trent apologized for the way he had handled the cabin scenario—making me feel "less than" is the way he put it—and I admitted I was being selfish. But it had been such a turn-on thinking about having sex with him when dozens of my classmates were just a stone's throw away. He said that was the same thing that petrified him.

It was that night I began to understand things from his perspective, and I think he began to understand things from mine. The complexity of what we had, and what we had to hide, was far more stressful than any other part of our relationship. After we had *really* talked things through, we had the most amazing sex of my life. My orgasms were stronger, longer, and more intense than any I'd had before. I knew then how much I loved him. Not just the sex—him.

That was the first time I had ever told anyone how I actually felt about Trent.

"Why do you suppose your sex was so much more intense that evening, Brianna?" Linda asked after a long silence. I had to think about that for a while. Linda didn't interrupt, she didn't hem and haw, and she didn't look at her watch. She just looked into my eyes and waited. I told her I thought maybe it was because by finally allowing ourselves to understand how difficult the relationship was for the other, we grew even closer. I said it more as a question, as if I were asking her if I got the answer right. She didn't offer an opinion as to whether she thought I was right or wrong, and she didn't shit all over me for expressing how I really felt about Trent.

She sat quietly for some time before replying. "That is a very profound insight, Brianna. You demonstrate a wisdom and maturity that goes well beyond your years. I can certainly understand why a sensitive man like Trent would fall in love with you."

Oh my God, did that hit me. I cried. I mean, I didn't just cry, I lost it. I had been waiting for months to hear someone, anyone, say, "Hey, I get it."

I told her everything. I told her about how we clicked, how we were made for each other, how everything felt so right. I even told her—and not because she pressured me to but because I wanted to—how amazing the sex was between us. I told her exactly how I feel about Trent. Exactly what we shared. I kept waiting for the hammer to fall, for her to say, "Okay, Brianna, that was a cute little fairy tale. Now let's cut the bullshit and get serious. You're a fucking child. You can't possibly understand anything about love. So let's get over this nonsense and move on." But she didn't. And for the first time since Trent abandoned me, I felt validated.

"You are a very fortunate young lady, Brianna," she said as we were ending our session and I was getting ready to leave. "Not many people get to experience that kind of love. Consider yourself among the very few to have ever known such wonder." There seemed to be a note of sadness in her voice, as though maybe she's never known what it feels like to really love or be loved in the way I have.

SO, AS BAD AS THIS Starbucks shift has been, life isn't. I'm not sure where this leaves me, though, or what the next step is. What I do know is there's at least one person in the world who believes me—believes in me. What an awesome feeling that is. It kinda makes it feel like even though I've lost Trent, I can still hold on to something of what we had because it wasn't bullshit like everyone else tells me. It was real.

Early in our first session, Linda told me that one of the reasons she's working with me now is that Doctor Philips, the head honcho guy, was reviewing my case and found some things about the way Tracy had been dealing with me to be disturbing. That's the word she used, "disturbing." I'm not sure what she means by that, but I'm okay with it.

She also says that Doctor Thackery, Trent's shrink, would like to meet me. It's not completely up to me or him, though. First, Linda has to know for sure that it will help me and be confident that I'm ready to do it, and she says she won't know that until we've spent more time together. And then there's Mom and Dad. Neither Linda nor the other doctor will even consider it unless my parents are on board. And there's not much hope that that'll ever happen. So I doubt it will.

I don't know what they expect to get out of me meeting with Trent's shrink anyway. Linda already told me he won't answer any questions about how Trent is doing or pass along any messages. She says he wants to meet with me because he thinks Trent and I are having an equally difficult time getting to the place we need to get to—a.k.a. getting over each other—at least that's my interpretation of it, and he may have a way to help us do that.

In the meantime, Linda wants me to write a victim impact statement. She says it's *not* to be a love letter or anything like that. I'm to really think about the hurtful things Trent did and how they've affected me. Maybe now that I've been able to tell Linda all the good things we had, I'll be able to get out some of the bad instead of feeling like I have to defend my feelings and Trent.

I like Linda.

She told me that Alfred Lord Tennyson said: "'Tis better to have loved and lost than never to have loved at all." It may be better, but it's certainly not easier. Maybe it'll get easier, though. Linda says it will. And I think back to Davy's fortune cookie . . . but first it will be hard.

CHAPTER THIRTY-EIGHT

In my first year of graduate studies, I was sitting in Abnormal Psych class and the prof said something that piqued my curiosity and bothered me: "There is nothing of true value in life that does not come at a high price. Anything that has worth is only ever achieved through hard work and discipline and is seldom realized in one's lifetime." Here in my cell, a lifetime later, I'm beginning to understand this. The road back, the road ahead, the road to healing, will not be, nor has it been, a leisurely stroll through a spring meadow. It will be a long, hard climb to the summit of a mountain I have never traversed. It took a lot of pain and difficulty to weave this web of self-destruction, and it will require much more to unravel it.

In retrospect, there have been few things in life to which I have given significant energy. My studies were not particularly difficult. I have never invested substantial blood, sweat, or tears in any previous endeavor. Like many others, hard work is not something I'm overly familiar with. I have drifted along like a log broken free from a timber raft, winding aimlessly, taking the path of least resistance.

I suppose it starts now. It's the waste that comes from idle living that makes life so empty. Directionless. Purposeless.

The emptiness of wasted lives is revealed in every aspect of prisondom, reflected in men who have no sense of purpose, no sense of worth, and little sense of self. It's contagious and a fight to walk a different path. I long to walk a different path.

Doctor Thackery has been using a method of therapy with me lately that I'm unfamiliar with but beginning to get the gist of. Logotherapy works from the assumption that each human being has intrinsic value—a God-given purpose—that is often lost or misplaced as life kicks the shit out of you. Its goal is to assist the patient in the rediscovery of that purpose, to give us something to live for. It examines our sense of worth and seeks to renew our faith in ourselves.

It's absurd how powerful self-deceit can be. Claire and Robert have just left. I love the vulnerability they share. Robert told Claire in minute detail exactly what he shared with me during our previous visit. I expected no less.

As I look at Claire in light of the knowledge of the pain I have brought to her, shame engulfs me like flames at an auto-da-fé.

I look deep into her eyes and feel a new awareness. She knows more of the pain I have suffered in childhood than I have ever told her.

During the winter I turned eleven, we were skating. Our farm had a small pond fed by a creek that flows from the Scioto. It had been cold for weeks prior, although there had been no snow. The pond was completely frozen over, as was the narrow creek, and without snow to block our path, it became a skating rink of infinite length. Miles of unexplored ice just waiting to be scored with fresh skate blades. Claire woke me early one Saturday to go with her on an adventure that would take us almost four miles toward the Scioto. The day was brisk and cloud free. There is something about the sun on a cloudless, Midwest day in the dead of winter that warms you even when the mercury never rises above freezing. Bundled up like Inuit babies in a papoose, we set out.

I remember the day as much for the conversations Claire and I had as for the beauty of the hoar frost on the trees lining the creek. The day was majestic. Ice crystals clung to the trees like ivy to the walls of Oxford. Claire reached out and took my hand. We skated in silence, the only sound our skates cutting against the glass beneath our feet.

No sooner had we begun our adventure than she stopped me and looked into my eyes. "I have a question I need to ask you." She paused and took a deep breath. "Is Santa Claus real?" I was as ill prepared for that question as I would be for the next one. I had no clue how to answer her.

I remembered the Christmas Eve, almost two years earlier, when I asked Mom the same question. Her avoidance of a direct answer was the only reply I needed. She acted as though I had asked her where babies came from. Mom told me that the spirit of Christmas was real, as was the love families share and the way we show that love to each other at Christmas time. She said the spirit of Santa Claus, which fills children's hearts with joy, is also very real. What she didn't tell me until I prodded much more aggressively is that, no, Santa himself is not real. It didn't hit me as hard as I thought it might. After all, if you're asking, there is a very good chance that somewhere in the recesses of your mind, you already know the answer. But as I went to bed that night, sleep didn't come easily. I knew there would be no sound of hoofbeats upon our roof, no jolly fat man coming down our chimney, and no presents from the North Pole under our tree. And that saddened me somewhat. I didn't want to steal that wonder from Claire. Mom had also given me strict orders not to tell Claire what I knew.

All of this ran through my head as I prepared to answer the question my dear sister posed to me. On that perfect Saturday morning, with just three days remaining before his long sleigh ride south, I had to determine whether I would be the one to steal the dance of the sugar plum fairies from Claire's dreams.

"Trent, is there or is there not a Santa Claus?" she demanded.

"Why would you even ask such a silly question, Claire Bare?"

"Because some kids in my class say he's not real and only babies are dumb enough to believe that he is."

Fair enough. "No, Claire, Santa is not real."

She didn't say much. We continued skating in silence for what seemed like a very long time.

"I didn't think so." That was all she said. She didn't inquire as to why. She didn't seem overly sad either. She even seemed somewhat relieved that now she knew.

"I have another question, Trent."

"Shoot," I said, full of confidence. After that one, I could tackle anything.

"Does Uncle Jimi hurt you when he sleeps in your bed?"

I froze. Everything froze. I stopped skating. As though the ice had fallen away from beneath my feet, I felt the freezing water grip my very soul. She looked up at me, waiting for a response.

"What a stupid thing to ask, Claire," I said as I pulled my hand away from her and sped off. She never asked another question about it, and we never spoke about it again. Not until today.

Robert, Claire, and I sat in the corner of the visitors' lounge. The conversation we had been having up to that point had been difficult. Claire wanted to know why I would even consider jeopardizing everything I had going for me for a good fuck. She was angry, but even more than angry, she was hurt. I tried to answer her questions as best I could, attempted to explain myself without justification, was as honest with her as I know how to be, which is certainly not absolute, but she seemed to understand. She painted a vivid image of what Aaron and Stevie had been thinking. My heart sank as I listened to her describe their questions, their confusion, and their pain.

The same fear gripped my soul as it had thirty years earlier when she finally asked, "What did Jimi do to you, Trent?" The look on her face said she already knew, or at least suspected. And today she didn't let me skate away. For almost thirty years, I had refused to answer that question. My resolve to lie disappeared. I summoned everything inside of me and told her and Robert everything I could remember, everything I'm not blocking from consciousness, and there is still much of that.

The first time it happened, at least the first time I can remember, I was startled awake. Jimi was lying behind me, spooning me, his arms wrapped around me. He was in the throes of an orgasm when I awoke. It was the pinching of my shoulder that woke me. He was shaking, convulsing, and breathing erratically. I doubt he even knew he had been pinching me. It was a spontaneous reaction to the intense explosion of his orgasm. He wasn't inside of me yet; that would not happen for at least a year.

My underwear was bunched around my ankles, and his erection was buried between my thighs and rubbing up against my scrotum. I had no idea what was happening.

"Uncle Jimi, are you okay?" I asked. He yanked his cock from between my legs and gave some kind of incoherent answer. Then he rolled over to face the wall and pretended to sleep. I felt his cum between my legs and all over my scrotum and penis. I touched it with my hands and tried to figure out why my underwear was around my ankles and why pee felt like that.

Claire held my hand and squeezed it as I told her of dozens upon dozens of horror-filled nights. She was beside herself. She sobbed—at times uncontrollably—for the little boy who had slept just a wall away from her for so many years. I have no idea whether any of the inmates and their guests who were close by wondered what the hell was going on at our little table, nor did I care. Claire needed to hear these things as much as I needed to get them out.

She attempted to talk, but nothing came. Robert sat in disbelief. He held my other hand, weeping for the brother of his bride whose life had been so thoroughly decimated by the monster under the bed—in the bed. He too was silent. What does one say when hearing such unbearable anguish?

There are moments in life when silence speaks loudest, when nothing is more appropriate than something, when the wisest of men draw still, and the voiceless rule the day.

So we sat together, silent, broken, waiting. Waiting for that moment that eventually comes even in the midst of tragedy, when the breathing slows, the fog lifts, and light returns to provide direction.

Claire tried for a time to tell me what Robert eventually did: that they have been to see Gerald. That he lives, and breathes, and speaks. A medical mystery is in the making, Claire says. As they stood at his bedside, Gerald lay hovering between consciousness and coma. He began showing signs of revival a few days ago. It began one evening when a nurse noticed his eyes moving beneath his eyelids. They immediately placed monitors back on him and observed brainwave activity where previously there had been none. When Claire and Robert arrived later that day, he was moaning as tears rolled down his cheeks. "He was calling out," Claire said as she continued to hold my hand, "for you."

Now sleepless, I lie on my bunk, looking up at the graffiti on my ceiling, somewhere in the early hours of the morning, aware of three things only: that I'm loved profoundly, that I have received a measure of healing in the revelation of my abuse to the one I hold most dear, and that for reasons unexplainable, Gerald lives.

If, as I'm coming to understand, there is an ultimate purpose inherent within every human being, if each man, woman, and child has a measure of value—of purpose—if there is meaning in each life, I wonder whether everything in life is that way. Is there a greater purpose behind the pain I have endured at the hands of Gerald and Jimi? Is there ever a reason for such suffering? I wonder, too, about the suffering that I have brought to my victims. Is there something of value from the wrong I have wrought that they may grow from? Can good rise from the ashes of evil? Do I possess the strength to allow good to come from this suffering? As I ponder these thoughts, I am unable to rest.

Earlier, Robert and Claire told me they had stood in Gerald's hospital room, asking questions of the doctor that he could not answer, for he is as baffled as they are by Gerald's reemergence. Claire stood holding Gerald's hand, willing life to grab him.

"Dad, I'm here," she whispered. "It's Claire."

His eyes fluttered and opened. There was no awareness, no eye contact, and no clarity, but there was Gerald. Claire tells me she thinks she felt him squeeze her hand. She also thinks he attempted to look at her. But she knows he croaked in a voice unused for months, "Trennnnnnnnt." Then as quickly as he awoke, he returned to slumber. And just as he had been doing earlier, he wept.

Before they arrived to visit me this afternoon, they stopped in to see Gerald. The nursing staff told them he had a restless night. He woke many times yelling, startled, and confused. They don't know how to care for him. His condition is foreign, like a strange, newly discovered species of animal. So, they observe at a distance. They give him water through a straw. Unaware, he drinks.

He sleeps, he dreams, he cries, he wakes, he screams, he sleeps.

Claire told me a neurological specialist has been consulted, and they will begin brain scans, MRIs, and cognitive awareness testing soon. This half man, half zombie, all Dad, that she gazes upon bewilders her.

It has messed with her psyche. For months she has mentally and emotionally prepared only for death. Now she's attempting to prepare for what life there may be. Life without quality, perhaps. She talks of bringing Gerald to live with them if he ever gets to the place where he can leave the confines of his prison.

I must begin to prepare for what life might be like for me as well. For in not much more than a year, I too shall leave the confines of my prison.

As sleep finally descends, I wonder whose prison is worse.

CHAPTER THIRTY-NINE

"Breathing in, I know I am breathing in. Breathing out, I know I am breathing out." I ring the small brass bell that sits next to me and between us as we emerge from our meditation. There is much I would like to accomplish in our time together today. Cognizant of this, I remind myself to go slowly. Haste where something as fragile as the human psyche is concerned is always the enemy. Yet I have seen much growth in Reynolds, growth that spurs him toward wellness. Now, in this moment, as he brings his full attention to the matter at hand—his wellness—I face the proverbial fork in the road. One direction will lead us toward dealing with living as a man with an incurable disease. I choose the other.

Many years ago, as a young medical student, I met a man—a mentor, really. I was entering my third year, and he was finishing his residency at Johns Hopkins. He took me under his wing and assisted in my growth, not only as a student but also as a man. He drew my attention to wasted lives. We watched as students around us wafted in and out of programs, majors and minors, relationships, and our own lives. Like a child's kite, something tethered them to the ground, but otherwise they were directionless.

Passion, my mentor told me, is like a ship's rudder. Without it, we have little direction. Purpose, he said, is the anchor that provides stability to our passions. The evidence was right before our eyes. Fellow students dropping in and out of disciplines, in and out of classes like coffee shops, professors changing focus midstream. All around and on every side, men and women live their lives blindly, driven by their passions with no sense of purpose. Ask any of them, and most would tell you they feel content, happy, even fulfilled. Probe deeper, however, and purposelessness was sure to bubble to the surface. Unsure as to the purpose behind our directions, we move from relationship to relationship, from job to job, city to city, spouse to spouse, friend to friend. A lifetime later, we ask not "What did I do?"—for that is easily identifiable—but "Why did I do what I did?" And for that there is often no answer.

It was my friend and mentor who introduced me to logotherapy, meaning, and love. Leland and I have been partners—lovers—for close to twenty-five years now. Like all couples, we have our struggles. He likes the bedroom warm; I prefer it cool. I enjoy my pipe; he detests the smell on my clothes and skin when I sleep next to him. He finds me more attractive as I get older; I find myself drawn to men somewhat younger.

I have told Leland of my attraction toward this man who sits next to me in the large, comfortable chair in my office. He understands. He guides. He still mentors me. The love we share has grown so far beyond a simple lust of the flesh. He knows I would do nothing to jeopardize that love. I have placed safeguards to prevent crossing that "thin red line," as Reynolds likes to call it. The line he crossed that caused our paths to cross, the line that separates practitioner from predator. The first safeguard is disclosure. The moment I realized this attraction—this countertransference—I told the good doctor, Leland Philips, my lover, my mentor, and my friend, of my attraction. Only when we insist upon hiding the truth from ourselves and those closest to us does it have the ability to trap, to consume, to destroy. For evidence of this, I need to look no further than the man sitting right before my eyes. Exposed, truth flourishes. Hidden, it is extinguished like a candle deprived of oxygen.

Leland wasn't shocked, offended, or even hurt when I told him of my attraction to Reynolds. He was grateful that I have enough faith in the strength of our love that it can handle this level of honesty. Revealing this to Leland is all that is required for him to rest in the knowledge that we are good. My affection for Reynolds is nothing he himself needs to be worried about or even privy to. It is not his concern. I'm able to stand firmly next to him as we journey together on this road toward his healing.

I'm cautious to limit physical contact between us to a pat on the back or a gentle squeeze of the arm, but for my own sake, I will not hug the man or otherwise show outward affection. In our environment, it would be most unusual to do so anyway, not to mention careless.

In our individual practices, when Leland was still practicing, before he accepted the role of chief medical investigator, we worked with many men suffering the ravages of HIV and AIDS. There was a time when my focus was to assist these patients with coping strategies: how to navigate life without infecting others, how to talk with friends and family about their condition, and how to find happiness amidst the horror. All helpful, all acceptable, and all simply Band-Aid solutions. Unless asked, I seldom discuss these genuine concerns with the pos generation any longer, nor will I with Reynolds.

My focus with this dear, wounded soul who sits next to me shall be upon the rediscovery of purpose. His purpose. As we probe the depths of his unconscious mind, this will surface.

We get there—to his inner consciousness—much easier these days than we did months ago. Today after a brief meditation, an invitation for him to know that there is nothing in this place that will ever harm him, we can plunge like scuba divers into the depths of his secret world.

We have done as much introspection into his childhood sexual abuse as need be for now. If required, we are able to pluck the lie and permit truth to grow in the fertile soil that remains. Further exploration does not seem to be required. And so, we focus on deeper pain, pain that only a father's hand can bring.

I share with Reynolds the wisdom of Viktor Frankl, "that even in the most absurd, painful, and dehumanized situation, life has potential meaning, and even suffering is meaningful."

In the safe, calming environment induced through hypnosis, we enter this "suffering that can bring meaning."

Hypnosis is, without question, the most misunderstood and controversial method of psychological treatment. The myths and misconceptions that surround hypnotherapy stem largely from ignorance and entertainment hypnotists. Entertainment hypnotism is essentially a theatrical performance and has about as much in common with bona fide clinical hypnosis as many Hollywood movies have with reality. Psychological hypnosis is a genuine phenomenon that has valid use in clinical practice. The simplest explanation is that it places the patient in a state of highly focused attention and concentration. It is often accompanied by intense relaxation and heightened suggestibility.

There are visible and auditory cues that suggest to the seasoned professional when a patient has reached this state. Their breathing becomes deep, even, and tranquil, and their body rests comfortably still. Like the Sanskrit language, a melodious, almost musical harmony of cadence indicates a patient has reached a place of heightened suggestibility. The patient's speech becomes effortless, almost lyrical, as the words rise and fall. When Reynolds arrives here, I'm confident we're ready to begin. In this place, I'm able to guide Reynolds through memories often repressed.

"I am swimming in our pond with Claire and David Walsh, a neighbor from the farm next door. He is four years older than me. I'm twelve. David loves to pick on me. He's a bully, has been for as long as I can remember. Claire and I are ignoring him. We didn't invite him to come, and we really don't want him to be here. But he watched us swimming from across his fence, and ten minutes later he's wearing his swimsuit, splashing water in my face, and telling me I'm nothing but a useless chicken fucker.

"Claire hates David. She hates him for all the same reasons I do but mostly because of the way he picks on me. He doesn't pick on Claire, though; he hardly even knows that she exists. We're trying our best to ignore him, hoping he'll get the hint that he's not welcome and leave. He doesn't. Instead, he swims over to us. 'Hey, useless chicken fucker, wanna race to the other side of the pond?' It's not really a question; it's a command. Claire is told to count down.

"'Three, two, one, go!' she shouts, and we're off. I'm a pretty good swimmer. Mom says in another life I was probably a fish. David certainly was not. He's big and slow and fat. He's falling behind as we near the center of the pond. Suddenly, I feel him clutch my leg and pull me back. Then he grabs my head and pushes me under. Because he's so much taller, he can stand on the bottom of the pond, whereas I cannot. I'm out of breath and in desperate need of air. I begin to choke and gulp mouthfuls of dirty, stagnant pond water. Finally, he allows me to surface. David laughs as I gag and gasp, dog paddling my way closer to the edge, where I can stand and catch my breath.

"He leaves us alone for a brief moment, then returns and says, 'Sorry, chicken fucker. That was really mean. Let's race again. I promise I won't dunk you.'

"I say no, but it doesn't matter. Claire counts down, and off we go again. I'm almost to the other side. David is behind me. He grabs me again, and I kick him hard. He disappears under the water. I can feel him grabbing me and pulling. When he comes up, he has my swimsuit in his hand. He swims away with it and throws it on the bank behind Claire. She goes to retrieve it, but David forbids it.

"'Go get your bathing suit, chicken fucker. What are you afraid of? Your little tiny chicken cock is so small, no one will see it anyway.' I go to retrieve my suit. He laughs hysterically. I feel his stare and my shame as I leave the water, naked and embarrassed. As I pull it back up, bent over with my ass exposed to David and Claire, he throws a rock that hits me in the butt. He laughs even harder. 'Did you like that, hairless chicken fucker?'

"'You're a big, stupid chicken fucker,' I say. He runs up onto the bank and begins to beat the shit out of me. I try to leave, but he won't let me.

Claire runs to the barn to tell Gerald what's happening. He comes to the pond to see for himself, then sends Claire back to the house. He watches for a while. David sees him and runs away.

"'David, what's going on?' he demands.

"David stops and returns. 'Trent swore at me,' he says. Gerald grabs me off the ground, stands me in front of David, and orders me to fight. I stand there and do nothing. He tells David to hit me if I won't hit him. David punches me softly in the center of my chest, afraid of what Gerald will do if he really hurts me. He should have no fear of that.

"'You call that a punch? Hit him!' Gerald orders, and David does, somewhat harder, in the shoulder this time. I flinch a bit but remain standing. 'Do I have to show you how to throw a punch?' Gerald asks, then he drives a fist into my stomach that doubles me over and knocks the wind out of me. 'Now fucking hit him!' he shouts at David.

"David punches me hard, an undercut that catches me square. Blood spurts from my nose. 'Again,' Gerald says. I feel the sting as my head slams to the side. My eyes water. I can't see. 'Again!' Another fist smashes into my mouth. I can taste the blood. 'Again!' My ear explodes. The ringing blocks out all sound except for, 'Again! Again! Again!' I cower on my hands and knees, trying to shield myself from the onslaught of blows.

"When it finally stops, I wait for a long while before I lower my hands and look up. Through my tears, I see David spreading the wires in the barbed wire fence, crawling back through to his farm, and Gerald rounding the corner of the barn. They both disappear out of sight. When asked at supper that evening, Gerald explains to Mom that I 'got into a little scuffle with the neighbor boy.'"

While he is still in this state of vulnerability and suggestiveness, I invite Trent to explore the emotions uncovered by this memory.

"I feel small, alone, empty, betrayed, lost, scared, confused, weak, cowardly, angry, defenseless, worthless, hopeless, naked, ashamed, and powerless, like a pathetic chicken fucker," he says. Next, we examine the truth. Reynolds acknowledges that he was small, alone, had been betrayed, and had every right to be scared and confused. He was, in fact, powerless.

We establish a mood conducive to deeper relaxation, vulnerability, and suggestibility before we go further. Once he is in this deeper place, we can bring to the surface deeper truths: his powerlessness doesn't equate to weakness. "Trent, you are strong."

"I am strong," he repeats.

Being angry does not mean he's bad. Confusion isn't hopelessness. Confusion is the inability to understand. Under the circumstances, this is completely understand*able*. Hopelessness is that place where all is lost. Being beaten up, even at the hands and encouragement of one's own father, while awful, does not have the power to remove hope.

"Trent, you have reason to be hopeful."

"I am hopeful."

He is ashamed, and rightfully so, but he has done nothing worthy of this debilitating emotion. Therefore, his shame is not in himself; he is ashamed of his father. And the little boy has every right to be. One by one, we pick away at the lies and expose the truths buried beneath.

When he emerges from hypnosis, truth remains as the lies fade into the horizon. He is a little more aware, a little more connected with truth, a little more prepared for honesty.

Purpose is built upon honesty. The little boy Trent was, and the man he is, have made a profound connection. This is the wonder of hypnotherapy. It combines the strength of the unconscious mind with the insight of the conscious mind. Woven together, they form something stronger than either are independently—id and ego working in harmony. Gestalt.

This is not a new or unique truth. The wisdom of Solomon, the wisest of men according to scriptures written 2,500 years ago, states this most eloquently: "A cord of three strands is not easily broken." The third strand of this cord is the role that I, as Reynolds' therapist, am privileged to play, and together we make a formidable team.

We move on to another, much more exciting chapter in his life. A new twist has developed. As I watch him sort through the implications of his actions, I'm as intrigued as I am amused. Reynolds has informed me that in a moment of impulsive, pseudo bravery, he mailed a packet of six letters to his father—letters that I specifically instructed him were for his eyes only. At the time, this action seemed innocuous enough. However, in light of recent events, it could alter the landscape of their relationship.

From everything we know, there is little chance that Gerald will ever regain the cognitive ability to read or even comprehend the letters should they ever reach him. Nevertheless, a few short days ago, his death was imminent as well, and that has changed. Today, he is breathing on his own, he wakes occasionally, and he calls out for his only begotten son. As tragic as this has the potential to be, I can't help but be amused at the potential outcome. As part of our therapy, I have read each of these letters, and I'm fully aware of their explosiveness. Even so, something within them gives me hope. The words are truth. And when truth rises to the top, it provides a unique perspective. From the top, we see things differently than we do from the bottom. For perspective is not what you are looking at; it's where you are looking at it from.

I laughed out loud when Trent told me what he had done. He was more than a little confused at my reaction.

"And you find this somehow humorous?" he asks.

"I find it very amusing, Trent. Look, you can still prevent Gerald from getting the letters, should he ever revive and should you ever choose to. It's as simple as asking your sister to find the packet and return it to you, or dispose of it before he arrives home, which there is little chance of happening. But within those letters, you have exposed every lie, have been more truthful than you ever would have been had you expected him to actually read them. You held nothing back. I think you would agree it was a helpful exercise, was it not?"

He nods.

"Now you find yourself in the midst of a dilemma if Gerald continues to improve, a dilemma that you should never have had to face and never would have had you simply been content to keep the exercise an exercise. Instead, you sent them. You chose to pit fate against almost one hundred percent odds, and now the odds have changed. Personally, I find that funny. We always have the power to choose, and now you have another choice to make."

Ordinarily, I would have encouraged Reynolds to do everything in his power to keep those letters out of Gerald's hands. Ordinarily, I would have admonished him for sending them in the first place, and I would have taken this action far more seriously. A couple of things keep me from doing so. There is, as yet, only a remote possibility of Gerald ever being able to read them, and more profoundly, Reynolds is not the same man who I began working with more than two years ago. He is stronger and more courageous. So instead, I encourage Reynolds not to make a hasty decision about the other choice he now faces. "The letters are out there. The easy thing is to pull them back. But I have never seen a lie do for any man what the truth could not do better. Six letters awaiting Gerald are filled with truth. Your relationship with him over the years has been based on lies. Lies upon lies upon lies. 'Do what you've always done, and you'll get what you've always got,'" I remind him.

I go to one of the books I keep on my bookshelf, thumb through it, then hand it to Reynolds. "Read this," I say as I pass the book to him.

He reads it aloud. "A lie cannot stand forever. Because there is no history so old, so impervious to revision, that the simple truth doesn't establish itself sooner or later. Like gravity the consequences of truth can be avoided for a while. Sometimes a little while, sometimes a great while. But in the end that which is false crumbles, falls away, and only the truth is left. So long as that truth has been once stated, no matter how feebly, under whatever pain."

I return *Actes and the Monuments* back to the bookshelf. "Perhaps this catastrophic fuck-up is serendipitous," I say. "Maybe this is the opportunity to change the entire course of your life. Think about it like this; your relationship with your father—"

"Gerald."

"I'm sorry. Yes, your relationship with *Gerald* is nonexistent. There is nothing but hatred, disgust, and mistrust. You despise everything there is about the man, and as far as you're aware, the feelings are reciprocal. So, what have you got to lose? It's not as though you're going to create a rift between you and Gerald. A rift would simply fall into the vast chasm that already exists there. You can't make your relationship worse. Maybe, Trent, just maybe this is not the worst thing. Maybe this is the opportunity of a lifetime. How courageous are you?"

We end our time together there. We have resolved nothing concerning the choice that lies before him. It was not my intent to do so. It was fodder for thought, something to demonstrate that one cannot damage that which is irreparable. Reynolds will ponder this, mull it over, and reach a decision on his own.

What *does* stir hope in me is the new strength I see within this broken man. A compassionate connection with the boy who never cried wolf. The boy who silently stands idle while the beast corners and then devours him. Unknowingly, Reynolds is preparing to defend the boy who could not defend himself. And in this I find much to smile about.

I watch a new determination grow within the boy inside the man. The boy who could not conceive of standing up for himself a relatively short while ago. The man who finds it inconceivable to trust anyone of equal position or power. The man unable to partake in relationships with anyone who could stand against him the way David and Gerald did beside the pond. The way Jimi did in his bed. The boy who is the man, who loves the girl he will never have. The man who desires to but cannot break free of the bonds that tie him to forbidden love.

He is ready for this too. And soon he will break forth from the cocoon he has wrapped himself in to protect him from the predators—the other predators, like him, only worse—who hold him captive to lusts and desires he does not want but to which he is enslaved. The man is ready for this fight, and the boy is ready to break free. What a glorious day that shall be.

I AWAIT FURTHER CORRESPONDENCE FROM Doctor Knox. She has been working with Reynolds' victim. In our most recent conversation, I learned that Linda agrees with me regarding the psychic union that we are confident exists between the victim and offender. However, she's not prepared to subject B to the rigors of deep hypnotherapy at this point, which is understandable. Twice now her patient has been under the care of a professional therapist who has abused their power for personal profit, one in a way that is unacceptable although not illegal, the other both unacceptable and illegal. In my estimation, one is not much worse than the other.

Doctor Knox reports that her patient's progress was indeed significantly thwarted while under the care—and I use that term very loosely—of her previous therapist. As a result, Linda is exercising extreme caution in the management of her patient. She has invested tremendous effort into establishing trust and building rapport. For the time being, this is where her energies will lie. I have complete confidence in Doctor Knox's ability to assess her patient's readiness to undergo a procedure as invasive and deep as sedative-assisted hypnotherapy. The success of hypnotherapy depends upon the trust established between patient and therapist. The greater the trust, the greater the success. There is no flexibility in this equation and no trade-off. You cannot have one without the other. For these reasons, Doctor Knox has my full support.

Leland is not only my partner; he is also indirectly my boss. As the chief medical investigator, he is responsible for the oversight of each therapeutic practitioner in the state. This has never posed a problem between us. We have been able to separate our personal and professional relationships.

As previously noted, it was Leland whom I contacted regarding the concerns I had for B's safety after my initial contact with her former therapist. Leland took immediate action, reviewed the situation with his board, and appointed a board member to investigate. The result was to have the patient immediately removed from the therapist's caseload. As a further precaution, Ms. Mathis has been placed on probationary restriction and is being monitored much more closely.

Leland has also served as an advisor with regard to my request to attempt to sever the psychic union between Reynolds and Barnes. I was confident that he would see the situation from my perspective, provide the necessary support, and pave the way for this to occur. I was wrong. I am not unsatisfied with his decision, and I fully understand his concerns. I learned long ago that setting ego aside for the benefit of the patient creates a win-win scenario, and there is tremendous benefit in crossing the aisle, so to speak, to view situations, especially those I'm so close to, from another's point of view.

From Leland's perspective, the conflict of interest my involvement would present far outweighs the necessity for me to be a part of the process, especially if other options are available that may yield the same result. And he feels there are.

Moreover, he brings a valid concern that has not occurred to me: any contact I have with the victim could be indirectly interpreted as a breach of Reynolds' no-contact order, and therefore be punishable by extension of his prison sentence. He has since outlined a process that the advisory board suggests would serve as a viable option.

Doctor Knox will conduct the procedure, assisted by Doctor Philips, who will observe the process via video link, alongside the patient's mother. If he feels at any point that the patient is in distress, he will discontinue the process, and Doctor Knox will bring the patient out of the hypnotic state and assist her through the reintegration process. The method of hypnotherapy required for the complete severance of psychic union disorder is much more involved than that which Reynolds and I have just come through. This approach requires the patient to be in a subterranean, trance-like state, which will allow the power of suggestion to delve deep into the unconscious mind. Let me be perfectly clear about this. It is still only the power of suggestion. It is not mind control. If the patient does not want to respond to any suggestion, she simply will not. The ability to control another human being through hypnosis is a scientific impossibility. If that were not so, the most carnal part of who I am would probably overrule common sense and I would be a multi-millionaire, surrounded by gorgeous young men in a private resort on a tropical island.

Once the patient is comfortable and willing to proceed, the therapist begins by asking a series of questions. The questions are random to begin with but become more specific and focused as we near the target. Ultimately, through logic and deductive reasoning, the patient herself concludes that, in this case, for example, what she truly desires is a healthy, balanced, age-appropriate relationship that will bring her lasting joy. As the patient embraces these desires and makes them her own, this once impenetrable wall is removed.

Back in the realm of consciousness, she can rationally and logically take steps to fulfill this new desire. The successful breaking of the psychic union is realized when both patients have chosen to live their lives in accordance with the decisions to which they have committed themselves. And soon, Reynolds and I too will round this corner and face this—together.

CHAPTER FORTY

Aside from Trent's arms, this may be my favorite place in the world. The fresh snow that is now falling covers the garden outside my window like a blanket. Moonlight spills through a break in the clouds onto the walls and floors, filling my safe place with a warm glow. Beyond the window, the moonlight sparkles like sun-kissed water droplets on the ocean. Millions upon millions of diamonds glisten in the new layer that carpets the ground. Outside, it's brisk and sharp. Inside, the warmth envelops me like a cloak.

My attention is divided between the beauty of the outdoors and the task before me. Linda has asked me to write a victim impact statement.

When this whole thing came crashing down around me, a police officer suggested I could write one—that I *should* write one. But the pressure was way too much. The police told me I would be helping them to punish Trent, give him what he deserves. My lawyer said the same thing. But I didn't think I could, so I didn't do it. I didn't think I knew how at the time. I mean, I know what a victim impact statement is, but so many things were happening all around me, and I was so fucked up by what had just happened that I wanted to distance myself from the whole mess as far as possible.

A couple of sessions ago, Linda said she noticed in my file that I had refused to write one. I told her I didn't refuse; I just didn't know how to go about doing it. At the time I was terrified and confused, and I simply felt unable to. Mostly, I didn't want to hurt Trent more than I already had. I told

Linda that I wanted to just pretend it didn't matter, and even thinking about writing one felt overwhelming. I didn't have a clue where to begin or what to write. Linda took her time with me, like she always does. She pointed out a bunch of good reasons to write one and good reasons not to. Ultimately, she said if the victim impact statement wasn't helpful for me, then it was a waste of time, and to do it for anyone other than me was wrong.

She said that when the police get involved in a case of child abuse, they are so focused on getting the offender, making him pay as high a price as they can, that they often do so at the expense of the victim. Not intentionally. They do care about the victim and want what is best for her. But what they really want is to make the son of a bitch who committed the crime suffer as much as possible. And if that causes undue pain and suffering for the victim, it's a small price to pay for what they call justice. But Linda also said that what many people mean by justice is revenge. It's not completely their fault, she said. That's just how they're trained.

Linda tells me that when children or teens who have been abused first come forward, their whole world explodes. She's got that right. Suddenly your closely guarded secret is everyone's business. When it's a high-profile case, like a student with her guidance counselor, news and media get involved and it's overwhelming. Most people just freeze up. It's the brain's way of protecting us, she says. And when the object of exposure is something as personal and private as your sex life, it completely messes with your head. Yup, that's for sure.

Linda says at first when you think about writing something like a victim impact statement, it feels overwhelming. There's way too much coming at you. She says it's like eating an elephant.

"Do you know how to eat an elephant, Brianna?" I shake my head. "One bite at a time, just like a hamburger."

She also told me that writing a victim impact statement as soon as the abuse has been exposed is like reading chapters four and five of a twelve-chapter book. You have no idea what's going on or what the outcome is going to be. A victim impact statement written before the *impact* is just a statement.

She tells me she doesn't have a lot of faith in victim *statements* because they are usually so full of reaction and pain that they contain a lot of emotion but little truth. Describing what occurred in an abusive relationship doesn't describe the impact of that abuse. And how can anyone know the truth of the impact before it happens? Good question. She says that now, because it has been more than two years since Trent went to prison, I have felt much more of the impact and am far better equipped to write a statement that is both helpful and truthful. She's big on truth. Linda says that victim impact statements shouldn't be used to indict criminals; they should be used to help the victim heal. And that's why she thinks it might be a good idea for me to write one now.

So here goes . . .

> I went to see Mr. Reynolds for help, and I got hurt. I asked him to teach me how to be a better person, and he taught me how to give a blowjob. I trusted him with my innermost thoughts, and he used those thoughts to expose my vulnerability to his advantage. I wanted to learn to love myself better, and he taught me how to love him. He used his power to make me powerless.
>
> You taught me things I wasn't ready to learn. You made me feel things I wasn't ready to feel. You betrayed my trust and misled me. You convinced me it was love when it was only lust . . . I think.
>
> You made me a pariah in my school. I thought I was once confident and strong, and you made me doubtful and weak. People used to treat me like I was like them. When they see me now, they only see the girl who was fucked by the guidance counselor. Teachers are afraid of me, and I'm afraid of them. My dreams used to revolve around things I hoped to gain out of life, things I could do to make the world a better place. You made me dream of only you. I have to see a fucking shrink because of you.
>
> I have lost friends because of what you did to me. I have lost focus because of what you did to me. I used to think I knew exactly what I wanted out of life. Now all I think of

is you. I was a pretty honest person when I met you. You made me into a liar. All of the dozens and dozens—hundreds and hundreds—of lies I told to keep our secret turned me into something I despise. Mom and Dad and even Davy don't trust me because of what you did. I stopped living for myself so I could live through you. My life became your life, but did yours become mine?

I quit volleyball to spend my days with you. I gave up Saturday morning hot yoga because you wanted my heat next to you. I quit babysitting so I could be your baby. I gave up my best friends, Jenny and Amanda and Deb and Robbie, so I could be exclusively your best friend. I lied to them over and over to live the lie that was us. I wanted love, and you promised love, but did I really get it? Did you really give it?

I wish you could know the confusion that wracks my life. I find myself loving you and hating you at the same time. I bought everything you sold. I convinced myself that what we shared was real. Now I don't know if it ever was. I only wanted to be happy, and you only made me horny.

You took the most private part of my life and exposed it to the world. You promised to take care of me but then you left. You abandoned me. You pulled the rug out from under my feet and left me lying on my back naked, alone, and miserable. You stole my virginity, my innocence, and left me guilty and stained. You fed me and then left me starving for what I could no longer have. You opened my eyes and then left me blind. You gave me a taste of sweet nectar, but it has become bitter. You showed me how to stop and smell the roses, but they have withered and died. The melody we shared that was once music to my ears has become a cacophony of clamor. Our song has become my funeral dirge.

I'm in the midst of writing this victim impact statement when I realize several things. What began from a third-person perspective quickly became too personal to be left to a narrator, and suddenly I find myself writing as if Trent is right here with me and I'm able to tell him how much he really hurt me.

I'm not pissed, though, not even sorry, just utterly confused.

More importantly, I notice I don't have a clue whether or not these things I'm writing are true. I measure what I write carefully, well aware that I have promised to be honest with Linda and myself. But I can't even tell if I am. And I don't know how to tell if I am or if I'm just full of shit. God, this is so confusing.

I feel like I'm falling victim to the victim impact statement. It's supposed to be an accurate list of all the losses, all the pain, and all the damage that has been inflicted upon me. So I try to write from that perspective. I name this pain that is no doubt accurate, but it only reflects the action—the event—it doesn't reflect my reality, for I would gladly sacrifice all those things for what we shared.

So, I guess in some sense I'm being truthful, but only truthful to the details, not to the impact. So, is it an impact statement, or is it just a grocery list of pain and loss? I'm trying to separate my feelings from the facts.

This is far more difficult than I ever imagined, and it leaves this statement feeling empty and cold. Maybe it's not my statement that is cold and empty. Maybe the separation of feeling from fact leaves *me* feeling cold and empty. And maybe it's the separation from Trent that leaves me frozen—isolated—confused. That seems more like it.

I just can't do this. I'll ask Linda for some direction and trust that she can provide whatever I'm obviously missing. The more I try to write about the impact our relationship has had upon me, the more confused and frustrated I get. I hate the confusion but love the man who brought this mayhem into my life. And *that* is the honest-to-God truth. It's the only thing I know for certain.

You would think that after all this time, after all these losses, I would have a better grip on reality, a better understanding of the damage Trent has done, but I don't.

Time heals all wounds, they say. Who the fuck are "they"? Whoever they are, they know nothing of my wounds. Time heals? I doubt it. And if it does, how much time will it take?

Three minutes and fifty-seven seconds. I don't understand time. It seems to be one of life's greatest variables. When you want it to pass quickly, it drags like a weight, and when you want it to stand still, it races like children on their way to a parade. "Unforgettable," by Nat King Cole; that's our song, and I love it. But *my* song for us—my guilty pleasure—is "Love Story" by Taylor Swift. When I hear her sing about her forbidden love, she's singing about ours. And for three minutes and fifty-seven seconds, I'm Juliet awaiting Romeo.

I used to wait for him by the picnic area at Glen Echo Park. He would always text when he was about five minutes away. Then I would put in my earbuds and crank "Love Story." By the time he pulled up, I would be pretty much on the verge of tears and fully in love. It was a ritual, I suppose. I think that's the only thing I ever lied to Trent about. He would ask, "Whatcha listening to?" and I'd say, "Oh, the usual." Which, I suppose, wasn't a total lie 'cause I usually listened to it just before he came. But for some reason I didn't want to tell him. I don't know if it's because I thought he'd make fun of me for being a Swiftie, or if I thought he'd think it was dumb to be listening to a song about forbidden love, or maybe he would be offended that I considered "Love Story" equal to, or greater than, "Unforgettable." I don't know. What I do know is that I felt like Taylor Swift knew what I felt and that maybe we were the only two people in the whole wide world who knew that kind of love.

When we met at Glen Echo, we didn't just race off somewhere to make out like high school kids; we enjoyed the park and each other. One of our favorite spots was the bridge that spans the creek near the foot of the stairs along the main path. When the sun breaks through the treetops and reflects on the water, it's stunning. Sometimes we were like a little old married couple. Trent would bring a loaf of bread, and we'd dangle our feet off the bridge and feed the ducks and swans that gathered around. My favorite was Lame Duck—our name for her. She was a small mallard with a deformed beak, so she couldn't really pick up a piece of bread. I guess it was a bit like making fun of a disabled person, but it was funny.

We would toss a piece right at her, and she'd keep trying to pick it up until it got water-logged and sank. Then she'd look up at us and honk as if she was pissed off, and oh my God, we'd laugh.

I suppose that love comes and goes. Trent did. But as I sit here looking at this victim impact statement, trying to discern fiction from reality, it's memories like these that make it so difficult to discern. Where did we—he—cross the line? Was it wrong for us to be at Glen Echo Park together? Was it wrong to walk hand in hand through the trees? Was it wrong to feed the ducks with our pants rolled up and our feet dangling over the edge of the bridge? Was it wrong to laugh at Lame Duck's feeble efforts? (Yeah, that probably was.) Was it wrong to share the songs we loved or the places or the food, or the city? If so, at what point did it become so? What makes love forbidden? Taboo? Illegal? These are the questions that are getting in the way of me being able to see what others seem to see with such ease.

It's like when you're riding in a car and you're looking at the beautiful mountains in the distance, then a bug gets splattered across the windshield right where you're looking. You keep trying to see the beauty of the mountains, but your attention keeps getting drawn to the fucking bug spatter, and you can't fully enjoy the scenery because of the bug. That's what writing this victim impact statement is like. I'm trying to see it clearly, but there's this bug that keeps bugging me, keeps drawing me away from what I want to be doing—what I should be doing. I know I should think Trent is that bug on the windshield, but it feels much more like he's the beauty I can't see because of the bug that is this victim impact statement.

Linda says that having my "safe place" is a good idea, just as long as it doesn't become the party room for my wounded ego. What she means is that it's a good place for me to think, meditate, relax, and heal, but it shouldn't be the place I run away to, where I hide and wallow and feel sorry for myself. As I sit here tonight, looking at this task before me, I don't think I'm feeling sorry for myself. But then again, I'm not sure what I think. I think my effort at this statement stinks. I think I know what's expected of me, but in good conscience, I don't think I can do what Linda wants me to. I'm not giving up on the victim impact statement per se, but

I need some clarity, some direction. Linda knows a lot about this kind of stuff, so I doubt she'll be too pissed off at me if I tell her I kinda hit a wall. And she'll probably be able to help me. That's the type of thing Trent was always so good at too, helping me when I hit the wall.

I put my earbuds in and sing along.

So I sneak out to the garden to see you.
We keep quiet 'cause we're dead if they knew
So close your eyes,
Escape this town for a little while.

CHAPTER FORTY-ONE

Awareness exists. I'm emerging, like a bear from hibernation, from sleep, a state, a darkness that reveals another darkness. One from long ago. A hidden darkness, a deeper darkness. Pain, almost forgotten, now rises to the surface of my consciousness like a bubble, its face revealed.

I must tell him. He must know . . .

"DANIEL! DANIEL!" FEAR GREATER THAN any I have ever known and anything I would ever know grips me, holds me, paralyzes me. "Daniel!" I call until my throat aches. There's no response. Everything I know and love about my home, my life, and my world I grow to despise in this moment.

When you are born and raised on a farm, it's your blood. It's as much a part of you as you are of it. You can't survive without it any more than it could survive without you. Even when you leave, it keeps calling you home, like the whispering wind through the willows. *This way, over here,* it calls, and you know that's where you belong. It was my father's before it was mine and my grandfather's before it was his. But it will never be my son's.

The very thought of him stirs within me an anger so deep it rattles my bones. I'm born of this earth and borne to it, blood, sweat, and tears. For so many years, I longed for nothing more than to grow, live, and die upon and within this soil. But life, as it has a way of doing, can reduce a man to dust, can strip from him everything that gives life and reduce him to ashes. This land has so stripped me, and I weep for my loss, as I wept long years ago.

The day begins beautifully, pure, and crisp. There are moments in this space of unconsciousness when everything is as clear as the ice on that fair day, even though I look through this glass darkly. Daniel is my world. We love the farm as we love each other. He teaches me to fish and to hunt, to swim and to skate. I'm sure there are times when he wishes I would leave him alone, give him some space, some room to breathe, but he never says so. He never makes me believe I'm unwelcome, even when his friends all gather for Sunday afternoon hockey outside on the frozen pond. They might exclude me, but I can always count on Daniel to call my name.

I'm not particularly good at skating and even worse at hockey, but when the team captains are chosen, if Daniel is one, I'm always his first pick. That Sunday, I allow the goal that will see us, the Reynolds Renegades, defeated four to three by the Wailing Welshmen. Once the others all leave, Daniel tousles my hair and says, "It's okay, champ. We'll get 'em next week." But there would be no next week. Not for Daniel.

Muskrats build their dams along the edges of ponds, creeks, and rivers. In the winter, when the water freezes over, they keep the entrance open with twigs and sticks. The ice near them always remains thin. Daniel is skating behind me and keeps poking my butt with the end of his hockey stick and bugging me about how I, "the great Ken Dryden"—the goalie I pretend to be because, well, he was the best—could possibly let a puck moving as slowly as *that* through my legs. "And it was for the win," he chides.

He is only teasing me. He's not angry, and the little nudges he gives are those of affection more than anger or even disappointment. It bothers me, though, because I'm the one who cost us the game. Feeling slighted, I grab his stick and chuck it toward the edge of the pond.

"You threw it, go get it," he says. I oblige and take off after it. As I'm getting close, the ice beneath me gives way and I fall through. The sudden shock of the cold water takes my breath away. I'm unable to breathe, unable to speak, unable to call for help. I sink below the surface once, twice. Daniel is there in a flash. My head never bobs beneath the surface a third time. His strong arms lift my cold, wet body effortlessly out of the water.

I am safe.

Daniel skates over to where his hockey stick lies, bends over to grab it, stretching so as not to make the same mistake I did, as I huddle, knees to chest, shivering to the core. Then in the blink of an eye, he's gone. One moment he's there, the next he's not, like a magician's disappearing act. I look desperately for him. My brother, my world.

I shout.

I scream.

Nothing.

It's the sudden cold of shock and fear that is your greatest enemy in such moments. And it is the stories you hear of those who drown under the ice that paralyzes you when your head first dips beneath the frigid water. At that moment, it's so easy to become disoriented. One simple movement away from the hole, and you never find your way back. In the confusion that shock brings, your effort to correct your mistake and navigate back toward the opening unwittingly pushes and pulls you even farther away. Like when you're playing baseball as a fielder and a ball is hit in your direction. At first, you run toward the ball until you realize it was hit harder than you think, so you run backwards, but by that time it's too late, and the ball bounces behind you. Anyone watching from a distance sees exactly where you should go, but when you're in the middle of it, you have no way of knowing.

I can see him under the ice.

I know exactly where he needs to go to find his way out, but I'm powerless to help. I don't know whether he can see me, and I hope he can't. But for a single moment—and yet an eternity—I know our eyes lock.

The terror in his eyes haunts me to this day. And for far too long after that, each time I close mine, all I can see are his.

I could have saved Daniel, but like the baseball player, I react too late. At that moment I'm too cold, too confused, and too scared. I think about it now, just as I have thousands of times before, away from the moment, when you can think with some degree of logic. I could have lowered my stick through the hole in the ice and nudged him with it, the way he had been nudging me mere seconds before. He would have felt the nudge and grabbed the stick, just as I had. And he would be here now.

Mere seconds before, everything was fine. Like anyone who's been in a car accident will tell you, it all happens so quickly. We were playing hockey, the other kids went home, we were heading home, and then Daniel was gone.

Hours later, our father finds me skating around and around in dark circles, frozen to the core, well after the sun has dipped, like Daniel, beneath the horizon. Dad asks me where my brother is. I can't speak. My voice is gone from shock, from screaming, from crying.

At his funeral, our mother falls. The pain shared by each of us weighs upon her to the point of collapse. She can't stand above the weight of our loss. This is the birth of my father's hatred toward me. I begin to experience that hatred as he looks upon my mother, a crumpled mass, a mess. Hatred that I have carried over to my son.

At thirteen years old, Daniel's life was over. At ten, mine felt as though it was too. I killed my brother. It's my fault, of that there is no question. I threw his hockey stick. I made him come to rescue me. Because I needed saving, he died. There's nothing I can ever do, nothing I ever will do, to make up for that.

I play the scene over in my head so many times it makes me dizzy. If only I had closed my feet a split second sooner, I would have saved the goal and been the hero. Daniel would not have been smacking me on the butt with his stick, and I would not have grabbed and thrown it. I would not have had to retrieve it, I would not have fallen through, Daniel would not have had to save me, and he would not have fallen through. It would have been just another Sunday afternoon on the farm. We would have sat down to a wonderful roast beef dinner, like always, and life would have been, as it always had been, perfect.

But I threw Daniel's hockey stick.

WHEN HE WAS BORN, TRENT looked so much like the baby pictures of Daniel that Mom kept everywhere. As he grew, he looked more and more like him. The same blond curls, the same smile, the same laugh. Everything about him is a reminder of Daniel. Daniel, my brother, do you still feel the pain? Every time I look at him, I see Daniel. God, I miss Daniel. Lord, I miss him so much.

I think—no, I'm certain—that from the moment Trent was born, he was a constant reminder of how desperately I missed Daniel. How desperately I wanted him back. He was a constant reminder that I'm the reason Daniel died. As he grew and became more like Daniel, I despised him more. He would treat his sister with the same love and compassion that Daniel had shown me, and I would hate him for it. I would look upon him and see only Daniel.

I made a choice—I'm sure it was before he was three years old—that he would never replace Daniel, that he would never know of Daniel. And that he would never be Daniel. I wanted him dead. I despised him. Each time I looked at his face, it was like Daniel was mocking me, pointing at me, accusing me: *Gerry, you let me die. I died for you. You killed me, Gerald. You, you, you!*

It was nothing planned. I didn't want to hate my son. I didn't want to hurt him. I only wanted Daniel, the brother I had lost. And Trent would never replace him. Never. And so, every good thing he ever did—ever would do—I took from him.

Everything he does, I compare it to Daniel, and he can't hold a candle to my brother. He's not as smart. He's not as skilled. He's not as loving or as strong or as helpful or as good of a brother—or person—as Daniel. He's a terrible son compared to Daniel, just as was I in my father's eyes. From the moment Daniel died, I could never measure up. Neither can Trent. The more he acts like Daniel, the more I despise him, and they're so alike in almost every way. I feel like somehow he knows who Daniel was, like he knows Daniel better than I, and that stirs within me a deeper hatred and contempt toward him. In every glimpse of Trent, I see Daniel, and I hate him.

It caused something inside of me to react violently. The older he grew, the more the hatred rose. On his fourteenth birthday, when he was for the first time older than Daniel would ever live to be, I hurt him bad. If Daniel wasn't alive, Trent didn't deserve to be.

Trent had wanted to spend the day with friends. It was his birthday, after all, and what kid wants to spend the day hauling bales with his old man on his birthday? So that's exactly what I decided Trent would do. All day long I threw bales at him hard enough to knock him over, and a few times right off the bale wagon. I would drive the tractor forward a few feet, stop, get off, and throw the bales that were lying in the field up to Trent, who was standing on the bale wagon. It was his job to stack them in columns. It was important that each row be straight so the top row wouldn't fall over. Trent could never make them straight enough for me. He could have used a level and plumb line, and it wouldn't have pleased me. When the hay wagon was piled as high as he could reach, which was not as high as they should have been, we would head back to the hay shed to restack them and then start the entire process all over again.

We were on what would be our last trip of the day. I had effectively taken the entire day from him. As the sun was setting, we pulled into the shed. Trent was exhausted. We climbed to the top of the stack in the loft of the shed, far above the floor. He was standing at the edge of the stack nearest the last of the hay bales. I was operating a block and tackle rigging system that allowed me to grab a bale and glide it from one end of the shed to the other. It required little effort to swing the bale from my end to his. A little shove would easily do the job. With the final bale of our load in place, I put all the strength I could muster behind the bale. It hit Trent with such force, it knocked him off the stack and out of the loft. I heard the heavy impact of his body hitting the hard-packed dirt some twenty feet below. I didn't really want to kill the boy, not at that time anyway; I only wanted to teach him that although he might be older than my brother ever was—the uncle he didn't even know had existed—he would never replace him.

When Louise returned home from the hospital that night, she told me that Trent had suffered a fractured collarbone and a serious concussion. They were going to keep him in for a few days for observation. I wasn't disappointed; I was relieved. He remained alive to torment. Happy birthday, Trent.

AS I'M WAKING UP, AN awakening begins.

I emerge attempting to comprehend what kind of monster would do this to his son. I'm nauseated. I spent my life tormented, first by the loss of my brother and then by the horrendous acts I carried out upon my son. Each act of undeserved hatred I would inflict upon Trent now eats a little deeper into my soul. It consumes and destroys all sense of manhood. What kind of father could do this?

Self-hatred rages through my being like bitter poison.

Is there a road back? Is it possible to make up for the horrendous man—I can't use that word; no *man* would ever do what I have done—demon I have become? If I could live a dozen lifetimes, I couldn't repair the devastation my actions have wrought. This comprehension leaves me undone. I long to scream, "Forgive me, please. I'm so deeply, profoundly, penetratingly, severely, intensely sorry," but I know the emptiness, the futility of those words. Yet I long to tell him. I have to tell him. He must know.

My daughter, all that remains that is good, comes to me in these dreams. She speaks to me words of love and compassion, of joy and hope. I see her clearly as though I could reach out and touch her, as she can me. And she does. She touches me. Each touch brings warmth and love. With each stroke of her hand upon my brow, I melt, and this barren land that holds me becomes a little less so. I hunger for her touch like a wolf for its prey. Her touch is here. It's real; I feel it, then it's gone, and the darkness overtakes me again.

Strangers come. They poke and prod and move me. I think they're trying to help, but I resist. I see faces, some familiar, others not. They come and go, just as I do. I'm aware that I'm not physically coming and going. Somehow I'm aware that I'm unable to move, but I keep coming and going from one state, one reality, to another. I'm unable to choose where I come from or where I go to. When my mind retreats toward distant memories, I attempt to flee like a dog from a cruel master. I'm aware, however, that I'm the cruel master, and it's from my very self that I wish to flee. In and out of this dream-wake state.

CHAPTER FORTY-TWO

It was probably well after midnight when I got up to pee. I heard noises, unfamiliar sounds, coming from Trent's room. The old boiler in our farmhouse made a lot of clunking and clanging. I'm sure that's why they didn't hear the squeaking floorboards under my footsteps. I poked my head into his room and froze, transfixed by the puzzling scene before me. At thirty-five, I would have known exactly what was going on, but as a child, I didn't have the foggiest idea. So I watched. It was dark. The only light came from a large sodium-vapor lamp outside in the yard. Trent's bed was a silhouette against the window. My first thought was, *Charlie's bouncing up and down, playing with Trent,* although the noise I had heard was definitely not canine. I was about to say something when I heard Jimi make an unholy, guttural moan. I knew immediately it was him by the tone. He made similar sounds when laughing really hard. I stood mesmerized. He moved up and off Trent, the covers fell back, and his erection was fully exposed against the light from the yard. I had never seen a man with an erection before, and I didn't know such a thing was even possible. When you're an eight-year-old girl, just to see a boy's penis dangling like a deflated balloon from where his "front bum" is supposed to be is weird enough. The idea that it could get hard and point straight up had never dawned on me. Then he laid down and covered himself and Trent. That's when I heard the whimpering. This time I thought for sure it was Charlie, whimpering like he had when his nose was full of porcupine quills. "Shhh.

You're okay, Trent. You're okay. Now go to sleep." Jimi stroked Trent's head, whispered to him, and tried to settle him.

Back in my bedroom, I tried to put together the scene I had just witnessed. Nothing made sense. I imagined that perhaps Trent had hurt himself and Jimi was trying to help him. I imagined Jimi perhaps beating him for wetting the bed, like Dad had done so often, and that would make sense because he would have peed all over Jimi, and that certainly would have made him mad. What I finally carried into the sleep that was rapidly overtaking me was that Trent must have had a nightmare, and Jimi was comforting him so they could both get back to sleep. Yeah, that must have been it. I could sleep with that.

THE DRIVE HOME FROM BRIAR Ridge is always difficult. It's the time I'm usually hit with the reality that my brother is in prison. Somehow it's so easy to put the notion right out of my head. If anyone knew Trent the way I know him, they would find it as inconceivable as I do. But today, after hearing Trent tell the horrors of Jimi's actions, I'm beyond distraught. Robert keeps looking over at me, probably trying to figure out if I'm on the verge of an emotional collapse. I wish he would stop looking and just pay attention to the highway.

We have timed the trip from the 270 onto the 33 as well as when we take Highway 22 across to the 23, then straight through town, bypassing the 270. It's about twenty minutes longer via this route, but today I don't care. "Please take the long way home," I ask—I demand. I suppose when I asked Trent the question, I had prepared myself for . . . I don't know what I had prepared myself for, certainly not for what I heard. Maybe that Jimi had fondled him the way Trent and I had each other—a bit of childish experimentation, I don't know. What I do know is that nothing could have prepared me for what Trent told me.

Our bedrooms on the farm were right next to each other. In fact, had there been no wall, our beds would have pretty much been touching. As I remember now all the sounds and bumps that I heard and felt over the four years that Jimi lived with us, on and off while his marriage was in the shitter, I'm dumbstruck.

As a kid, the sleeping arrangement really didn't strike me as completely unreasonable. There were only three beds in our house. Mom and Dad shared one, I was a girl, and boys don't sleep with girls until they're married (everyone knows that), so that left Trent's bed. It was not even questioned where Jimi would sleep the first night he showed up with his little suitcase in his hand and a tear in his eye.

Some nights after Jimi moved in, I heard rustling, moving around, thumping, and even grunts and groans coming from Trent's room but never thought much of it. As time goes by, you get used to noise. It fades into the background and eventually you don't notice it. Ask anyone who lives near John Glen International. After a while, they'll tell you, you don't even hear the planes.

Mom and Dad's bedroom was downstairs on the main floor and on the other side of the house, so it's not surprising that they never heard anything, even the times when the wall next to me would thump, thump, thump, sometimes for ten minutes or more. The little girl I was knew that somehow, something was amiss, but I had no idea what and could not, for the life of me, figure it out. As we grew older, I might have put two and two together had Trent given any indication as to what was going on. But there was nothing in his behavior or mannerisms to suggest anything was out of the ordinary.

He never cried wolf.

I sit here, looking through my tears at the snow coming down, making the world pure again, and think, what a farce. There's nothing pure about it. I think about the clues, or lack thereof, and wonder whether I'm looking for a way to justify my ignorance. If I didn't know, couldn't have known, then there was nothing I could have ever done to help. I want this to be true. I don't want to think, not even for a split second, that there's some way I could have known, something I could have done.

And I wish I didn't know now what I didn't know then.

When we were children, I once asked Trent if Jimi hurt him, and he told me to shut up and mind my own business, so I never asked again.

I try to imagine what it was like for Trent to have someone so powerful have such complete control over him. I try to imagine Trent fighting to save his own sanity, his purity. He was never a fighter, though. I try to imagine Trent's victim feeling the way Trent did in Jimi's clutches, and I cannot fathom it for even a moment. Did she feel the same way?

When Trent was in high school, grade ten I believe, he would often stand up against the kids in his class who would pick on Raymond Clark. Ray had terrible acne, and his breath and his body odor were often overpowering. Trent didn't particularly like Ray; it wasn't like they were pals and hung out or anything, but he couldn't stand by and watch the others pick on him either, so he often came to Ray's defense. The problem with that was twofold. One, Trent became the target of abuse in the same manner as Ray was. Two, Ray began to think of Trent as his friend, and this association was not something that Trent relished.

During gym class one day, a group of guys were standing in a small circle, six of them and Trent. Trent had a pack of gum and offered a stick to each of the guys. There were only seven pieces in the pack. Raymond was standing just beyond the circle, which was his usual place, an attempt to pretend he was welcome without being overtly present. Trent pulled the last stick of gum out of the pack for himself and was about to pull the wrapper off when he noticed Raymond. He tore the piece in half and gave half to Raymond. Trent says it was really no big deal, but Ray just glowed. For a moment he was one of the guys. That lasted for about ten seconds before the taunting from the very guys to whom Trent had given gum began.

"Reynolds, what the fuck, man?"

"Why the fuck would you give a piece to Reeking Ray?"

"What are you two, fags?"

In my estimation, that small act was one of Trent's finest moments, and I love him for doing it. It wasn't enough, though, and Trent held on to that for years.

Raymond took his own life the summer between grades ten and eleven. While he never spoke about it, I know Trent well enough to know that he wishes he would have done more—truly befriended Ray, perhaps. But he was the only one who stuck up for Ray. He often stood up for others but never for himself. And I suppose that is why he's never said anything about Jimi.

I also think that he may have been afraid to tell anyone. Dad would probably never believe him, and for Trent to even suggest to Dad that his best friend was sexually abusing him might have sent him into a flying rage.

The thing that keeps haunting me, however, and the thing I don't want to do, is allow this new knowledge to change the fact that Trent's abuse explains or justifies his behavior, his own abusive nature. It doesn't. But God, I wish it did. I could jump into Trent's corner and be his champion. "It's not his fault! The devil—Jimi—made him do it." But I can't go there. I will not go there. Robert would never let me, and what fills me with so much love for Trent is that he would never let me either. As far as I know, Trent has never blamed anyone but himself for his crime. He's not an altruist, but he is a realist.

ROBERT, THE BOYS, AND I have been spending most every evening at Glendale with Dad.

"Miracle: ˈmirək(ə)l· *noun*· a highly improbable or extraordinary event, development, or accomplishment that brings very welcome consequences." That fits, even though the medical team who hover over him, now unceasingly, won't use that term. To me, it's the word that most aptly describes what's going on with Dad. He can talk. He can move. He pushes his call button, interminably. This drives the nurses crazy. But a few short weeks ago, he was, for all intents and purposes, dead. Today, he is very much alive. So I'm going with miracle.

When Dad first began to wake, there was little evidence of much cognitive activity. His brain patterns were anything but normal. MRIs reveal scattered lines of activity exploding in every direction, jumping and sputtering like a car whose engine is flooded. You keep cranking it, the ignition is firing, but the connection isn't quite being made, so it won't run. Once it does start, it sputters and coughs and chokes before things begin to settle down and run smoothly. That's how Doctor Morrow explained it. And while Dad's "engine" is certainly not running smoothly, the pinging, rattling, and knocking settle a bit each day. Surprisingly, his heart—sometimes it's easy to forget that that's what started the whole situation in the first place—is relatively well. They inserted a pacemaker, and things seem to be functioning within the "acceptable range," whatever that is.

A physiotherapist has begun strenuous activity with his limbs. Because Dad has been immobile for months, his muscles have atrophied. Before he is able to attempt to walk again or even hold anything, there is much recovery to be done. So, three times a day, she comes in and works his fingers, his hands, each of his joints, and pulls his arms and legs into contortionist positions, all to help him regain mobility. He fights it at times, but at others he resigns himself to her care. I think he enjoys her soft, smooth skin touching his. He also has a speech therapist who is helping him form words, articulate and enunciate, so he can carry on more intelligible conversation.

Stevie has a much shorter attention span than Aaron, which doesn't always serve him well during our visits. Dad's speech is often slurred, at times almost incomprehensible. I'm not sure whether this has to do with his cognitive impairment, the medications he's on, or both, but it makes it difficult to understand him, and if you're not paying full attention, it's easy to misunderstand what he's saying. While Dad was receiving an invasive procedure, we were all waiting outside his room when Stevie asked, "What kind of medicine do they give Grandpa for his sore ass?"

"What?" Robert inquired, more shocked by the question than the inappropriate noun.

"Grandpa said he doesn't like the medicine he has to take for his sore ass," Stevie said, somewhat incredulous, as though we had missed the entire conversation.

The light eventually went on. "Oh, Stevie," Robert says when he finally stops laughing. "It's medicine they give Grandpa to relieve pressure around his *thorax*."

Dad rarely remembers our conversations. I have told him many times what happened, explained about his heart attack. At times he seems to understand, at others, not so much. He wonders where Mom is, wonders why she hasn't come to see him. Each time I tell him she's dead, it's as if he's hearing it for the first time. He becomes distraught, as though they'd actually shared something worth caring about, which they hadn't in almost a decade. I try to explain to him that they had been divorced for years before she died, and they'd had little to do with each other for quite some time. That doesn't seem to compute.

He wonders who is taking care of the farm and doing the chores. "Make sure to keep the bull out of the pasture. That horny bastard'll kill the cows." I try to explain that we no longer have cows or the farm and that he lives in four different places: a house here in the city, a beach house in Miami, his villa in Spain, and his yacht. Trying to get him to comprehend this is often an exercise in futility. His mind can't grasp much of what is going on or even who he is.

He talks about people long gone, some of whom I have never heard of. He refers to someone called Daniel. I have no idea who Daniel is, yet Dad speaks of him as though they share an inseparable bond.

Mostly, though, he talks about Trent. He asks for him continually. "Where's my boy? I miss my son so very, very much. I need to talk to Trent. I have to tell him . . . He must know . . ." Whenever Dad talks about Trent, it's as if they had the kind of father-son relationship you only see in movies, like Marlin and Nemo in that movie my boys liked so much. I only told him once that Trent is in prison. It upset him so much that I'm hesitant to broach the subject again. So, when he asks now, I tell him that Trent is away and will come as soon as he can.

I have no idea what to tell Trent. I'm sure it would piss him off to hear that Dad suddenly seems interested in him.

THE WORST STORM WE EVER had on the farm was during the summer I was in grade eight. There was a record-breaking heat wave for almost three weeks before it finally broke. To protect the cows from the intense heat, Dad kept as many as possible in the barn, shaded from the relentless sun. The storm hit late in the afternoon, building from the west and creeping toward the farm.

That unforgettable day began to cool rapidly. As it cooled, hail began to fall. Gently at first. Trent and I went outside as much to cool off as to gather the hailstones that were beginning to pile up in the yard. We had no idea this was the making of a full-blown, category-four tornado, but Dad suspected it. For the first time in weeks, the wind began to blow. As it did, a wall of cloud formed and stretched from the ground right up to the blackening sky. Its edges were tinged with a menacing dark green. And then, as quickly as it arose, the wind and hail stopped, and it became eerily quiet. Mom called for us to come inside. We ran to the house, where Mom and Dad were preparing for the worst. Dad had closed all the shutters, and Mom had stuffed old blankets and towels in the cracks of the walls and under the door jambs, where the wind often blew in on cold winter days. Dad said we needed to go to the cellar and wait it out.

I have always hated the cellar. There are no stairs; we use a ladder to crawl up and down. It's dark and dank and smells of rotting potatoes. There are only three lights in the basement, and you have to pull a string to turn them on and off, but you can't turn the one below the trapdoor on until you're in the hole. I hate it.

Once we're in the cellar, it begins. We hear the rain and hail begin to fall again, like the hoofbeats of a thousand cows—a stampede hammering away at the walls of the house. The wind builds to an ear-piercing crescendo. At that moment, the lights flicker and fail. Dad sends Trent back up to find the flashlight he forgot to bring down. Trent retrieves it and begins to climb back down the ladder when Dad says, "Get your ass out to the barn and check on the cows."

As Trent's dark silhouette disappears from view, the wind shakes the entire house—and my heart—as the door opens and then shuts. Moments later, a cacophony of ear-splitting booms drowns out the wind and the thundering rain. The banging eventually stops, but the wind and rain continue. It's thirty minutes of continual bombardment before the storm subsides.

Once it stops, we climb out of our dungeon, and Dad pulls on his big rubber boots and heads out to examine the damage. The barn remains standing, although one wall is pretty much gone. He finds it the next morning, resting between the fence and the house. Two cows are dead, and Trent is nowhere to be found. Mom and I are hysterical. Dad, not so much.

When Trent gets home after ten o'clock that evening, Mom is so relieved, she bursts into tears, but Dad is livid. Dad's pissed because two of his cows are dead, and it was somehow Trent's responsibility to ensure their safety. Trent says nothing, but his place in the family is firmly established. He gets the message loud and clear—Dad's fucking cows have more value than his son.

Now, how am I supposed to tell him that Dad keeps calling out to see his beloved son?

Doctor Morrow explains that these types of cognitive distortions are to be expected, and Dad may or may not ever be able to remember things as they actually are. So I hold his hand and tell him how much I love him and how happy I am—we all are—that he's doing so well.

He fawns over my boys when they come with us to see him, as though they are the most precious little guys in the world. Before this, Dad was always cold and aloof toward them. "Children should be seen and not heard, or better yet, *not* seen and *not* heard," had always been Dad's modus operandi. Now he's compassionate and kind. I like this new side of him. The boys also love this newfound affection their grandpa shows them. They revel in it.

TONIGHT, AS I LIE CLOSE to Robert, snuggling in his arms, I chuckle. The chuckle turns into a giggle, then into gales of laughter. Robert asks multiple times what's so funny, but I can't get it out. When I'm finally able to control myself, I roll toward him and ask as sincerely as I can, "How's *your* sore ass, Robert?" We both roll in fits of uncontrollable laughter.

Laughter, after these long months of intense pain, is just the medicine I need for my wounded heart.

CHAPTER FORTY-THREE

Once again, I'm becoming far more familiar with the infirmary than I would like. I feel like shit much of the time. The nursing staff say it's a reaction to the medication I'm taking for this disease that exists within me. They have changed my entire regimen. I'm told that in a week or two, I should feel like a new man. God, I hope so. Between spending as much time as I do on the toilet—where much of my introspective work is currently being accomplished (turns out I *can* multitask after all)—in the infirmary, visiting with Claire—which is the best part of this miserable existence—and Doctor Thackery's office, I have little time for much else. Who would have ever thought that time in prison could go as quickly as it does these days?

My release is just months away, and it feels as though crossing out days on the calendar is finally making a difference.

As I prepare for life on the other side of these walls, I have a sense that I will get there a better man than the one who came in here, perhaps a better man than I have ever been. A short while ago I thought my progress had little to do with me and everything to do with Doctor T. I'm beginning to realize that I'm as responsible for my well-being as for my misery. So I take some credit for the hard work I have done and this new man I'm becoming.

Prison, any prison, will destroy a man if he allows it. And I have, for far too long. It has much to do with my intrinsic need for self-pity and self-sabotage. But this too is beginning to recede, like a ship on the horizon. Attitude, as I'm learning, can alter one's entire outlook. "Everything can be taken from a man but one thing: the last of the human freedoms—to choose one's attitude in any given set of circumstances." Viktor Frankl's breakthrough work in logotherapy is helping to reshape my warped sense of perception. This therapeutic approach was developed through his experience as a concentration camp prisoner in Auschwitz and Dachau. I am one beneficiary of his suffering.

I spend long hours each day immersed in meditative practices, positive self-talk, reading, and journaling. These exercises cleanse my mind, allowing years of distortion to float away like debris in a current. They leave me able to view life from a much healthier place than ever before.

I'm not even as hostile toward Gerald as I once was. And I never imagined for a moment that that was even remotely possible. Sometimes I get pissed at myself for even considering not hating Gerald with all that is within me. Then I'm reminded of what a controlling force that hatred has been in my life, and I'm once again grateful for this new perspective.

I had convinced myself that hating Gerald was the one thing in my life I had zero control over. I'm astonished how this hatred, which has consumed me for a lifetime, is actually controllable. Not that I ever want anything to do with the man; I certainly do not. But that the very thought of him no longer turns my stomach is a win for me. Who he is and what he has done no longer devours me.

On that front, there have been multiple recent developments. Gerald has been making great strides in his cognitive awareness. Apparently, his mind is as sharp and abhorrent as it ever was. He is learning to do life again. He can feed himself. While he can't dress himself or walk yet, it's only a matter of time. Claire is looking to place him in a private, long-term care facility, where I am sure he will have an entire complement of staff to cater to his every whim, twenty-four/seven.

There is a bigger development than that, though: I have taken a stand against Gerald. While it involves doing nothing, it may be the most proactive and perhaps cathartic thing I could ever do.

I have chosen not to have Claire intercept the letters I sent.

This decision was not made lightly. Doctor Thackery and I have weighed the pros and cons. There are many very good reasons for not allowing Gerald to get his hands on them. There is but one good reason for allowing him to: it will be the single biggest act of bravery I have ever taken against him. I have allowed Gerald to shit upon me my entire life. I don't know why he hates me so much, and I don't care. However, I think it's important for him to know what his hatred has done to me. I expect nothing from him in return. In fact, if he were to respond, I might never acknowledge it. His reaction means little to me. But he should know.

The reason Doctor T had me write the letters was for me. The process had little to do with Gerald. It was a venting exercise, a place for *me* to express *my* anger, *my* rage, and *my* hurt, nothing more. His receiving the letters does nothing to take away from the purpose of the exercise. In fact, it brings a small measure of solace to think that, as unlikely as it is, he might recognize the devastating effect his brutality has wrought in my life. Again, however, I have no expectations from him in return.

Expectations are deadly. When you tell someone you love them, you *expect* to hear, "I love you too." When you help a little old lady across the street, you *expect* to hear her say, "Thank you, sonny." When you spend your entire day helping your father organize his workspace, you *expect* to receive acknowledgement for a job well done. When none comes, it removes the desire to help again. When you expect to be disappointed and instead receive endorsement, it's a pleasant surprise. When it comes to Gerald, I have learned to never expect validation. I have not been disappointed.

Something is happening inside of me, as if I'm emerging from a lifetime of sleep. Not sleep, per se, but something is waking in me that brings with it new life, new hope.

When a newborn cub emerges from its den in the spring after winter's hibernation, she sees a world that for her had never existed. I feel something of this. Aware that my emergence from this place is yet a winter away, nonetheless, I have hope. Hope for a spring thaw that will bring with it a world of unforeseen and unexpected beauty. This is not to be confused with any form of expectation. Hope and expectation, as much as they may seem similar, are juxtaposed. Expectation anticipates based upon probability. Hope lies inside unconfident possibility without promise. My hope is that exodus from this place will coincide with a fresh beginning, that this purpose of which I'm learning so much about will serve as a catalyst for new adventures.

There are certain realities I must accept, however. I will never again be employed in a position of trust. The education, expertise, and experience from a lifetime in the mental health and education community will be as useful to me as this disease that lurks within.

Which brings about another consideration. I'm still a youngish man, by many standards. I will need to adjust to the fact that I will never again have a sexual relationship with any sense of normalcy. In the environment where I currently reside, this poses little concern. However, once these walls are nothing more than a sad reminder of choices poorly made, this will surface as an unwelcome reality. My heart sinks like an anchor at this awareness. And this sadness leads me directly to thoughts of Brianna.

Sundays had become "our day." We lied, moved scheduled activities, and rearranged our lives to make it happen. Nothing would keep us apart on that sacred day. It was often the only full day of the week we could spend together. We filled those days with music, reading, dancing, cooking, eating, and lovemaking. We shared a compatibility and comfort I have never known with another woman. It's the fond memories of days with Brianna that fill me with dread when I think of my positive diagnosis. I have attempted to push this into the recesses of my mind, but the closer I am to life on the outside, the more difficult it is to keep it there.

I don't delude myself that life outside of here will yield Brianna; it most certainly will not. But that I may one day again have the opportunity for a sexual relationship is a reasonable probability. With HIV, however, everything changes. I find it interesting that Doctor Thackery rarely talks about this aspect of my life, even though we seem to cover almost everything else.

I say I *think* of the possibility of a relationship other than one with Brianna, but that very thought leaves me cold. I have no longing to be with another. This is something that Doctor Thackery and I have explored at length. He has proposed a deep hypnotherapy technique that he would like to attempt. He feels confident it will help me break the intense emotional attachment with her that I can't seem to overcome. He believes a kinetic bond, or something of that nature, has been established between us that he may be able to help remove. If I want to.

Of course, the correct answer is obvious: "When can we start?" But the truth is that I like these thoughts and memories of Brianna that I can't shake. And while it may be better not to have them pulling and calling me like a sinful temptation, I enjoy them. They give me a sense of, for lack of a better word, *manhood.* Having been under the good doctor's care for as long as I have, this should immediately raise red flags. The fact that it doesn't should sound the alarm and be all the more reason to consider his proposal.

In good moments, I know that life would be better if thoughts of her didn't consume me. But I often feel like they are the very thing that keeps me sane in this place. In the deepest part of who I am, I recognize the futility of this thinking and know full well that the best thing for Brianna and me would be to submit to this treatment. And so, with a heavy heart and a sigh of despair, I will. God knows I don't want to, which is all the more reason that I must.

CHAPTER FORTY-FOUR

The chief medical investigator asked me to accept a new patient. I wasn't reluctant to agree, as her condition is of particular interest to my current field of study. The patient, an eighteen-year-old female victim of child sexual abuse, displays evidence of psychic union disorder. Her case has been highly publicized in the *Dispatch* as well as in many local news broadcasts. The abuse occurred at the hands of the guidance counselor at Glenwood High School, who is currently serving his prison sentence in Briar Ridge. The victim, Brianna Barnes, had been receiving counsel and support from the offender over a period of five months. She was fifteen years of age when the abuse began. The abuse lasted for just under a year. A motor vehicle accident brought the abuse to light, and the offender was charged and shortly thereafter prosecuted.

Prior to my involvement, the victim had been the patient of a social worker, where the emphasis seemed to be more upon the victim's sexual exploits than her sexual exploitation. When this came to the attention of the chief medical investigator, Brianna was immediately removed from the social worker's caseload and placed into mine.

Brianna is a well-spoken, intelligent young woman who found herself groomed by the victim and falling in love with him. The offender's file suggests that while he has admitted his crime and has accepted full responsibility for the abuse, he too declares that he remains deeply in love with the victim. Dialogue with the offender's psychiatrist, Doctor

Edmond Thackery, has revealed that while his patient is making significant progress in cognitive awareness and rehabilitation, Thackery believes psychic union disorder is a contributing factor in the slow remediation of the offender's affection for the victim.

Doctor Thackery and I have approached our respective patients with the recommendation of using neural hypnotherapy as a method to disrupt the psychic union and expedite the healing process. Interestingly, both patients, while having the cerebral discernment to understand why this technique could be integral to their healing, have shown resistance to its implementation. This, of course, serves to corroborate the diagnosis.

I have attempted to validate Brianna's authentic feelings for the offender and have emphasized that the hypnotherapeutic process would not stop the love shared between them; it would simply provide the cognitive strength for each of them to choose a healthier path. I further emphasized this by illustrating that the recommended therapeutic approach is not the opposite of a "love potion" and has no ability to make them fall "out of love" with each other. It will only provide her with a clearer understanding of the effects of psychic union disorder and, therefore, give her the ability to make her own decisions, which is something she seems incapable of doing. This awareness has allowed her to relax and give greater consideration toward the treatment.

In a recent session, I suggested Brianna write a victim impact statement as therapeutic homework. As I suspected, it revealed substantial evidence to support the PUD hypothesis. Throughout the impact statement, she wavers between emotion and fact. She displays tremendous insight into her abuse and then immediately attempts to rationalize it by the love shared between her and the offender. She came to me very frustrated and, in her words, "Completely confused about how to write this fucking thing."

After reading as much of the statement as she had written, I asked Brianna whether we could talk about what was going on in her head and heart as she wrote. She revealed a depth of insight that is rare in such a young person. I applauded the effort and energy she had invested into such an accurate depiction of the impact. Her response was that the impact statement hardly even made sense. "It jumps from here to there, from truth to lies, from love to hate. It's just a confusing mess."

"Yes, it is," I replied. Then I explained to her something so glaringly obvious that she had been unable to recognize it. "While you're digging, searching, and fabricating to find all the 'proper' signs of abuse, the truth has been screaming at you." She was still confused, so I asked her to list some things that culture suggests are indicators of child abuse. This she could do easily: unwanted sexual advances, threatening to harm the victim or loved ones if the abuse is revealed, forced sexual exploitation, and the list went on.

"Did you encounter any of these with Trent?"

"No."

"What did you experience?" I could see the wheels turning. She had written it dozens of times throughout her victim impact statement but had yet to make the connection.

"I don't know!" she finally said in exasperation. "I just felt so confused."

"Bingo," I said.

"What?"

"Why do you think that sexual abuse has to be all about the sex?"

"Doesn't it?"

"What do you think?" We spent considerable time on this topic. We were able to agree that the greatest impact her relationship with the offender has had upon her is complete and utter confusion.

And this too is abuse.

Confusion is a dis-ease of knowledge. I have a hypothesis regarding this that I often see in my practice, yet the cause is such a new phenomenon that for it to have a label is still years away. Nevertheless, I foresee a day when cerebral-limbic imbalance syndrome will be included in the DSM. The contributing factors of C-LIS have not been scientifically studied, and the compilation of data will be years in the making. Nevertheless, I have witnessed such a shift in cerebral thinking patterns within my patients that I must conclude the hypothesis has some merit.

The limbic system is a complex array of nerves and networks in the brain, involving several areas near the edge of the cortex, and is primarily concerned with instinct and mood. It controls basic emotions—fear, pleasure, and anger—as well as basic drivers: hunger, sex, dominance, and care of offspring.

The cerebral cortex is the largest region of the cerebrum in the brain, and it plays a key role in memory, attention, perception, cognition, awareness, thought, language, and consciousness. The two are inextricably linked.

In this information age, the cerebral cortex receives information at a rate unprecedented in history. Each of us holds within our pockets a device that gives us instant answers to concrete questions: what is the temperature in Bangkok? How many US dollars in a euro? What is the preferable wine with lobster thermidor? The point is, this influx of knowledge stored in the cerebral cortex was not acquired via neural pathway connections. We skipped a critical step. We didn't learn anything; we simply gathered knowledge. In a sense, the conscious mind is becoming like a spoiled rich kid, getting anything she wants without having to work for it. This, of course, has consequences. In society, we see it played out regularly. Some have gone so far as to associate it with "affluenza." But it goes far beyond such a careless portmanteau, which is only symptomatic of a much deeper root cause.

While the cerebral cortex is fed this diet of data, the limbic system attempts to keep up. And this is where things take a turn. Every acquisition of consciousness demands emotional input. The temperature in Bangkok will elicit some form of emotional reaction, albeit perhaps very small: "God, it's 104 degrees. Sure glad I'm not there" or "I could handle that for a while." Our limbic system has a say in every message our cerebral cortex receives.

The sheer volume of knowledge entering our heads at unprecedented rates is causing cognitive distortions within the limbic system. Serotonin released with each new influx of knowledge shoots through our brains, looking for something to attach itself to, and finally, finding nothing of reason, seeks the most reasonable facsimile and settles there. The result is an emotional state of utter confusion. We feel sad about the very things we should feel happy about and often happy about the things that should bring us misery.

The preferred current medical solution is selective serotonin reuptake inhibitors, which are designed to bring a sense of balance to our lives by making us, for lack of a better term, catatonic. This wonder drug, "Fuckitol," relieves all symptoms associated with our emotional imbalance and induces a zombie-like state.

The more the limbic system is forced to find an answer to this unsolvable riddle, the more ground it loses. Consequently, the limbic system atrophies while the cerebral cortex artificially and exponentially grows. The way this plays itself out in our culture is through misunderstanding, misinterpretation, and confusion about matters that should be glaringly obvious. If my hypothesis is correct, Brianna may be as much a victim of cerebral-limbic imbalance syndrome as she is of Trent Reynolds.

Once consent has been granted, Doctor Thackery and I will attempt to restore this imbalance within our respective patients through neural hypnotherapy. While I don't have Edmond's expertise or success record in using this technique, I'm confident that it is a reliable solution to the obstruction and will yield immediate, measurable results.

Brianna's emotional response to the suggestion that confusion is the primary impact of her abuse, and therefore that her victim impact statement is completely accurate, was profound. She broke down and wept. This was only her second such reaction in our therapy. We investigated this response together. Her reaction validates my presupposition that C-LIS is a factual disorder, but more so that confusion has been the principal result of her abuse.

Brianna is beginning to experience the relief that comes with the realization that she is not stupid, nor was she duped into giving herself away. If a choice is beyond one's capacity to make, it's not a choice. It's a reaction to something that the brain has no possible means of interpreting in any other way. This is the absolute power an offender has when grooming a child.

As this priming continues, the victim becomes increasingly powerless to choose, and without the ability to make a choice, they must submit. Brianna found herself in the midst of something that she had no way of knowing how to deal with. Confusion reigned supreme, and her inability to decide became her decision. She has come to recognize that she is neither dumb, gullible, nor a slut. She is, in fact, in love. It was not a cognitive decision, but the result is the same as if it had been. Her response was the only one she could have had.

Our session today ended with Brianna confessing that while the deepest part of her longs to not love Trent, she still revels in thoughts of his affection and pines for him daily.

I set aside my therapeutic hat to become the friend that she needed in the moment. I held her close as she wept at the prospect of letting her love for him go. I remained silent as she released years of pent-up emotion. She told me how he had made her into a better person, kinder, more compassionate, and more open-hearted.

The love they share is as real as any I have known. So I question the process we are proposing to relieve her of it. I'm fully cognizant of the fact that neural hypnotherapy has no ability to change one's emotions; it only gives the patient the ability to choose those emotions. Yet part of me wants that choice to be for each other, for love.

I understand the implications of this desire and the potential it can have for bias in favor of that which is so despised in our culture. It's easy to stand on the sidelines, shouting for impartiality, when you have nothing invested in the game. But in those moments, as I held her in my arms, I became all too aware of her perception of loss. It has less to do with innocence, security, and passion, and more to do with friendship, companionship, and love.

CHAPTER FORTY-FIVE

Mom didn't have many friends, and those she had weren't overly close. For as long as I can remember, she was quiet and soft-spoken. She kept to herself, and while she put up a formidable front, she was the textbook submissive housewife—most of the time. Her picture would fit perfectly beside the definition of "still waters run deep." It was not at all unusual to find her intensely contemplative over mundane things. She was compassionate and thoughtful and, unfortunately, all too obedient. Somehow I think that during their wedding vows, the only thing she heard of the "Do you promise to love, honor, and obey" part of the ceremony was "obey." There was little love or honor in their relationship, and I'm sure Dad's selective deafness kicked in right around the time the minister said, "forsaking all others." In many respects, I suppose we were not much different from most farm families.

The way Dad treated Trent bothered Mom deeply, but most often she remained faithfully compliant and quiet.

The first and only family vacation we took while we were still on the farm was to the Poconos in Pennsylvania. I wrote a report about it years later in junior high.

I was six years old and had never been out of the state. For some reason I thought that state lines were magical, at the very least something physical. In my mind's eye, something would change dramatically between one state and the next; else why would there be state lines? I was certain that once we hit the Pennsylvania border, it would be like entering an entirely new world.

Trent and I shared this misconception. We pleaded our case with Dad. Trent leaned over into the front seat of our old station wagon. "Dad, can we pleeeeeease stop at the border and see what it's like?" Dad completely ignored him, like he didn't even exist.

About twenty minutes later, I asked the same question, probably using the same words.

"Of course, sweetheart. How come you want to stop, though?"

"We just want to see it." He didn't answer, but I know that if I had said, *"I* just want to see it" and not *we*, Dad would have given some pleasant reply. When we stopped and got out, Trent and I looked all around. Obviously, Dad had missed something.

"Where is it, Dad?" Trent asked.

"What the hell are you talkin' about?"

"The border? Where's the border?"

"You're standing on it, you idiot."

"I can't see it."

"What the hell is wrong with you? Did you expect it to be a line like on the map, you moron?"

That's exactly what we expected. We returned to the backseat, crestfallen, trying to figure it out. Not only was there no line, there was no difference. The trees were the same, the road was the same, even the sky was the same. If you're going to have a border, we thought, there should be some reason for it. Trent and I were dumbfounded. The difference, of course, was that Trent was ridiculed mercilessly about it. Mom sat quietly while Dad taunted. She knew her place.

We arrived at our campsite. It wasn't one of the good ones, like those in Lehigh Gorge State Park. It was one we could afford, on the far side of the Delaware water gap. There wasn't even any water to play in. Within the first hour of our arrival, Trent got lost. I mean *really* lost. A park ranger brought him back to the campsite late that night.

Mom and I were gathering firewood while Dad and Trent set up the tent. Once we got back, I asked where Trent was, and Dad said, "Dunno. He'll be around here somewhere."

About twenty or thirty minutes later, Mom started getting worried and wanted to go looking for him, but Dad shut her down. "The dumbass just wandered off. He'll come back. It's not that big of a place."

Well, he didn't. Dad wanted Mom to start cooking supper, but she refused until Trent came back. He took her by the hand into the tent they shared, and when they came out, she began supper.

"Hey cutie," Dad said. "Why don't you and I take a lookie and see if we can't find that useless brother of yours?"

We headed down a path together, but Dad seemed more interested in finding blueberries than Trent. He was whistling "She'll be Comin' 'Round the Mountain" and popping blueberries into his mouth like they were candy. "You should try these, kiddo. They're grrrrrrreat." He said it just like Tony the Tiger, expecting me to laugh along with him.

As the sun began to set, I started to cry. He picked me up and asked what was wrong. Even at age six, I was smart enough to know that he didn't seem to give a rat's ass about Trent.

"I'm scared for Trent," I said. "What if we don't find him?"

"Oh, sweetheart, we'll find him, and if we don't, I'll get you a new brother. A better one."

"I don't want a new brother. I want Trent!"

We "looked" for another ten minutes or so, and then Dad said, "Well, we should get back. Mom will have supper ready soon."

When we got back to the campsite, Dad ate ravenously while Mom and I sat there in tears. Eventually, after Dad drank a couple of beers, he wandered back down the road and called a park ranger from an emergency phone we'd passed when we arrived. They found Trent almost four miles from our campsite, shivering cold, covered from head to toe in mosquito bites, and hungry and scared to death.

Trent and I slept in a little pup tent next to Mom and Dad's bigger one. I have never heard Mom before or since tear strips off Dad the way she did that night. She went ballistic on him. We could hear her screaming like she was standing right next to us, shouting into our ears. If there were bears anywhere nearby, they would have been frightened into the next county. I lay there next to Trent, thinking how happy I was that he was back with me, safe and sound.

The next morning, Dad had red marks about the size of Mom's fingers around his neck. And for the next few weeks, Dad trod very carefully around my big bother. Trent and I have never talked about it, but from that moment on, I knew he held very little importance in Dad's eyes. I'm sure Trent knew long before that. Not often, but when she needed to, Mom had a way of being able to get through to Dad that no one else had. She didn't know about much of the cruelty Trent had undergone, though, and I'm sure that added ten years to the life of their marriage.

After Trent went to prison and just before she died, Mom was often delirious due to the immense amount of morphine they were giving her. At first I attributed it to the morphine when Mom told me that I was the strong one in the family and that it was now my responsibility to watch over Trent. As I think about it now, however, I realize it may have been a moment of absolute clarity.

Robert and I continue to visit Dad every day, or at least we try to. The boys are getting a little bored, so we often don't bring them. It's a hospital, after all, and there's only so many days in a week that you can expect an eleven- and twelve-year-old to maintain a semblance of hospital decorum. Stacy babysits most evenings, but when she can't, they come with us.

Dad improves a little each day. He's using a walker now. He's only made it to the nursing station so far, but he claims he'll be running to the liquor store by the end of the week. He can feed himself and use the toilet, usually on his own. That was such a humiliating experience for him. As his cognition improved, the realization that someone else had been wiping his ass embarrassed him to no end.

He's been growing by leaps and bounds in his cognitive awareness as well. He remembers each of us as soon as we walk in and smiles from ear to ear. He's the same old Dad in some respects, and yet in others he is radically different. It's not uncommon to be in conversation with him and, rather than him having to dominate the entire discussion like he once did, he falls into a quiet, contemplative funk. When asked if something is bothering him, he'll say, "No, no, I was just thinking." It's not bad; it's just different. I'm not used to seeing him with that thousand-yard stare. It will probably clear up as he progresses, but it lends a certain sense of depth and serenity to him that I'm growing partial to.

I've been bringing him magazines to read. He can't read for any length of time without getting a headache, but he enjoys flipping through them, looking at the pictures, and reading the short accompanying blurbs. I've brought him numerous magazines that I know he loves: *Esquire*, *GQ*, *Men's Health*. I even snuck him in a *Maxim*. His favorite has always been *Yachts International*, although I don't think he's even touched it since I brought it in. He doesn't speak at all about *The Endeavor* either. It's like somehow the luster and mystique of what was once his greatest passion has subsided. He remembers nothing of his heart attack on the yacht, and he rarely mentions Judy. He does ask about Trent, though—endlessly. He's no longer surprised when we talk about Trent being in prison. He is fully aware of the circumstances around his son's offense and doesn't seem disgusted like he was prior to his heart attack. He's more understanding, as though he somehow feels responsible. It's often when we speak of Trent that Dad gets quiet and morose.

He's not one hundred percent, not by any means. We were talking about Trent just the other day—I'm sure Dad knew we were talking about Trent, anyway—and yet he referred to him as Daniel. Obviously both oars aren't fully in the water yet, but the improvement on a daily basis is pretty remarkable.

There has been talk of moving Dad to an extended-care facility. He doesn't require the care of a full-fledged hospital any longer. His needs are no longer acute; they are rehabilitative—physiotherapy, speech therapy, cognitive therapy, and such. Dad has grown fond of many of his caregivers and, surprisingly, they of him. It's going to be a bittersweet day when it comes. More sweet than bitter, I'm sure, but transition is always difficult.

Robert and I are researching long-term care homes, trying to find one that is a good fit for Dad's needs. His occupational therapist says he will only need to be in a rehabilitative environment for a month or two. After that he should be able to return home and have homecare workers provide the support he needs.

Rehabilitation is a slow process, and adaptation is hard on everyone. Doctor Morrow continues to be amazed with Dad's progress. He's been written about in four or five medical journals. He's had some of the top neurologists in the country read his file and share their opinions.

Interviews with medical experts are being set up so they can try to figure him out. I'm not sure what they expect him to tell them, but he has agreed to meet a few.

They also want Dad to participate in some psychological examinations. I was sure that he would quash that idea. Mom had asked him to see a family counselor with her years ago, but he wouldn't consider it. "I don't need none of them goddamn head-shrinker quacks telling me what's wrong with me."

Surprisingly, Dad is far more open to the idea than I ever imagined he would be. "Who knows?" he said. "Maybe they'll find something in there that could do with a good scrubbin'."

"See, there is a God," Robert said with a smirk. And so, along with each day comes a little more improvement, a little more clarity, a little more insight, and a little more Dad.

I don't know what tomorrow will bring for any of us, but if it's at all like today, it won't be a bad day at all.

CHAPTER FORTY-SIX

The idea of a breakthrough is rarely synonymous with work in psychiatry. Recovery—healing—occurs at such alarmingly slow intervals that the therapist is fortunate to even notice progress with a patient. Breakthroughs in one's work in an institutional environment such as Briar Ridge are even less common.

Most often, by the time an inmate is paroled, we have just scratched the surface of the issues that brought about the problematic behavior. One hopes the patient will continue to seek treatment upon release, but that is seldom the case. More often than not, especially when the inmate chooses not to continue therapy on the outside, we see him return in short order to begin once again, and from an even darker place than when he was released. This is the cycle in which the prison psychiatrist lives. You do not work in such a place for the satisfaction or reward of seeing patients' lives improve significantly with any regularity. If one is looking for the kind of reward that comes from seeing a job through to completion, he becomes a carpenter or a dentist. So, on the rare occasions this happens, we enjoy the progress and work all the harder to ensure the inmate has every opportunity for success once they leave our care—although after their release, the odds of hearing from them again are remote. When I witness the steady, rapid growth of an inmate like Trent Reynolds, I do everything in my power to ensure his success.

When Reynolds first came to me, he was a weak, fear-filled, anxious, passive-aggressive, psychologically broken young man. Today when he comes into my office, as he will shortly, he arrives courageous, confident, and full of purpose.

The journey to this place has not been easy for him, nor is it by any means complete. Recovery is a lifelong process. But as I reflect upon the man he was in relation to the man he is becoming, I have every reason to believe that recidivism is not in the cards for him. Rather, he will go on to make the world a better place for himself and others. In my line of work, it doesn't get much better than this.

There are two immediate hurdles to overcome. We will work on one today, and the other Reynolds may get to face in short order. Gerald Reynolds, the patient's father, continues his recovery at a startling rate, even faster than what I'm seeing in Reynolds. So, "the race is on," so to speak. While I'm no longer concerned that his father's recovery will have a life-altering impact upon Reynolds, it will definitely leave a mark. Seldom have I worked with a man who has suffered such abuse, sustained over such a long period of time. This has left an indelible wound within Reynolds. While the scar tissue is forming and the wound is becoming less sensitive, the day will come—if not before his release, then certainly shortly afterwards—when the two men will face each other, and I am concerned about what the results of that confrontation will be.

The letters Trent wrote as an exercise for reflection were mailed to his father several weeks ago. He decided not to intercept them. As Gerald's condition has so significantly improved, it will be only days now, no longer weeks or months—or never, as previously thought—before he receives them. What the spillover of that will be remains to be seen. It promises to be volatile, to be sure.

One benchmark of life change is when a patient responds counterintuitively to past normal behaviors. I have witnessed this with Reynolds' attitude to the fallout of the letters he has mailed. He no longer lives in the fear of how his father will react; he lives in anticipation of it. Like a boxer who has been pummeled into the canvas round after round, if he remains standing by the ninth, he often gets a second wind, throws caution to it, and comes out swinging. No longer afraid of his opponent, he welcomes him. He has taken the worst that his opponent can dish out and now stands ready and prepared to defend his territory, and sometimes he comes out the victor.

When Reynolds and I discuss the letters, he no longer fears his father's reaction. This newfound courage arises not because he doesn't give a shit but rather because he does. In his father's eyes, Reynolds has always been a coward.

He spent the early years of his life struggling to gain his father's approval. When he finally came to the realization that that would never happen, he spent the remainder of his life either running from him or doing his best to avoid him altogether. As they grew further apart, the distance gave Reynolds the space required to evaluate. All attempts to comprehend the extent and depth of his father's hatred have left him wanting. He has never found answers, yet he continues to seek them. Even if found, the answers will do nothing to repair the damage done, the mistrust, or the understandable anger that lives within him, but they will at least provide insight into the man who caused the wreckage.

Reynolds isn't looking to reconcile with his father; profound devastation seldom yields such outcomes. But he is looking for understanding. What Reynolds is searching for from his father is not remediation; it is closure. Closure is a much misunderstood and misinterpreted concept in the therapeutic world. It has come to mean the end: the problem is solved, the curtain called, and the proverbial fat lady has sung. But it does not mean this.

If a rabid wolf is chasing you and you run into your home and slam the door in his face, the wolf doesn't disappear. He remains, just as angry, just as rabid, and just as intent upon sinking his teeth into your flesh. However, as long as the path between you is blocked, he can bring no harm. The opportunity to do so was removed when you closed the door. Closing the door thwarted his power over you, but it did nothing to remove his desire to overpower you. I use the term "closure" in this context. Reynolds' confrontation with his father will do nothing to change his father; he doesn't possess the power to do that. The only thing he has the power to do is open or close the door on the wolf. It is his choice.

With the great strides Reynolds has been making in his self-talk, reading, meditative practices, and his seeking to discover purpose and the embracing of his inner child, he is emerging from the murky waters of his abuse much better prepared to stand against the onslaught of exploitation, should it be hurled at him again. As he so eloquently stated, he longs to look his father in the eyes and be able to say, "I'm not the worthless piece of shit you made me out to be and wanted me to believe I was." If he can do that, this piece of the puzzle that is his life will be set in place. Closure will commence, and he will be able to move forward.

This naturally leads to the second hurdle Reynolds faces—that we face together—the one we shall approach momentarily: the neural psychic union that holds him captive to his victim. It has taken some time, more than I expected, for Reynolds to embrace the idea that his love for his victim is not a volitional choice. It's much deeper than that. The problem, as created by the development of this psychic union, is that the emotional connection binding them has been so reinforced and is so overpowering that neither of them have the strength to choose whether this is something they truly want or whether they might both be healthier choosing a different path.

The idea of two people being so fully in love that they can do nothing to prevent that love may sound hopelessly romantic, but clear away the quixotic fantasy and one quickly realizes they are little more than slaves to their passions. With the ability to decide removed from the equation, this starry-eyed compulsion soon creates far more problems than it solves.

I'm delighted that Reynolds has consented to engage in deep neural hypnotherapy as an attempt to assist him in breaking the psychic union between him and his victim. I emphasize the word *attempt.* The state created through hypnotic induction creates an environment of hyper-suggestibility. It carries no guarantee, and the outcome remains completely within the patient's control. I counseled Reynolds that this, while highly recommended, must be solely his decision. Furthermore, I have not discussed, and will not discuss, his victim's therapy with him. Therefore, he is completely unaware that she too will soon undergo this same process.

The ability to choose is taken for granted in our culture. One need spend only a short while in prison to witness how the removal of choice affects a person. In this environment one has no choice over the simplest of things: what clothes he will wear, what food he will eat, or where and how he will spend his time. The removal of these basic choices can become almost paralyzing. Reynolds' choice to undergo this process is the second most important one he will make regarding his victim. The first is choosing to live without love for or from her.

CHAPTER FORTY-SEVEN

I walk through these corridors that have become so unwelcomingly familiar over the years, flanked by my escorts. As often as they have had to take me from cell block H to Doctor Thackery's office, you'd think it would become just another innocuous part of their routine, yet each time they insist on making sure I know what a worthless piece of shit I am. I suppose this *is* the routine: to make the prisoner miserable.

Today, Doctor T is going to attempt to hypnotize the one I love out of me. Of course, he doesn't put it in these terms, but the result is essentially the same. So, as I walk closer to this destiny, I feel an apprehension that hasn't been here in months. I'm not as concerned about the procedure working as I am about it failing.

I seem to have no ability not to love Brianna. I'm all too aware of the many reasons I shouldn't, yet I seem incapable of choosing otherwise. I have made many decisions that were as difficult as or more difficult than this one should be, so why I can't do this baffles me.

There are dimples on Brianna's lower back, just above her flawless ass, that when she lies on her stomach and arches look like the edges of her perfect smile. I miss those. I miss kissing them. I miss nuzzling against her soft, warm thighs. I miss looking deep into her stunning blue eyes and the look of concentration upon her exultant face when we are in meaningful conversation. I miss the smell of her hair, the way she giggles, the way she wrinkles her nose before a sneeze, the way she blushes when I tell her how wonderful she is. Sometimes these memories leak down my cheeks, and I will sorely miss each one.

I'm fully aware that the hypnotic spell I'm about to undergo has no more power to relieve me of these memories than it does to create them. But given the choice not to have them consume me day and night, I will choose, and the memories will fade. As it is currently, I seem to have little choice. When thoughts of her come, they force every other thought out like a bully taking over a sandbox. I'm powerless to keep them away. The hope this procedure offers is the power to choose whether I entertain these thoughts—this love—or not. Once I have this ability, I must choose not to indulge those feelings. Otherwise I will be in the prison of her love forever. And while that prison is infinitely better than this one, I'm no less a captive.

Tweedle Dee and Tweedle Dum leave me outside of Doctor Thackery's office. When I open his door, I realize some things have changed. The chair that I have always sat in during our session has been replaced with a comfortable-looking chaise lounge. It has a large burgundy velvet pillow at one end and a matching blanket. Next to this chair stands a stainless-steel surgical tray upon which is a large green rubber strap, cotton swabs, alcohol pads, a syringe, and a small glass vial. Doctor Thackery's appearance too has been altered. He is wearing a white lab coat over his usual casual dress attire.

"Good morning, Trent. How are you feeling? Are you ready for this?"

"I'm pretty okay," I tell him, all the while staring at the medical tray. "I think I'm as ready as I'll ever be."

"Perhaps I should have given you a bit more of a heads-up about what we're going to be doing," he says, keenly aware that my eyes haven't moved from the medical equipment on the tray.

"Well, if this is supposed to be helping me relax, it isn't."

He laughs and then invites me to sit. I sit on the edge of the chaise lounge, unsure of how to proceed, waiting for an explanation, I suppose. Little comes. He sits on a medical stool—another new addition—next to me, and I look past him, my eyes still fixed on the tray next to him. Finally, he clues me in.

"I have prepared a benzodiazepine injection that will help you relax as you undergo the hypnotherapy." If I didn't trust the good doctor as much as I do, I would bolt. As it is, I say nothing. He explains that very little will be different from our regular session. Once he administers the sedative, I'm to lie back on the lounge, get as comfortable as I can, and then we'll go through our breathing exercises and meditation, as we always do. When I feel like I'm relaxed enough, I'll give him permission to begin, and he'll induce hypnosis. He reassures me once again that it is not as though he can force me to tell him anything. My deepest, darkest secrets will not be revealed. I remind him that there are none that he doesn't already know about, and we share a chuckle.

Upon his request, I roll up the sleeve of my jumpsuit as he prepares the injection. It's easy to forget that a psychiatrist is a medical doctor long before he's a shrink. After he administers the sedative, I lie back upon the lounge. It's relaxing. My head rests comfortably upon the large, soft pillow. Relaxing music fills the room and my senses. My eyes close, and the bell rings.

"Breathing in, I know I am breathing in . . . Breathing out, I know I am breathing out . . ." I recognize the tension in my body and mind and let it go. All fear, stress, and anxiety are lifting. "Breathing in, I receive all that is good and wholesome, loving and pure . . . Breathing out, I expel all that is misery, emptiness, wretched, and evil." I appreciate the revelation that I'm completely relaxed and at rest. The benzo is working its magic. My mind and heart are purged of darkness and infused with light. I am at one with this place, myself, and my doctor.

CHAPTER FORTY-EIGHT

Recognizing when a patient is in a deep hypnotic state—open to the power of suggestion—becomes much easier over time. All the indicators in Reynolds are there: he is breathing deeply, his eyes are moving slowly under his eyelids, his body is completely at ease, and his chest is rising evenly, slowly, and smoothly. What I want to suggest to Trent in this hyper-suggestive state is that his love for himself is of utmost importance, that it's difficult to love another until he can love himself. I will invite him to acknowledge that loving Brianna isn't the best way to love himself or her, that his love for her is associated with pain for her, pain for her family, pain for himself, and pain for his family. Love and this kind of pain are not meant to co-exist. He can choose a better path.

I make these suggestions to Reynolds over and over and then invite him to repeat after me: "I want to love who I am. I *can* love who I am. I choose to love who I am." When he is able to receive this, we move on. "I want Brianna to love who she is. She *can* love who she is. She chooses to love who she is." We move forward. "I want to be free to choose who I love. I *am* free to choose who I love. I choose who I love." And then again. "I choose to love myself. I choose to love my family. I choose to allow myself to choose whom I love. I choose to allow Brianna the choice to choose her love." And still further. "I let go of my hold on Brianna. I allow her to let go of her hold upon me. I let go. She lets go. We let go." And further yet. "Love is a choice. I choose to love myself. I choose to allow

Brianna to love herself. We choose to love ourselves. We choose to love or not love each other. We choose."

We continue repeating these simple yet profound ideas until I know that Trent believes he has this choice. And then with no fanfare or theatrics, we begin to move back toward consciousness.

Bringing a patient out of deep-state hypnotherapy requires as much patience and care as it does to enter it. "Breathing in, I know I am breathing in . . . Breathing out, I know I am breathing out . . ." And slowly we reemerge.

When the bell rings, I invite Reynolds to open his eyes and sit up. In his post-hypnotic state, we don't talk about the outcome of the process. It's pointless to do so. Neither of us has any idea what that outcome will be. Instead, we talk about what the experience was like. We talk about how relaxed he remains, how he is becoming the person he has always wanted to be.

Afterward, we enjoy a cup of ginseng tea together and talk about trivial matters: fly fishing, the Stanley Cup play-off race, the upcoming Masters tournament at Augusta. We avoid politics, religion, or systemic correctional institution failures. I inquire about his nephews and his sister and how he is coping with the loss of his mother. And when he's ready, we talk about Gerald.

CHAPTER FORTY-NINE

Doctor Thackery seemed a little hesitant to talk about Gerald's recovery. To be fair, there was a time not so long ago when I skirted the issue altogether. I suppose I'm not the man I once was. Thoughts of Gerald certainly stir no warm fuzzies within me, but nor do they wrack me with fear, hatred, and dread as they once did. It's with great respect and gratitude toward Doctor T that I can view my relationship with Gerald from a position closer to neutrality.

I tell Doctor Thackery that Claire and Robert have been visiting less these past few months. I think there are several reasons for this. I'm in a far better place than I once was. Claire, being the perceptive woman she is, recognizes this and invests her energies elsewhere. I don't begrudge her this in any way. I do feel a sense of guilt for how much of life she and Robert have put on hold in order to visit as often as they have.

The other reason is Gerald, who has required much more of her time and care than he did when he was lying comatose, on the brink of death. Not so long ago, this would have bothered me greatly, but it doesn't affect me the way it once did. I get to choose my response to disappointment. The decision to choose my attitude is freeing, like floating on my back in the middle of a crystal pool on a warm summer day, not unlike this hypnotherapy experience I have just come through. The benzodiazepine must still be in my system.

I tell Doctor T that Gerald is being transferred to Ridgewood Terrace this week. Ridgewood isn't the exclusive nursing home I would have expected from him—from Mom, yes, but from Gerald? Absolutely not. It's a modest residence filled with elderly middle-income patients who are afflicted with everything from Alzheimer's to Parkinson's. I'm surprised at this choice. I would have expected Gerald to insist upon a place like Gold-State Manor in Upper Arlington, where he would have his own luxury suite and a full complement of staff at his beck and call, a place filled with people just like him: recovering, needy, and rich. Instead, he'll be only a short distance from Robert and Claire's home. There's an inkling of something in me that wants to give Gerald some form of kudos for this. Definitely, the sedative still lingers.

CHAPTER FIFTY

Reynolds chooses his father as the topic we will focus on in our remaining time together this morning. I sit and listen as he speaks for the first time about trying to understand the hatred Gerald has displayed toward him throughout his life. Prior to this, he has shown interest only in the *what* of their relationship, seldom the *why*. I note this, and he continues. He is interested in what he could have done to elicit such responses from his father. In doing this, he recalls events from his childhood, then realizes we have explored these ad nauseum and they offer few answers.

He wonders out loud about what might have happened in his father's life to cause such an adverse reaction to him. He supposes, presupposes, and ponders but comes up empty. Nor can he find anything that explains his father's hatred, malevolence, and violent behavior.

As I listen, I wait for the realization to hit him. It doesn't, so I prompt him with a question. "Trent, what if this has *nothing* to do with you?" As he thinks about this, I tell him about an old therapeutic practice where the patient is encouraged to take their frustrations out on an inanimate object—a pillow or a punching bag. The patient is invited to unleash their pent-up anger and hostility on the object as an expression of their outrage. The punching bag has done nothing to deserve the abuse and has no association with the mitigating factors; it is simply the recipient of the patient's anger.

"Perhaps," I suggest, "Gerald's lashing out has nothing to do with you. Perhaps you have little or no connection to the source of his anger. Perhaps you were just the recipient. Perhaps you were nothing more than his punching bag." This is a difficult concept to grasp at the best of times. When one's life has been completely decimated for no reason, the pain is no less; in fact, it is often much more than if one had deserved every beating incurred. Reynolds' response is immediate. At that moment he seemed to grasp that he may never understand something for which he was not responsible.

Here in my office, after Reynolds has returned to his cell, I reflect upon the success of our recent session. He is displaying specific indicators of choosing well.

CHAPTER FIFTY-ONE

Dear Gerald,

By now you will have read the many "love" letters I have sent. I don't regret sending them. As you will note, early in the first letter I said that they were not to be sent, that they were to be a therapeutic exercise for my own healing and sense of well-being. So, why did I send them? The short answer is, you're supposed to be dead.

But I have a better one. While here in prison, I have grown. I've grown more than I could have imagined. The coward I once was is gone.

I spent my life in fear of you. Fear became my trademark, a pattern that defined me. I wore it like a target for anyone to take aim at. My entire life, I have been afraid of what others think of me, what others might do to me, what others did to me. But that stops here and now. I want you to know how your evil heart has affected me. You came so close to destroying me. Let me rephrase that: I came so close to *allowing* you to destroy me. You couldn't imagine the many times I wanted to die after one of your unprovoked attacks. I allowed your evil to convince me that I was worthless. In this worthless state, I entertained the idea that I had earned what you dished out. I know better now. I didn't earn it, and I certainly didn't deserve it.

I have given great consideration to it, and still cannot fathom what deranged part of you would permit you to treat me with such utter contempt, nor do I care. I care only that I never give you permission to do it again. There may be some hidden part of your life that no one knows about, some obsession with evil that lingers in the corner of your life that compels you to shit on others. I have no idea, and once again, I don't give a damn. What I do care about is that you know I'm recovering. I told you that I was almost murdered in this place. My recovery from that event occurred at light speed compared to my recovery from you. The aftermath is somewhat similar though. The attempt on my life leaves a residue, a disease that consumes me much like the memories your continual barrage of abuse would have done had I not made a conscious effort to no longer permit it. Unfortunately, I have no power over this disease, but I do have power over the way I respond to it, just as I have power over how your castigations affect me.

The only consolation that has come from my experience in prison is that I have used the time I have to commit myself to doing some things with all the energy I have. Doctor Thackery has invested much of his life in helping me sort out mine. I do not take his investment lightly.

Nothing that has value comes easily. I have value. So I spend hours each day working to improve who I am, to discover something buried beneath the shit, to become something other than shit. And incrementally, I am.

I have discovered that my life has a purpose. It's not yet as honed or as polished as it will be, but it's beginning to take shape. My purpose is rather simple and somewhat, I confess, existential at this moment: to become the best person I can possibly be. What that involves is infinitely more complex. In its simplest form, it involves acquiring an honest view of reality, a willingness to see things as they truly are and not only as I would like them to be. It involves choosing to be a bit better today than I was yesterday. In its uttermost complexity, it involves forgiving you. As I said, my purpose still lacks. Forgiving you is a long way off, but for the first time in my life, I have a desire to want to forgive you. The desire to *want* must come before the desire to *have*, just as the desire to *have* must come before the object of desire is attained.

Lest you flatter yourself, my desire to want to forgive you has little to do with you and everything to do with me. I want to be able to forgive you so that I can live in harmony with life and experience some semblance of peace within my soul. Holding onto this bitterness hurts me more than anyone else, including you.

Claire tells me that your recovery has been rapid. A piece of advice: now that you've been given this second chance at life, perhaps think about someone other than yourself for a change. You should know better than most what a fragile thing life is.

Did you have any great revelations as you lay hovering between life and death? Any significant insight into your own misery or the misery you inflicted upon me? Any desire to be a better man than you've been?

You're off to Ridgewood Terrace, Claire tells me. How nice for you. Someone new to wipe your ass. Or have you surpassed that stage by now? I must admit, I was pleasantly surprised to hear that you're not going to Gold-State. I'd like to know whose decision that was. I assume Claire's. Maybe it was decided while you were still in and out of reality. I can't imagine that Ridgewood was your first choice. Nevertheless, I'm certain it will take a great burden off Claire not to have to drive clear across town every evening to see you. So, if you did have anything to do with it, thanks. Anything that makes Claire's life easier brings a measure of comfort to me. God knows you and I have seldom made life easy for her.

I'm writing this to let you know it didn't work. You tried your best and failed. I'm going to come out of this thing, this place, a better man than I came in. I don't mean prison; I mean life. It was your ambition to see me fail. And when I was first arrested,

I admitted defeat. I was ready to fly my tighty whiteys—standard issue in federal penitentiaries—from a flagpole and give up. Surrender is my default, my place of comfort, it's what I have always done best. Surrender is easy. As I said, nothing of value comes easily. It's sinking in; I have value, as much as you may beg to differ—as much as you have tried to convince yourself and me otherwise. I finally know that as truth, and I will be damned if I'm going to allow you to devalue me any further.

What you think of me, Gerald, means little. What anyone thinks of me is not my concern. I'm learning to mind my own business and not waste my time on what is none of mine. As a result of my crime, my reputation—or what little is left of it—is loathsome. I have come to terms with that. When I leave this place, I will only be free in the eyes of the law. Society has branded me for life. My reputation is that of the lowest form of life. Another thing I have learned from my good doctor: reputation is only what others think of me; character is who I am. I can't change my reputation, but moment by moment, my character is changing—growing.

So, go ahead, Gerald, recover. Get healthier than you have ever been. You've taken your best shot, and I'm still here. I didn't die like you wanted me to. I may be down to 145 pounds, but I'm stronger than ever. So if you wanna go, let's dance. I'm armed with something I've never been able to use against you before—self-respect. I don't have much of it, but I have a lot more than I ever had before, and it has given me a glimpse of the man that I hope to be one day, the man you never taught me to be, the man you never wanted me to be.

I don't write these words in anger or in arrogance. God knows I've got nothing to boast about. I write these things out of love. Not for you but for myself.

Maybe one day we'll talk,
Trent

CHAPTER FIFTY-TWO

Mom and Linda had a long talk a couple of days ago. I'm eighteen now, so I really don't know why Linda felt compelled to include Mom in my therapy stuff, but she did. I'm not pissed off about it or anything, but Linda is *my* therapist. Maybe it's because I wasn't an adult when the shit hit the fan, so my parents still get a say in the matter. Who knows?

Weird, when you turn eighteen you think that somehow everything will be different, look different, feel different. But it isn't. Everything's exactly like it's always been. Well, I suppose not everything. When I went to see Linda this morning, things in her office were different.

Linda told me a while ago that she wanted to do this hypnosis thing on me to see if I could break out of the . . . I don't know what to call it—love spell—that Trent has over me. She calls it a psychic union disorder. Some kind of connection she thinks Trent and I have formed. I don't really understand it. In my head, I have this image of something creepy, Like the blood pact made between Tom Sawyer and Becky Thatcher. Like they think that Trent and I cut our thumbs and held them together so that our blood mixed, and now we have this mystical bond. I mean, I know they don't really think that, but they believe something has happened between us so we now have a connection that joins us whether we want it or not.

When we got to Linda's office today—Mom came with me—she introduced me to Doctor Philips. He's like a shrink for shrinks, I guess. I talked to him on the phone once. He's the one who set me up with

Linda in the first place. He's a psychiatrist, so he's allowed to give patients drugs, whereas Linda, being a psychologist, can't. That's the only difference between them that I know of. We talked a bit. He explained what he was going to do to me and why. He seemed nice. He gave me the sedative to help me relax. Shortly after that, he and Mom left. Then Linda helped me to prepare for the hypnosis.

She had me take off my shoes and lie back on a comfortable recliner that sits in the corner of her office next to a big window and what looks like a tall bonsai tree. I relaxed and listened to soft music while the drugs did their magic. They were pretty sweet.

After about twenty minutes, I felt like I was floating. It was like I couldn't feel the chair under me, like I was suspended in midair. It wasn't at all like being drunk or even like a pot high. It was totally chill. We did some deep breathing and meditation exercises, like the ones Tracy taught me. Linda was very familiar with the practice and made a couple of suggestions that were helpful. She said she was glad that Tracy had taught me how to do this, 'cause it can be really helpful.

Linda began talking calmly and quietly. I guess I was expecting her to dangle a pocket watch in front of my face or something, but she just talked. She began by asking me questions about things that happened when I was a kid and then about my relationship with my parents and Davy and then about Trent. She asked me to repeat things—like the self-talk that Tracy taught me—over and over, about loving myself and my ability to choose what I want in life and my being willing to let Trent go and his choice to let me go.

I don't remember a lot of what went on. I was very relaxed, almost sleepy. I think it was the sedative that Doctor Philips gave me. I would have told her anything she asked, which I suppose means that I might have been open to anything she suggested.

When it was all over, we didn't talk much about the hypnosis other than her asking me how I felt.

The purpose was to break this psychic union, although I don't feel much different, kind of like turning eighteen didn't feel any different from being seventeen. But just because you don't feel different doesn't mean you aren't. I was expecting that suddenly I wouldn't have feelings for Trent or that I would come out of it hating him—like so many people think I should—but I didn't feel much different at all. When I asked her about it, Linda didn't seem to think it was important. She said we would explore that at another time. So we talked about school and my upcoming prom and things like that.

Jake Simonson asked me to prom. I haven't said yes yet. I'm not sure what's holding me back. He's really nice, and I probably should. I probably will. Not a lot of guys are interested in me other than trying to get inside my pants. Ever since Trent, most people treat me like I'm a slut. I guess they think that all Trent and I ever did was fuck. That's all that seems to matter to most of them. But Jake's cool. We've hung out a bit after school and stuff. He comes by Starbucks when I'm on shift. Sometimes he'll wait 'til I'm on break, and we'll have a latte together and just hang.

Jake's not one of the popular guys at school, although pretty much everyone knows who he is. He's involved in a lot of stuff, like I used to be. He plays basketball and volleyball and works on the prom committee, so I guess he's somewhat popular. When we hang out, he never brings up what happened between Trent and me. If I bring it up, which I don't—well, not very often—he'll listen and stuff. He doesn't interrupt and say, "Yeah, that Mr. Reynolds, what a piece of shit," like everyone else does. That's one of the things I like about Jake.

He says he used to go see Trent sometimes when he was in grade ten. It's kinda weird 'cause I really only know him as Trent, and Jake only knows him as Mr. Reynolds, the guidance counselor. Sometimes it feels like we're talking about two different people, even though they're the same. And I suppose in some ways, Trent was two different people. Two-faced? Hypocrite?

Jake told me that when he was in grade ten, Trent gave him some advice about this girl he liked. It was hilarious; he told Jake almost the exact same thing he told me about Rusty, that he had nothing to lose by asking her out. "If she says no, I'm in the same position I was in before I asked her out, but if she says yes, well, that changes everything." I laughed when he told me. He asked what was so funny, so I told him Trent had given me the same advice, almost word for word.

"Did you take his advice?" I asked. That's where our stories diverge. Jake didn't. I told him what happened when I asked Rusty out, and we both laughed. He said the girl he likes is definitely not a lesbian, but she ended up with someone else who eventually broke her heart. So he's been waiting for her to heal before he puts any pressure on her.

"Maybe you should ask her to prom," I said.

"I did," he whispered.

Then it got *really* quiet between us. When I looked into his eyes again, they were misty.

"Brianna, I have liked you since the day you walked into Ms. Thatcher's Geometry class on the first day of grade nine. When all that stuff happened between you and Mr. Reynolds, my heart broke for you. Maybe I should have said something or did something a long time ago, but I'm kind of a chicken. That's why I didn't ask you out when Mr. Reynolds told me I should. When everyone found out about what was going on with you and him, when it was all over the news and the school and stuff, I went home and cried for you. I got so mad at myself. There have been so many nights when I laid in my bed, thinking about you and what happened, and asking myself if I would have had the balls to ask you out way back in grade ten, maybe things would have been completely different. Maybe you would have said yes, and nothing would have ever happened between you and Mr. Reynolds, and you might have been spared so much. Sorry for dumping on you like this. I've been holding this in for a long time. Brianna Barnes, I really, really like you. Would you please go to prom with me?"

So, yeah, I'll go to prom with Jake Simonson. When I told Linda, she smiled and said that sounded nice. It does sound nice. It's going to be nice. Jake is nice. Who knows?

When I told Mom that I'm going to prom with Jake, she cried. So did Dad, but he's always been a softie. I think for them it's such a big deal because they think that maybe, just maybe, their daughter can have a normal life post Trent. And who knows? Maybe she can.

CHAPTER FIFTY-THREE

Dad's suite in Ridgewood Terrace is quaint. It's small, but it has a beautiful family room with a comfortable sofa, two recliners, and a little balcony that overlooks a cute garden with a waterfall and bird baths. It will be nice for him to sit out there when the weather warms up. His recliner is one of those that can lift at the touch of a button to help him stand. He no longer uses a walker, and he doesn't use his cane as much as he should. He fell the day after he got here. It wasn't a big deal to him; he wasn't hurt at all, but in this place, a fall is a cause for great concern. So he's been placed on fall alert, which means if he doesn't have visitors, every staff member who walks by checks in to see if he's okay. Dad often wanted to be the center of attention, but lately that seems to have changed. He certainly never wanted this kind of attention, and it's driving him a little wonky. Otherwise, he's adjusting well.

When Robert and I were checking out extended-care homes, we looked at all the best places in town, as Dad had seemed to gravitate that way once the money poured in. But it was Dad who suggested Ridgewood because it's pretty much right around the corner from our place. I can walk here in ten minutes. I was surprised, actually. It's not like Dad to think of others before himself, but he insisted.

His recovery continues to be remarkable. He takes all his meals in the dining room on the first floor with the other residents. He no longer requires any help when eating, and he's on a regular diet. His physiotherapist works with him three times a week for two hours per session. Their time together is divided between the therapy pool and the workout room. Debbie, his PT, says that he's doing really well. She attributes this to his age. At sixty-one, he's one of the youngsters in Ridgewood. She also says the fact that his health was excellent prior to his heart attack has contributed to his rapid recovery.

Cognitively, he has also made great strides. The lapses in memory, aside from the actual event and the time he was in a coma, are gone. I think he has memories of things that were going on internally while he was in the coma, but those are closely held secrets. He remembers many things that were foggy and unclear to him just a few weeks ago. He clearly recalls Mom's death, their divorce, the success and sale of Reynolds' Baling Systems. And Trent.

Dad is back.

He wants to begin meeting with his accountants and investment agents, although Doctor Morrow is encouraging him not to rush and to make regaining his health his primary focus. "Otherwise none of these other concerns matter," he says. Stress is the greatest enemy to Dad's recuperation, and with him doing so well, Doctor Morrow wants nothing to interfere with that progress, so he has forbidden Dad a cell phone and Internet access, at least for now. Amazingly, Dad seems okay with this.

He is far more even keeled than I've ever known him to be. Not so long ago, if anyone had told him what he could or couldn't do, he would have flown into a rage. Dad has always had a sharp, quick intellect and a lightning-fast temper. Tell him something he didn't agree with and he could reduce your argument to rubble in no time flat, explaining in minute detail why you were wrong and stupid and why he was right. That part of him seems to no longer exist. He has emerged from his coma far more considerate of others than he's ever been. The person he seems to consider most and be most considerate of is Trent.

TRENT WAS PREPARING HIS DEFENSE for his grad thesis. The title was *The Psychology of Transition: From Poverty to Affluence.* His interest in the topic was piqued primarily because of our experience and the adjustments we were forced to make after the sale of Reynolds' Baling Systems but also because of trends that his research revealed in many who have had similar experiences. Mom and I attended his defense together.

It was the one thing that Trent hoped Dad would be interested in enough to attend. I think he felt the topic would have been appealing to Dad and that he might even begin to understand a thing or two about why we all reacted so differently to the sudden change. He went to Dad's place one evening to invite him. I think he probably knew before he ever extended the invitation that Dad wouldn't go, but I doubt he expected the response he got.

Mom and Dad had been divorced for a few years, and Trent wanted me to go with him to Dad's place. He hated being alone with Dad, who usually treated Trent much better in mixed company, so I agreed. I got a call from Dad the day before, inviting us to make an evening of it. "Why don't you come for dinner?" he said. I assumed Dad was inviting *us*.

When I got to Dad's, I asked where Trent was.

"I have no idea," he replied. "Let's eat."

"Shouldn't we wait for Trent?"

"Dinner's getting cold," was Dad's even colder reply.

His chef served us a wonderful dinner in the small dining room across from the large one. We were about halfway through dinner when I got a text from Trent asking what time I was planning to arrive at Dad's. I excused myself from the table and texted him back, saying I was already there, that Dad had invited me for dinner, but he had made it clear when he invited me that both of us had been invited. Trent said Dad told him to come at about 7:30—after dinner.

I returned to the table and asked why Trent wasn't here.

"I told him to come, but you know how that brother of yours can be," he said. And that was it—topic changed. Dad stretched dinner out as long as he could. We were still eating dessert at about 7:45 when Trent arrived. Dad's assistant invited Trent in and took him into the study, where he sat alone, waiting while Dad lingered as long as possible around the table, enjoying an apéritif after dinner, and insisted that I stay put until he was ready to leave. The volume of his voice increased after Trent's arrival, so he would know what a grand ol' time Dad was having with me.

It was after 8:00 when Dad finally wandered into the study, positioning himself as he walked so that I was forced to stay behind him. He didn't even sit down; he just stood in the doorway.

"What can I do for you?" he said. Not "Hello, son," or "It's nice to see you, Trent," or "Sorry for the misunderstanding over the dinner invitation." Just "What can I do for you?" as if Trent were a door-to-door salesman. He made it very clear that his evening was being interrupted.

Since Dad didn't sit down, Trent stood up and told him about his thesis topic and defense and invited him to attend. He added information about it—where it was to be held, the date and time, and a brief synopsis of the topic.

"All the information is here," he said as he handed Dad a postcard that explained it in detail. Dad didn't even glance at it, just folded it in half and then in half again like it was a piece of trash, before setting it on the fireplace mantel.

"Thanks," Dad said. Then he stepped aside, indicating that their meeting was now over, and Trent was welcome to take his leave.

As I watched Trent's car pull out of the driveway, something in me snapped. For most of my life, I'd allowed Dad to walk all over Trent. But something happened at that moment. The words Mom had spoken to me on her deathbed whispered in my ear: "Claire, you're the strong one." I froze for a moment. I'd watched Dad treat Trent like shit throughout our lives. Those words came again, but this time they screamed. "Claire, you're the strong one. Look after Trent!"

A courage I had never known, a righteous anger, boiled inside. I grabbed my father by the arm and swung him around to face me. The look of disbelief on his face emboldened me. "How dare you treat my brother that way?" I shouted. "Trent is as much a part of you as I am. I have watched you belittle him, walk all over him, and drive him into the ground my entire life. But it stops here and now. You tell me you love me so often it's become meaningless. You want to prove your love for me? Then start treating my brother—your son—like he's part of the family. Until then, I want nothing to do with you."

Then I did something else I'd never done before but should have done years earlier: I slapped him across the face and stormed out of his house.

I called Trent and told him what I'd done, and we met at a coffee shop near Dad's. "You shouldn't have done that," were the first words out of his mouth as I sat down across from him.

I was still fuming. "Why the hell not? You certainly didn't stand up for yourself."

"And just what would I do, Claire? Punch him in the head and tell him that if he didn't come to my thesis defense, I'd never speak to him again? Listen, Claire, I appreciate you looking out for me, but nothing is ever going to change between Gerald and me. There's no point in ruining your relationship with him by getting between us. That won't solve anything. He's always been good to you. Don't fuck that up."

"That's where you are dead wrong, Trent," I replied. "He can't be good to me and bad to you simultaneously. Treating you like the enemy hurts me in ways I can't even begin to describe."

Trent reached across the table, took my shaking hand in his, and looked deep into my eyes. "Thank you, Claire. I love you."

I sipped my watered-down Americano as the silence between us did what silence often does: gave us time to settle, calm down, and regain perspective. I took the vibrating phone from my purse, looked at it, then let it go to voicemail. I wasn't even close to being ready to talk with Dad.

It was more than a month before we spoke again. Dad made promises that I accepted as authentic. It took several months before our relationship was restored. Trent was seldom brought up, and when he was—always by me—Dad was cordial. He did show up at Trent's thesis defense. He didn't sit with Mom and me, though, which was to be expected, since things weren't exactly smooth sailing between them. At the small social gathering afterward, he was nowhere to be found, but he was making an effort, and I give him credit for that.

Ever since that blow-up, I've had a little less difficulty navigating the turbulent waters between Trent and Dad. I still find myself having to support each of them through their dysfunctions, but it has been a bit easier. I love them both dearly and have never been able to figure out the disdain. On occasion, I have asked why he treats Trent and me so *differently.* His answers never satisfy. "You're a woman, and Trent needs to learn how to be a man." That's about the extent of any answer offered. I think

Dad is aware of how obvious it is to any outside observer how shitty he treats Trent. I just don't think he cares. Trent, of course, doesn't treat Dad much better. Playing the chicken-and-egg game with them is useless. I have no idea what precipitated what, and I don't care. When I get caught in the middle of this hate dance, I feel as if I'm spinning.

The change in Dad after I slapped him was temporary and forced—for my benefit only. But the change I see in him now has nothing to do with me and everything to do with him. And what a beautiful thing it is. He often asks how Trent is holding up and expresses genuine concern for him.

On our way home from visiting tonight, Robert said he was surprised by how interested Dad seems to be in Trent. He thinks Dad has really changed. Time will tell.

I stopped in at Dad's house on our way to see him this evening and gathered all his mail. It's amazing how much junk mail can pile up in more than two years. I'd had all the bills and anything that seemed important forwarded to his accountant last year, separating the wheat from the chaff, so to speak. So everything else was pretty much junk. But it wasn't mine to throw out or go through, so I dumped it all in a large box and stuck it in the back of the SUV. While he's not supposed to do things that stress him out, I think it'll do him some good to start going through the months of junk mail that has piled up.

CHAPTER FIFTY-FOUR

Several weeks ago, Reynolds emerged from our hypnotherapeutic experiment with a new comprehension. I believe he has emerged well. As expected, initially there was little evidence of perceptive change. However, in recent days, as he continues to engage in the hard work of self-discovery, purpose, and attitude adjustment, he has made significant advancements.

Recently, we have been exploring his feelings and attachments. He has been making good choices. If he talks about him at all, he speaks of Gerald, his father, almost sympathetically. The hard work he has been doing on perspective—right views, right thoughts, right attitudes—seems to have given him a different lens through which he sees not only his own life but also the lives of others. He speaks of his relationship with his sister, as he most always has, with love and affection. When he talks about his victim, he speaks with a clarity that was previously absent.

Reynolds' difficulty has never been acknowledging or owning his crime. His cognitive distortions have most often surfaced around his feelings for his victim, which were the target areas of our hypnotherapy and precisely where I'm seeing evidence of true clarity. Reynolds is developing a fresh perspective toward his victim. He imagines a future for her that is full and rich and absent of himself. He is expressing a genuine hope for her happiness without him.

Psychic unions like that which have held Reynolds and his victim captive are not easily identifiable. Their successful severance is much more difficult. In discussions with Doctor Knox, we have both recognized identifiers that suggest incremental steps are being made in the right direction.

I have been working with Reynolds for the better part of three years now. He is up for parole in just under two months. In our most recent sessions, we have been discussing his release plans, but we have also spent much of our time reflecting on the prison experience.

When he arrived at Briar Ridge, he was completely ignorant of the penal system. He had never even known anyone who served time. He was an anomaly. Most people who find themselves in this place are intimately acquainted with the day-to-day operations of prison life. Many of those serving their first stint have a working knowledge of the system through friends and relatives closely connected to it. If Reynolds had had some awareness of the system to begin with, he would have seen many of the red flags pointing to his attack, which were all around him. In his ignorance, he walked right into it without any forewarning. Reynolds has learned many things about this system that, while he may wish he had never needed to know, will serve him well.

Once he leaves this place, Reynolds will re-enter a community that knows virtually nothing about the world from which he has so recently emerged. Back in mainstream society, he faces numerous hurdles, not the least of which will be culture shock. Just as the man who has never experienced a prison environment experiences culture shock upon arriving here, he experiences the same when he returns to society. The adjustment to making choices again can be as difficult as the adjustment to losing choice.

Because he has qualified for early release, Reynolds will leave here a parolee, with many restrictions governing his movement. He has now served close to three years of a four-year sentence and will remain on parole for another full year. While in the community, he will be under the watchful eye of a community parole officer who will see him up to four times per month.

He is further required to obey the law at all times. An infraction as simple as not wearing his seat belt could have dire consequences. The greatest difference between prison and parole are the bars. He will be, for all intents and purposes, still serving time; only the place he serves it will have changed. As part of his case management team, one of my responsibilities is to prepare community assessments for various potential people with whom he can live in the community. Until he reaches the termination of his sentence, he is not permitted to live alone.

His sister, Claire Durst, and her husband, Robert, have requested and applied to have Reynolds live with them indefinitely. This seems like a solution that will serve Reynolds well. His community parole officer will conduct the assessment in the Dursts' home and make the final decision based on her findings. The support the Durst family has given Reynolds throughout and even before his incarceration has been exemplary, and I foresee no issues in their approval.

Many restrictions will be placed upon him with regard to the places he can go and the things he can do. He cannot go to schools, parks, playgrounds, swimming pools, or other places where children under sixteen are likely to be. This doesn't concern me. Reynolds has never demonstrated any affiliations with the typical pedophiliac profile.

It is apparent that Reynolds feels a sense of humiliation in having to be a burden upon his sister's family yet recognizes his limited options. Humiliation is not a bad emotion for a recently released prisoner to experience. Humility provides a sense of indebtedness. Far better this than the sense of entitlement prisoners often carry into community life. The posture of humility provides the ambition to work hard to redeem oneself and increases a sense of gratitude for the support given.

We have spoken of future employment opportunities for Reynolds. He is aware that his charges disqualify him from future work in the field where he has always found employment. The prison world shields a man from having to think about such things. The very structure of prison creates a barrier around how he is going to live once he emerges from this existence. In fact, for most, it serves to remove these considerations altogether. Reynolds has often expressed his concerns about future employment. There is no means to prepare oneself for outside work while inside. Trade education services were removed from the system years ago to cut costs, and education in the prison system doesn't go beyond high school equivalency. For a man of Reynolds' education, training, and life experience, the system offers nothing. Further obstacles are stacked against all convicted felons the moment they walk out of the gates by the very nature of their status.

Applying for a menial job at Walmart or McDonald's often involves a Google search of the applicant's name. Therefore, even jobs that have no required criminal record check do in fact have them. The prisoner often finds himself unemployable.

Nevertheless, I have great hope for Reynolds. While there may have been no means to provide retraining or re-education for him, we have been engaged in the re-tooling of his mind, and he shall be far better prepared to leave this place with an attitude that will assist him greatly in meeting the many challenges he is sure to face.

The judicial system does far more to break a man than it does to restore him. Seldom is a man who has any accurate estimation of himself able to emerge from this environment with his head held high. As mentioned, a sense of humiliation often clothes those who leave here. When that humiliation grows into shame, self-pity, and self-loathing, this can destroy a man.

"Wholeness is brokenness owned and thereby healed." Reynolds has worked diligently to own his brokenness. Within our culture, things that break are either mended or, more likely, thrown away. Unfortunately, people are no different. If they are perceived as irreparable, they are tossed. In this case, those thrown away don't end up in a landfill; they end up in places like Briar Ridge, where they incur further brokenness, and many, unfit for any other existence, wind up never really leaving. The healing I have witnessed through Reynolds' diligent efforts will serve him well in the reintegration process.

In my earliest notes, I described Reynolds as either a narcissist or an empath. I'm pleased to report that I see him emerging as the latter. The more introspection and inner work he does, the more he is able to accurately see himself, his victim, and the consequences that have resulted from his crime. Our most recent work sees Reynolds expending very little energy on past ruminations of his relationship with his victim. Any discussions about her revolve around her personal well-being and the effects that his crime has had upon her. This is a massive leap from where we began, and it suggests a favorable evaluation of the neural hypnotherapeutic treatment.

The hypnosis seems to have had a gestalt effect. Not only have I witnessed change in the target area, a dramatic shift has also been taking place in Reynolds' perceptions about his father. He is demonstrating a desire to come to the other side of the table, so to speak, to see himself the way his father does—as someone who, for reasons he is unable to comprehend, is unworthy of love. Reynolds' approach to this is realistic. He recognizes that his father's hostility toward him began at such a young age that Trent did nothing to earn this lack of love. Therefore, the fault lies not within Reynolds but within his father. For the first time in many years, however, he is expressing a desire to understand why.

The work I do in Briar Ridge is frequently unrewarding. Once a patient leaves, I lose all contact with him. And when I'm completely honest with myself, I often experience a sense of relief when this occurs. With Reynolds, however, I feel a sense of loss.

Reynolds will spend these next few weeks preparing for his release. He will be meeting more often with his parole officer in preparation for his parole board hearing. He will be doing exit interviews and release documentation, all of which will take priority over our sessions and may interfere with our regularly scheduled therapy. This is the point at which I take a backseat to other matters in his life. Our time together is rapidly coming to an end as he prepares for life on the outside, which is bittersweet.

And in this I greatly rejoice.

CHAPTER FIFTY-FIVE

Dear Trent,

I just finished reading the last of the letters you sent. They were the most hate-filled and horrible attack against a man that I've ever heard. The more I read of your hatred, the more anger fills me. How in the hell could anyone be so heartless and cruel? How could anyone say and do things that would cause so much hurt? Your words cut through me, into me, and destroyed me. You speak of hating me, wishing I would rot in hell. I'm filled with a hatred and burning anger I have never known before. I can't even find words to express my rage.

The picture you paint of me is pure and utter evil, like I have been the devil himself out to destroy you. How do you suppose that makes me feel? Did you think for a moment that I would feel anything other than revolted at your description of me? You have made it very clear that I am to blame for so much of what has happened in your life.

And I am.

This hatred, anger, and rage I feel is *not* toward you, Trent; it's fully, in every way, toward me alone. I'm totally responsible for ruining you, and now I'm the one who is ruined.

I don't deserve to have you even hear me out, but I hope to God that you might be willing to.

What I have done to you, you have stated exactly right. You held up the mirror that I have been forced to look into. I hate the man who is looking back at me. The more I read, the more I realize how much pain I have brought to you, although I certainly didn't have to read your words to know this. From the moment of your birth, I have recklessly abused you. I know that to say I'm so very, very sorry does nothing to remove the damage I have done, and it doesn't even begin to describe the deep pain that fills me.

Oh, Trent, even writing this hurts so much. But I owe you the truth. I never wanted or planned to teach you anything. Had I known that you admired the way I washed my hands, I would have never washed them in front of you. I wanted only to hurt you. And today my entire body is wracked in pain and sorrow for what I have done to you.

Even as I write this, tears stream down my face. Sorrow as deep as the ocean fills my soul. I am broken.

As I sit here, I try to imagine what it will be like for you to read these words, and every attempt to explain why I have been such a terrible father to you makes no sense. There is no reason any man or child should ever be treated the way I have treated you. No reason whatsoever. Yet if you will listen to this broken man, I will attempt to explain.

In recent months as I lay in darkness, somewhere between life and death, much has been revealed to me. As you so clearly pointed out, I have always been a hypocrite. But while I lay between worlds, I had many encounters with a force—I will call that force God, if I can be so bold. I confess I've never clearly understood the Almighty. But he/she/it/they showed me things I never knew.

Do you remember the parable Jesus told of the pearl of great price? I'm sure you learned about it in Sunday school: "The kingdom of heaven is like unto a merchant man, seeking goodly pearls: Who, when he had found one pearl of great price, went and sold all that he had, and bought it."

It's not my intention to push my spiritual beliefs upon you in any way, but please, dear Trent, hear what I heard. We have been taught our entire lives that in this parable, the merchant man, the one who was in search of the treasure, represents us. We go through our lives seeking, and one day, somehow, we stumble upon this pearl of great price—God. We sell everything, give up everything to purchase Him and inherit eternal life. In my unconscious state, I was shown something that has completely changed how I understand this. In each of the parables of Jesus, the "man" is always representative of God. Why should it be any different with this parable? I think it has often been interpreted backwards. God, as in each of the other parables, is the merchant man seeking, and you are the pearl of great price. In his infinite love, God found you, Trent, a treasure of infinite worth, and gave everything in order to purchase you.

I have always hated it when someone says, "God told me . . ." because it warns the other person that an authority greater than either of them has spoken, and so you cannot disagree. In this instance, however, I say with some degree of confidence that God seemed to speak to me in that dark place between worlds. He said, "How dare you treat my pearl of great price, my priceless treasure, my Trent, the way you have? You, Gerald, have been an abomination to me."

That was the moment I began to emerge from lifelessness. I lay for months on the bridge between this life and the next. The tipping point was my response to God's correction. I understood. I saw with new eyes what I had done to you throughout your life.

I wept. I wailed. I howled for the son I have destroyed.

When you and Claire were young, the way she worshiped you should have made me proud, but instead it made me angry. She would follow you, imitate you, and want to please only you. Your heart was so pure and flawless.

You were six years old the day this was made perfectly clear to me. It was the first day of school, warm and sunny, the sky radiant, cloudless, and blue. The breeze was soft and warm, and so were you. We all stood on the front steps of the old farmhouse. When Claire saw the school bus raising dust a mile down the road, she clung to you, pleading for you not to go, not to leave her alone. Your mother and I stood at the top of the steps as you tried to make your way down the driveway with Claire attached to you. Mom turned to me and smiled. "Do you ever wish you had an older brother or sister, someone who means as much to you as Trent does to Claire?" I remained silent, an anger burning deep inside me.

When you realized you wouldn't make it down the driveway with Claire hanging onto your leg, you sat down with her in the fresh green grass next to the driveway. You held her little hand in yours and looked into her sad eyes. We heard every word you spoke to her, although you were trying to whisper. "Claire, I'm becoming a big boy now, and you'll be a big girl pretty soon. When we get bigger, we have to do big people things. School is a big people thing. You have to do bigger people things now too because you're getting bigger, just like me. You must stay here and help Mama with the things that I can't because I have to go to school. Pretty soon you'll get to go to school with me. But right now, you get to stay with Mama and help her with the things I can't do anymore because I won't be here. Do you think you could help Mama get the laundry off the clothesline?"

She nodded and smiled at you. "I can be a big help to Mom," she said. "I'll get the clothes, then fold them, and I can even put your clothes in your dresser so they'll be there for you to wear to school tomorrow. Then I can help Mommy make supper, and when you come home from school, I can show you all the big people things I did with Mommy. And you can show me all the big people things you did at school."

"I promise I will, Claire," you said. "I love you, big girl." You gave her a long hug and a kiss. Then she walked hand in hand with you down the driveway and stood watching and waving until the school bus disappeared from sight. She remained fixed in that spot until Mom went to get her. When Mom got there,

Claire was still waving, tears streaming down her face, and she kept repeating, "I love you, Trent. Have a nice day at school."

When you got home from school that first day, Claire ran with Charlie at her side as fast as she could to meet you. She hugged you, then you walked back up the driveway hand in hand as she told you every detail of her day, full of all the new things that come with being a big person. And inside my heart was only rage.

I must now share with you why. I have hidden a part of my life from the entire world.

Daniel.

I kept everything about Daniel hidden from the world. Not even your mother knew about him. I lost Daniel when I was ten years old. It was the darkest, most painful day I have ever known. Daniel was my older brother. He was almost fourteen when he died. It was an accident, an accident that I caused. I will spare you the details for now, but if you should ever want to know, I'm prepared to answer any and all questions you have.

What I would like you to know now is that I was Claire to your Daniel. I worshiped my brother. He was my world. My everything. When I saw the love, compassion, and adoration Claire had for you, it mirrored what I had felt for Daniel. My brother. My friend. My everything. The way she would follow you, and imitate you, and cherish you was so much like I'd been with Daniel. Your understanding, patience, and kindness toward Claire was the same as Daniel's toward me. Everything about you was Daniel, and I was unable to accept it—unable to accept you.

Your wavy blond hair, your large, penetrating blue eyes, the small cleft in your chin, the shape of your nose, the sharp, square cut of your jawline, your high cheekbones, your straight shoulders and posture, the way your permanent smile curls just at the edges of your lips. Looking at you was like looking at Daniel.

As you grew, you looked more and more like him. His mannerisms became yours. The way you would stretch after waking first thing in the morning, the way you would sit with your legs crossed, folded over your thighs, your gait as you walked, the way you turned your head. Everything about you was Daniel. I didn't know how to deal with it, so I attempted to make you into everything he was not. I crushed your spirit because it was strong, like Daniel's. I ridiculed your humor because it was rich and full, like Daniel's, I insulted your intelligence because it was sharp, like Daniel's. I wounded your heart because it was kind and warm and full, like Daniel's.

The older you became, the more like Daniel you became. When you turned fourteen, the age that Daniel would never be, I couldn't imagine him growing older and didn't want you to either. Your life continued while his didn't. He died at that age. You became more.

When you turned sixteen and got your driver's license, I despised you because you could then take Claire all the places Daniel could never take me. You became the man Daniel never did. I stopped Daniel from becoming that man, and I did everything I could to stop you from becoming one too. My horrible selfishness destroyed you, and it destroyed me. I'm so very sorry that it took a near-death experience for me to recognize this.

This letter is already pages long, yet it feels as though I haven't begun to scratch the surface of the many things I long to tell you—need to tell you—should you choose to hear them.

You speak of being a coward. How could you have been anything but? I placed you in situations where, as a young child, you couldn't respond except through cowardice. My violence demanded you cower to exist. It is me who is the coward. Trent, your letters took courage to write. I know that your intention was never to send them, but I'm grateful you did. I needed to hear your heart, your brokenness, your pain. Trent the man is not the person I tried to make him into. You have been through a fire designed to destroy you, but you have come through stronger.

I'm sorry, Trent. I'm trying to find words that adequately express the sorrow I feel for the harm I have caused you, but I come up empty. As I reflect on the words in your letters, self-disgust rises within me like vomit. My brokenness makes it difficult to write, difficult to breathe, difficult to comprehend. I cannot find the right words.

In that place where light and darkness do not differ, I experienced the chance to start again. I suppose something like Ebenezer Scrooge's visit from the ghost. Reading your letters brought that experience from the darkness into the light, and they demand a response. And I'm responsible to respond. Response-*able*. This letter is my first feeble attempt to respond to you with a flicker of a hope that you could possibly extend mercy to me.

For reasons I may never know, mercy was given to me as I lay near death. I was given a second chance to redeem myself. Redemption is the gift of mercy. Until that moment, I knew nothing of mercy. Now I know that mercy can't be taught; it can only be received or rejected. While I didn't deserve to have it extended toward me, it was, and I have chosen to receive it.

The very nature of mercy is that it's undeserved. And I deserve none from you. Nevertheless, if you graciously choose to extend it toward me, I will receive it with more gratitude than it's possible to express.

With deepest regret and sorrow,
Gerald

CHAPTER FIFTY-SIX

Mom and Dad went on a date! It's kinda freaky to think that your parents are divorced and suddenly they're dating again. When Dad brought Mom home, they were laughing like high school kids. Dad came in, and we all played Trivial Pursuit. Davy won, like he usually does. I think he takes the boxes of cards up to his room and memorizes them. Who could possibly know that Katharine Hepburn was nominated for thirteen Academy Awards and won four? Davy, that's who. He's crazy smart that way. Dad was still here when Davy and I went to bed. I can't say for sure, but I think he may have spent the night. His car was gone by the time I got up, but I'm pretty sure I heard them making love at about two in the morning.

I really hope that things work out between them again. They have always said that they were best friends before they started dating and got married. I think it's a good idea to spend your life with your best friend, although best friends can change.

When I was in grade school, my best friend was Lisa Montgomery. From the first day of grade one, we were best friends. We had sleepovers all the time, went to Girl Scouts together, and took figure skating lessons together. But by grade five, we were becoming different people. Our interests changed. She started liking boys way before me. Maybe 'cause she was an early bloomer. She had the biggest boobs in school by the time we entered grade six, and a lot of boys began paying attention to her. She started dating a boy who was in grade eight when we were still in grade six, and that's when we started to drift apart.

In middle school, Jenny, Amanda, and I were best friends and stayed that way right up until high school. That's when Trent became my best friend. But now that Trent's gone, Jenny and I are closer again. So, I'm thinking, why couldn't Mom and Dad become best friends again? And who knows? Maybe it will work out for them this time. I hope it does. It's kind of a romantic thought. Mom and Dad together, then apart, then together again because their love for each other is stronger than the things that drove them apart.

I fight hard inside not to feel the same hope for Trent and me. Linda says that I shouldn't fight to not think about Trent. She tells me to relax and be okay within myself, that I might be expecting too much of myself.

Expectations are overrated.

When I tell her I still think about Trent a lot, she doesn't freak on me. I guess I still think that something magical should have happened when she hypnotized me, and I expect her to be disappointed if I'm not completely over him. But she isn't. I mean, I think something happened. I don't think about him all the time anymore. I kinda expected that any thoughts post hypnosis would have been negative thoughts, but they're still mostly good ones. Damn expectations.

It's hard balancing my thoughts these days. I think about Jake almost as much as Trent. *All* the thoughts I think about Jake are good thoughts, and only most of them about Trent are. Jake knows that I still have a lot of feelings for Trent, and while I can see it bothers him, he's pretty cool about it and supports me more than I deserve.

Jake took me to see Beach Slang last weekend. Pretty great band. I've always liked indie punk but kind of set it aside while Trent and I were together because it wasn't his fave. I mean, it's not mine either, but I like it.

When Jake first asked me to go, we were talking about music and stuff. He's into Tenement and Liturgy and Girlband. I never took him for an indie punk guy, but it was a pleasant surprise. At least he's not into Green Day and Rise Against. I told him what I was into, or what Trent got me into. When I think about it, I kinda let Trent dictate to me what was cool and what wasn't. It's not that I don't like Pink Floyd or the Doors or Miles

Davis, but I'm starting to ask myself, do I like them because *I* like them or because Trent liked them?

Beach Slang was awesome. I don't slam or anything like that, and neither does Jake, and we didn't take E like probably 90 percent of the kids there, but we really enjoyed it. I like Jake a lot.

I used to talk all the time about how my relationship with Trent wasn't based solely upon sex, and I still don't think it was. But shit, we sure had a lot of it. Almost every time we were together, we had sex. And in some ways, as I think about it, whenever we were together, everything we did was leading up to it: the nice walks we would take, the dinners we planned and prepared, the movies we watched, the drives we took, the music we listened to, the games we played, at the end of it all, we wound up fucking. Don't get me wrong; I loved it and wanted it, but it was like all those things were in preparation for what we both knew was coming. All roads lead to orgasm. Like a maze that you do in one of those puzzle books to kill time while waiting to see the doctor. You take a pencil and start going down a path on the paper. When you realize that where you're headed won't take you to the little square at the very center, you try a different path until you solve it. With Trent and me, the solution to the maze was always sex. When we reached that point, we knew we had won and the maze had been solved.

Jake hasn't even tried to kiss me yet. We have spent a fair bit of time together. When we part ways, he talks about how much he enjoyed our time together, then he says goodbye, and that's it. We've only even hugged a couple of times. I don't know what he's waiting for. Maybe he thinks I don't want to kiss him, or maybe he's scared to because he knows how intimate Trent and I were, or maybe he wants to wait 'til I'm more over Trent. I don't know.

Part of me is excited to kiss him, and part of me is scared. I have been thinking about what it's going to be like and doing my best to prepare myself not to compare his kisses to Trent's. I guess I'm also scared that kissing him will be like betraying Trent, which is totally stupid. I don't owe Trent anything. It's not like we're still going out.

It's good to be sort of dating someone else. Jake is so kind and timid. He's kind of like a puppy. He's smart and funny but not in a show-off sort of way. I once told him I think he's really smart. He blushed. "Half of appearing smart is knowing all the things you're dumb about and staying away from those things," he said. See? Smart.

We're going to the Metropolitan Library together tomorrow. Jake is preparing for a paper he has to write for English Lit class on fiction writers who have developed into successful screenwriters, so he's researching Margaret Atwood, one of his favorite authors. I told him I'd like to go with him, and he smiled. So we're hanging out together again. Linda thinks it's a great idea for us to hang out together and for him to research Margaret Atwood. She's one of Linda's favorite authors.

In our sessions lately, Linda has been helping me understand how to live my life without someone I love. We've been going through how to cope with loss, and that has been very helpful. I've been thinking a lot about loss lately, about losing things and people, like Trent. I'm realizing loss takes all kinds of different forms.

As children, we lose our teeth, only to be replaced by newer, bigger, stronger, more practical ones. Socks are often mysteriously lost—or stolen by the dryer phantom. We lose toys at about the same time as we lose interest in them; otherwise we wouldn't lose them. We lose phone numbers and our memory. We lose friends and luggage and money in vending machines and library books and our homework and wallets and cell phones and track of time. We lose our virginity and our best friends. Sometimes we lose our virginity to our best friends. And sometimes losing things is an important part of growing up.

Linda says it's often only after we lose things that we realize how valuable they were or that they didn't actually have as much value as we thought they did. But until they're lost, we can't know. She also says that our "life buckets" can only hold so much. When they're full, we either have to take something out to make room for other things we want to put in them or wait until we lose something before something more can be added. Losing Trent kinda felt like the bottom fell right out of my bucket, but I think it's back, and I can start putting things into it again. I think I'd like Jake to be in there.

The other thing Linda said that kinda shook me is that she doesn't think we need to be together much longer. She says that I'm adjusting well, and she's very proud of the work I've done to heal from what may have destroyed many others. She says I'm strong and adaptable. I guess I am. It's weird, though. I've been seeing a counselor for almost three years. If you include seeing Trent, it's been, like, five. I hardly remember my life without one. Well, I do, but you know what I mean. I guess Linda is taking me out of her bucket to make room for someone who needs her help more than I do. It doesn't feel the same as when Tracy, my other therapist, dropped me. That felt like I was being rejected and thrown out. This feels more like I've graduated or that we've finished or something. And in some ways, I do feel like some things have finished.

Prom is a few weeks away. A chapter in my life is wrapping up so that the next one can open. I've been accepted to OSU to begin pre-vet studies in the fall. Jake is going there as well to begin a program in early childhood education. I doubt we'll have any classes together, but I'm sure we'll hang out and stuff. At least I hope we will.

We will. He likes me.

CHAPTER FIFTY-SEVEN

Picasso dropped by my cell to tell me he's being shipped out to a farm on the west coast. He leaves on the next "con air" flight, probably tomorrow or Friday. Con air is nothing like Delta or United. The DOJ owns a fleet of jets whose purpose is to transfer inmates from one institution to another. Essentially, they are little more than a prison with wings. And the prison farm is not what one typically associates with the word "farm" either. It's certainly nothing like the one I grew up on. In theory, farms are communal living centers for minimum-security prisoners, those who have served most of their time but are still not considered safe enough to be on parole in the community. Picasso fits this description well. He has served sixteen years of a twenty-four-year sentence, and his adjustment to community living will take some time. The farm is a good place for this to occur.

Pic has been a pretty good unit manager. It's not an official title. The actual unit rep is Ralph. His job is to ensure law and order are kept within the unit and to serve as a liaison between the COs and the inmates. That being said, since my arrival in PC, Pic has always been the one who has kept law and order on the unit. I'm not going to miss him, but I don't look forward to the pissing contest that will determine who will rule the roost next.

Picasso's not the only one leaving here soon, though. I have been approved for parole and will be leaving this horror show in just over a month, so I'm not too concerned about who will take over after he's gone.

I'm going to be living with Claire, Robert, and the boys for the next year or so. I have no say in the matter and am grateful for their hospitality. I will still be on parole and, therefore, not permitted to live alone until my parole warrant expires, just under one year from my release date. Community support is what they call it. In reality, it's having a babysitter to make sure I don't park my white panel van outside of a grade school and rape little kids.

During their visit yesterday, Claire and Robert spoke enthusiastically about my living with them, like I'm a long-awaited, honored guest. She told me that they and the boys can hardly wait for me to arrive. I appreciate their enthusiasm, but I can't help but feel as though I will be a burden. I couldn't ask for a greater support system than Robert and Claire, but I know I will be somewhat of a burden. How could I not be?

When I consider the many inmates in this place who have no support whatsoever, those whose families have disowned them or those who have burned so many bridges that they are completely alone, I know I'm blessed. But there's something unnerving about having to be so dependent upon others. That in itself isn't the crux of the matter, though. It's not their gracious generosity that's the problem. It's being forced into a position of utter dependence that stirs unrest within me. Incarceration is hard, but so is being released, or so I'm finding.

When I walk through that heavy iron gate, past the three rows of sixteen-foot, razor-wire-topped chain-link fence, I will be walking into the unknown. I have no job and no prospects of one, no car, no bank account, and very little savings. Any friends I had are all but gone, except for Bryan, and he'll be overseas for quite some time yet. I have no mother, I never had a father, and I have no phone or personal address. No Skype, no Facebook, no Twitter, no email address, no driver's license. The clothes I have stored in boxes in Claire's basement will no longer fit. I will leave here pretty much a blank canvas, which isn't all bad.

A fresh start is what I have needed for many more years than those I've spent in prison, and now I have it. Doctor Thackery suggests that having nothing is usually the best way to start: "Nothing doesn't weigh much and, therefore, doesn't weigh you down." Especially if that "nothing" includes expectations. There are many things about life that I have learned and have had to unlearn since arriving at Briar Ridge, and now I will have to learn many things again.

I have become a different person in prison—surprisingly, a better person. This has nothing to do with the system itself and has everything to do with Doctor Thackery's sacrificial investment. It's with much thanks to him that I have become a man. I look at life from a completely different perspective. I'm more considerate, by which I mean that I consider better. I'm better able to consider. Consider-*able.*

And so, I give consideration to the sacrifice that men like Doctor Thackery and people like my dear sister have made for me. While the investment Claire has made in my recovery is without question sacrificial, and I could elaborate upon her sacrifice endlessly, I wasn't always so generous as to call what Doctor Thackery has invested sacrifice. After all, he's being paid to work with the likes of me. But I know better now. There have been many hours of such deep concentration I would see beads of sweat form upon his brow as he gave himself fully to the formation of my manhood. Cathexis. So much wisdom bestowed, so many hours in research and preparation before I ever walked into his care. He isn't paid to do this to this extent. He didn't need to do this; it was a gift—charisma. A sacrifice, something holy. And I am the beneficiary of his sacrifice, like soldiers who return to their families because a martyr threw himself upon the grenade tossed into his comrades' trench.

My healing, while far from complete, comes at a high price for those who long to see me well. I shall not receive their gift ungraciously. I will commit to becoming a better man day by day by day. I will see Doctor Thackery one more time, perhaps twice, before I leave Briar Ridge. Unlike Picasso—who has done me no wrong—I will miss my good doctor, who has done me so much good. I consider how I can possibly go about repaying Doctor T for all that he has done, and I know exactly how. It's simple, really. I can take this man I have become—am becoming—and do manhood well. Some of that must start with Brianna.

Consideration of Brianna has taken new form. Until our story broke, I considered her only my lover, the one whom I loved. Once our relationship became a public fiasco, she was considered by everyone, except me, as my victim. After much consideration and even more introspection, I recognize how she was both my lover and my victim—something that was inconceivable for a long while.

I consider that her choice, her power to consider us, was infringed upon by the authority of my power. I can't relegate her to having no choice in our relationship; to do so would be an insult to the intelligent young woman she is. But I have become able to consider and accept that the influence I had upon her decision-making process was certainly greater than it would have been had our relationship been age and context appropriate. As a result, I'm here, and she bears scars that will remain throughout her life.

I consider her desire to give herself fully to a young man whom she may choose to love someday, and I recognize that while she may be able to do this, she will only be giving herself fully *again*. This she must carry, and so must I. Such knowledge gives pause for consideration. I consider the help she came to me for initially and didn't receive—at least not the way she desired to. Instead, she received that for which she was ill prepared. In the wake of our collapse, it's my sincere hope that she has received preparation for life from a healthier counselor than I, that she is growing in wisdom and self-discovery, and that she is healing and able to move forward with her life and dreams.

She will graduate from high school at about the same time as I walk out of here. Another hope is that my release will not be a burden on her, that there will be no fear associated with her knowing that I'm back in the community. I will not visit our old haunts: Glen Echo Park, Palace Lanes, Westbank Walkway, Thompson Library at OSU, Haden Falls, Buca Di Beppo's, Lindey's, and Scioto Valley Coffee. These would serve as severe reminders of us, places I have a desire to visit, and therefore will not. Placing restrictions like these on myself is catalytic toward my continued healing, probably our continued healing.

To say that my desire to be with Brianna has been removed completely would be a lie. To say that my desire to see and be with her again is less than my desire for her and my own personal well-being would be the truth. Living truthfully, I'm finding, is a much easier and better way to live. Living truthfully requires far less energy than living a lie. Being honest with myself and others is freeing, life-giving. It's not always comfortable, but it's always right.

In my life, being consider-*able* must also include the ability to consider Gerald, who lives and speaks and breathes. Claire says that Gerald continues to amaze her, medical science, and himself. She tells me that he is different, that he has changed. I don't want to give him the benefit of this doubt; therefore I must. This is part of the changed me that I'm working hard to become. This newness of life must permeate every corridor of my being, Gerald included.

Approaching every aspect of life from this new perspective is not easy, but it is necessary. Along with a new perspective, I must entertain a new way of thinking, then a new way of processing those thoughts, after which must follow a new way of acting upon said thoughts. These actions precipitate patterns that are becoming habits. The old ones die hard, and the new ones rise hard.

Claire told me that Gerald's doctor has recommended that while he heals, he remain as free from stress as possible. Therefore, he has forbidden communication with his investment agents, his advisors, and his accountants. She tells me, wonder of wonders, that Gerald seems to be okay with this. He doesn't even inquire about how his plethora of investments are doing. She also tells me that since all of Gerald's financial issues are handled through his offices, she dropped off the stacks of junk mail that have gathered over the months for him to browse through. "His Easton Mercedes catalog shouldn't be too hard on him," Claire says. She made no mention of the letters I sent, so I must assume that they arrived amidst the bundles, uninterrupted. Well, if he finds them among all the Walmart, Dicks Sporting Goods, and Target fliers, they should increase his stress level a bit, I would think, which gives me more to consider.

Considering how Gerald and I have navigated our lives with respect to each other over the years, how does this new me deal with any of the repercussions that may arise from my correspondence? As I consider this,

I'm forced to acknowledge a fear of Gerald still lurks within me. He has proven over and over that there is much for me to be fearful of.

My concern is less about his reaction to the letters than it is about any future interactions. As a soon-to-be guest in Claire's household, I must give consideration to several factors concerning Gerald should he choose to disown me, which I'm quite certain he will—or has. My crimes are impetus enough; add to them my furious rants, which he certainly has read by now, and I hold out little hope of ever hearing from him again. Not that I have much of a desire to do so. However, this new life I live attempts to never say never. And with Claire being so involved in his life, I foresee a day in the not-too-distant future when our paths will cross. While it's easy enough to say I'll cross that bridge when I get to it, I don't want Claire to be stuck in the middle of Gerald and me like she was during so many of our childhood years. I'm certain this concern has not been lost on her either. As a guest in their home, this is something I need to give great consideration to.

Consider, consider, consider.

So, I consider possible ways to defuse the situation, as much as I am able. There are a few possibilities. I can make myself scarce whenever Gerald visits. I can put a smile on my face and make like a child—seen but not heard. I can engage Gerald in polite, emotionless conversation, or I can attempt to be the man I purport to have become and work toward resolving some of the tension between us, using the skills I have learned and the promises I've made to myself. I dislike the latter option passionately, which suggests it's likely the best of the four. I'm learning that the difficult path is often the higher ground, that the path I find most bitter is the right one to take. That I don't even like to consider it is a powerful indication that it's the right choice. Each of these falls within my ability to choose, and choosing well is what I have committed myself to doing.

Writing letters from prison is not like writing on the other side of these walls. There is no option to sit at my laptop and eloquently express myself. Each letter is handwritten, which is fine. In fact, I have come to enjoy this long-lost practice. But as a result, there are no copies to refresh my memory. I still have no regret about sending the many letters I wrote to Gerald. However, concern arises from the new perspective that I have adopted. Would I say the same things the same way now that I'm a different man—a man? No. Would I still have been truthful in the letters? Yes. Would I have included sins of omission? Perhaps not. But the tone of the letters, that would be different.

I had one intent: to hurt Gerald. I wanted him to feel and to know the pain I have felt and known. Because the letters were never meant to be sent, I considered only my woundedness, which was selfish. Had I ever intended for Gerald to read them, I would have written differently. And if I'm honest with myself, they probably would have lacked much honesty. So, when I say I don't regret sending them, that is only partially correct. I'm thankful for the truth I was able to pen. Doing so was catalytic to my healing. Nevertheless, the way I spoke those truths lacks any sense of respect for the worth and value of another human being, which, as I have come to understand, I have a measure of, and if I do, others must as well. It's Gerald's worth as a human being that I have neglected in my letters. Consideration of Gerald's intrinsic value as a man is something I gave no consideration to whatsoever.

Intrinsic human worth, value, and purpose are not to be confused with respect. Respect must be earned and can also be lost. I'm all too aware of this. I have lost more respect than I care to consider. The long, hard road back to earning it again is a path I'm just beginning to forge. I have no respect for Gerald. In my estimation, he has earned none and lost much.

Respect here in Briar Ridge is something one finds very little of. The mighty, like Picasso, do not earn respect; they demand it. Demanded respect is no respect at all; it's nothing but fear. The guards also demand respect, but like Pic, they are merely feared. I have feared Gerald for many years. The letters he now has will reveal to him that in my fear of him, there has been no respect. I hold out little hope of ever respecting the man who was to have been my father, but I won't fear him any longer either.

As I consider my release into the care of the one I love and respect more than any other, I'm filled with gratitude. As I consider future encounters with Gerald, I have some trepidation and concern. The person I was, who committed the offenses I have, who lived in fear of his father, whose life was filled with regret, remorse, and shame, came into this place a boy but leaves a man. I have grown twenty-five years over these past three. I am learning to live life as a man, to think like a man, to reason like a man, to choose like a man. I have woken from childhood, reemerged differently. I look at everything through a new lens, almost as if I have been reborn. Born again?

Each day looks different. It has a different feel, as though life prior to this was another person's life, a child's life. I can be with the child I once was. I can talk with him, calm him, understand him, instruct him. My emergence from childhood doesn't diminish or replace the child I have been for thirty-five years. I walk alongside him, providing care, nurture, and guidance. Trent the man serves as a guidance counselor to Trent the boy, who needs much. My new role is to protect the boy I was and help him understand the world and his place in it from a perspective of truth and accuracy, of which there has been little—to help him grow. Because Trent the boy lives in the body and psyche of Trent the man, he is often unable to see the world clearly. He can't because he remains a child who has not grown with the time that has passed or adapted to life as it changed all around him. He has been stuck as a ten-year-old for twenty-five years.

He really does exist, and yet if Trent the man is to live, one day Trent the boy must not. With Trent the man to guide him and help him grow, Trent the boy will do so. As he grows, he will become closer and closer to the man I am, and one day we shall merge and become one. That will be a good day for us both.

Of course, I must give great consideration to this disease that, little by little, is consuming me. Being HIV positive, even with the knowledgeable, widespread destigmatization of the disease, is a sensitive matter. I'm concerned about the fear that Stevie and Aaron may have about being in close proximity to their uncle. While neither Claire nor Robert have expressed any concern, I must consider this situation. It's something we must discuss together. Claire has never brought up the matter, other than to express her heartfelt sorrow for my condition. I haven't told her or Robert how ill I have been, how I'm often nauseous during the day, or the diarrhea that visits, often with little warning. I'm sure much of this has to do with the prison diet and will improve along with the ability to eat healthier. Nevertheless, it seems to ravage me from the inside and is something I need my sister and her family to be aware of.

As of late, Doctor Thackery has provided some excellent counsel and wisdom about my diagnosis. Of course, I'm far from the first patient he has worked with in the pos community. His work among inmates who have this condition, while not an everyday occurrence, is not unusual either. Moreover, he volunteers at a local AIDS hospice and has seen his share of men in their final days of its grasp, something I have never witnessed and hope never to see. He has provided risk-reduction counsel and given some good advice about dating, future partners, and strategies to inform women I may one day desire to have a relationship and relations with. When I asked him if my sex life was over, he almost laughed. "Of course not! Today, there are multiple ways to have safe sex." Staying compliant with my meds and maintaining an undetectable viral load is the best way to ensure that I never transmit the virus. He says that this method of prevention is for my protection just as much as it is for any future partners.

I have shared with him my concern for Claire and her family, and he has debunked many of the stereotypical false assumptions about the disease. He has also recommended a reputable therapist to provide psychosocial stabilization counseling for Claire and her family as a means of coping with my condition—another thing for consideration. My family shouldn't have to suffer through or undergo treatment for what I have wrought upon them, but they do.

I have regular blood tests to ensure that my CD4 count and my viral load are within the acceptable range. My CD4 count has occasionally dipped below 300, which is unusual and more than a little concerning, as 200 or less indicates that the HIV has become AIDS. This would explain why I'm feeling so tired and sick and weak. It would also suggest that, for whatever reason, the current cocktail of TDF, 3TC, and EFV drugs I'm taking aren't doing their job, which may mean having to switch medications again.

Doctor Thackery has set me up with a friend of his, Doctor Sullinger, who is an HIV specialist. I'm scheduled to see him within a few days of my release. Doctor T tells me that Doctor S is one of the most respected HIV specialists in the country, and he will determine in short order whether the virus I have is resistant to any medications—which is unlikely, but if this is the reason for my low CD4 count, he will prescribe alternative treatment that will be helpful. I'm told that no matter how low my CD4 count drops, it's easily treatable, and once we find the right medication, it will shoot up again, my viral load will drop, and the chances of me infecting another person or succumbing to the disease altogether will become negligible. I'm continually being reminded that a person diagnosed with HIV today has roughly the same life expectancy as a person who is HIV negative. However, I also know that this virus makes me more susceptible to several health risks that I must remain aware of, including cardiovascular disease, kidney problems, and bone density loss. I'm fully aware that HIV is not what it once was, although this nagging cough that will not seem to go away concerns me.

As I prepare to leave this place, I will take some things with me, and HIV is only one of them. I will take certain new understandings of the word *demoralization*. This place specializes in keeping a man down, making him less than, reducing him to little more than a number. But I will also take with me a sense of purpose, a new perspective on living, and a new, fuller, richer sense of freedom's value. And with that an appreciation for those who have given themselves so that I might experience this new freedom in a way that is life giving. I consider those who have given so much of their lives to the betterment of my own, and I am filled with gratitude.

CHAPTER FIFTY-EIGHT

Dear Trent,

It's been a very long time since you and I have had any form of communication, and we won't have any now, but I thought I'd write anyway. A couple of years ago, way back when Tracy was still my therapist and Linda wasn't even in the picture—not that you'd know either one—she suggested that I write you a letter, one that I will not send. Just something to help me get all this stuff that's inside out. At the time, I didn't understand what she was talking about or feel that it was necessary, but lately I've been thinking about it, and you know what? I think it's a good idea.

First of all, I should tell you I'm not mad at you, and I don't hate you, but I don't think I love you anymore either. Believe me, this is as much of a shock to me as it may be to you. Not so long ago, I didn't think I would ever get over you. Thoughts of you—of us—consumed me. There was not an hour, let alone a day, that went by when you were not first and foremost in my mind. But as time goes by, the intervals between how much you consume my thoughts grow longer, lengthening like these days of spring that are quickly approaching summer.

I want to begin by saying that I'm so sorry for what happened to you after the car accident. I can honestly say that never in my wildest dreams did I imagine you could or would have to suffer the way you have for nothing more than being my boyfriend. I guess lurking in the back of my head, I knew that what we were doing was illegal, but I didn't have a clue that it would end the way it did.

You knew, though.

So, why did you do it? Was it worth the risk? Was I worth the risk? I guess in the depths of my heart, I still like the feeling that comes when I think that you loved me so much, you risked everything to be with me. To be honest, I feel kind of honored that this might be true. But I also feel like, in some ways, you were, I don't know, so stupid. I mean, seriously, Trent, were you so naïve as to think that we could get away with it forever, that the day would come when everyone, including my parents, would just smile and say, "Oh, how wonderful it is that they're so in love." So, the part of me that's sorry is also tempered with a part of me that just doesn't get it—doesn't get you. God, I hope one day you'll grow up.

The one thing in our relationship that I do have to own—you taught me the importance of owning my shit, thank you—is what happened at your trial. I allowed my lawyer, the police, my parents, and the pressure from everyone around me to convince me that it was okay to lie. It wasn't, and it's one of the biggest regrets of my life. I think the lies I told in that courtroom did as much or more damage to me than anything you ever did. I carried that with me for way too long.

Linda, my new therapist, has helped me to forgive myself for what I did. She thinks you and I shared something unique, rare, and special, by the way. It's largely because she validated the feelings I have—sorry, *had*—for you that I've been able to make so much progress in getting over you.

When I fell in love with you, I was a child. I felt like an adult, you treated me like an adult, and so I behaved and believed I was an adult, but I wasn't. Why didn't you honor and respect the child Brianna the way you did the woman you forced me to become? I would have respected *you* far more if you had.

Linda tells me that while what you and I shared was very real, I couldn't process it with the maturity that the depth of our love demanded. Does that make sense? It's starting to, at least for me. I fell in love with your superior intellect, your sense of humor, your life experience, the wonderful dinners, the depth of our conversations, your fast car, the amazing sex, your home, your music, and dreams of a future together. But these were all things that I should have known nothing about at ages fifteen and sixteen. How could I be anything but in awe of you? I don't know if you knew the power that you held over me, but you should have. When I should have been dating guys with acne and homework and dreams of playing in the NHL, I was dating someone who had left those things behind years ago. How could any high school boy measure up to you? Did you know all of this and choose to pursue me anyway? Did you use that power to overwhelm me, to seduce me?

I'm not expecting an answer, and I'm aware that I will never get one, but God, I'd like to know. I would like to know—to believe, I suppose—that I was more than just a conquest to you. I hope I was. Otherwise I'll feel so stupid. So duped. So foolish.

I would like you to know that you did hurt me—in a lot of ways. You forced me to grow up much sooner than I should have, and in doing so, you stole some of my childhood. And I will never get that back. Like my virginity, it's gone forever, and that hurts. I don't begrudge giving you my virginity, though. I gave it to you freely. You were a wonderful and passionate lover. The way you used to . . . ah, I better not go there. You taught me well, and I will cherish the things I learned, and I can't wait to enjoy that kind of passion with someone again. It may be sooner than you know.

But you also hurt me when you left. You abandoned me, Trent. You taught me to completely depend upon you, and then you vanished. Of course, I know you didn't choose to leave, but it doesn't change the fact that you did, and that brought a level of pain I had never known before, or since. I wish I could make you feel the emptiness I lived with month after month after month.

The nights I cried myself to sleep, missing you, are too many to count. I was on antidepressants for almost two years. They didn't help.

School was hell for the rest of the year after you left. Teachers and students ostracized me. Suddenly, most of the guys thought that because you had been fucking me, they stood a pretty good chance as well. Do you have any idea what that's like? Of course you don't.

I'll just say it's awful. A lot of the girls at Glenwood treated me like I was a slut too. Can you imagine what that was like for someone who had been "the nice girl" her whole life? The pain and shame from that was almost unbearable.

In some ways, the teachers were even worse than the students. It was like I had been infected by a sinister disease. They would almost run away from me, even teachers like Ms. Thatcher, whom I always thought really liked me. When I got back—I stayed away from school for almost a month after you were arrested—I was treated with mistrust and suspicion. It was like I had become someone completely different. I didn't feel like I had totally changed, but shit, everyone else seemed to feel I had. I almost changed schools, but something you taught me kept me there. Remember how you used to say, "The problem with running from your problems is that you take the biggest problem, 'you,' with you"? So I stayed. At first it was really hard, but now I'm glad I did.

The media attention made life almost unbearable for a while. I don't know if you get the news, the *Dispatch*, or anything like that in prison, but we were a pretty hot item for a while. Of course, they didn't mention me by name or have any pictures of me, but you got lots of notoriety. I guess that's another thing that confuses me, Trent. Knowing how dangerous what we were doing was, you did it anyway. Why? Really. I mean, what the fuck was going through your head? I'm sure you've asked yourself that question more times than I have, but I can't get my head around why anyone would give up as much as you did for us. I hope you can get the help you need to sort things out for yourself. I don't know if they offer any such help in prison. I doubt they do, but if so, I hope you take advantage of anything they have for you.

You should know that I don't wish you ill at all. In fact, I wish you well. I hope you can find new meaning and purpose in life after all that you've been through. I've tried to imagine what life must be like for you in there. I used to lie awake at night crying for you and praying for you, that you would be okay. That's still my hope for you, that you will be okay.

I'm sure the road you will travel after all this will not be easy, but I hope you can find peace and some sense of happiness in your life as you prepare to leave that place. I think you'll be getting out soon. My therapist, Linda, says the police will tell me when you're being released because, as your victim, I'm supposed to know when you're back into the community. God, I hate that word, "victim." I am not a victim. I made choices, you made choices, and we've both suffered for the things we chose. You certainly more than I, but we both paid a far higher price than I'm sure either of us ever imagined.

Things are pretty much back to normal for me these days. I thought you might be happy to know that. I sure am. I graduate next week. Amazing how fast time flies, huh? I'm sure you don't feel the same. I'm looking forward to prom and to getting on with my life. I've been accepted at OSU in the pre-vet program. For the first time in a long while, I'm excited about the future. I've been in touch with Doctor Cho at the Lake Darby Veterinary Clinic. He says I'm still welcome to do my residency with him when the time comes. I'm pretty psyched about that. I think he followed our "situation." He seemed a little surprised when Dad and I dropped in a couple of weeks ago, but he was very nice and seemed genuinely happy to see me. So, thank you for introducing me to him.

Oh yeah, Mom and Dad are back together! You probably didn't even know they split up, although we talked enough about how stressed things were at home that I'm sure you suspected it was imminent. Anyway, they split up a few months after things went south with us, and they were apart for more than two years, but they decided to try and make a go of things, and so far, it seems to be working out great. That's another thing I'm psyched about.

A lot of good stuff has been happening in my life over these past few months. I'm so used to bad shit happening that I'm a bit cautious whenever something good happens—like the universe is setting me up to be shit on again. But Linda has been helping me to feel safe again. I'm lucky to have her in my life, and it's one of the reasons I hope you can find help too. She has been a lifesaver for me. I don't know what my life would have been like had she not stepped in. When I first started seeing her almost a year ago, I was still pretty fucked up. I had another therapist for a while, Tracy. She was okay, but she was a bit of a piece of work too. She spent more time telling me how I was supposed to feel than listening to how I was actually feeling. And more time wanting to know the intimate details of our sex life than almost anything else. Once I started seeing Linda, I realized how wrong things were with Tracy. To be honest, I think Tracy was getting turned on when I told her about sex with you. Weird, huh?

Linda did this thing with me to break what she called a psychic union that she thinks you and I had. Some kind of connection that was preventing me from getting over you. Weird again, right? Anyway, another doctor gave me a shot to help me relax and then Linda hypnotized me. Other than being very relaxed and pretty high I didn't feel much different, but she walked me through some of the choices that I had made and showed me some that I could still make. Not having to love you was one of them. When I came out of it, I didn't feel any different, but over the last few weeks, I've been able to do something I never seemed able to do before: stop thinking about you all the time. I don't mean to hurt you, but you have no idea how good that feels. I guess the reason I hope you get the help you need is that I know how much it has helped me to have someone in my corner who understands me and wants to see me be the best person I can be. That's what Linda has been for me, and that's what I hope for you.

Before I wrap this up, there's one more thing I want to tell you: you're a good man, Trent Reynolds—as fucked up as you may be. You have a kind heart and so many other amazing qualities. I wish that things had turned out differently for you—for both of us. I really do. Not that I wish we were still together. I guess I'm glad we're not. I suppose if I was older or you were younger, I'd probably feel differently. But you taught me so many things that I'm happy I know. You taught me how to love. Not just another human being but how to love myself and appreciate who I am. Much of that got lost in the chaos that ensued around us, but it's still there, and I'm grateful for it.

I only wish you the very, very best in life and hope that the road ahead is better than the one behind. Part of me will always love you. Goodbye.

Love,
Brianna Barnes

P.S. I've met someone whom I think you'd like. Actually, you know him, Jake Simonson. Remember him? You gave him some excellent advice a few years ago that took him almost three years to act on, but he finally did, and we're together now. We're going to prom, and he'll also be going to OSU in the fall, so hopefully we'll be together for a while. And who knows . . . ?

CHAPTER FIFTY-NINE

Dear Trent,

You and I have always had the type of relationship where we could tell each other anything. I love that about us. But there are some things that have more meaning—more impact, more value—when put on paper. First, I want you to know how welcome you are in our home. I know that if our situations were reversed, you would move heaven and earth to help me. You always have. So, it's not like I think I'm doing you a big favor or being overly gracious or anything of the sort. I'm simply doing the only thing I can do. I couldn't live with myself if you were somewhere else and weren't spending the next year or so with us. And I can say with absolute certainty that Robert feels the same way. I know that you probably feel as though you're going to be a burden on us, but please, for God's sake, get that faulty thinking out of your head. I know you think that way because that's the way I would think if things were reversed, but you couldn't be more wrong.

Robert and I are also fully committed to helping you get the help you need. I have been researching HIV specialists as well as psychologists who specialize in helping adult victims of child sexual abuse. I have found a few that I think may be really helpful. So, I hope you don't get pissed at me, but I already made a couple of appointments for you. :-) I've seen the incredible change in you since you've been working with Doctor Thackery, and I realize how important it is that you continue to grow.

Trent, I love you more than pretty much anyone on the planet and will do everything I can to help you. Once again, this is nothing that you wouldn't do for me.

My heart breaks when I think of the secrets you have been forced to hold in your head and heart all these years. I won't dwell upon this. I try my best not to, for when I do, it eats away at me, and I begin to think all kinds of crazy thoughts. A million woulda shoulda couldas flood my head and erode the healthier things that I need to focus on. But I want you to know that when I think of the things Jimi did to you, I get sick. I have actually had to excuse myself from the classroom, from social gatherings, and even get up in the middle of the night to puke when thoughts of what he did enter my head. It's one of the reasons I can't allow myself to think about it much.

I can't fathom what those nights were like for you. I think you must have felt the way a kitten feels when a fox enters the barn and corners it. I remember being only five or so the first time I saw that happen. The options for the kitten were limited: fight, flight, or freeze. Until it was cornered, it tried to run. Once it was backed into the corner, it didn't fight. I'm sure it knew how useless that effort would be, so it froze. The terror in its eyes and the pleading, pathetic mews as it cried and resigned itself to the inevitable still haunt me. I have often wondered if this isn't exactly what you felt each time you heard Jimi creep into your room and felt him slither into your bed.

In our visits, you have often talked about the self-pity demons that possessed you and that you don't want me adding fuel to that fire. I promise I will do my best not to do that. You have made it clear what a destructive force that has been in your life. So, please know that I don't feel sorry for you, although I'm so sorry that my big bother, my friend, and my hero had to endure the agony of those terrible experiences for so many years. And as much as there is a part of me that's glad I didn't know about what was happening to you, I'm so sorry I didn't.

Okay, on to better things.

Stevie and Aaron are so pumped about you coming to live with us. They can't stop talking about it. They've pretty much planned your "Uncle Trent" week in August. Just a heads-up. I hope you still like roller coasters, as you're starting at Cedar Point Amusement Park in Sandusky and then are off to Crystal Rock Campground and the water park nearby. Good luck. Robert and I have been made aware of the restrictions placed upon you about being alone with children and have signed a consent for you to be with the boys regardless of whether or not we're present. On that note, the idea that we'd be concerned about you being alone with the boys is absurd to both of us. You do know that we trust you implicitly, right?

A community parole officer was by the other day to do a community assessment of us. The boys had to be here as well. He went into detail about your crime and made certain that we were all aware of the conditions of your parole, and he insisted we notify him should you breach any. I understand the rationale for such precautions. But for you? I know this guy deals with criminals who are constantly looking for ways to get around or break the law. I also know they have to paint every prisoner with the same brush, but wrapping my head around that is far easier said than done. How does one do that?

These last years have been the hardest of my life, so I can't imagine what they've been like for you. I'm not mad at you. I was, though. There was a time right after you went in when everything around me seemed to be falling apart. Mom dying, Dad's heart attack, and your absence left me in absolute despair. I was mad mostly because when I needed you the most, you weren't here for me. Over the years, I had come to depend on you for almost everything. Robert thinks you and I are probably a little enmeshed, and he may be right. But in the darkest days of my life, when the one I leaned on whenever dark clouds were overhead was gone, I kinda fell apart. I never let you know that. Whenever I saw you, I did my best to be strong and courageous because I knew you were facing far more than I was. Now as the clouds appear to be lifting, I'm less hesitant to trust hope again.

Remember that poem Dad had mounted above the fireplace in the old farmhouse? It was called something like "Footprints in the Sand." God, I hate that poem. I mean, if the poet was actually being carried by God through the darkest times in his life, wouldn't they seem like the best times of his life? After all, could there be a better place to be than nestled in the arms of the Almighty? I've never understood how so much of the world can embrace the obviously ridiculous. It sounds nice, but the moment a person walks through abject horror, they want someone there, not empty rhetoric.

I have a spiritual theory that I'm beginning to think sums up much of life—a Forrest Gump-ism, if you will: "Shit happens." That's it. Life is hard, and some people get dumped on more than others, and we deal with it. God doesn't show up and sweep us into his arms to soothe the pain. We walk through it, hopefully with those we love but sometimes all alone, then we carry on. I guess I feel like I needed you, my savior, to show up and help me through the darkness of these past years, but you were a cause of much of the darkness and walking alone through your own. That's where the anger with you came from. I needed you, and you couldn't be there for me.

We have hardly spoken of your HIV-positive status during our visits. I want to attribute that to the fact that the prison visitors' lounge isn't the best place to have such conversations, but that wouldn't be altogether true. I simply haven't known how to talk with you about it. I guess there's been so much stigma associated with the disease that I've been a little fearful for—and to be honest, a little fearful of—you. As mentioned, I've done a fair bit of homework, and with the drugs available today, a person with HIV can expect to live as long as a person without and be just as healthy. Did you know that? There's even a very low risk of you infecting another person as long as you stay on your treatment plan. I know you know this. I'm writing this more to reassure myself than anything. The boys also know about your status, and it doesn't bother them at all. They just want to be reassured that you won't die anytime soon.

Over the past couple of years, Robert has suspected that you would likely need a place when you were released, so we've been fixing up the basement. It doesn't have the big wall of glass and sliding doors to take you out onto the balcony like your thirty-second-floor apartment did, but it's bright and open. We've got your furniture and stuff all set up. I think you'll find it a cozy place to live for a while. It will be completely your space. Robert even built a separate entrance from the back.

If all goes well, you'll be here next Thursday. The boys are pumped about that because Friday pizza nights have returned by popular demand. You'll hardly recognize the boys. Aaron is almost as tall as I am. His voice is beginning to change; he squeaked at me a couple of times last week. Stevie has had a growth spurt and is even taller than Aaron, which pisses Aaron right off. When they scuffle, though, Aaron still comes out the victor. But the boys, as opposite as they are, seem to be getting along better over these past months. I think what happened to you took a greater toll upon them than any of us realized, and it's taken a long time for them to sort through it.

Dad is doing amazing. His health is pretty much back to where it was prior to the heart attack. I know of no way to describe it other than miraculous. On Monday he'll be leaving Ridgewood Terrace and moving home, if you can believe it. He has arranged to have a nurse come in once in the morning and once in the evening, just to check on him, but he's almost completely self-sufficient again.

While physically he seems to be 100 percent, some things about him are very different. He's far more thoughtful than before, and he doesn't talk nearly as much as he used to. He's also less anxious and more deliberate.

Here's a question: do you know who Daniel is? Dad referred to him a lot while in the hospital and a few times since. I have no idea who he's talking about, and I get the sense he doesn't want me to. And yet, whoever this Daniel is, he and Dad seem to be very close.

When I was there last week, he said he'd received some mail he'd been expecting his whole life. He didn't elaborate, and it appeared he didn't want to discuss it, so I didn't push it, but whatever it was, it really shook him.

I told him you're getting out next week. I hope that's okay. He said he was happy for you and asked if it would be okay to see you at some point. "No rush," he said, then added that if you don't want to see him, he completely understands that as well. Then he did something I've never seen him do. He cried, Trent. Sitting there in his recliner, he put his head into his hands and sobbed. After a bit he composed himself, apologized, and said he couldn't explain it, but every now and then he gets really emotional. Then he said something else that I never expected I would ever hear from him. He said he would like to see someone who can help him deal with some of the things in his past.

"Like a psychologist?" I asked, probably much too quickly and definitely much too enthusiastically. Dad just nodded. Can you believe that?

I often wonder what happened to him all those months he spent in a coma. I'm trying not to get my hopes up, but I think maybe our whole family might be on the mend. I hope so. After all the years of hell, how wonderful would it be to have a bit of heaven shine down on us, huh? I know you probably don't feel the same. Heaven for you likely doesn't include Dad, and I understand that. I wish I could do something to help mend the relationship between you two, but I'm fully aware that's out of my hands.

Robert and I have discussed how we're to navigate the tumultuous waters that surround you and Dad and realize that we'll soon be right in the middle of the whirlpool. We've agreed that we'll do everything we can to support you, but we won't isolate ourselves from Dad. I have no idea what that's going to look like. I hope you can understand this. I suppose it will take some time to figure it out. Please be patient with us as we do.

Once life is a bit more stable, I'm sure Dad will start gallivanting around the globe again, so I doubt he'll be around much, but we want to be able to have him over. One of the reasons Robert set the basement up the way he did is so you can put some distance between yourself and Dad if and when he comes over, if and when you want to.

But I do want you to know that I'm tired of walking on eggshells between you two, and I'm going to try not to do that. You both seem to have changed a lot as you've trudged through this shit. Both of you have kind of grown up. I know that it probably seems like a near impossibility, but it would be nice to be a family at some point, whatever that means.

Trent, you've been the most influential person in my life. When we were kids and I was deathly afraid of thunderstorms, it never dawned on me to run to Mom and Dad for protection. I always went to you. Remember that horrific storm when I was in grade five? It was the same summer Rascal died. Probably around two in the morning, the thunder began to shake the windows. The lightning flashes were in such rapid succession that the inside of my room looked like a disco dance floor. I was about to run to your room when the loudest thunderclap I had ever heard in my life paralyzed me with fear. Seconds later, you were there. You lifted the blanket from over my head and crawled under it with me. You held me and stroked my head as I shook in your arms. "It'll be alright Claire, it'll be alright." you said, and it was. When the storm finally ended, you didn't let me go, and we eventually fell asleep together with you holding me tightly. My protector, my champion, my best friend, my big bother. I couldn't have asked for a better person to help me navigate life, and if I can do some of the same for you now, I would be honored to hold you until this storm passes, the same way you held me.

I love you more than words can express,
Claire Bare

CHAPTER SIXTY

Dear Trent,

I'm sitting here in my study at home as the fire burns in the fireplace next to me. I've been reflecting upon the many months you and I have spent together. When I first suggested that you write to your father and tell him of the horrors his actions wrought upon you, I did so because I have often found this to be a helpful practice in my own life. Hence this exercise I'm currently engaged in.

As you know—although I doubt you took it seriously at the time, for if you had, our paths may never have crossed—when you're studying to be a therapist, you're required to go through your own therapy. Early in my therapy, the man who provided my counsel suggested the practice to me that I passed on to you, of writing letters we'll never send to those who have impacted our lives. I have continued this practice over the years and have found it to be very cathartic. Unlike you, however, I have always followed the instruction not to send the letters. I still find it amusing that you did.

I'm sure you can imagine some of the judgment and abuse that I encountered as an openly gay man growing up in the ruthless 1980s. Being able to receive good counsel from a compassionate straight man taught me the value of therapy. Being able to write letters to so many who rejected my orientation proved lifesaving.

These letters, however, don't always have to be to those who have caused damage in our lives. Sometimes we write to those who have been inspirational as well.

This is one such letter.

There are some things I would like you to know. First, I'm so very proud of the work you have done in our time together. More so, however, I'm prouder of the work you did when we weren't together. The time a patient and therapist spend together is useless if the patient is unwilling or, in some rare cases, unable to do the hard homework assigned to him. You did. Each time we were together, you proved to me how serious you were about your recovery by the hard work you put in between sessions.

Few things are as disappointing to a therapist as watching a patient come week after week with no change in his thinking patterns or behaviors. It feels like an utter waste of time. The work you put in made my job rewarding. Thank you for that. As I have observed, the work you put in has made your life much more rewarding as well, and for that, you are most welcome.

We approach each relationship with certain biases and prejudices. When you first came into my care, I expected resistance and distance. My bias was that, as a therapist yourself, you would want to demonstrate to me your intellectual prowess as an equal. Instead, you showed up as a man broken, vulnerable, and ready for change. I suppose the nature of your crime, the public attention it received, and your wounded inner child had stripped you of almost everything necessary for arrogance. And so, you arrived as a blank canvas. What a treat that was. Thank you for taking off your counselor's cap and submitting to the role of patient. We both gained much through that exchange.

As the events of your childhood began to unfold, something stirred in me that doesn't often happen. Not only did I become empathetic to your situation, I also became sympathetic to it. My heart broke for the horrific abuse you endured. This surprised me to some extent. As I'm sure you can imagine, psychiatric work in the DOJ is rife with stories of neglect, abuse, and childhood trauma. You don't end up in prison if life has been a bed of roses. Well, few people do. But as you shared of your abuse, it struck a chord in my heart and contributed to the compassion I have for you. Somewhere in this process, I began to care for you and feel for you in ways that are not healthy. The same emotions that brought you to me were beginning to surface within me.

Countertransference, as you know better than most, can be a deadly affection. Thankfully, I have a man in my life who I can take all my struggles to. I wish you had had the same in yours. My partner is an outstanding therapist in his own right. Ours is a relationship of complete openness and transparency. I was able to share the feelings I was developing for you with him. He was understanding and supportive in helping me to remain professional throughout our therapy. I dare say you probably had no idea that I had developed an emotional attachment to you. One of us dealt with our countertransference as we were trained to do, and the other did not.

I'm so grateful for the supports I have in my life that you didn't have in yours. I would also like you to know that this is the only thing that placed you on one side of the bars and me on the other. You and I are not so different, Trent Reynolds.

As we explored your childhood wounds, I recognized a number of issues that had eroded your manhood. You know what many of those are now. Your childhood sexual abuse stopped you from being able to grow into your sexuality. This sexual paralysis prevented you from developing healthy, age-appropriate affections and relationships. Your wife's affair was her painful cry that she wanted to be loved by a man, something you were incapable of doing. Your early childhood expressions of sexuality with friends of your sister and others were little more than misdirected passive-aggressive outbursts. Your relationship with Brianna filled the emptiness and longing for something you could never have with someone your own age. As I'm sure you'll agree, had your relationship not been thwarted, she would have soon outgrown you in her need and ability to love and be loved. As a result of your emotional paralysis, she would have eventually sought a man capable of truly loving the woman she was becoming and not just the child she was.

The man I write to now has developed a fuller, more comprehensive understanding of himself and is equipped to grow and flourish in future relationships. And in this pursuit, I wish you all the success in the world. You have a new understanding of who you are, the scars you bear, and the path required to ensure you never repeat your mistakes. Godspeed as you go.

Over recent months, we have explored your sense of purpose. I cannot tell you how excited I am for your future. If you hold onto these truths like a treasured possession, they will serve you well throughout your life. Nothing gives a man more reason to get up in the morning and more satisfaction as he lies down to rest at night than having a purpose to live for. You have this, Trent, a priceless treasure. Never let it go.

I shall now take this letter and deposit it into the fireplace, then reflect warmly upon you and the new life you are leading.

With great fondness and admiration,
Edmond Thackery

CHAPTER SIXTY-ONE

Dear Trent,

In my first letter, I was scarcely able to scratch the surface of all the things that I would like to say to you. While I hope I covered some of the important things, others I neglected altogether, and I would like to tell you more now, if you would be so kind as to receive them.

I feel as though so much has been shown to me about how screwed up my life has been that I hardly know where to begin. As your letters make so clear, for the better part of my life I paid little attention to the one I call God, but I feel as though he has given me a new lease on life, and I must respond as a different man, a better man. I don't expect you to believe this. But my greatest hope is that, over time, you will see the change in me and perhaps then come to believe.

While I was fully aware of the shit storm I was bringing to your life with each act of rage I poured out on you, I felt powerless to stop it. I gained a deep, wicked, and unquenchable satisfaction with each blow I dealt you. I can't explain what it was or where it came from. All I know is that a messed-up part of my own emptiness received some sense of being built up as I tore you down. The shame and horror that fills me as I consider this now rests like a heavy weight on my chest, and I can barely breathe.

In the blackness of my unconscious state, for the first time I saw my life as it really is, as if the blinders I had put on to keep me from seeing who I truly am were ripped off. What I saw sickened, horrified, and terrorized me. My spirit crumbled to dust.

When you were the age where you began to realize how inconsistent my treatment of you was compared to Claire, your mother, and every other living creature, I despised you even more. I wanted to undermine your compassionate, Daniel-like joy at every turn. When I couldn't do that with words, I hurt you physically. When that failed, I used neglect and every other form of abuse that I could think of. Logically, this appears to be completely intentional, but it was as if a force outside of me compelled me do those terrible things. As I read these words, I recognize it may appear as though I'm once again trying to avoid taking responsibility. This is the last thing I want to do. I know your demise has been entirely my doing. I was very aware of the destruction I was bringing upon you, and I did it on purpose. Like an addiction, my powerlessness came in my lack of will to refrain from doing it. I think this is what I've been trying to tell you.

I'm convinced that if I had not worked so hard to crush you, you would not be sitting in prison today. Knowing this breaks my heart. Not only have I been a source of anguish and pain to you, I continue to be. Undoing what I have done is impossible. The only thing I can hope to do is be a better person moving forward. The past is just that, past. All I have is today. And today I can do something different, be someone different.

I'm sure you remember that beautiful fall weekend the year you turned nine. The weekend I almost shot you. Had my friends Mike and David not been along on our hunting weekend, I likely would have. It was certainly not my idea that we take our children hunting with us, but because they insisted, I brought you as well. I didn't want them to know of my hatred for you, so I needed to play the part of caring father.

That first evening we sat around the campfire, us men drinking beer, you kids drinking hot chocolate. You had made it clear to all of us that you couldn't understand how anyone could enjoy killing a defenseless deer. Mike patted you on the head and said, "That's because you've never done it, Trent. There's something amazing about your first kill, and once you've done it, the thirst can't be quenched." You looked at him—excuse the comparison—like a deer in the headlights. You couldn't grasp the idea that anyone could get pleasure from harming something else. Rather than coming to your defense, though, I made fun of you and said only men could understand the thrill of the hunt, not a little girl like you.

We got up with the sun the next morning and set off in search of our prey. The three of us, our kids in tow, each took a different path around the northern edge of the large lake. You were the first to see and point out the large, sixteen-point buck just barely moving through the mist toward the water's edge. I told you to get down on your stomach and shut up. You did as you were told. I shouldered my rifle, loaded the chamber, and tuned in my sights. I had him locked in, and just as I was about to pull the trigger, you shouted, "Run, deer, run!"

With deep shame, I remember what I did next like it happened yesterday. First, I smacked you on top of the head with the stock of my rifle, hard enough to flatten you to the ground. You grabbed your head and cried. I looked at you with dark hatred and told you to shut your fucking mouth. When you looked up at me, you were staring up the barrel of my thirty-thirty. I held you in my sights for an eternity. I hate this about myself, but I wanted so desperately to pull the trigger, to end your life like I had Daniel's, to remove you from the face of the earth like I had Daniel. I shook with rage. Had Mike not come around the bend and into view, I may have killed you right there on the spot. For many years I was angry at him for preventing me from doing the deed. Reflecting upon that action—that intention—makes me sick to my stomach. I wish I could explain to you the hatred I held. I wish even more that I understood it. All I can say is something deep within me forced me to do things I despise.

In one of your early letters, you said I would be too ashamed to ever fill out the application to visit you in Briar Ridge. I have taken that step and have just received my acceptance. I would very much like to come and see you, although I understand that you may not want to see me. If you would agree to this, though, please let Claire know, and I will get there as often as I can before your release, which I know will be soon.

The next issue I must address with you is Jimi. And I confess that I do not know how to go about doing this. I'm at a complete loss. How do I tell you that I suspected what he was doing but turned a blind eye to it and pretended to be totally oblivious? I never encouraged him or heard about it, and in that sense I didn't know directly. He never spoke of it, and I never inquired. I never knew what he was specifically doing, but I strongly suspected and did nothing, which is as good as knowing. If I had known, would I have done anything about it? No. And that confession sickens me to the core. What can a father say to his son after that?

Daniel showed me how to live, and when he died, a part of me died too, the part that might have possessed something of decency, something of love, something of character. I have lacked a sense of character my entire life. Reputation, well, I've always wanted that, but I have willingly chosen to forego developing not only my character but also yours, both of which were my responsibility.

In another letter, you spoke of your friend, Bryan, saying he credited much of his manhood to his relationship with his own father and then asking, "Who taught you how to be a man?" That was my job, and I failed you miserably.

As your letters progressed, I noticed a man emerging. It seems that you are in good hands with Doctor Thackery. I'm so thankful that you're finding your way to manhood. I'm entirely aware that you did this not only without my assistance but despite my interference. How I wish things had been different—that *I* had been different.

Another realization is dawning on me: I am unable to deal with my own dysfunctions alone. I have made an appointment with a psychologist. My hope is that if I'm as truthful with her as I'm becoming with myself and with you, there may come some understanding and breakthroughs toward healing.

The decision to live more honestly means amends must be made. Another confession: I have no idea how to go about mending the lives I have destroyed—yours or mine—but I'm committed to learning how. I'm aware enough to know that I can't purchase your affection. That would be far too easy. This path is not an easy one. It seems few things of real importance are.

In several of your letters, you spoke of hoping that I would die. In many ways, that would have been easier, even preferable. Nevertheless, for reasons beyond our control, I do live, and I want to live better than I have. Much better. I hope that as I learn to live better, those around me will live better too. I completely understand your death wishes for me. In fact, I would have been surprised if you had any other feelings. A part of me feels that if it would bring any sense of resolution or peace to your soul, I would grant your wish. But if I have learned anything from these evil years I have lived, it's that my death would solve nothing. You wouldn't receive peace from my death, just distance. Perhaps that would be enough for you, but I carry another hope inside of me: as you and I share this planet, we will one day, perhaps, at some point, be able to enjoy it together. That may be a stretch, I admit, but it's the longing of my heart.

Your letters speak of regret and loss. My life is filled with this pair. My regrets are more numerous than the sand in the sea, and they involve many people, but primarily two: Daniel and you. It has been more than fifty years since I lost Daniel, yet the memory is as fresh as the day it happened. His bright blue eyes, identical to yours, call out to me from under the surface of the ice today as clearly as they did the day I watched him fall through it. Your bright blue eyes, identical to his, so often searched mine, pleading to know what you had done to deserve the beating you'd received this time. My heart is filled with regret. I regret each harsh criticism, each slap across your face, your head, your bare bottom, each blow that made your blood and tears flow. I regret allowing Jimi to set foot in our home—your torture chamber. I regret throwing out Mr. Snuffles as much as Daniel's hockey stick. I regret not attending your high school graduation, your college graduation, your thirtieth birthday celebration, every high school ball game, every event I held you back from attending, only to inflict pain upon you. Trent, I have been worse than an absentee father; I was abusive to the extreme. I wish there was something beyond words, something that could repair the damage. The words "I'm so sorry" ring as empty to me as I write them as I'm sure they do to you as you read them.

I have lost many things in my life, but only three matter to me now. Your mother and Daniel, there's no getting back. Maybe one day, however, God willing, through your mercy and his grace, which I call upon, as undeserving as my pleading may be, I will have the son I brought so much pain upon back in my life. If I could have that, I could die a happy man.

Forgive me for ending this on such a bold note. I have never told you this. In fact, as you stated in your third letter to me, the first time you had a man tell you he loved you was your friend, Bryan, as he said goodbye before you went away. I'm so sorry it has taken so much time and pain for me to come to this realization.

I love you,
Gerald

CHAPTER SIXTY-TWO

It's almost unfathomable but I leave this place tomorrow. As I do, I'm prepared as never before to face the world on the other side of these large iron gates.

Reflecting upon these past years, I recognize certain events that have shaped the man I am today: horrors lived through, lessons learned, and manhood acquired. I leave scarred, both physically and emotionally, yet better equipped to face the uncertainty of life ahead.

Over the past two weeks, I have received numerous letters and visits from various people. Among those letters came one from Claire. Even though I see her regularly, her letter was a blessing as rich as each of the many visits she has made throughout my incarceration. As she said, some things carry more weight on paper than they do when spoken. I can't begin to express the power of the written word. The love and compassion Claire and I have always shared was underlined and emblazoned in her words. She has, once again, gone above and beyond in preparing for my arrival. The support that she and Robert have been and promise to be stirs a depth of gratitude within me that I'm as unable to express as I am to repay. So I must accept it for what it is—a gift.

I had my final session with Doctor Thackery last week. It wasn't a session of learning and development. It was, instead, a celebration of things learned and developments made. He was as kind and gracious in our farewell as he has been throughout our therapy.

A few days later, I received from him a letter that was "not to be sent." His humor is not lost on me. I can almost see the smile on his face as he decided to send it. I think he may also have sent it as a way of pointing out the value of letters meant to be unsent that, nonetheless, are.

Unlike those I sent to Gerald, Doctor T's letter was filled with grace and love, not hostility and rage. He reminded me of how much I have grown through our time together, and yet his letter served as a wise reminder of how fragile growth is and that it's much easier to stifle and stop that growth than it is to empower it to flourish. He encouraged me to embrace the things I have learned and continue to pursue character. Resting on my laurels is a sure way to lose purpose, self-worth, and meaning.

Having a definite sense of purpose has breathed life into my soul. When we first met, Doctor Thackery asked me what I hoped to gain from our time together. The answer leapt from a deep and hungry place inside, a place longing for a sense of meaning. In that first session, I said to him, "More than anything, I want to wake up one morning, look at myself in the mirror, and be able to say, 'I like you.'"

"That is a destination one can only arrive at through hard work and determination," he replied, "not something easily achieved." At the time, I had no idea how right he was.

This morning, after shaving for the last time in front of that dented, chrome-like piece of metal that distorts my face like a carnival house mirror, I looked at myself and noticed how I have aged, how pallid and sunken my face has become. Then I stared for a long time into the eyes of the man in the mirror and said, for the first time in my life, "I like you." And I meant it. I continued to look into the eyes of the man who was, such a short time ago, little more than a boy, and I watched as tears of joy streamed down my face. The tears came not from the joy of my release tomorrow nor from the knowledge that I had survived what I never expected to, but rather because I really do like the man staring back at me.

I owe so much of this new appreciation of self to Doctor Thackery and to my sister, but I must also give much credit where it is also due—to myself. I never could have arrived here without their support and encouragement, but the hard work done to get me to this place, I alone have had to do. Hard work takes different forms. One of the more difficult hurdles to overcome has been in the area of self-talk. Catching those things I say to myself—about myself—was no easy task. Years of believing I was a worthless piece of shit and either openly saying those very words or thinking them did not serve me well at all. Daily, hourly, and sometimes moment by moment, I catch myself and stop the negative, accusatory comments. At one time not so long ago, I would have found the idea of being self-congratulatory an arrogant expression of self-aggrandizement. I no longer feel that way. I have worked hard to become who I am today, and I deserve the recognition I give myself. As a man who now possesses a certain amount of self-worth, I can acknowledge this and receive it. This is in no way an act of arrogance; it is in every way an accurate assessment of who I am today. I can hold my head high, aware that while I may have a long way to go, I have also come farther than I ever thought I would. I'm also committed to doing the hard work ahead, much of which has to do with Gerald.

Gerald. My father. Where do I even begin with him? I have been so resistant to give him any benefit of the doubt about his disposition, his misery, his demons. I have refused to give consideration to any perspective other than my own.

I received a letter from him almost two weeks ago and another just days later. You think you know a person, and in one fell swoop, that's all blown away. The information he shared with me in those two letters was, to say the least, shocking. I had prepared myself for what I fully expected to be his reactions to the many letters I sent him. Even as I looked at the return address on the envelope prior to opening it, I was prepared to hear his wrath, his rage, his defense of self, and further accusations. I gave serious consideration to not even opening them; afraid of what I might find. A lifetime wouldn't have been enough to prepare me for what was actually inside.

Gerald killed his brother. I had no idea he ever had a brother, Claire had no idea, and as far as I know, Mom didn't even know. I'm at a loss for how to process this sudden influx of information and the emotions that accompany it. I have considered this, day and night ever since, and find myself at once confused, sympathetic, and somehow even sorry for him.

A sudden understanding has dawned on me. They say "knowledge is power." Somehow, though, this new knowledge seems to have left me powerless. Powerless to process this new understanding and powerless to defend against it.

I find my head and heart wracked with how this new man I am should respond to the new man Gerald claims to be. If I can change the way I believe I have changed, why can't he? If we've both grown as I know I have over these months, what am I to do with that?

Gerald has pleaded with me for an extension of grace and mercy. Having been the recipient of so much myself in these last few years, how can I not extend it? He asked for permission to visit me. I didn't reply because I did not know how to. In my second-to-last session with Doctor Thackery, I brought the letters Gerald had written in order to gain his wise counsel. He read the letters while I listened to a Gregorian chant and meditated. When the bell rang and I opened my eyes, his eyes were misty. He offered few words, but those he did offer were full of wisdom.

"It occurs to me," he said, "that the door of opportunity has swung wide open, and now you have some momentous decisions before you. You are in the proverbial catbird seat. Being in such a great position gives you all the power. And at the risk of being cliché, 'with great power comes great responsibility.' Your father is a broken man, Trent. I suggest you tread gently. You know what it means to be broken and can appreciate, I hope, the sensitivity of the matter at your feet, which is where your father has placed himself. He sits in that lowly place, pleading for mercy, for understanding, for undeserved compassion. It's yours to grant or to withhold. Choose wisely."

He reminded me of the way he had laughed when I first disclosed that I had sent the letters. Then he spoke of the enormous power that truth possesses. "Truth has the power to free a man completely. The words in the letters you sent were raw and filled with passion and anger but also with truth. They have given your father the opportunity to be free for the first time in many, many years. You alone, Trent, now hold the keys to his freedom. You can throw them into the ocean and he will remain captive forever, or you can unlock the door and set him free. Your father's destiny lies in your hands."

And so it does.

I have tried to lay aside the vivid memories of abuse at his hand, memories of beatings and neglect and furious outbursts. I'm powerless to let them go, but I know that if I don't set him free, I will never be completely free either.

I have made my choice. Gerald will be free, and so will I. *We* will be free. I look at the man in the funhouse mirror again. If he wants to be free, the man I want to be must grant his abuser's request, and I shall.

I consider how to proceed with this knowledge. Claire must help me to ensure my motives remain pure and my goal in focus. I have one purpose with regard to Gerald—freedom. I must look him in the eyes and be able to tell him with complete honesty that I indeed forgive him. I must do this, but I cannot do it alone. At one time there was no want of any desire to forgive, then a want for that desire emerged. Today, there emerges a desire to forgive the man who was, for my entire life, unforgivable.

I sit here on the edge of the rock-hard, unforgiving plastic mattress in my cell and in the cold reality of what will, by this time tomorrow, be only memory.

I speak words I never thought I would speak. "I forgive you, Gerald." I say them again. "I forgive you, Gerald." And again, "I forgive you, *Dad*."

CHAPTER SIXTY-THREE

Just as he has for the past ten months, when Stevie wakes up, he runs downstairs to wake up Trent. He is delighted that his uncle has come to live with us. It's pizza night, and Trent has promised to take the boys shopping to get the ingredients we'll need. But this morning, Stevie runs back upstairs horrified. Once he calms down enough to speak, he tells me that Trent is hanging over the toilet, vomiting blood. This is the first time Stevie has recognized how sick Trent is. Robert, Dad, and I have known for some time.

Trent has been to every specialist available. Dad has spared no expense in trying to help, but Trent has AIDS now. His CD4 levels have been plummeting since he was first diagnosed. In much the same way as Dad's recovery was a medical mystery, Trent's continual and rapid decline has his doctors completely baffled. His spirits are up, but the same can't be said for his white blood cell count. He has been poked, prodded, examined, scrutinized, observed, studied, and categorized, all with no improvement. He has good days and bad days. Today looks like another bad one.

His good days are spent rich and full. He looked for work for quite some time until he began to get really sick. The Internet is a wonderful tool if you're looking to gather information, not so much if you're looking to keep that information from being gathered. In every position Trent applied for where he was invited to interview, upon returning from the face-to-face meeting—Trent usually felt very positive about how things had gone; he has always made a good first impression—he was turned down. The scenario became obvious. After the interview, they Googled him. The moment Trent's name was typed into the search bar, the next candidate on the list was called. It was a discouraging process for him, although one that Doctor Thackery had prepared him for.

So lately Trent has been investing his life in the people around him, which has proven to be most rewarding. Dad hired him to look after some of his investment portfolios. He is able to do that from home, which allows him the freedom to spend his days doing things of real value. He has been a godsend in our home. The boys can't wait to arrive home from school to see what Uncle Trent has concocted. His investment in their lives is teaching them so much about what it means to be blessed and to be a blessing to others, which I suppose is exactly what Trent's new purpose in life is all about: to be a blessing to others. He could write a book on the topic.

He spends much of his not-so-good days in the apartment that Robert built for him in the basement. He's aware that he's now mildly contagious and stays away from the boys and us whenever he's in the throes of one of his coughing fits. He spends those days on his computer, making more money for Dad.

The first weeks he was with us were an amazing time for everyone. His health was still pretty good, and watching him and Dad together still brings tears to my eyes. Three days after his release, Trent asked if it would be okay to have Dad come over and said that perhaps he and Dad could make dinner together. Once I picked myself up off the floor, I said, "Just like old times?" He said he was serious. He needed to talk with Dad. He even called him that.

Dad arrived at about 3:00 that Wednesday afternoon. When he walked into the house, he and Trent stood face to face. I had learned from Dad that Trent had sent him several scathing letters and was prepared for the worst. What I wasn't prepared for and will never get out of my mind's eye is what happened next. These two men whom I love and admire, these two adversaries, stood like gunmen ready for a showdown, peering deeply into each other's eyes, waiting for the other to make the first move.

Trent stepped forward first, inviting Dad. Then they embraced. They held each other. First, Dad began to shake, then the sobs began. Who would have ever imagined that brokenness could be so beautiful? Soon, Trent began to cry too. They held onto each other like soul brothers and wept. Through a veil of tears and brokenness, Dad finally blurted out, "I'm so very, very sorry, Trent. Will you please forgive me?"

Since that time, Robert and I have learned so much about the pain and suffering that our father and brother lived through, about hidden pasts and hopeful futures. Dad now speaks often of his brother, Daniel. He speaks of him as a hero, a giant among men. Dad felt toward his big brother the same way I feel toward mine.

Trent and Dad spend long days together. On days when Trent feels strong enough, they hike together and travel. They are trying to make up for years of lost time. Saturdays belong to the four men—Trent, Dad, Aaron, and Stevie. Dad loves on Aaron and Stevie the way he never could with Trent. He spoils them rotten, and Robert often gets pissed when he does. Dad just says, "Spoiler alert, Robert, life's too short to get upset about good things."

Dad and Trent are seeing a psychologist together. She has been monumental in their healing relationship and most supportive. Trent tells me that she has shown him it's not that Dad *wouldn't* love Trent as a child; he *couldn't*. In much the same way as Trent had been emotionally and sexually paralyzed by the abuses he suffered, Dad was unable to handle the reminder of Daniel that Trent represented.

At first, I was shocked at how willing Dad and Trent were to overcome the vast chasm of pain that had been between them. I couldn't fathom how quickly they each seemed to be able to set aside their bitterness to embrace the other. As we have talked, though, I realized that so much of the healing work they both did occurred long before they stood face to face in our home, and none of it was easy. Trent was able to forgive Dad while he was still in prison. He gives much of the credit for this to Doctor Thackery.

Dad says he was forced to face the horror of himself while he lay unconscious and near death. He still doesn't tell Robert or me much about his self-discovery while unconscious, although I'm certain Trent knows more. Much of their healing occurred through letters that Trent and Dad had exchanged when Trent was still in Briar Ridge. I had no idea they had been communicating. Every time I see them laughing together, I'm filled with a sense of wonder and joy. I don't remember one time as we were growing up where either of them was laughing while they were in the same room.

"HEY, SIS." TRENT SMILES WEAKLY at me now that he has made it up the stairs and into the kitchen. I hand him a cup of coffee, but he declines. "An apple-ginger tea would be great, though. And where's my boy? I think I scared him a bit this morning."

I put a tea packet into the Keurig and put my arm around my brother as the hissing and spurting tells us his tea is almost ready. "He went with Robert to the store to get stuff for pizza night. Says he's worried about you and that you're not allowed to leave us again." I give him a squeeze. "He's right. You're not allowed to leave us again."

"Well, if I have anything to say about it, I'll be a pain in your ass for years to come. I'm doing everything I can, Claire. It's the meds that need to do their job."

Trent is beginning a new experimental drug cocktail, one designed for people like him, those who for some unknown reason are resistant to the standard HIV regimen. The regular ART meds don't seem to work for Trent. He's tried every one on the market, but nothing seems to elevate his CD4 levels. While we're all very concerned about this, Trent doesn't worry much about it. He's so focused on his new mission in life that everything else, including his personal well-being, takes a backseat. These days, Trent lives to do whatever he can to make other people's lives a bit better. He says if he can't make himself better, maybe he can do that for others. He does whatever he can each day to bring a smile to the faces of those around him. And he does. Even in his emaciated state, he has a great sense of humor, and his optimism is magnetic. He's like he was as a child, only with a laser-like focus—determined.

We were in a long lineup at the Giant Eagle last week with a number of frozen food items already beginning to thaw. As per usual, the checker was being dumped on by every customer in line. Somehow it was her fault that half of Columbus had chosen to shop that afternoon, that her cash register ran out of receipt paper, and she ran out of five-dollar bills. By the time we got our cart unloaded and onto the conveyor, I could see the stress on her face and hear it in her voice.

Trent's smile alone calmed her. He read her name tag and then said something like, "You know, Renee, in another hour or two, your shift will end, those of us in this line will be home with our groceries put away, and for a short while, everything will be right with the world. You're doing a great job. Don't let miserable, small-minded people ruin a great day. You're not the cause of their woes, and once they're in their cars heading home, they'll find someone else to focus their anger on. Our lives are no more important than yours." He said all of this in a voice just loud enough for those in our lineup to hear.

She immediately relaxed. "Thank you, Mister," she replied. In that brief exchange, her world became a bit better. Trent seems to have developed a way of doing that for all of us every day, and I get to be the beneficiary of his gift.

As we were walking away with our groceries, the grumpy old man next in line, who had been muttering expletives under his breath, smiled and said, "It's a beautiful day, isn't it, sweetheart?"

SEASONS CHANGE. NOT LONG AGO, life was filled with pain and sorrow. Today, there's so much to be thankful for. One thing Trent has taught me is that pain and sorrow are things we choose. I don't have to live sorrowfully. The world will always be filled with sadness, but taking it upon myself is something I can choose to do or not. Lately I've been choosing to live without it, and I'm finding it's a much better way to live.

Aaron and Stevie worry too much about Trent. They were downstairs in his "pad," watching something with him on Netflix. I was carrying a bowl of popcorn down to join them when I heard the program pause and overheard Trent say, "Ya know, Aaron, there are only two types of worry in the world: worry you can do something about and worry you can do nothing about. If you can do something about the thing you're worrying about, then it's kinda dumb to keep worrying about it. Just do what needs to be done so you don't have to worry about it. And if you can't do anything about it, then it's pointless to worry about it 'cause there's nothing that worrying can do to change it, right?"

Aaron acknowledges this, and as I come around the corner, he looks at me and says, "Mom worries about you more than me and Stevie do."

"Then your mom needs a beating," Trent says, and that's when the pillow fight began.

We're all learning that much of life is out of our control, but the way we deal with the things life throws our way is within our control. We are choosing better, living better, and loving better.

CHAPTER SIXTY-FOUR

OSU is awesome! I'm loving my classes, loving volleyball, loving choir, loving freshman student council, and loving Jake. Jake has been a godsend. Seriously. We meet for coffee on Monday, Wednesday, and Friday before first class. We both have an 8:15 in Galvin Hall, so we get together about 7:30 in the Commons and hang for a while before our day begins. Starting my day with him makes every day so much better.

There are so many things to do in this place. I often don't get home 'til, like, 10:00 at night. So, Jake and I are talking about—well, I'm talking about it, Jake is mostly listening—maybe getting a room together in one of the student houses nearby next year. Mom doesn't want us to rush into anything, but we love each other, and I think we're ready. I'm not in a panic, and I don't want to pressure Jake into anything he's not ready to commit to, so I'll bide my time and see what happens.

One of the most amazing things about this place is that no one knows my history. I can introduce myself to others without having to worry about them going, "Oh my God, are you the girl who was raped by that guidance counselor?" I'm just Brianna, and I love being me. I mean, I really do. Linda has a lot to do with this.

What an amazing woman she's been in my life. I haven't seen her since I started university last month, but she said that I'm welcome to make an appointment every couple of months and drop in for an emotional check-up kinda thing. I'm all for that.

In our last session, we did what she calls a postmortem—a debrief. We went over all the things that we had covered in each of our sessions. I can't believe how much I've learned about myself and Trent and life. Everyone should have a shrink, or at least someone they can go to who's able to see their life from a different perspective. Looking at things from the outside gives you a completely different viewpoint than when you're on the inside. I know this seems like a no-brainer, but often we don't, or can't, see things clearly from our own perspective. Linda has been that different perspective I've needed for a long time.

I take all the shit that seems to weigh me down in life, drop it on her desk, and she helps me to sort through it, to look at it differently. It's like that "eating the elephant thing" she taught me about a long time ago. She's able to see all these different parts of my life from an outside vantage point and sort them out, line them up, and suddenly they don't seem so unmanageable anymore. I still have to do all the work, but she helps me see what needs to be done first. Once I get started, it seems to flow pretty easily after that. I guess my life is a bit like "syllabus shock." In the first days of university, when you get all your syllabi, you look at the momentous workload and it's easy to get overwhelmed. Once you lay it out in your calendar, though, it becomes more manageable. That's my life today—more manageable.

Trent was released from prison a few days before I graduated from Glenwood. I got a phone call from a police officer, letting me know Trent was being released into his sister's custody. Her name is Claire. He loves her so much. He used to talk about what an amazing person she is. I hope it goes well for them. The police officer told me that if I ever see him, I can call them and they will immediately arrest him. Why would I do that? Why would they do that? I mean, he's served his time, right? Do they really think he's going to stalk me, follow me into a dark alley, and rape me? It's like they see him as some kind of monster. I wish everyone could look at people for who they really are and not drop everyone into a category and label them for life. To the cops, Trent will always be a sex offender, and I will always be a victim. What the fuck is that? I suppose they're just doing what Linda helps me do, though—break things down into pieces and tasks that are small enough to handle. It's just that I'm not a victim any more than I'm a term paper, and Trent isn't a threat to me any more than he's a rapist.

It probably doesn't sound like it, but I rarely think about Trent anymore. In so many ways, I've moved on. I've grown up a lot, and I doubt that if the person I am today met Trent, I would be as in awe of him as I once was. I don't think we'd even date, and we definitely wouldn't end up as a couple. I'm not even sure we're the kindred spirits I thought we once were.

Distance gives a person perspective too. I see the things in him that I was attracted to, and so many of them are superficial. I might think that way about Jake one day too. I hope not, but when Trent and I were together, I couldn't see the situation anywhere near as accurately as I thought I could. I guess I've learned to be a little less trusting and a bit more suspicious of my own feelings. They can be deceptive. That's another thing Linda helped me see.

She says that our brains can't be trusted. The smaller part of our brains, the limbic system, which controls our emotions, is the part we often listen to, over and above the larger part, the cerebral cortex, which controls our rational thinking. We listen to the limbic system more because it screams louder. It calls for us to feed it, whereas the larger part just sits quietly in the background, doing the hard work. I have to learn to slow down and quiet the screaming baby—my limbic system—so I can hear what the part of me that actually uses brains is trying to convey. Linda tells me this is why we spend so much time in quiet reflection before we begin our sessions. I have tried to continue to do this on my own now that I'm not seeing her every week, and I'm usually pretty good at it. It's really helpful. As soon as I'm able to calm all the incoming noise of life, I get a clearer view of reality.

PROM WAS PRETTY SWEET. JAKE didn't do what a bunch of guys did—rent a limo and try to knock me off my feet. He borrowed his dad's Buick, spent the day washing it, and met me at the door, where he thanked Mom and Dad for allowing me to go with him. I think they liked that. It was like asking their permission.

After the banquet and before the dance, we went for a long walk together, through the park on the other side of Lakeview. He told me how beautiful I looked and how much he liked me, how much he thinks about me. It wasn't sappy like I'm probably making it sound; it was romantic. Just before we went into the dance, he said, "Brianna, can I kiss you, please?" I didn't answer him, I just pulled him close against me, and we kissed for a long time. I think I shocked him when I opened my mouth and stuck my tongue into his. It was a pleasant shock but a shock nonetheless. I felt him get hard against my stomach, and I started to giggle. He pulled back slightly. "What's so funny?"

"I'll tell you later," I said. Then we went in and danced most of the night together. The asshat had been taking dance lessons for three months before prom because he was afraid to look like an idiot on the dance floor. So, guess who looked like the idiot? Aside from that, the evening was amazing, and Jake *is* a great dancer. We kissed a few times on the dance floor and a fair bit when we went out to the garden next to the auditorium, and each time he got a hard-on. I tried to keep from commenting on it and giggling, but it was hard—I mean to keep from laughing, not his . . . well, yeah, both were hard. Jake didn't sneak a flask into the dance and get shit-faced like half the guys. He was a perfect gentleman all night long. Trent was always a gentleman too.

When we finally left the dance, at about 11:00, I asked Jake what he wanted to do next. He looked a bit confused, as if he was just going to take me back home, hug me in the driveway, and say goodnight like he always had. "Well, the night is young, and so are we," I said in a sappy voice.

"What would you like to do?" he asked. It was a bit like laying out toys for kids you're babysitting to play with, but he soon got the idea.

My family has a cabin in South London, just off the Jackson Pike Freeway. It's less than an hour outside of the city. Just before Jake arrived to pick me up for prom, I took the key and told Mom and Dad not to wait up. When we got to the cabin, Jake was nervous. It felt a little weird, I gotta admit, being the teacher rather than the student I had been until that point. Jake was fabulous. He was a little awkward and a little rushed but very good. I mean, when is sex ever really bad, right? He came twice before we actually got to the act itself and then twice during. So did I, so that's pretty good. I was pleasantly surprised at how quickly Jake could recover and go again. I guess it helps when you're eighteen, and not pushing forty.

I surprised myself at how little I thought about Trent when we were making love. A couple of times I wished that Jake would do some of the things Trent had done that would really get me off, but it wasn't like I was thinking about Trent while Jake was doing his thing or even wishing he was Trent. Since then, Jake has become very good and knows exactly how to push all the right buttons.

I'm pretty happy in our relationship. No, I'm very happy. There's no comparison. Trent was Trent, and Jake is Jake. I always wondered how people who have had many different partners keep from playing the rating game. I've realized that each person is so unique, so different, that you don't even think about previous partners when you're with the current one. At least I don't. Jake is kind and generous and compassionate and quiet. I like the qualities he brings to us and out in me. I'm more grateful each day that we found each other.

There is far more balance to our relationship than there ever was with Trent and me. Okay, I guess I do *some* comparing. But because Trent and I always had to hide from other people, there was a covert mystery and intrigue, but also a fear factor that became exhausting. We could never really relax with each other. As comfortable as we were, we always had to be on the lookout. *If my cell phone rings, how do I answer it? If someone sees us downtown, what do we do? If we plan a weekend together, how many lies do I have to tell to make sure all our bases are covered?* It was a lot of hard work. With Jake, our relationship isn't based upon deception and lies, so there's none of that, and it's so freeing.

I think the best way to describe me today is content. I was happy with Trent, but because of the nature of our relationship, we could never be content. We always had to be a bit on edge—sometimes a lot on edge. So there was always this tension. To me, contentment implies safety and security. I have that with Jake, and it feels wonderful.

CHAPTER SIXTY-FIVE

I have this son. He's a tremendous young man. He's thoughtful, warm, loving, inspiring, fun, passionate, merciful, considerate . . . and dying. I haven't had him for long, and I won't have him for much longer. And that breaks his father's heart.

When Claire first invited me over after Trent's release from Briar Ridge, I was filled with fear and anxiety. After all, I had much to be fearful of. All communications from him over the previous three years had been hostile and filled with rage, as I deserved. Communications prior to that had been almost nonexistent. I had not been a good father to him. I had been no father at all. The most appropriate descriptions for what I had been in my son's life are tyrant, oppressor, and despot. I had every reason in the world to suspect our first encounter after those three years had passed would not go well. Trent had every reason to make it not go well. Imagine my surprise when the prodigal father was embraced by the rejected son.

There are moments in life that one never forgets: where you were when Armstrong took his first step on the moon, the exploding of the Space Shuttle *Columbia*, the fall of the Twin Towers. In my world, these events now pale in comparison with the one that occurred in the foyer of Claire's home. That memory has been carved into the core of my being like lovers' names in the trunk of an old tree.

We stood in that spot for an eternity, staring into each other's eyes. To be honest, I was expecting his fist to fly toward my head, or worse.

I deserved worse. I will never forget Trent taking the smallest of steps toward me before opening his arms and welcoming me into his world. It was not the first time he had welcomed me there. As a child, he had often done so. But it was the first time I had ever accepted his invitation. And accept it I did! I grabbed him and held onto him and didn't want to let go. I squeezed him so tightly I thought his frail body might break. He held me tightly in return. Tears expressing years of pent-up sorrow broke like the levees of New Orleans when Katrina hit. And I wept for the pain I had brought to this man. My son, my heir.

I would love to say that at that moment, everything between us was restored. It was not. But it was the beginning of the healing that is, inch by inch, coming toward us, bringing us together like . . . well, like father and son. Many tough conversations have taken place between us in these months we've been reunited. United. *Reunited* would imply there had at one time been unity.

Trent had been out little more than a week when he and I were walking together through St. Joseph's Cemetery, where his mother rests. We sat together on a bench near the garden's edge, and he asked questions I had no answers for and likely never will, although they demand answers. "Why did you lie to me and then beat me mercilessly about who let the racoon into the house when I was five? How could you have sent me in search of a creek I would never find, knowing I would get hopelessly lost on our only family vacation? Why did you ridicule me, mock me, and call me down, over and over, in the presence of your friends—and worse, my friends? How could you break promise after promise after promise throughout my life? Why did you attempt to sever the close relationship Claire and I have worked so hard to have throughout our lives? How the hell could you have allowed Jimi to rape me hundreds of times as a little boy? Why did I sicken you so much?"

No answers can justify my actions, the man I was, the lunatic my son called Daddy, then Dad, then Gerald, then . . . nothing. There are no satisfactory answers. Doctor Jordan, our therapist, has helped me to accept forgiveness in lieu of answers—helped Trent extend even more grace and mercy toward his pathetic father. I'm learning there are some things I will never have answers for on this side of eternity. What snapped in me when

Daniel died? Why did that event unleash the monster that brought so much harm to his only son? How can I receive what I don't deserve? Grace is easier to extend than receive. And Trent has been far more extending of it than I have been able to receive it. Although this is something I'm learning to embrace.

Trent has been on a new antiretroviral therapy, an experimental one, and it seems to be working wonders. What a blessing this has been for our family. In the past few weeks, he has been able to keep down everything he's eaten, his appetite has increased, he's gaining weight, and he's feeling better, and we are increasingly blessed. Stevie and Aaron are running him ragged, and he loves it. They think it's such a thrill to have sleepovers at Trent's, even though it isn't more than twenty feet from their own bedrooms. They make blanket forts and have their version of wild parties: too much ice cream, popcorn, pizza, soda pop, and noise. And we all cherish each moment.

I have asked Trent to help manage a couple of low-rental housing properties I own near the city center. The families who live in these buildings are all low-income earners. Many of them have been hit hard by the pandemic and the recession, and most are living paycheck to paycheck. He accepted my offer on the condition that each apartment receive a complete renovation, the rent not increase, and tenants get the month of December rent free every year to offset the cost of the holiday season. My investment strategist hit the ceiling when I agreed. We were in his office when Trent made the proposal, and I accepted.

"Gerald, we will make no money. In fact, you'll lose thousands," my strategist said. Trent and I just smiled at each other as we walked out of his office, listening to him rant on. "This is the most asinine investment decision you've ever made. Keep this up and we'll all be in the poorhouse. In fact—" Sometimes it takes losing the things most precious in life to show us where our wealth truly lies.

I've been invited to go on the exclusive Uncle Trent's Week-Long Extravaganza with him and the boys at the end of August, before Stevie and Aaron begin grades six and seven. As history bears witness, these have always been highlights of the boys' year. We are going camping and then getting violently ill on "ginormous" roller coasters and water slides for an entire week. I may be getting a bit old for some of it, but to decline the offer would be like turning one's back on the King of England. So I'll muster all the enthusiasm I can and embrace this delightful adventure. If we survive, I've asked Trent to join me for a week at my villa in Valencia, Spain. It will be a vacation to recuperate from our vacation, so to speak. I hope it will also allow us to spend some time working on our own still fragile relationship.

Shortly after we were together for the first time since before his incarceration, Trent told me about his breakthrough in being able to look at himself and say, "I like you." For Trent, years of hard work had led to that most important accomplishment in his journey toward self-acceptance. I have one such moment I hope to hear before I die. It's simple, really: I long to hear my son call me "Dad."

IT WAS FATHER'S DAY. TRENT was in grade two. He made me one of those cards that kids make in class for their fathers. He had used blue construction paper, and I could tell he had invested a lot of care and time in the project. He had drawn me sitting on a tractor that was pulling a plow. He drew himself sitting on my knee. Both of us were smiling ear to ear. The sun above was just as you would expect a kid to draw it: a large, misshapen yellow circle with a dozen or so uneven lines coming out from the edges. He handed it to me. Beneath the picture, he'd written "World's Greatest Dad!" Then I opened it and read, "Me and Dad getting ready to plant the fields," but he spelled it "*feelds*." All I said to him was, "Don't they teach you how to spell in grade two?" He slunk off, completely despondent. Later that night, shortly after Jimi left to crawl into bed with Trent, I picked up the card and burned cigarette holes through the bright blue eyes of the picture Trent had drawn of himself.

Tears of shame stream down my face as I recall this now, just as they did when I shared it with Trent in our last counseling session with Doctor Jordan. Being forgiven for such acts is most humbling.

CHAPTER SIXTY-SIX

Spain is a remarkable place. It's made better when you're with people you like. It's almost unfathomable that I can say I am. Gerald and I have been enjoying the wonder of the Valencians and their beautiful homeland. These people bear a rich heritage. While we have done very few touristy activities, lazing around Gerald's villa is just fine by both of us. The boys wore us out. While it's been a few years since I've done the last-week-of-August-trek with Aaron and Stevie, I don't think I should be as spent as I seem to be. Maybe it's the jet lag as well as my age catching up with me, although it's more likely I'm still feeling the exhaustion that comes from having a CD4 level under 150, which I'm grateful is now back above 200. I'm feeling better than I have in quite some time, yet I'm woefully aware of what's going on inside of me. I feel it growing, festering, consuming.

Gerald is inside, sleeping, I suppose. I sit out here on the balcony, breathing the majestic Mediterranean. In the distance, I hear music, not of the local variety. It's a song I know well. Elton John's "Daniel" comes across the waves, probably from the yacht anchored just offshore. It brings back so many memories. And in a moment, I know what I must do. "Daniel, you're a star in the face of the sky." I begin here and now preparing for what is surely to come.

THERE IS A MAGICAL INNOCENCE in being twelve years old that I miss. I missed it when I was twelve too. So much of childhood stripped away; innocence, wonder, and dreams never realized. Anger toward Gerald still rises in me when I remember that age. I suppose it's one of the reasons I enjoy investing in Aaron and Stevie. The week we spent with the boys was spectacular. Seeing Gerald being both the father and grandfather I never had was simultaneously difficult and wonderful. He's trying so hard to make up for lost time. Too little too late, perhaps, but I give him an A for effort.

Stevie and I have always been a little closer than Aaron and I. I think it's because in so many ways, I see in him the boy I was—the boy I would have been, the boy I would have liked the chance to be. Stevie and I are a lot alike in terms of disposition and personality. There's a hope I have for him, one I try to instill in him, that he may find, early in life, his purpose, the reason he has been placed on Earth, and that he will work hard to fulfill that calling. I have the same hope for Aaron, but in Stevie, I can sense it beginning to reveal itself.

Like me, Stevie abhors the idea of killing. We were watching a movie together in the hotel the night before our camping trip wrapped up—Gerald caved and decided we should spend the final night of our exhausting vacation with the boys in a theme room at a hotel. We were all piled together on one of the king-size beds watching *Jumanji: Welcome to the Jungle*, and I could see Stevie cringing at the same parts that would have made me cringe as a child, some that still make me cringe today. Needless, senseless violence is unnerving and upsetting to us both.

Later that evening, Stevie and I were out for a walk together.

"I don't get it, Uncle Trent," he said. "Why do people like seeing other people get hurt?"

I told him that I don't get it either. "Hurting others is never the best way to get what you want or to solve problems. There's always a better way."

"Yeah," he said. "Like what those men did to you in jail. It didn't solve any problems, and they hurt you bad, didn't they?"

"Yes, they sure did, Stevie. But they only hurt my body. They didn't hurt what's important: my heart and soul. Those things are still in pretty good shape. I was able to protect those parts of me from them."

"I'm glad for that, Uncle Trent. I think when your heart and soul get hurt, it's sometimes worse, right?"

"Yeah, Stevie, it's almost always worse."

There was quite a long pause in our conversation before Stevie broke the silence. "But that's what you did to that girl in your school, Uncle Trent. You hurt her heart and her soul, didn't you?"

I felt like I had been set up then kicked in the stomach, like Stevie walked me right into it and trapped me with my own words.

I don't think about Brianna all that often. I have worked hard not to. But as I sit this evening, alone on the balcony of Gerald's villa, overlooking the perfect spot where the Turia meets the sea, with the taste of sea salt in the air, she comes to me, and Stevie's words whisper like the warm Mediterranean breeze: "That's what you did to that girl, Uncle Trent. You hurt her heart and her soul. And when your heart and soul get hurt, it's sometimes worse, right?"

There are times in life when I feel as though I'm making great strides toward wholeness and others when it feels like little has changed. When thoughts come of how my selfishness has hurt Brianna and left indelible marks upon her heart and soul, I want to revert to the person I was and self-flagellate. I fight this today, acknowledge my actions, and leave them in the past where they belong. I have paid the price for my crime; I have served my time. However, she may still be paying. She may always have to. It is thoughts like these that bring the heaviness.

There was a time not so long ago when these thoughts would have led me toward self-hatred, and self-hatred toward self-pity. Today, I pause, I breathe deeply, and I meditate. Breathing in, I know I am breathing in. Breathing out, I know I am breathing out: right perspective, right thoughts, right purpose, right action.

I can do nothing about what I have done; I can only be a better version of the man I am. Being a better me makes the world a better place and protects others from what a worse me might inflict upon them. And perhaps it protects Brianna, even without her knowing it, from attachments and emotional connections that may serve to bind and hinder her personal development. This is all I am able to do.

Knowing this reminds me that Gerald is powerless to change the pain I have suffered at his hand in days past as well. My need for mercy, for forgiveness, and for the compassionate understanding from others, like Brianna and Stevie, prompts me to further extend that toward Gerald. We are all grace givers and grace receivers. As I leave this balcony tonight, I will sleep well knowing I have done what I can to be the man I want to be, the man I have chosen to be.

THE FIRST COUPLE OF DAYS in Valencia were pretty much catch-up-on-our-rest days, and Gerald's villa is a spectacular place to do just that. A local couple, Carlos and Anita, run his household when he's in town. They do the cooking and cleaning and run errands. They are a delightful couple who seem to be energized by serving others.

I have learned that purpose in life is easily identified by what brings us the most joy. Carlos and Anita receive their joy from how well they serve others. I'm aware that Gerald compensates them well for the work that they do, but a good-paying job doesn't make you whistle and sing while you do it. These things come from a joy found deeper than what can be purchased. Being around these two is inspiring.

Being in this majestic land is also inspiring. Valencia is a city of unspoiled beaches and perfect weather, a place where gothic architecture merges seamlessly with modernity. It's saturated with museums and presents a rich tapestry of history. We spend our days enjoying the city and, yes, even each other. I have never shared in Gerald's extravagant wealth and have no deep aspirations for such, but I must confess the brief taste I'm getting is rather intoxicating.

We spend our days taking in all that this city has to offer but also spend much of the time in conversation and some of it in therapy. Our weekly therapy with Doctor Jordan is not canceled, as it was last week while we were camping with the boys; rather, we hold it via video conference.

When you have spent as much time as I have with one therapist, there is always an adjustment period under another. Each comes to you with a different approach and a slightly different perspective on the problems you bring forward. Doctor Jordan possesses tremendous insight into familial conflict and the breaking down of barriers. Like Doctor Thackery, she places great emphasis on self-discovery and self-actualization. I sit in amazement as Gerald eagerly devours all he can to become a better man—a better father. There are times, many of them, when he openly shares his own childhood fears.

It wasn't always this way. In a conversation we had last evening while overlooking the sea, Gerald confessed he used to think and act like a man who wasn't afraid of anything. He said it was Doctor Jordan who set him straight.

Early in his solo sessions with her she asked, "What are you so afraid of, Gerald?"

"I'm not afraid of anything," Gerald replied in a defensive tone.

Doctor Jordan laughed and called his bluff. "Really? So, you're out late at night, all alone, and this huge dog comes running around a corner, straight at you, baring his teeth, barking and growling, and you're not the least bit afraid?"

"Well, yeah, I suppose if that happened. But . . ."

"In the days before your vast empire, when there was no money to be had, you were never afraid that when you got to the end of the month, there would be nothing to pay bills, no money to buy groceries for your hungry children?"

"I guess so, but . . ."

"And you weren't afraid that your mother was going to be a vegetable after her stroke?"

"Well . . ."

"And you're not afraid that your daughter is going to see through the bullshit façade you wear and recognize you for who you really are: a man who neglected and abused his son because he was a reminder of the brother he lost? And you're not afraid that if you get to the other side of this existence, you'll meet Daniel, and he'll hate you because you froze when he needed you most? And you're not afraid that one day you're going to lose absolutely everything and wind up dying all alone?"

Gerald laughs as he recalls the bullshit he tried to pull "By the time Doctor Jordan was finished with me, I didn't think there was anything I *wasn't* afraid of." I laugh with him at his confession and admire his honesty.

That is the kind of no-nonsense woman Doctor J is. She is thorough and tough and insightful and takes the proverbial bull by the horns. She doesn't tolerate beating around the bush any more than she does lying. As a man who spent far too many years playing games in therapeutic settings, I know she's exactly what I need, what Gerald and I both need to keep making progress in our individual lives and in our relationship with each other.

I see growth in Gerald every day. Sometimes I find myself sitting across the table from him at dinner, wondering who this man is. Where has he been all my life? *This* is a man I would have loved to have shown me the road to manhood. I still long for that, for him to teach me how to be a man. Some days I think I'm close, others, not so much.

CHAPTER SIXTY-SEVEN

Uncle Trent and Grandpa took almost a month to get back from their trip to Spain, which was supposed to be only a week. I thought it was because they were having so much fun. But just before they got back, Mom told Aaron and me it was because Uncle Trent got really, really sick again. When Uncle Trent did finally get back, he didn't come here to live with us; he went straight to the hospital. I hate hospitals. I've spent way more time in them this year than I ever wanted to, and I'm not even sick.

Mom says the new medicines that the doctors gave Uncle Trent didn't help him like they were supposed to. Instead, they hurt him. Instead of bringing the number of cells back up like normal people, they pretended to bring them up and made everyone think they were coming up, but they were hiding them, and even though it looked like he was getting more cells, he was actually getting less. I don't know how many cells we're supposed to have in our bodies, but it must be more than the number Uncle Trent has. Aaron and me have the right number, though.

I asked Mom if I could give some of mine to Uncle Trent so he would have enough. She said that was a really nice thing to offer, but it doesn't work that way.

I'm really afraid that Uncle Trent is going to die, like Grandma did and like Grandpa almost did. I don't know what I would do if he did die. I would be very, very sad. I love Uncle Trent more than almost anyone in the world. And when he hurts, it kinda hurts inside of me too. Him and me, we're kinda the same that way.

And even though I know he really hurt that girl he was supposed to be helping, he didn't mean to, and it makes him sad to think that he did. It was bad what he did. That's why they threw him in jail. He told me once that it took him a long, long time to forgive himself for what he did to her. But to keep punishing himself for something that he is very sorry for and wishes he'd never done doesn't help anyone. He says that everyone makes mistakes—does bad things—and if we spend our whole lives wishing we had done things differently—better—we end up living only to die, and no one should live like that. I suppose living like that doesn't help anyone and hurts everyone.

Some things I just can't figure out, though. When I go shopping with Mom and she buys us stuff to eat, it's ours because she paid for it. When you pay for something, it becomes yours, right? And when it's yours, you're free to do whatever you want with it. Uncle Trent paid for what he did to that girl by going to jail and working to get healthier in his head and heart, then he got out. So he paid the amount they told him to pay, and now he should be free. But he's not really free at all. He's sick all the time because of what some really terrible men—when Mom can't hear, I just call them assholes—did to him. So he's still paying for something he shouldn't have to pay for anymore, and that's not fair.

When we go visit him, we have to wear these stupid yellow gowns and gloves and little masks over our mouths. I'm not even supposed to hug him, but I always do. Somehow it doesn't seem fair or right that even though Uncle Trent has paid for what he did, he still has to pay for it, and it might even cost his life.

Mom and Dad and Grandpa haven't said it, but I'm pretty sure they know that Uncle Trent is dying. I can tell. They're acting the same way they did just before Grandma died and like they did when we went to the hospital to tell the doctor he could take the machine away that was keeping Grandpa alive. They're so sad so much of the time, and they whisper whenever they talk about Uncle Trent.

It kinda pisses me off, 'cause I'm eleven now and I'm not stupid. If Uncle Trent is going to die, shouldn't I get to know?

Sometimes when I'm in my bed at night and I think of Uncle Trent, it hurts so much that I cry for him. I guess I cry for myself mostly, but I cry when I think about him. I'm really scared of losing him. I guess I'm more scared for Mom than anything. She has lost so many things since I was seven, I can hardly even count them: Grandma, then Uncle Trent when he went to prison, and a whole bunch of friends when Uncle Trent went to prison, and a bunch of weight when Uncle Trent went to prison, then Grandpa—almost. Then she got Grandpa back, and she was happier. Then she got Uncle Trent back and she was happier than I ever remember her being. But now when she thinks about losing him again, I can see in her eyes and in her face how much pain it's causing her. It's not fair.

Dad keeps telling me that when we think life should be fair, we're setting ourselves up to be hurt. Because life isn't fair, it never has been, and it never will be. But that doesn't change the hurt that I feel in my heart and in my head.

I worry for Mom mostly, though. I'm afraid she's going to get depression or something if Uncle Trent dies. And I know that when some people get depression, they kill themselves. I couldn't handle that. So I try to only think about one thing at a time. Uncle Trent is really good at doing that. He calls it "living in the moment." He says that all we have is this moment. Oops, now it's gone, so we only have this one. Uh-oh, now it's gone too. And he talks about things like when we think about what happened yesterday or what might happen tomorrow, we miss the magic of what's happening right now. And since the only thing that is real is right now, if we miss this, we miss out on life. We're not really living, and we may as well be dead.

Uncle Trent and I went for a walk around the garden of the hospital while Mom and Grandpa talked with his doctor. Well, I went for a walk; Uncle Trent got to drive his wheelchair. It's pretty sweet. It's red and has a pole on the back with a clear bag hanging from the pole. The bag is full of his medicine, which goes into a needle in his arm. That way he's always getting the medicine he needs to stay alive. His wheelchair has a turtle speed and a rabbit speed. When he's got it on rabbit speed, I have to run to keep up with him.

Anyway, we were talking about life, what's happening right now, and Uncle Trent was staring at the water that was trickling down this little creek through the garden beside the hospital. I asked what he was staring at.

"This is amazing, Stevie," he said. "Just look at how the water flows along its path. It travels over these rocks, around this small tree, through a maze of water plants, and under the bridge. Each trickle takes its own path, yet they all end up in the same place. But no one really knows how much of the water will get to where it's going or where it will end up because some of the water will evaporate, and some of it will splash out and dry on the rocks, yet it continues to flow. It has for thousands of years and probably will for a thousand more years. While its always the same, it's always different too. And the water we're looking at right now will never pass this way again."

It took me a while to figure it out, but I think I did. Our lives are kind of like that water. We move and trickle and flow. We start in one place, no one really knows where, and we end up someplace else, and no one really knows where that is either. Every decision we make changes the path that our life is on, sometimes just a little, and sometimes a lot. So it's really important that as we flow, like the water, we're aware of the things we say and do and the things we pass and go over and around and move through because we will never see those things again. Life is kind of like that stream. It looks like the same thing is happening over and over again, but really, it's all happening for the first time. I get that. And it helps me to "live in the moment," as Uncle Trent says.

CHAPTER SIXTY-EIGHT

Oh my god! Oh my god! Trent's dead.

I was in the Commons, having my morning coffee with Jake. He was browsing through the news on his iPad like he does every morning when he suddenly looked up at me and took my hand. Then he turned his iPad toward me. I froze, a thousand-pound rock landed in the pit of my stomach. The picture of Trent that stared back brought a flood of memories and tears. His penetrating blue eyes burned into my own. I tried to read the caption but could not. Everything was out of focus. The entire world was out of focus.

I'm sitting now in my big bean bag chair. Dad's den has, for the moment, become my safe place once again. On my phone I read the caption under his picture. I attempt to control my emotions, my breathing, my world. "Former guidance counselor and convicted felon of Glenwood High School dies at 41." The story goes on to talk about how he was gang raped at Briar Ridge and contracted AIDS. Why the fuck do they call him a *former* guidance counselor but not a *former* felon? They have reduced him to a monster. They have taken my first love and turned his entire life—our love—into nothing more than an act of brutal violence. I shake with anger and something much deeper as I read their summation of Trent.

I'm as shocked at how this news has affected me—impacted me—as I am by the news itself. I thought I was completely over Trent. I honestly did. Jake is a wonderful guy and an amazing lover. I have no doubt about the love that we share. We are in love, a love deeper and purer than I have ever known. But this new knowledge has shaken me to the core of my being. It has awoken repressed memories and feelings I thought were gone forever, no longer even possible.

"Funeral services for Trent Reginald Reynolds will be held at 10:30 a.m. on Tuesday, November 27, at Davis Shaw Funeral Home, 34 West 12th Avenue, Columbus, OH 43201. In lieu of flowers please . . ."

I stop reading. The rest doesn't matter.

CHAPTER SIXTY-NINE

In his final days, Trent and I walked through our lives together, reflecting upon the depth of our love and our lives. Our days were filled with the pleasant memories of youth—the difficult ones we let be. There has been enough reflection on those to last a lifetime. And when time is of the essence, looking at the shit is a poor expenditure of it. So we spent those final days together, when he was awake and alert, walking down memory lane. No, we didn't walk. We ran like children chasing a new puppy. And we laughed. Oh, how we laughed. We laughed until we cried. And then we cried until we laughed.

It's interesting how imminent death makes you so much more attentive to life. The autumn leaves are more vibrant, the sky vivid with color. The stars sparkle like polished gems. Everything is more intense, more invigorating. Somehow the imminence of death makes life more tangible. Appreciation for life is magnified.

And it was. Until the morning I held his hand and watched as the sun set for the last time in my big bother's life. Then everything went black.

I pushed the stop button on time, but it ticked on.

Powerlessness.

Few things in life are as horrifying as feeling utterly and completely powerless. It's been only a few short days, but the pain, the agony, the Trent withdrawal, they crush my soul like a vise.

When you grow up together, you never foresee this day. You don't think about it, plan for it, or even imagine it. Dad is taking it harder than any of us, except maybe for Stevie. Watching your child in such deep despair and agony for which nothing can be done tears a mother's heart to shreds. Losing Trent, if there were no other pain involved, would have been almost more than I could stand. Combine this with the pain my children, my husband, and my dad are going through, and it takes me to another place altogether. Numb. Uncomfortably numb. Torrentially numb. I thank God for the numbness, because without it, the agony would be too heavy to bear.

At Trent's funeral, Doctor Thackery is going to deliver the message. He has been such a blessing over these last few days. The night before Trent passed away, he came to visit him again, and then he went to Dad's place afterwards. He wanted to meet and get to know a little of the man who was, then wasn't, and is now again, father to the son.

Trent and I planned every aspect of his funeral together. He wanted me to sing "Hey Jude" at the top of my lungs the way I had years ago in London's Piccadilly Square. I graciously declined. "That," I told him, "was a once-in-a-lifetime performance."

Trent created a video with the help of his childhood best friend, Bryan. I don't know the contents of it, as he wouldn't say. What I do know is that it's for Dad more than anyone else. Had I known this a year ago, I would have been scared to death and probably sat next to the video projector to pull the plug if required. But there has been so much restoration between Dad and Trent that I eagerly await the dimming of the lights.

Robert will do the eulogy, and I know the "comedy hat" he wears from Monday to Friday will not be set aside. He and Trent have been close since they met in college. Trent has—had—the utmost respect and admiration for Robert. If this had not been so, Robert and I never would have met, for it was Trent who introduced us. He has always been very protective of me—just one more thing I love about him. I almost said *loved.* I will always love him no matter how long we are separated by heartbeats and brainwaves.

I don't remember even writing the obituary we penned together, nor the outline for the funeral service itself. I planned every step of it along with him, and yet it will be as fresh and new to me as it will be for every other person in attendance. Shock has value that way. Shock value. It protects us from intolerable pain.

As we ride together to the funeral home, I sit with Aaron on one side of me and Stevie on the other. The limo's dark windows keep the sorrow in and the sunlight out.

CHAPTER SEVENTY

I didn't bring enough fucking Kleenex. My pockets were stuffed, but I used them all before his family was even seated. Trent, I miss you. You've really gone and done it this time. You've abandoned me forever. My self-talk is useless this morning. I have to get through this. I can get through this. I will get through this. *Walking by his open coffin was the worst part,* I keep telling myself. I know how improper, how inappropriate and unholy it would be, but I so wish his eyes would have been open. To look into them one last time. To have him look into mine just once more is all I need. In the deepest recesses of my mind, I'm aware that we're over, that there's a man in my life who loves me and whom I love. So I will just call these emotions, this longing, this intense sorrow, shock. That's what it must be—what it has to be.

That's Michelle, Trent's ex-wife, sitting across from me. I recognize her from a picture he showed me once. *What the fuck are you doing here?* I suppose she could ask me the same question.

When we were dating . . . Oh my God, that must be his sister and his nephews. Oh God, I feel like I'm falling into a bottomless cavern. An endless pit of despair and darkness. *Breathe. Calm yourself. Relax.* He talked about them all the time when we were dating.

In the back of my mind, I always knew he would die first. I mean, he was twenty years older; of course he would. But I never pictured it like this. I was supposed to be sitting where they are. I was supposed to be his family. They were supposed to be my children—our children. I have to let this go. *Dammit, Brianna, snap out of it.*

CHAPTER SEVENTY-ONE

"Dearly beloved, those who are dearly loved by Trent, we have gathered here today to celebrate the life of Trent Reginald Reynolds. Trent was predeceased by . . ."

I've never understood why we have to go through the formality of who the dead have been predeceased by or who they're survived by. I mean, we know that, don't we? We're sitting right here. All of us. Everyone but Trent. He's lying in that box, at the front, under the lights. Spotlighted. The star of the show. He was always my star.

When he was eight years old, Mom was baking my birthday cake. I only like chocolate, and all Mom had was vanilla. There was very little—well, no—money, but the day before, Trent took his allowance and bought two Hershey's chocolate bars, the ones without the almonds. When Mom was beating the batter, he brought them out and offered them to her so she could melt them into it. I got my chocolate birthday cake, the best one I have ever had. Trent decorated the cake himself. On the top, he wrote "Happy 7th Birthday Claire Bare" and beneath that "The best sister any bother could have." He forgot the first "r" in brother, and until last week, I often referred to him as my "big bother." I will miss you so very much, big bother.

Bryan did a masterful job of Trent's video. Like Trent told me, it was really for Dad. Interesting, I thought. Funeral video montages are always pictures of the deceased. This one was not. A perfect reflection of the selfless man Trent had become. His frail, emaciated image, sitting upright in his hospital bed, filled the screen. Then in his calm, soothing way, he spoke about what it was like to be the pearl of great price—something of unsurpassed value. It was kind of weird. I don't think it was sacrilegious or anything, but he talked about how Dad had taught him that the pearl in the parable that Jesus taught was not us finding him; it was him finding us—a priceless treasure worthy of sacrificing everything to possess. Trent had been found. Found by something greater than himself.

He spoke of how important it is to find value in those around us and to repay debts of mercy, love, and grace. How to receive grace graciously—which is far more difficult than extending it. He spoke to each of us. He looked straight into the camera and called us each by name: Aaron, Stevie, Robert, me, and Dad. He also spoke briefly to Doctor Thackery, and tears welled in his eyes as he expressed the depth of his gratitude. Then he did something that surprised me. He said, "Princess, I will always love you too." I was baffled until I heard the sobs and gasps coming from the back of the chapel.

It was as though he was able to look through the camera and directly into our eyes—into our souls. When he spoke to Dad, he choked up. We all did. He began by saying a simple word I had not heard come from his lips in more than thirty years. "Dad," he said, "I love you. I'm so sorry for your loss. For our loss. But I have been found and have found you, my father, my friend, my dad." The video then faded into a montage of images. As the pictures blended seamlessly into one another, the song "Daniel" by Elton John played in the background.

Bryan told me later that Trent had been in touch with Gertie, Dad's aunt. She gave him a box of old photographs, many of them in black and white, and many of Dad and his brother, Daniel. Pictures of them playing together on the old farm, laughing together, unwrapping Christmas gifts together, skating together on the pond behind the old farmhouse, the same one Trent and I skated on and swam in together as children. Dad sobbed and choked and moaned but could not take his eyes away from the images. I think in those moments, Dad was finally free of the guilt and shame that had held him captive for a lifetime. The resemblance between

Daniel and Trent was uncanny. If I didn't know better, and if it were possible, I would swear it was Trent in those pictures with Dad.

When the video ended, there was absolute silence except for the sound of sobs and sniffles.

We had arranged an open mic time. Dad was the first up. He almost ran to the podium.

"My son," he said as tears and snot poured from his eyes and nose. There was no pretense, no composure, no best foot forward, just pure, raw emotion and love that had to be expressed. "My son, you taught me how to laugh and how to love, how to cherish each moment. You taught me how to live well and how to die well. I had you for such a short while. This regret I shall carry with me for a lifetime. But in the short while you were mine, we shared a lifetime. I love you. I miss you. Thank you for your forgiveness, for your mercy, and for your grace.

"When a person outlives a spouse, they become a widow. If you outlive your parents, you become an orphan. There is no word for a parent who outlives a child. There is no word because there are no words. It's not supposed to happen, and when it does, there are no words . . . I have no words." With that, Dad crumbled. Robert and Doctor Thackery helped him back to his seat.

I was stunned by who stepped up to the podium after Dad sat down: my Aaron and Stevie. Doctor Thackery lowered the microphone so they could be heard. The room fell completely silent.

"My Uncle Trent didn't deserve to die," Aaron began. "He should be alive today, celebrating my birthday." In the chaos surrounding recent events, we had all forgotten that Aaron turned thirteen today. "Uncle Trent gave the best birthday presents and the best birthday parties ever. When I turned eight, I was woken up in the morning by a puppy licking my face. It was Uncle Trent's birthday present to me." We all chuckled when he added, "Yes, Uncle Trent talked with Mom and Dad first. Remington has been my best friend ever since. Well, my best friend next to Stevie and Uncle Trent. Uncle Trent taught me how to take care of Remington, how to love him and teach him all kinds of tricks. I learned how to care about and love people better because of what Uncle Trent taught me too.

"Uncle Trent used to tell me that the most important thing I can do is be the best me I can be. That if I can learn to live a bit better and love a bit better every day, I will *be* a bit better every day. And someday I'll be pretty awesome. I might even stop beating the crap out of Stevie.

"Even when he was really, really sick, Uncle Trent found some way, every day, to let people know that they were important, that they mattered. When I was with him, I always felt like I mattered. And maybe that's why Uncle Trent lived, to help people see that they mattered. Yeah, that *is* why. It was his purpose, I guess. He used to say that everyone has a purpose—a reason they're alive. I'm not saying he was perfect. He wasn't. He hurt some people terribly, deeply, and paid a lot for that. And maybe that's why he changed so much. The hurt he brought to other people, he never wanted to do again. So instead, he changed and found a reason to treat everyone like they were important. He told me once that the people who are the hardest to love probably need it the most. I think he was right. And that, I think, became his reason for living: to make other people feel better about being alive. I wish he was.

"I suppose, when I think about it, Uncle Trent taught me that when you find something more important than yourself, you become a better person—a happier person.

"I don't like seeing you in that stupid box, Uncle Trent. You're not supposed to be there. You're supposed to be with me, with us. Death is so dumb, and I hate it."

That's where Aaron stopped. Stevie tried to talk, but like Trent, he doesn't like being in front of people, and all he could do was cry. That's all most of us could do.

At the interment, Doctor Thackery spoke briefly again: "Death only has no value if we give it permission to have no value. Yes, Aaron, it's dumb. And I hate it too, but just as each life has a purpose, so does each death. Finding purpose in death can be infinitely harder though, because it gets mired in grief and pain. We find the purpose of life and death as we look into ourselves, then beyond ourselves and into others. Out of the mouths of babes, they say. After what young Aaron taught us this afternoon, little else needs to be said. 'To make other people feel better about being alive,' That's a damn good reason to live.

"I met Trent under the most difficult of circumstances. His life had been torn from him. Yes, much of it by his own hand, but that does nothing to negate the pain of his suffering. As Trent grew, as we grew together, we learned how to navigate the circumstances of Trent's suffering. He didn't draw back from the difficult challenges he faced day in and out. He learned to walk amidst the darkness, to wade through it and, eventually, to rise above it. Healing happens in the soul. Reparation occurs only in the battle between evil and good that takes place internally. It changes the way a person thinks, the way they respond to the triggers, which may never go away. But in living well, we can find that the trigger no longer has to be pulled.

"A wiser man than I once said, 'When we are no longer able to change a situation, we are challenged to change ourselves.' And so, Trent did. And as he changed himself, he was able to change the world around him. Yes, Aaron, your dear uncle found his purpose, and it could never be said better than you said it. Trent's reason for walking this planet had become to help others walk life less encumbered, more empowered—freer to love and be loved.

"When I first met Trent, he was my patient; when I last saw Trent, he was my friend. Like so many of yours, my life has been enriched by knowing the man, Trent Reginald Reynolds."

I APPROACHED HER AS SHE was leaving after the reception. I caught her gently by the arm. There was no mistaking who she was. She was stunningly beautiful and completely broken.

"Brianna," I said, "thank you for coming. I know it would have meant a lot—means a lot—to Trent that you're here."

She broke down again and threw her arms around my neck and wept. "I know it's not my fault, but it feels like it is," she whispered. I held her close. We cried together.

She's right; it's not her fault. Yet if not for her, Trent would be alive today. But he lives in each of us now. Like Dad said, Trent has taught us all how to live better and how to love better.

This may have been the most surreal day I have ever lived. It was—is—the most horrible and beautiful day of my life. The words Doctor Thackery and Aaron spoke seem to have changed me somehow. Dad received today what he has waited an eternity for, and my heart bursts with pride for the children I have, the man I married, the father who gave me life, and the brother I shall never let go of.

I love Trent so much . . . I am so . . . I think we might . . . I know that . . . God, I hate words; they possess so little power to convey the heart. They fail when I need them the most. They abandon me when I call. But that too is okay, for nothing else needs to be said.

As we drive away from the funeral home, we leave Trent behind, but only his body, not the man we love.

Aaron sits next to me with Robert's arm around him. I sit staring at my father across from me. He has a look of peace on his face, a serenity I have never seen before. Stevie rests his head against my breast. Tears stream down my face as he strokes my hand. "It'll be alright, Mom. It'll be alright."

And so it will.

ACKNOWLEDGEMENTS

Finding the right words to thank all of those who have contributed to this work leaves me awestruck. Those who come to mind immediately are, of course, my children.

Kiera, I am in awe of how enthusiastically you embrace your position in life. Even amidst the never-ending day-to-day challenges that I know must feel endless. You amaze me. Hudson is blessed, as am I, to have you in his life. You are a wonderful mother and an amazing woman. I have never known another human being who radiates kindness quite the way you do.

Echo (NBBP), my heart swells with pride at the young woman you have become, the success you have found, and the obstacles you have overcome. You are the motivating force behind this thing I do with pen and page.

Courtney, the way you sacrificially pour yourself into the lives of your boys is inspirational. And as I watch that carry over to your grandson my heart smiles. Please don't think for a moment that even across these many mountains and miles, this isn't clearly evident. I'm so grateful to have been found by you.

The three of you have been the arbiters of grace and mercy in this old man's life. As Gerald says, "Grace is easier to give than receive." But I receive yours with so much gratitude. I have fathered far out of my league. Another gift of grace.

Hudson, my special little guy: each and every moment I spend with you fills my soul with joys unknown to me until you graced my life. Thank you for the gift you are to our family.

My mother and father were still alive when I began this work. Mom asked to read an early version, so I sent her one. The most memorable comment she made about it was, “Do you have to use the F-word so much?” I took a few out, Mom. Mom and Dad gave me much more than life; they taught me, by example, the value of unconditional love. That love has sustained me and taken me, more often than any could know, from the depths of despair to heights I could never have realized without them.

Mike, I'm not sure what I'd do or where I'd be without you. You hate this kind of stuff, so I won't say more . . . other than thank you, thank you, thank you!

Mrs. Taylor, I find it interesting that long after we've graduated from high school and have grown older than our teachers were when they taught us, we still refer to them as Mr. or Mrs. or Ms. You saw something in my writing when I was in grade ten, and you pushed me toward excellence. Thank you. You are a big part of why these pages exist. I suppose it's now safe to confess that I wrote most of my older brothers' English assignments. Oh yeah, and that provincial essay contest Joy won in grade eleven? Yup, that was me too.

Marilyn, ours has been a confusing relationship, made much more so by my hand. Had I had the courage to be more like Trent and less like myself in the early years, I know I would have spared you much suffering. Nevertheless, it's what it is, or perhaps more accurately, it was what it was. You have been more gracious than I could have expected and more forgiving than I deserve, and for that I thank you.

Ryan, in a world filled with trite meaninglessness, you have challenged me to be more, to rise above, and to pursue excellence. For that I thank you. I hope that in some small way I have challenged you toward that end as well. You are not all you can be, yet so much more than you think you are.

Harold, while I walked through the valley of the shadow of death, you walked with me through that darkness until the light you pointed me toward shone once again. And for that I'm filled with gratitude.

To the men and women of Miklat, you gave me the gift of recovery, which has resulted in so many other gifts that I would never have otherwise known, and my heart is filled with gratitude.

To my therapist, Ron, I've often felt that if people truly knew the wretched man who lives behind these blue eyes, they would run from me as if from a burning building. You know the worst parts of my humanity, and yet you have accepted me for the beauty you also see inside of me. You have guided me through the deepest parts of my shame, regret, and fears. Your unconditional support of me drives me to be a better me. Thank you.

And to Chris Weekes . . . Ditto.

I must also give a shout out to the Rainwriters: Bob, Doug, Chris, Edi, Elisa, Paul, Keith, and, before she passed on to her eternal writing studio, Loreena, the Dragon Lady. Your critiques of the first chapters of this book and my writing in general have sharpened it and made it better. You are my "punctuation police." Perhaps one day I'll learn the proper spot to place, a comma.

At 170,000 words I tortured numerous alpha and beta readers with early drafts of the manuscript. Your tenacity, perseverance and comments encouraged me to not give up and to get this thing to something a bit more palatable.

Several gracious people sacrificed their time and eyesight as advance readers: Don, Ryan, Harold, Sharon, Elisa, Scott, and Rick. Thank you for your investment, your ARC reviews, and your comments that served to strengthen this work.

After the ninth or tenth draft of this work sat for a couple of years, I decided the time had come, and I began the search for that all-important assistant captain, the dreaded editor. I will go so far as to say that fate intervened, and I met Dania Sheldon. Not only is she an award-winning editor, she's damn good. Dania, you received this manuscript with an enthusiasm and a professionalism that re-inspired me. Who else would find that single straight quotation mark at the end of an otherwise italicized sentence? You also brought a level of excellence to the characters, the pacing, and the narrative arc that I was not expecting. You make me sound smarter than I am. Not only is my writing richer because of you, my life is richer because of you. This story is so much better since our paths first crossed. You have somehow managed to polish it into something more than it was, making it, for better or worse, all that it is. Any errors that remain herein belong to yours truly.

My journey with the FriesenPress team began with Debbie Anderson who seemed to share an enthusiasm for this project that led me to believe it may be worth publishing. I was then introduced to Erin Cutler who has walked with me through the entire publishing process, answering my myriad of questions, pointing me in the right direction, and has served as a sounding board as I vented and stressed about the publication process. Kevin Miller did the final edit and created more work after I thought it was completely done, than I could have imagined. You found little things that in the end made a big difference. Many thanks. Lilian Knoops performed the final proofread and found a plethora of issues that somehow managed to slip by countless other eyes. My deep appreciation for your finetuned expertise. The interior layout and design were created by Geoff Soch. Thanks for not going with Times New Roman like you threatened.

The cover design and artwork were by Michael Lloyd. I am most grateful for your eye. You captured young Trent's sorrow with sensitivity and precision.

I'm further indebted to the writings of Carl Jung, Viktor Frankl, Jordan B. Peterson and, to a lesser degree, Sigmund Freud and Friedrich Nietzsche, whose works have impacted my life and this manuscript. Thanks also to Brené Brown for her outstanding work on shame.

There likely are others who belong on this page. But eventually it has to come to end. Please forgive me if you feel you have been overlooked and undervalued. If you do belong here, you've likely got my number. Give me a shout. There's not much I can do about it now, but maybe we'll have a nice chat and laugh about it.

I could go on thanking those who have played a role in the development of my life and thereby contributed in one way or another to the contents of these pages. but I shall stop with this: Sharon, my dear sister, you have been my number one beta reader and my number one fan. Your words of encouragement and support, not only throughout my writing career—as short as it has been—but also throughout my life—as long as it has been—have allowed me to believe in myself and in this craft. My most sincere and deepest thanks to you. I love you Nicely.

ABOUT THE AUTHOR

Brian Douglas grew up in Alberta, Canada, and has lived, at least for a short while, in each of the prairie provinces prior to making British Columbia his home in 2017. He began working as a short-order cook in the seventh grade and has really never stopped working. While his careers have changed, from dishwasher to therapist to lighting designer to hospital crisis counselor, for as long as he can remember, writing has always been Brian's greatest passion. He has three grown daughters, four grandsons, one great grandson, and a deep respect for the broken human condition. Brian holds a master's degree with a double major in clinical counseling and pastoral leadership. *They Flutter Behind You* is his first novel.

Printed in Canada